PURGE ON THE POTOMAC

BY DAVID THOMAS ROBERTS

ISBN-13: 978-0-998770-49-9 (Hard Cover)
ISBN-13: 978-0-998770-46-8 (Paper Back)
ISBN-13: 978-0-998770-48-2 (eBook)

Printed in USA by Defiance Press & Publishing, LLC
Proudly Published in The Republic of Texas

Edited by Janet Musick
Interior designed by Deborah Stocco

Distributed by Midpoint Trade Books

Bulk orders of this book may be obtained by contacting Defiance Press & Publishing at www.defiancepress.com or Midpoint Trade Books at www.midpointtrade.com.

Also available in audiobook format on Amazon.

Publicity Contact: mfoster@reliantpr.com

DEDICATION

This book is dedicated to my four grandchildren—Vivi Rose, Braeden, Aliza and Izzy, and to any of my future grandchildren in the hope that I have contributed in some small way to securing their God-given Liberty for them and future generations.

FOREWORD

The *Texas Crisis*–From "A State of Treason"

The United States of America had just endured its most serious constitutional crisis since 1860, precipitated by the unconstitutional actions of a newly elected president against Texas and the newly formed Tea Party.

President Tyrell Johnson was the first minority president elected in U.S. history, and the country believed he would be a healing and transformational president. Instead, his administration would go down as one of the most corrupt, divisive and inept ever to set foot in the White House.

Wielding the full power of the Executive Branch, President Johnson's Department of Justice and his attorney general, Jamail Tibbs, conducted unconstitutional operations against all his political opponents. Those actions would have made even Richard Nixon blush.

At the epicenter of the conflict were the grass-roots constitutional literalists, mostly located in the South, but especially in Texas. Identified as the Tea Party, they were designated political enemies by the administration.

An Islamic jihadist, whose sister was killed in a bombing raid by U.S. forces on a hardened nuclear facility in Iran, attempted to assassinate the president. Secret Service agents killed the would-be assassin, a master's student at Southern Methodist University, during the attempt. When they raided his apartment, agents found his laptop and discovered his master's thesis, which focused on the Tea Party.

The administration purposely kept the assassin's ties to Islam and Iran from the public but trumpeted his supposed ties and activism in the Tea Party. The administration fostered the notion that the assassin's attempt on the president was racially motivated and played into the talking points used to try to discredit Johnson's political opponents in the Tea Party.

President Johnson, keenly astute to political opportunities, swiftly seized on public sentiment and launched raids on Tea Party offices, individuals and donors, mostly without warrants, using the National Defense Authorization Act (NDAA) to classify these groups as terrorists with no habeas corpus protections. Under the careful orchestration of the attorney general, the FBI, Homeland Security and the Bureau of Alcohol, Tobacco and Firearms (ATF) jointly carried out operations that resulted in several unnecessary citizen deaths in Texas.

TV cameras captured a Waco-style raid by the ATF, showing a large Homeland Security tank slamming through the wall of a house owned by Houston resident Chuck Dixon, who was the president and founder of a large and successful Tea Party group. His wife and child were terrorized, and Dixon was arrested and transported to Ellington Field Air Force Base, where he was held incommunicado and interrogated for several days.

The level of outrage by the average Texan was vocal and intense. Texas Governor Brent Cooper, a staunch political opponent of the president, ordered the Texas Rangers to find Dixon and rescue him. Under the command of legendary Texas Ranger Pops Younger, the Rangers and the Texas State Guard found Dixon and rescued him. During the operation, Younger arrested the participating federal agents and a federal agent was wounded, infuriating the president and attorney general. Not to be outdone, the attorney general issued federal arrest warrants for Younger, the participating Texas Guard and, unbelievably, Governor Cooper!

The *Texas Crisis*, which had been simmering, was about to escalate and boil over.

A Justice Department prosecutor, who had become aware of the real identity and motives of President Johnson's would-be assassin, was able to secretly remove documents proving the man's real motives and get them to Governor Cooper. Several days later, the whistleblower and his wife died in a suspicious car accident in the Georgetown district of Washington, D.C.

Governor Cooper called for Congress to impeach President Johnson and remove Attorney General Tibbs but Congress, controlled by establishment Republicans, could not muster the courage or the votes necessary to support impeachment. An enraged Tibbs schemed with the president and cabinet members to put an end to the *Texas Crisis* by ordering a commando-style operation to arrest the governor and embarrass the state leadership of Texas. The attorney general became obsessed with the idea of the world seeing the brazen Texas governor doing a perp walk in handcuffs.

Special Forces sent into Austin, Texas by the administration to make the arrests and seize the capitol building and the Department of Public Safety created a global incident as federal agents failed; a Blackhawk helicopter was destroyed and Pops Younger and his Texas Rangers outmaneuvered the feds. In the operation, federal agents and U.S. Army Rangers were killed.

The sentiment of average Texans took on a more virulent hatred toward the administration, while the mass media painted the narrative of a state government out of control. The loss of federal agents and Army Rangers during the operation inflamed public sentiment in the media and on the U.S. Northeast and West coasts against Texas and its stubborn stance against the administration. How dared a sitting state governor demand the impeachment of a president, especially the first minority to hold the highest office in the country!

The media and politicians downplayed the demand as coming from a few irrational extremists, but soon the entire world was glued to the high-stakes chess match taking place between Austin and Washington.

Pops Younger advised the governor and top state officials to move to a remote west Texas location, the Swingin' T Ranch, in anticipation of the administration's next move. Secretary of State Annabelle Bartlett, her eye on the next Democratic presidential primary nomination, seized the opportunity to insert herself into the fray, attempting to be the hero who brokered a settlement in the crisis. She traveled to Austin to meet with the governor, unbeknown to the president.

But the attorney general learned of the secret location housing the governor and his officials. Consumed by the immense satisfaction he would receive by arresting the governor, he sent a full military and Homeland Security unit into Texas to capture them. With permission from Mexico, the raid was launched south of the Rio Grande. Adding insult to injury, the Tibbs dubbed the mission "Operation Santa Anna" after the Mexican dictator who sacked the Alamo and marched into Texas, only to be defeated later by General Sam Houston's army at San Jacinto.

Five Homeland Security choppers left Mexican airspace for the Swingin' T Ranch, but the raid went horribly awry. Governor Cooper and his wife Lyndsey were killed in the raid, along with several state officials, Texas state troopers and federal agents. The Texas Air National Guard downed two choppers as they attempted to escape back to Mexico and engaged the Mexican air force over both Texas and Mexican airspace, escalating an internal American constitutional crisis into an international incident.

More skirmishes at Texas borders between the Texas Guard and militia troops heightened the stakes even more. Upon orders from the administration to launch a full military operation into Texas, several generals on the Joint Chiefs of Staff refused and were arrested as they left a meeting at the White House.

When the bodies of the governor and his wife were flown to Austin for a state funeral, Pops Younger ripped off the American flags draping their caskets and replaced them with Lone Star flags. The scene was played repeatedly on world TV networks. As the new governor, Alvin "Smitty" Brahman, was sworn in, Texas became more defiant than ever as Brahman promised to call an emergency session of the state legislature for a special election to put an immediate referendum to the voters for independence. He repeated Governor Cooper's demand for the impeachment of the president and his attorney general, but Congress remained impotent.

The president declared martial law in Texas, going so far as to shut down the federal background check system so Texans could not purchase guns. Governor Brahman responded with an executive order lifting federal background checks in the state.

Even the United Nations recognized the growing conflict and scheduled an emergency Security Council meeting.

The president announced that any referendum on independence would be both seditious and illegal, announcing that the entire state of Texas was in "A State of Treason!"

"The Deep State"—(noun) A body or group of people involved in the secret manipulation and control of government policy.

- Anonymous

CHAPTER 1

"There are decades where nothing happens; and then there are weeks where decades happen."

> *- Vladimir Lenin*
> *Communist Revolutionary,*
> *Father of Leninism (version of Marxism)*

A mericans were about to be jolted out of their winter Sunday early morning slumber as if a massive earthquake had hit the entire country at once...

On a dark gray, bone-chilling Sunday morning in late November in the nation's capital, only two people braved the cold, nasty twenty-three-degree weather to visit the Vietnam Veterans Memorial on the National Mall. The Mall was eerily quiet except for a few Canadian geese honking as they kept together in small clusters to keep the water moving and thus from freezing in the center of the Constitution Gardens pond. Several hardy joggers were scattered on the concrete paths that meandered through the park, and large wet snowflakes lightly descended to the ground.

Chris Vasquez and his sister Connie were bundled up in large wool coats and scarves as they made their way several blocks from their hotel to find a long monolithic granite structure, a memorial to those who died in the Vietnam War. This was their first trip to Washington, D.C. from Texas, and there was some trepidation about their feelings when they finally saw *his* name—their family name—on the memorial. They would be the first in their large family to see the memorial that honored their grandfather and other veterans of that war.

It felt as if they were carrying the weight of the grief and ultimately the pride of their entire family as they carefully walked down the salted, wet concrete path. When they arrived the night before, the bad weather had not dampened their mixed feelings of anticipation, pride and sadness.

The wind howled through the Mall, whipping the flags wildly and causing the brass swivel snaps to clank against the stainless steel poles. After about twenty minutes of looking for the name of their grandfather, they finally found it on the tenth granite panel. They both pulled off their warm gloves and touched the etched name, carefully outlining each character with their fingers, neither one saying a word. It was a seminal moment for both, seeming to last minutes although, in reality, it was much shorter.

Their quiet reflection and solitude in the moment was about to be shattered...

Less than a couple of thousand feet away, on the south lawn of the White House, Marine One was taking off without much fanfare. It had been a busy week for the first female president of the United States. Annabelle Bartlett had just finished a highly contentious meeting, to be continued at Camp David, with her chief of staff, Milton Weingold, and several others close to her.

Despite what the public usually saw on television, the Secret Service and the Defense Department typically "scrambled" the presidential helicopters so as to create some ambiguity regarding which chopper the president was on. For that reason, there was always more than one chopper, just like there was more than one limousine in a presidential motorcade. In a presidential motorcade, there were typically five or six blacked-out SUVs, only one of which contained the president. The Secret Service played a shell game of sorts, so that any would-be assassins or terrorists would not know for sure which vehicle actually contained the president. This tactic was also known in defense circles as the *"hide the president"* shell game.

Marine One operated on the same premise, usually deploying five of the same exact choppers taking off simultaneously from the south lawn. But, on this crisp morning, there were only three choppers slowly lifting off the lawn, swirling the snowflakes. Camp David was only sixty miles from the White House as the crow flies, and the president would be there in less than twenty minutes,

The three choppers took off into a south wind heading, banking slightly as they changed direction to head up the Potomac in a northwesterly direction toward Camp David. It was a flight path that took them directly over the Mall and the Lincoln Memorial.

The thundering thump-thump noise of the three choppers in the quiet morning got louder and caught the attention of the siblings at the memorial.

"Wow, that must be the president. Look!" Chris pointed to the south lawn.

"Oh, very cool!" Connie fumbled for her smart phone to get a picture or video. "What's that?" she shrieked as she looked up.

Across the reflecting pond at the Mall, she pointed to what looked like a very large bottle rocket streaming smoke as it climbed slowly and erratically into the sky. The smoke trail emanated from two men at the edge of the trees.

"What the hell! Look over there, too!" yelled her astonished brother.

There were so many of the streaming rockets that they couldn't count them, and the missiles came from all directions.

Before the siblings could say anything else, it appeared all three choppers moved in an asynchronous fashion, banking wildly in the sky at different and contorted angles. Suddenly, the chopper farthest to the south exploded into a huge fireball, dropping from the sky, falling like a meteor onto Seventeenth Street just yards from the World War II Veterans Memorial.

"*Oh my god, oh my god, oh my god!*" screamed Connie.

Two shoulder-to-air rockets hit the second chopper. Smoke billowing, it was coming down hard right in their direction. Connie and Chris began running north to escape the falling chopper as it crashed into the southwest corner of the reflecting pond and hurled wreckage half-way up the steps of the Lincoln Memorial.

The third chopper was still airborne, but it twisted like a drunken whirlybird. Unable to stay airborne, the pilots lost control, and the chopper slammed into the world headquarters of the American Red Cross a block away. Strips of aluminum foil fell gently to the ground with the snowflakes as barely deployed anti-missile chaff used for anti-aircraft missile defense landed in the reflecting pond and on the partially snow-covered ground.

Hiding behind a park bench, the siblings slowly stood up, both in shock.

"Holy crap, did we really just see that?" Chris said, partly to himself and partly to his sister.

"Chris, was the *president* in one of those?" Connie cried.

"I don't know, but we better get the hell out of here." Chris looked around, wondering what the foil strips were that were falling all around them.

For a few moments, there was an eerie silence, as if nothing had happened and they were the only two who witnessed this unthinkable calamity. The crackling noise of the burning wreckage was the only sound besides the honking of startled geese that had lifted off from the pond and were trying to circle back to their original places in the water.

The wreckage burned brightly, reflecting off the low cloud cover and bathing the Lincoln Memorial in an ominous orange glow.

Connie and Chris continued to stare at the wreckage, then instinctively they began to walk briskly north, turning every few feet to look back in the direction of the wreckage. Two different pairs of men in ski masks ran past them, then several more a block ahead of them. In the chaos, it seemed natural that people were running away; it did not strike Chris and Connie until later that the masks the men wore might be for a different purpose than just shielding their faces from the brutally cold air.

When they reached Virginia Avenue two blocks away, Connie stopped. She turned to look back.

"Chris, I don't see any movement around the wreckage," she cried. "What if *she* was in there? *Did someone just kill the president?*"

"We've gotta go, sis. We've got to go!" he stated firmly, putting his arm around her to encourage her to keep walking north away from the carnage. They could not know that President Annabelle Bartlett, the first woman president of the United States, lay dead in the burning wreckage of the Marine One chopper at the foot of the Lincoln Memorial.

Sirens from all directions screamed as ambulances and police vehicles rushed to the scene in the gray fall morning. Before most people had had their first cups of coffee, America was about to be rocked to its core...

CHAPTER 2

"To die for an idea: it is unquestionably noble. But how much nobler it would be if men died for ideas that were true."

> *- H.L. Mencken*
> *(1880-1956) American Journalist, Editor, Essayist,*
> *Linguist, Lexicographer, and Critic*

With only a few months left in President Tyrell Johnson's second term, a news flash came scrolling across every cable and network news organization at 11:26 a.m. Eastern time. The Senate had arrived at its decision in the president's impeachment trial.

The entire world had been mesmerized, both entertained and disgusted by the process. Many thought this entire trial was a black eye on the country, as Secretary of State Annabelle Bartlett was handily leading in the polls after an easy primary and, if elected, would surely pardon Johnson anyway.

People stopped what they were doing to get in front of a television, on their smart phones, or anywhere they could to access live coverage of the final vote. The Senate, according to its constitutional authority, was required to take up the impeachment trial offered by the House.

The Senate had chosen to conduct the impeachment trial behind closed doors with no live news coverage. The public, the press, and especially the network and cable news providers were livid, not so much because they were missing history, but because they were missing gargantuan ratings opportunities.

Strangely, and at the outrage of the Republicans, the Senate had not required the president to be present during the reading of the verdict. After almost three weeks of testimony and sharp sniping between Democrats and Republicans, the verdict was to be read *in absentia*.

To the most knowledgeable Beltway insiders, this fact told them everything they needed to know regarding the outcome.

"President Tyrell Johnson, you are accused of multiple abuses of power resulting in the deaths of American citizens, issuing unconstitutional executive orders, obstruction of justice, contempt of Congress and various misdemeanors. Mr. President of the Senate, will you please read the verdict?" said the senate majority leader from the podium.

It was common for the president of the Senate, who was actually the vice president of the United States, to be seated by the podium for an event of this magnitude; however, Vice President Doolittle had been busy on the floor of the Senate, maniacally whipping votes to acquit his boss.

Members of the Senate and their staffs were under intense and incredible political pressure. The Democrats were using every advantage they could muster, threatening Republicans on other legislation, and occasionally threatening those in their own party who were inclined to vote against Johnson. Senators had come out of the Senate chamber looking as if they had either been without sleep for two days or had seen a ghost. The browbeating was as intense as it was effective.

Doolittle slowly took a piece of paper from the majority leader and walked around the podium seated above the lectern, fully aware of the theater it provided.

Despite the previous ban on live coverage, the Senate leadership allowed the press to cover this final aspect of the impeachment trial. They were obviously confident in what was about to be the penultimate moment.

Opening the letter and adjusting his reading glasses, Doolittle looked down at the paper to take a second look, then looked above his reading glasses at the members in the chamber to hushed anticipation from the floor.

Would this be the first time a U.S. president would be successfully convicted as the result of an impeachment proceeding?

Nixon would have surely been convicted had he not resigned and received a full pardon from Gerald Ford. Clinton was able to dodge perjury charges about his many rendezvous with Monica Lewinsky in the White House and his subsequent lies under oath. During the Reconstruction Era, after the War for Southern Independence, President Andrew Johnson, whom most associate with impeachment, barely escaped being removed from office by one vote for refusing to follow an unconstitutional act passed by Congress—an act which, interestingly enough, was later overturned by the United States Supreme Court.

Heightening the drama for this current trial was the fact that Johnson's attorney general, Jamail Tibbs, the central lightning rod of the *Texas Crisis*, was successfully impeached and was facing sentencing for high crimes against the United States. Tibbs' impeachment vote wasn't close, but many expected Tibbs to be the main scapegoat for Johnson. Johnson was in the last few weeks of his second term, but the impeachment was being pressed by Texas and many southern conservatives in Congress for his role in authorizing military action against Texas without Congressional approval.

Proponents of the impeachment needed sixty-seven Senate votes out of one hundred to convict Johnson. To provide cover for Democrats from the south, the leadership had passed rules to allow for a secret ballot to the vociferous outrage of the general public and the press.

The Senate held its breath.

"Mr. Majority Leader, the Senate has voted 66-34 to impeach. The impeachment *does not* pass. The president of the United States is *acquitted* of all charges, including high crimes against the country and all misdemeanors."

The Senate erupted into chaos, much like in 1868 when one senator from Alabama and one from Ohio actually traded punches on the Senate floor.

Now the world's attention suddenly shifted to Austin, Texas, where the Texas State Legislature sat in a special session called by Texas Governor Brahman. The legislature was scheduled to take up the referendum approved by Texas voters that called for a binding referendum to be voted on by their legislature for Texas independence.

CHAPTER 3

"History is the version of past events that people have decided to agree upon."

> *- Napoleon Bonaparte*
> *(1769-1821) French emperor*

Texas Governor Alvin "Smitty" Brahman called a special session of the legislature to consider the independence referendum that Texas voters passed in response to an armed incursion by the federal government.

The session was specifically scheduled to coincide with the reading of the verdict in the impeachment trial of former President Tyrell Johnson.

Now, with Johnson's acquittal, the drama that was about to unfold in the Texas Capitol was palpable. Seemingly, every news agency in the world had cameras in the chamber and their lights were bathing the podium in front of the chamber.

Governor Brahman, the slightly pudgy, former rice farmer from El Campo on the Texas coastal plains, strode to the podium with several aides, Lieutenant Governor Tommy Wilson, and Texas Rangers Commandant Pops Younger.

Brahman pulled a short piece of paper from his pocket and put on a pair of glasses to read it. He stared out at the joint session of the Texas Legislature and the jam-packed gallery. There were so many reporters that the sergeant-at-arms made special provisions so all the news teams could be accommodated, with some uncharacteristically on the floor, roped off from the main body of the legislature.

The large room fell silent as Governor Brahman cleared his throat to speak. The news had spread quickly about President Johnson's acquittal, and most already knew.

"President Tyrell Johnson, the same person who authorized hostile federal interdiction into Texas resulting in the deaths of so many Texans while they were simply exercising their God-given right of self-determination, has been acquitted of all charges," Brahman stated matter-of-factly. "Ladies and gentlemen of the legislature and my fellow Texans, to say we are disappointed is a colossal understatement."

The joint Texas legislative session erupted into temporary chaos, including yelling, screaming and threatened fisticuffs, much like the chaos on the U.S. Senate floor just moments before, divided mostly by party lines.

"Order. Order. Order!" yelled the Speaker of the House, swinging his huge gavel so hard many thought the heavy mallet end would break off with each successive strike.

"The citizens of Texas asked us to put their referendum before the legislature for a vote. I implored the legislature and my fellow Texans to allow the impeachment process to run its course. With this verdict, our disappointment in Congress and the Senate cannot be overstated. I warned the rest of the country, absent a conviction of the tyrants involved in the unconstitutional armed federal incursion into our state, that I would call a special session and the vote would proceed. Texas will be patient no more."

The governor stepped back to the microphone to drop one last devastating bomb to the audience.

"The vote was 66-34, one vote shy of conviction," said Brahman, visibly disgusted. "I'm horribly embarrassed as a Texan to inform you that sixteen Republican senators…" he paused, then continued, "…including our esteemed senior Texas Senator Kevin Simpson, voted against impeachment!"

The legislature again erupted.

"That turncoat son of a bitch!" screamed a state legislator from West Texas.

"His vote was the deciding vote in determining President Johnson was not responsible for his crimes committed against Texas and the Constitution. Wherever you are, Senator, there will be hell to pay!" the governor promised.

Suddenly, a chant rose up from the joint chamber…

"Amanda! Amanda! Amanda!" The chorus became louder and louder.

"Remember Chuck! Remember Amanda!" followed.

Then suddenly came the chant, "1789, 1789, 1789!"

The various news crews covering the legislature's reaction to the impeachment proceedings were packed into the gallery above the legislature. Many of them were lost regarding the significance of the chants.

Texas flags with 1789, some handwritten with black markers, appeared in the gallery above the floor of the legislature.

When Homeland Security had been ordered to shut down the referendum vote, Amanda Flores, a University of Houston co-ed, fashioned a Lone Star flag with the letters 1789 hand-stitched on the white bar. Flores was attempting to cast her ballot on Texas independence at a downtown Houston Jewish Center polling place. She was shot and killed by federal Homeland Security troops while holding the flag.

Chuck Dixon, a Texas business owner who was a Tea Party patriot organizer and whose arrest lit the fire that became the *Texas Crisis*, was a hero to everyday Texans. Dixon tried to save Flores but, when she was killed, he picked up the flag on a pole and waved it in the face of federal troops attempting to stop the vote on direct orders from the Johnson administration. The scene of Dixon shot dead, leaning up against a concrete planter with that flag furling in the wind, became the symbol that led to the impeachment hearings for Johnson.

Brahman had demanded the impeachment of Johnson, Tibbs and others, promising that Texas was going to take up legislation that would begin the permanent separation process.

"Tomorrow morning at 10:00, we will proceed with the will of the people. God bless Texas," said Brahman as he stomped off the riser.

When a CNN reporter stuck her microphone in front of Governor Brahman as he was being shuffled off the floor by Texas Rangers and Department of Public Safety officers, he halted.

"Governor, what is your next step now that President Johnson has been acquitted?" asked the bleached blonde reporter with oversized Botox lips.

"If the rest of the country thinks this is settled, I've got a message for America," Brahman stated flatly.

"What's your message, sir? What do you want the rest of America to know?" she asked.

"We hear you loud and clear. Has America gone mad? Is this really the will of the people? Congress is totally impotent. I am stunned at Congress' willful dereliction of duty to bring President Johnson and his corrupt administration to justice. I'll just leave it at that—for now," he shouted.

"Sir, sir, a few more questions!" she persisted as he headed for the rear of the chamber with his entourage. "Your own Texas senator, a Republican, voted for acquittal!" she yelled at the top of her lungs.

Brahman stopped in his tracks, despite the efforts of his security detail to hustle him out of the chamber. He turned around slowly and took a few steps back to the reporter.

"History is full of people like Simpson. The question is, what was his quid pro quo for his vote? I don't envy him when he returns to face his constituents," Brahman snarled as he turned and walked out.

She turned to the camera. "There you have it; the Texas governor has sent a message to the rest of America," she said to the news anchor.

The next morning, Texas had a decision to make that she hadn't had to make since 1860.

CHAPTER 4

"It is very comforting to believe that leaders who do terrible things are, in fact, mad. That way, all we have to do is make sure we don't put psychotics in high places and we've got the problem solved."

- Thomas Wolfe
American Author (1900-1938)

The demonstrations that filled the streets of places like Chicago and other major urban areas during the impeachment proceedings had turned violent. Fourteen law enforcement officers lost their lives at the hands of leftist radicals, anarchists and racial groups who claimed the impeachment hearings were racially motivated against President Johnson, who was an African-American.

After the announcement of Johnson's acquittal, those demonstrations turned into celebrations; however, the looting of businesses, the burning of police cruisers, and random shootings continued.

Mayors and police chiefs across the country adopted a policy of non-aggression when it came to protests that turned violent, essentially ceding entire city districts to protesters so as not to provoke more violence. Politically correct stand-down instructions were the order of the day.

Governor Brahman would have none of it, ordering Texas law enforcement officials *not* to stand down from the anarchist-type activities that typically followed these protests, instructing everyone who would listen that protestors who broke the law would be arrested immediately. Brahman's orders would be tested over the next three nights in Dallas and Houston as hundreds of arrests were made, but there was none of the burning or looting seen in other major U.S. cities.

With the impeachment hearings over, the media focused on Texas' next move. Brahman had given the U.S. Congress an ultimatum to impeach Tibbs and Johnson or else, but only Tibbs was successfully impeached. Editorial staffs of major newspapers and political pundits were extremely critical of Brahman and displayed open editorial hostility to the reaction from the Texas Legislature.

Senator Kevin Simpson's offices in Austin and Washington were flooded with calls from outraged constituents, as well as from many non-Texans who called to vent their hostility.

"It is important that our country begins to heal from the *Texas Crisis*. This administration is in its last months in office," stated Senator Simpson, a sixty-four-year-old former prosecutor and attorney, on ABC's Sunday talk show. "Soon we will go to the polls to elect a new president. I see nothing positive coming out of impeachment. I understand Texans' frustration because I'm a Texan, but public polling shows the country is against the impeachment and, if we want any chance as Republicans to win in November, we have to put this chapter behind us."

"Senator, it would sound to many Texans like you are putting politics ahead of the administration of justice," said the host.

"Look, if it was a cut-and-dried case based on the evidence, the Senate would have convicted easily but, as you can see by the final vote, the facts were highly contested," Simpson answered.

"Well, sir, it wasn't broadcast live so, to most Americans, it wasn't obvious. The final vote had sixty-six in favor of impeachment, *one* vote short. *Your* vote, Senator… That's sixty-six percent of your body that voted in the *affirmative* for impeachment," was the host's comeback.

"The vote was…" said Simpson.

"Senator, how will you deal with your constituents who, in a recently conducted poll among Texans, recorded an astonishing eighty-seven percent in favor of impeachment?" interrupted the host.

"Well, sir, I have no idea of the validity of that poll…" stated Simpson before becoming visibly agitated that the host was starting another question before allowing him to answer the previous question.

"It's a reputable, national non-partisan pollster, as you are fully aware, Senator. In fact, you've quoted these folks' polling data as recently as this year in several speeches you've conducted," retorted the host.

"Listen, I believe deep down that we just need to move on. The crisis was a horrible thing. The impeachment itself is another stain on our history. We have so much that needs to be done in healthcare, jobs, the economy and trade. The impeachment was becoming a sideshow. This president was at the end of his term. It's likely the next president would pardon him anyway. We will have a new president in a matter of months, so why put the country through this?" said Simpson.

"The administration of justice is a sideshow?" asked the host sarcastically, surprising Simpson, since this host was a typical liberal media type.

Simpson's face reddened against his light complexion and snow-white, short-cropped hair. He adjusted his red tie on his white collar, trying to pace himself carefully in his answers, as he knew all too well that his pale face betrayed his anger or excitement easily.

"It is time for the country to move forward. It's that simple," he repeated.

"But your constituents obviously believe differently. Is this a case where an elected representative knows more than his constituents?" asked the confident host, who now was feeling as if he had Simpson boxed in.

Simpson paused, then replied, again measuring his words carefully, "The people elected me to do a job. This is a representative republic. My job is to represent them in the United States Senate to the best of my ability. Not every vote I make will resonate with every Texan. I'm elected to interpret and judge the various laws and issues that come before me. That is how a representative government functions."

"So, in this case, your judgment is that you know better than your constituents?" asked the host.

"Well, I agree that many of my fellow Texans wanted the president impeached. We successfully impeached Tibbs," came the side-stepped response.

"So they should be happy with that? Is that what you are saying?" pressed the host.

"I'm saying I was privy to evidence they didn't see. The impeachment hearings were not public, as you know," answered the senator.

"That's a whole other issue in itself. Were you in agreement with the decision to hold these impeachment hearings in secrecy? Isn't that against the accepted tenets of a constitutional republic?" queried the host who was, in essence, correcting Simpson on the actual form of government that exists in the United States.

"I agreed with the leadership to close this to the public. First, the hearings themselves would likely have taken two to three times the length necessary due to grandstanding from both sides of the debate, just because it was on television," reasoned Simpson.

"But…" started the host, who was now being interrupted himself.

"Not to mention, sir, that holding these hearings in private in the Senate chambers was in our national interest," interrupted Simpson.

"Is it not in the national interest for our citizens to know the possible level of malfeasance in our federal government? Doesn't the public have a right to know?" countered the host, almost sounding like a conservative media pundit.

"Well, sure, but the accused also has the right to a fair trial. I'm not sure if that would have happened had this whole process been public," responded Simpson confidently.

"I want to get back to one thing, Senator, before we stray too far. Is it your belief that you are supposed to vote the overall will of your constituents on any issue that may come before you, or…" said the host.

"My job is not to vote a particular way just because of *mob rule*. They elected me to represent them by using my good judgment on the issues, even if it goes against their wishes," said Senator Simpson to a visibly shocked host.

CHAPTER 5

"How strangely will the tools of a tyrant pervert the plain meaning of words!"

- Samuel Adams
(1722-1803) known as the "Father of the American Revolution"

Z ach Turner had seen enough.

The leader of the *Free Texas* movement was deeply involved in the *Texas Crisis* from the beginning. He was a close friend of both Stan Mumford and Chuck Dixon, the two citizen-heroes of the Tea Party who were killed by federal agents. Their deaths lit the match that ultimately led to the Texas referendum vote and the impeachment trial of the U.S. president and his attorney general.

From the standpoint of the current crisis, Zach was actually much further along in his belief that Washington, D.C. was, in fact, *unfixable*. Despite Mumford's and Dixon's pleas, they could never get Zach to become active in the Tea Party.

It wasn't that Zach didn't believe in limited government and adherence to the Constitution; he just flatly refused to believe the bureaucrats in D.C. would ever return to a true constitutional form of government. He also subscribed to the theory that, throughout history, most failed democracies committed suicide as elected politicians figured out they could keep themselves in power simply by redistributing the contents of the Treasury in exchange for votes.

For Zach, and many more like him, the only answer was a complete and total separation of Texas from the United States. He had dedicated his post-military adult life to an *independent* Texas.

More hardcore than either Mumford or Dixon, Zach seemed to attract those types who were similar to him in thinking and in life experiences. At six foot two and now thirty-six years old, this Navy SEAL veteran of sixteen years looked like he could still walk right back into active duty and complete any mission he was assigned. Zach worked briefly for the CIA after his stint in the Navy, but was so disillusioned by the direction of the agency, the unlawful missions, and the meddling of the bureaucrats that he abruptly resigned and moved back to Texas from Langley.

Back in Texas, the tall and muscular blond started his own corporate security business, which kept him involved in his former element and around similar alpha males who worked for him. Zach was the quintessential man's man.

Zach spent any spare time he had building the *Free Texas* organization and working to legitimize both the idea of an independent Texas nation and the overall credibility of his group. Opponents likened *Free Texas* to secessionists, often calling Zach and his group racists, which was somewhat ironic considering that Zach's marriage to an African-American woman was seven years strong and included a son named Colt.

Whatever "list" the administration kept on political enemies, Zach was now on it. But it was not only the administration that had him in its crosshairs. He had aroused the ire of almost every establishment politician in Texas, both Democrats and especially Old Guard Republicans.

Most politicians run from bold ideas. Only the most ardent of believers allowed themselves to be seen with Zach before the *Texas Crisis*. Politicians, always looking for political cover, couldn't afford to associate with Zach, who the left and moderates labeled a right-wing extremist. Politicians from some of the most conservative and rural districts in Texas were warming to Zach quickly. Politicians from those parts of Texas found very quickly that the image of Chuck Dixon with the *1789* Lone Star flag was emblazoned in their conscience, never to go away, and a good politician would capitalize on that fervor.

Although Zach was affable to all, he had a very tight circle of friends and associates he trusted. He trusted very few people, and absolutely *nobody* in any level of government was among them, with the exception of Texas Ranger Pops Younger.

Zach's business was primarily geared for oil company executives who had to travel in various world hot spots such as Venezuela, Colombia, and the Middle East. Zach had developed a well-known and respected network of operatives in those regions and even in the U.S. who were as good as, and probably markedly better at, advance planning for those executive visits than the State Department or Secret Service. He was well paid and he shared most of the profits with his dedicated crew. They were extremely loyal to Zach and trusted him implicitly.

Zach had built the offices of Turner Invincible Security on ten acres just outside Katy, Texas, about forty miles west of Houston. The small building, constructed of shipping containers that had been set in concrete, welded together and lined with concrete cinder blocks with few windows, was more like an above-ground bunker than it was an office building, therefore earning it the "Bunker" moniker from Zach, his staff and friends. Inside, the space was full of electronics, computer monitors, servers, and guns... lots of guns.

The office was completely off the grid. It was powered by solar for electricity, supplemented by propane-powered generators. The propane tanks were buried underground in concrete boxes where they could not be seen. A well supplied water. Nothing in the Bunker was connected to any utility.

Three of Zach's staff were sitting at one of the small conference tables in the Bunker as he strolled in, flanked by his two best friends, who were also on the payroll and served with Zach on the same SEAL team.

Zach removed his shoulder holster and set it on a large hook on the wall, along with dozens of other guns carefully placed on pegs on the same wall. He poured himself a cup of coffee and sat down with the others.

"Sons of bitches let him off..." started one of the men at the table.

"Did we expect anything else? But that damned Simpson... We all know *what* and who he is." Zach stared off into the distance.

"Oh, oh," said Will, one of Zach's two best friends, "I can see that brain is in full lock-down mode and working overtime. What happens next, Zach?"

Zach sat quietly for a few seconds that seemed to last an eternity. "They launched a federal military strike on the governor and deployed troops to try to prevent a *non-binding* referendum vote. Brahman's next move is likely to call for a *binding* vote," he said.

"There's no way they are going let that happen, guys," stated Will.

"The strategy will be the same by the feds, but the tactics might change," replied Zach as he stood up, yawned and stretched his arms behind his head, revealing a SEAL tattoo on his substantial left bicep and the Lone Star flag on the other.

"What is the most likely scenario the feds could muster to stop a binding vote for secession in the legislature? Are they going to launch a military strike on the Capitol building? Seems unlikely to me," said one of the men at the table, half-jokingly.

"I can't see how that would play well nationally. Bartlett is going to win the election. She portrayed herself as the peacemaker during the entire crisis. I think we all need to understand they will use covert actions to prevent this," said Zach.

"Makes sense. Zach. If that was our operation, how would we do it? We need to put ourselves in their shoes," replied Will, stroking his goatee.

"You have to get to those who are voting," Zach replied, as if he had already thought through this process.

"The state legislators? How so?" asked another.

"Everyone, and I do mean *everyone*, is vulnerable to *something*. Hell, these votes could be bought or they could be coerced. *Nothing* is sacred to those in D.C. You can bet this would be an operation out of Langley. If it was me, and if my ultimate mission was to defeat this vote in any way possible with no holds barred short of killing off legislators, I would start looking at who is most vulnerable and likely to cave with pressure, or those who are susceptible to the *wrong* kind of exposure," Zach surmised.

"Well, you could buy votes. That's the simple answer. When that doesn't work, you either find a hidden skeleton or you threaten family, or both. It would depend on how much time they have to influence things," shot back Will.

"Just remember, you don't have to turn the *entire* legislative body," reasoned Zach. "Just as the last presidential election turned in four swing states and was ultimately decided in six counties, you can affect the outcome by picking off just the right mix of legislators, state senators, or party leaders. Seriously, guys, this would be a chump mission compared to some of the crap we've been through in Afghanistan, Iraq and other parts of the world."

"The power of persuasion!" yelled Will, holding up his 9mm Glock to the laughter of everyone at the table.

"We are all persuaded and motivated by *something*," Zach continued, ignoring Will's shenanigans. "Langley will figure out what buttons to push and with whom, and it won't take them long. I bet they have dossiers on most of them anyway."

"So, if you had to predict…?" asked Will.

"You're asking me if politicians have the *huevos* to make the right decision, even if it's not politically correct? Ha! Remember, just because a politician is from Texas doesn't mean he has the interests of his fellow Texans at heart. Hell, look at Simpson. He's a carpet-bagging, sorry waste of oxygen," lamented Zach.

"Give me five minutes with Simpson!" said another man at the table.

"Five minutes? Hell, that's overkill. Give me thirty seconds with that sorry scumbag!" answered Will.

"You never know, fellas," said Zach, as if he knew something they didn't know. "You may get that chance sooner than you think."

The focus and demeanor suddenly changed.

"So there IS a Plan B in that crazy mind of yours?" asked Will, relieved.

Zach reached around to a side table, pulled out a black backpack, and unzipped it. He pulled out several documents and began to lay them on the table in front of the small group. Immediately, the group abandoned their chairs to get closer to the documents.

Zach had an uncanny ability to define and plan missions with incredible detail, fallback options, and risk assessment while he was a SEAL. It wasn't uncommon for those in command to define the mission and then cut Zach loose to plan it. He was an expert at detailed mission planning. He had never had a plan rejected by command and had never had a failed mission with the SEALs that he personally planned and executed.

In a matter of weeks, the entire country would come to understand the breadth of Zach's talent.

No one said a word as the crew anxiously pored over Zach's documents.

Will laid a document back down on the table after reading it and turned to Zach. "Give me an order, sir!"

CHAPTER 6

"All we ask is to be let alone."

- Jefferson Davis
President of the Confederate States of America

P ops Younger strolled into the ornate reception area of the governor's office. Already famous among law enforcement professionals, Pops was now a living legend among everyday Texans and the rest of the country for the scene that was broadcast live worldwide on the International Bridge in Laredo during the *Texas Crisis*. Pops had walked into the chaos and gunfire that erupted on the bridge to confront charging Mexican federales, calmly shooting several with the two ivory-gripped revolvers he pulled smoothly from his western-style holsters as the federales plunged more than a hundred feet to the Rio Grande below. It looked like a perfect stunt scene out of a well-orchestrated action movie, except that it was real.

Most people in Austin had never seen Pops without his trademark Stetson hat, his cowboy-cut denim Wranglers, and alligator cowboy boots. His handlebar mustache seemed to be as old as he was, but those close to him always commented on his steel-blue eyes and homespun wisdom. Legend had it that he had brought two fugitives to justice simply by staring them down as they pointed their weapons at him. That icy stare shot fear into the criminals, enough for them both to surrender their weapons to Pops without him saying a word. Nobody really knew how old he was, but some guessed him to be as old as eighty. He was ornery as a rattlesnake, except when it came to women.

"Howdy, Margaret, how was your weekend, darlin'? Damned cold this morning, ain't it?" Pops greeted Margaret, the governor's executive secretary.

"Sure is, Mr. Younger, but it may be colder in *that* office than it is outside!" she quipped back.

Pops never was much for ceremony, even in its simplest forms, and he detested most politicians. Margaret knew not to ask him to wait in the reception area while she notified the governor he had arrived. Pops was a Texas icon, surviving the administrations of six different governors, both Democrat and Republican. The one commonality between them all was that every one of them grew to love and respect Pops despite any differences they might have had with his old-school conservatism. Women especially were not put off by his chauvinistic nature and, oddly enough, most of them considered it chivalrous.

He also didn't need an invitation. Pops rarely elicited small talk, and about the only time you could get him to opine on current and political affairs was around a campfire at deer camp. Pops was Texas' version of Yogi Berra in cowboy boots, full of a unique, special wisdom and simply genius anecdotes. Pops had no tolerance for politics or politicians and, if he was coming to the capital, even without an appointment, then by God the governor was going to see him.

As the large oak doors swung open, Governor Brahman had just finished lighting a cigar. He didn't say a word as Pops strolled to his desk and sat down in the large leather chair, made from Axis deer and longhorn steer hides, opposite the desk. Governor Brahman took a long draw on his giant box-pressed Cuban stogie, leaned back in his hide-covered chair, and let the smoke billow out slowly. The governor's office always smelled like fine cigars and leather with a hint of the finest Kentucky bourbon.

"Good morning, Pops," said Brahman.

"What's good about it, Smitty?" asked Pops, who never called anyone by his official title.

"Well, damn, Pops, I guess you know where we stand this morning. I should've figured you'd be the first one in my office."

"I know this," said Pops, who was visibly agitated, "we've got a bunch of spineless weasels in the Congress and one especially from Texas."

"I know. I've never been more disappointed in my life with a Texas' senator. I thought Yankee liberals from the Northeast would be difficult to top!" lamented Brahman. "But you gotta be impressed with the PR campaign the media waged for Johnson."

"Hell, the impeachment hearings for Johnson were a joke and we didn't even see them! A certain senator should be tarred and feathered, then hung on the lawn of the Capitol. Somebody in D.C. must have some damned *goat* pictures on a few of these scoundrels." Pops stood to gaze out the window.

Brahman took another deep draw on his cigar. The former Texas Speaker of the House had ascended to the governorship immediately following the deaths of former Governor Brent Cooper and his wife, who were killed during the ill-conceived and failed federal arrest raid ordered by the administration that ignited the *Texas Crisis*.

Brahman had become a very popular figure among Texans as he stood up to President Johnson and Washington, D.C., just as his predecessor Cooper did. Not nearly as good-looking as Cooper, who strikingly resembled the original Marlboro Man, he became just as popular quickly during the *Crisis* as he promoted a non-binding referendum on Texas independence to voters despite the administration's heavy-handed unconstitutional tactics to stop it.

"Give some credit to that old warhorse Annabelle Bartlett, Pops. She managed to be the voice of reason, complaining how the impeachment hearings were tearing the country apart," said Brahman.

"Hell, it'll probably get her elected," quipped Pops.

"Pops, you know good and well she's going to get elected, no matter what. That's already been decided," answered Brahman.

Pops walked over to the coffee bar and grabbed a coffee mug emblazoned with the state seal to use as a spit cup for the pinch of Copenhagen between his bottom lip and gums. The governor knew he was about to get some of Pops' unique wisdom and insight. At that point, it was best to just shut up and let Pops talk, and Brahman knew it. This was about to be one of those rare moments with Pops that endeared him so much to those who knew him.

Looking down at his cowboy boots, Pops moved his left foot, then his right, in small circles as if he was kicking dirt around on his ranch, despite the fact he was standing on broadleaf pine wooden floors in the governor's mansion. He spit some tobacco and saliva juice into the cup, then twisted his thick handlebar mustache, deep in thought. Next came the slight tilt on his Stetson as he pulled it down slightly lower above his left eye.

"Smitty, folks are madder than hell. They stirred up a damned hornets' nest. It's like a box of BBs fell on the floor. You ain't never gonna get 'em back in the box," Pops said in his slow Texas drawl. "If I was that dirt weasel

Simpson, I'd be damned sure afraid to go back to my hometown right about now. We're sittin' on a tinder box, Gov. It wouldn't take much for the whole enchilada to blow up again."

"Well, crap, Pops, we had one hundred eighty-nine Texans die simply trying to cast a vote for a *non-binding* referendum on Texas independence!" retorted Brahman. "Seventy-eight percent to twenty-two percent, then the legislature refuses to take up the referendum and pass it. I'm pretty angry myself!"

"Some folks think Bartlett will salve all wounds," responded Pops. "I don't buy it. She's worse than that scalawag Johnson in some ways. Pure evil through and through. I don't know how folks don't see it. It's as plain as sunlight hittin' your face in the morning."

Again, Brahman drew down deeply on his cigar. His office now had a three-foot-thick haze of cigar smoke clinging to the ornate tin ceiling as the two antique ceiling fans in the room barely turned.

"I'm working on the timeline now to call the legislature back into session. We better get this one right, Pops."

"Damned straight, Smitty," shot back Younger.

"The good people of Texas will find out soon enough if their elected leaders have any balls," said Brahman.

"Governor, I have a lot of faith in my fellow Texans, but that damned legislature ain't much better than those sons of bitches in D.C. Politicians are lower than a snake's belly, no offense intended."

"None taken," chuckled the governor.

Pops sat back down and Brahman now stretched his legs as he put his black snakeskin cowboy boots up on the desk. They both just sat there and thought for a few long moments. It was as if just the fact that they were in the same room together, smoking cigars and dipping tobacco, that put them both at ease despite the enormity of the last few months' events. Both had felt a strong loyalty and duty to Texas for their entire lives. Now, two giants of Texas lore, one as iconoclastic as a figure straight out of the 1880s and the other of more recent vintage, sat there together, just the two of them, quietly pondering the uncertainty of Texas' fate.

After a few quiet moments, Brahman said, "That was a helluva storm, Pops."

Pops knew exactly what the governor was referring to, and it wasn't the weather.

"Sir, what's bearing down on us right now will make that look like an afternoon squall," replied Pops.

More moments of silence ensued as Pops peered over to the west wall of the office, the only wall without windows to the downtown Austin skyline. For a moment, Pops seemed to be taken aback, then he flexed his slender frame as if realizing he was in the presence of royalty or some antiquity of historic or religious importance.

Recognizing this was the first time Pops had seen the large framed item that adorned his west wall, Brahman offered, "I sure as hell hope he and that little gal didn't die in vain."

Pops kept staring at the now famous item, a Texas Lone Star flag with the black numbers *1789* hand-stitched in the white bar. The flag was covered with dark stains...

Blood... from Chuck Dixon and Amanda Flores.

Pops walked over to the flag and stood just beneath it, then rubbed his mustache with his right forefinger, trying to hide the fact that he was struggling to hold back tears.

"It would be a damned tragedy, sir. Damned tragedy, indeed..." said Pops as his voice trailed slightly.

After a few more moments of silence, Pops seemed to gather himself and his entire demeanor changed. "Gov, you can say a lot of things about Texans, but forgetting history ain't one of 'em."

CHAPTER 7

"During times of universal deceit, telling the truth becomes a revolutionary act."

- George Orwell
Author & Journalist

The emergence of populist Republican candidate Roger Hilton over the spring and summer months jolted American politics. Although he was more of a populist and not exactly conservative, the far-right wing of the party was forced by public sentiment to eventually get behind him over traditional candidates who were congressmen, senators and governors. A businessman, he was an outsider who had never held political office.

Former Secretary of State Bartlett was always one to make the most of her political opportunities. There was nothing contrived about her. To those who knew her well, she was cold, manipulative and cunning. Very few politicians in American history had her knack for sensing when to seize the narrative. She was now in her sixties, and the political seeds she had sown over thirty years were about to be harvested in a big way.

As President Johnson wound down the last few months of his lame-duck presidency, he was more than happy to broker a back-room deal with congressional Democrats. He had no problem with allowing Attorney General Tibbs to be impeached as the scapegoat for the feds' incompetence and ultimately the death of a sitting Texas governor and his wife in the *Texas Crisis*.

Johnson and Bartlett had always had an uneasy co-existence. Johnson had come from behind to win the Democratic primary eight years before.

Bartlett thought it was her turn, as did most of her party establishment. The Democrats, who made history with the first African-American president, now wanted to do it again with the first elected woman for the leader of the free world.

Bartlett had gotten the lion's share of the credit, albeit mostly undeserved, from the media for brokering a temporary pause to the hostilities of the *Texas Crisis*. The Bartlett machine then kicked operatives around the country into gear to lock up the Democratic nomination long before the convention, with no serious threats from other candidates.

Hilton, on the other hand, was in a supreme battle with a dozen candidates. The Republican primary was especially harsh, inflicting permanent damage on each candidate who slogged through the state primaries. Hilton did not carry the Texas primary. Senator Roberto Perez from Texas did, bolstered by his support for the referendum.

In each televised debate, Perez was excoriated by the moderators, Hilton and the other candidates for supporting the Texas referendum. Hilton labeled Perez as "Treasonous Bob" and the pseudonym stuck. Surprisingly, Perez' affinity for the Constitution enabled him to win seventeen states, but he fell significantly short of Hilton's delegate count majority.

Hilton's attraction came from the voters' disgust with both political establishment machines and the dysfunction of the federal government. Surprisingly, despite the fact that voters were fed up, the vast majority of Republicans nationwide did not support the Texas referendum, but they also were strongly against President Johnson's actions during the *Texas Crisis*. Hilton often crowed that Perez did nothing to avert the crisis that led to bloodshed, even to the point of blaming Perez' support of the referendum directly for the deaths of federal agents and Texas citizens.

Most political experts and prognosticators predicted a close general election, with the final tally in the Electoral College coming down to the swing states of Florida, Virginia, North Carolina, Ohio and Pennsylvania.

The *Texas Crisis* was a central subject of both campaigns; however, for the most part, both candidates agreed Texas had no right to conduct such a vote. Hilton, especially, was very measured in responses to questions about the crisis, states' rights and the loss of life in an attempt to gain independent voters who polled against the Texas referendum.

Bartlett was quick to take credit, at any opportunity she could, for ending the crisis.

This presidential election broke all spending records by a couple of billion dollars. Despite the serious flaws, associations, and questionable dealings in their pasts that would have sunk candidates in previous election cycles, the country appeared to be entering a new political era where anything was accepted.

A country where the average voting-age adult couldn't even name the three branches of government or give two examples of the Bill of Rights was about to choose from an entrenched political hack and an outsider who could become the first *tabloid* president.

A key component of the Bartlett campaign strategy was to distance herself from Johnson, but especially from Johnson's Attorney General, Jamail Tibbs. Tibbs was a fierce personal enemy of Bartlett's. She reveled in the fact that he was impeached and made no bones about his complicity in the ultimate deaths in the crisis. Bartlett, however, was not dismissive whatsoever regarding the feds' authority to attempt to shut down the Texas referendum.

As the Florida votes came in, Hilton had an early lead, larger than anyone expected. As the night wore on, Bartlett began closing the gap. Election returns from South Florida in the Miami/Dade area were solidly in her favor, typical for the Democrats. By 10:00 p.m., most of the networks were ready to call a huge upset for Hilton. Fox and CNN were already projecting Hilton as the winner, although his lead had shrunk to four points with only the Jacksonville metro area to report. Because of Jacksonville's military presence, it was safe to predict Hilton would carry this last major precinct, and thus Florida.

MSNBC broke into programming to declare Bartlett had carried Jacksonville, erasing Hilton's lead and delivering the first major blow on election night. Bartlett won Florida, not totally unexpected, but from far behind in a staunchly conservative area that hadn't voted Democratic since JFK.

Pundits now focused on Virginia, North Carolina and Pennsylvania, whose polls closed at or near the same time as Florida's.

Bartlett's election headquarters in Arlington, Virginia was abuzz. The crowd went from despair to elation when Fox, CNN and ABC changed their projections to declare Bartlett the winner.

Bartlett watched from her expansive hotel suite with her handlers, strategists, and largest donors. In the corner of the room, drinking a glass of Dewar's and water, was Nils Ottosson. Ottosson was an executive with a lobby firm on K Street that just happened to be owned by Säkerhet Intelligent Systems, AB (translated into English to "Certainty") and was well known in Washington, D.C. circles as CIS.

CIS had won several database contracts for their work on the U.S. Census. The lobbying firm CIS America was well known to Beltway insiders. It was one of the most prominent of the hundreds, if not thousands, of lobbyists registered to influence votes and government contracts.

Ottosson was a known ladies' man and partier, and the Bartlett campaign headquarters environment was beginning to be described as giddy, perfectly suited for a good time. Though he was married, with his wife and two children in Stockholm, Ottosson never acted like he was married while he was in D.C.

"This is going to be a great night," claimed Ottosson in broken English to two twenty-something females who were deep into their own private conversation and countless selfies they were taking with the crowd in the background.

At first acting like they had not heard him, they finally looked up and one said, "So far, so good, but it's only the first one in!" she said, gleefully referring to the Florida results.

"Trust me, it's going be a *great* night!" he claimed, holding up two full glasses of Dewar's, one in each hand.

Laughingly, the second girl said, "Well, we're glad you're so confident. There's still a long way to go."

Ottosson was dressed in an Armani suit and displayed a little bit of charm, even if he was approaching middle age. The first girl took a couple of steps closer. She sensed his confidence, but also figured he must be somebody important.

"Two drinks at once?" she asked.

"I'm already celebrating our victory!" he shot back coolly.

"Do you know something we don't?" she replied wryly.

"Let's just say that the Electoral College will be decided before the polls move west across the Mississippi," he said confidently as he sipped from one of his two glasses.

As the election night sped on, Hilton took early and sometimes substantial leads in some of the key swing states, but amazingly couldn't sustain those leads in any of them. A trend began to emerge where key counties that traditionally voted Republican were won by Bartlett very late in the election count. As many as six key Republican counties swung Democratic in Pennsylvania which, along with northern Florida, may have been the shockers of the electoral map this election night.

On the strength of pulling out a win in every single swing state, former Secretary of State Annabelle Bartlett swept to victory. What most pundits believed to be a very tight race turned into three-hundred fifty-two electoral votes to the populist Hilton's one-hundred eighty-six. It was a landslide. Ninety-seven electoral votes swung to Bartlett in six states alone where Hilton was expected to be very competitive and where his early election return leads evaporated and turned into last-minute Bartlett victories.

Far worse for the Republicans, they barely hung on to a majority in the Senate and lost the majority in the House handily.

Experts called Bartlett the "closer" for her ability to come from behind late on election night in key states to win.

The United States of America had elected its first woman president.

CHAPTER 8

"It is enough that the people know there was an election. The people who cast the votes decide nothing. The people who count the votes decide everything."

- Josef Stalin
Communist Dictator of the Soviet Union
(1878-1953)

Zach Turner and his wife settled on the couch after a home-cooked dinner, after they put their son Colt to bed. Kymbra Turner was already cozy in her flannel pajamas and was ready to settle in for the night with Zach to watch the election returns. Zach had prepared her that the deciding results might not be apparent until deep into the night.

By 10:30, Zach became so agitated that he couldn't sit still.

"Something ain't right," he told Kymbra as she struggled to stay awake. She had chased after Colt all day, along with housework, and the election results were not enough to overcome her fatigue.

"Damn, they are starting to call it," Zach said in a distressed voice.

Kymbra had just fallen asleep, but Zach's tone shocked her awake.

Zach scooted up onto the edge of the couch, clicking the remote to check all the major election coverage on Fox, CNN, ABC and others.

"I'm telling you, this stinks," he growled.

"Yes, it does, baby," said Kymbra, knowing how disappointed he was as she played with his short-cropped hair.

"Not for the reasons you think, sweetheart. She has either got to be the luckiest candidate in history or something else is going on here. I mean, heck, she was down in almost every swing state, some with sixty or seventy percent of the precincts already reporting. That just doesn't happen."

"Well, it did this time. Zach, you can't get yourself so worked up," she said soothingly, knowing that her protests about his anger would likely be ignored.

Zach's cell phone rang.

"Turner," he answered. He never said "hello." He looked at his watch as he listened for a few seconds. "Right. 0700 at the Bunker."

Kymbra knew it was useless to protest, but tried anyway. "Baby, try not to get so worked up. I can see your mind already working overtime. What's going on in that head of yours?"

"I just don't understand this. It doesn't look right. The odds of that happening like it just went down is astronomical, yet everyone is praising Bartlett for the great comeback. I don't buy it," he said as he stood up and began to pace around the living room.

"You're scaring me... Zach, there's nothing you can do."

"It ain't right. Somebody has to look into this. Not one pundit on TV said a damned thing about the odds of this happening. Something happened. I don't know *what* happened, but I don't trust it one damned bit."

"My hero," she said, "always taking on the weight of the world at any opportunity he can." She stood and put her arms around him, kissing him on the cheek, partly in genuine admiration and partly to calm him.

"I can't be the only one who sees this," he kept saying.

"Come to bed, baby. I'll settle you down," offered Kymbra in the sexiest voice she could offer.

"I can't take this. I've got to find out. I've got to do *something*."

As they crawled in bed, Kymbra snuggled up to Zach and started kissing him slowly, all over. She was determined to put him at ease.

He tried his best to get into their lovemaking, but his mind wandered at times. Shortly afterward, Kymbra fell asleep. Zach quietly got up from bed and went back into the living room where he turned the election coverage back on.

"This stinks. I don't trust it," he murmured to himself.

Finally, Zach went back to bed, crawling carefully under the covers so as not to wake Kymbra. But he couldn't sleep; as he lay on the pillow, his brain ran in circles.

Staring at the ceiling, he continued to rerun the election in his head as he tried to discount the deep nagging feeling that the election had possibly been *stolen* somehow—some way.

CHAPTER 9

"Democracy consists of choosing your dictators, after they've told you what you think it is you want to hear."

> *- Alan Coren*
> *English Humorist*
> *(1938-2007)*

President Bartlett entered the Cabinet Room at the White House almost thirty minutes late for her first Cabinet meeting, in keeping with the bad habits of her predecessor Johnson. Bartlett didn't seem fazed whatsoever by her tardiness with the cameras and press there to get their opportunity to see Americas first female president presiding over her first Cabinet meeting.

"Thank you, ladies and gentlemen," she remarked, pausing for a full half-minute so the photographers could get the most out of this photo op before she took her seat.

Dressed in her trademark utilitarian-style pantsuit, cut to minimize her sizable pear-shaped derriere, Bartlett finally took a seat as the press took a few minutes to clear the room.

"Madam President, sitting on the table in front of you is the approved agenda for today's meeting. Would you like to take these items in the order suggested?" asked Milton Weingold, her chief of staff.

Bartlett read for a few seconds before replying, "Let's first get an update on the *Texas Crisis* please." That was not in the top three agenda items she had previously approved.

Weingold stood up, taking out a different set of papers from his leather briefcase. Only Weingold and the president knew this was to be the central topic of the cabinet meeting.

"The Texas Legislature failed to take up the referendum passed shortly before the impeachment hearings. Our strategy will be to lean on the monied interests, call out favors and, of course, use the power of certain persuasion to get the Texas Legislature to kill its referendum if it comes up again, and all signs point to that happening. The referendum almost died in committee, but was not successful on the floor. However, our guess is that, since the legislative session is adjourned, the governor will likely call back a special session to try again. We fully expect this and have prepared accordingly," Weingold told the group.

"For now, this whole hare-brained idea down there is not dead yet, but it is on hold," he said, looking up over his eyeglasses to survey the entire cabinet with a wry smile, like a professor looked at his class to make a point he didn't want them to forget.

"Madam President has talked personally to Governor Brahman and they have assured each other that both state and federal law enforcement officials will stand down as this process, wherever it takes us, continues." He paused.

There was grumbling at the table, most of it inaudible but registering just the same.

"Would someone like to say something?" asked the president, irritated that anyone would dare question her strategy.

Since this was the first Cabinet meeting with the president, there was some reluctance to be the first to speak. Attorney General Laura Scripps-Mosey stood.

Scripps-Mosey was one of Bartlett's first nominees and was proud of the fact that she was the first openly gay U.S. attorney general and a double minority. Scripps-Mosey was a controversial figure, a black woman criticized on many fronts, even in her own party, for her decisions and judgment as an urban district attorney from Baltimore.

"Madam President, doesn't the public still want to see justice for the loss of life, especially for the federal agents and U.S. military personnel who died in Texas? Let's face it, the arrest of FBI agents by state police, especially by that cowboy, hasn't left the public's consciousness."

"Laura, I appreciate your concern, and I'm sure many of you here today feel the same. We are formulating a plan to keep this situation from escalating. My predecessor, and your predecessor in the Justice Department, I might add, elected to take a head-on approach to this." President Bartlett paused to let her words sink in. "I have a different plan. You saw how we got this silliness defeated by calling in favors and applying the exact amount of political pressure where it had the most effect. There will be a time and place for that, and I promise you we will not forget. I know the players down there fairly well from prior dealings. I will ask you all to trust me on this as we will be including each of you in specific roles for dealing with the de-escalation of what was essentially a manufactured crisis," Bartlett stated confidently.

"Madam President, I want to offer to you and everyone here my suggestion that we no longer refer to this situation as *The Texas Crisis* or refer to it as a crisis in any way, since hostilities have been settled," Weingold added. "I just think it's time to change the narrative."

"Great suggestion, Milt. Let's all adhere to that directive," agreed President Bartlett.

In unison, most of the Cabinet said, "Yes, Madam President."

"Each of your staff will be getting talking points on how the administration is dealing with Texas. Please make sure your entire staff is fully cognizant of these directives," said Weingold authoritatively.

Most pundits were taken by surprise that Bartlett tapped Weingold for her chief of staff. He hadn't been directly involved in any of her campaigns, but he was a staunch Democrat and an ultra-progressive supporter from New York. Weingold had graduated from Harvard Law School and was the dean of NYU Law for twenty years before going into private practice. He had been instrumental in two other campaigns that resulted in wins for Democrats in a New York gubernatorial and U.S. Senate race. He was Jewish, wore thick, black-framed round glasses and was known as a no-nonsense political operative. In his mid-sixties, he never married and was known for wearing three-piece Brooks Brothers suits, always accented with some version of a red bow tie.

The next item on the agenda was the replacement of several of the military Joint Chiefs who had been arrested for dereliction of duty and failing to carry out orders from the president during the Johnson administration's failed Operation Santa Anna. The operation, which attempted to exercise a federal arrest warrant to snatch the governor of Texas, failed miserably and resulted in an international incident with Mexico, and the deaths of the Texas governor and his wife.

It was a huge national embarrassment to the Johnson administration and ultimately resulted in the impeachment of Attorney General Tibbs and the unsuccessful impeachment of President Johnson.

Bartlett was torn by the prosecution and case against the former Joint Chiefs, as she was diametrically opposed to Tibbs' plan. She felt that, if she had been allowed to continue to mediate the stand-off, bloodshed could have been avoided. There was absolutely no love lost between her and Tibbs.

Like many of this old political warhorse's enemies, he totally underestimated her and he paid the price for it.

CHAPTER 10

"Our job is to give people not what they want, but what we decide they ought to have."

- Richard Salant
(1914-1993) former President of CBS News

The election of Bartlett was a watershed moment for the Supreme Court. Three justices who sat on the Supreme Court were more than seventy-six years old. The Court, which had leaned slightly right over the previous twenty years, was at a precipice. Any one of these justices could retire or die at any moment.

Two of the three justices who leaned conservative had indicated they were weary of the demands of the Court and were ready to retire, hoping for a Hilton victory so they could retire knowing that any new nominations to the Court would likely be in their mold. Now, with a Bartlett victory, they had decided as a group to stick it out four more years. There were major cases that were making their way through the federal district courts that could change the entire course of America. The United States, which was being fashioned more and more as a European-style socialist state, was only a few Supreme Court decisions away from completing the transition.

The Court's interpretation of the 2nd Amendment, which had stood since 1789, had been successfully weakened incrementally every time some lunatic killed random victims in a mass shooting incident. The left was salivating at the chance to permanently alter it, leaving it so weakened that it wouldn't have the same intent as the Founders had crafted.

The *Texas Crisis*, with the resulting deaths of federal agents and U.S.

Army Rangers, had swayed public opinion to begin to "federalize" all police forces and threatened to dismantle state-run militias and state guard organizations that operated at the behest of their respective governors. The largest and most organized of this type was in Texas, and the rest of the country was stunned to learn a full military unit in a state operated independently of Washington.

Supreme Court Chief Justice Clarence Noyner was considered to have a brilliant legal mind and was the bell cow of the Court for conservatives. Noyner, appointed by a Republican president, had served the Court through six presidents. Originally thought to be a moderate, Noyner became increasingly conservative and was the object of ridicule by the left on a regular basis. Noyner had cast the deciding vote in most major cases.

Noyner, at seventy-seven, was a large, round man who wore bifocals when on the bench. He was balding, with a few strands of hair literally combed over and seemingly pasted to his head. Mostly jovial in social situations, Noyner didn't suffer fools when it came to legal briefs, unprepared attorneys who appeared before the Court, or even his fellow justices. Whether he was in dissent or writing for the Court, his fellow justices usually chose him to write the opinion. Most legal scholars believed him to be a brilliant justice, even those who didn't agree with his opinions. There was no doubt that Noyner was one of the brightest legal minds to ever sit on the Court.

Originally from the panhandle of Texas, Noyner graduated from the University of Texas at the top of his class and then attended Harvard Law. He met his wife of forty-six years in Austin. Noyner clerked for another conservative icon, Chief Justice Matthew Kelby. Many considered Noyner the most influential Supreme Court justice in one hundred fifty years.

"The car will be here to pick you up at 2:00, Your Honor," said the attractive, dark-haired, green-eyed female clerk who brought him his briefcase stuffed with legal documents.

Noyner was headed for a well-deserved vacation after the election during a recess in the Court's schedule. Even on vacation, Noyner still worked, as evidenced by his well-worn brown leather briefcase—that went with him everywhere—that he got as a gift from his parents when he graduated Harvard Law School.

"Okay, Jenny, thanks for putting these case files together for me."

"Your Honor, are you really going to work while you are on an offshore fishing boat? I would get seasick trying to read papers. Heck, I'd probably get seasick even if I wasn't reading on a boat that never stops rocking!" she teased.

"Well, there's the boat ride for a couple of hours out to the fishing reef and a couple of hours back. It's therapy, young lady. It's what I love to do," Noyner replied.

"That's what makes you so good at what you do, sir!" said the clerk innocently.

"Ha, I wish it were that easy, my young friend. But you will learn that in time. You will be an outstanding lawyer in your own right!" he told her.

"Well, thank you so much, sir. Again, the car will be here in a couple of hours."

Supreme Court Justice Noyner arrived at the private executive aviation terminal in a black Escalade driven by a single driver. Noyner's SUV was waved through a private electric gate, then pulled onto the tarmac and parked right next to a brand new, white-and-polished-aluminum Falcon 900 private jet.

The jet had one engine running to keep the air conditioning circulating, as Noyner was the last passenger to arrive. The driver got out and opened the rear cargo door of the SUV as two employees of the executive airport picked up the chief justice's bags and loaded them on the plane.

Noyner struggled somewhat to get his heavy body to climb the six steps onto the plane. He paused momentarily to look at the tail of the plane, which had the CIS logo painted on it. He paused again on the last step; a small part of him wanted to step back down. He was more than a little curious why they were taking a CIS jet. His host, a Republican senator, told him the plane was provided by a major donor who was also going.

Noyner didn't know CIS was the donor.

"Well, there he is!" said Senator Robert "Bob" McCray, who was already sitting on the plush leather couch in the plane's cabin with a scotch on the rocks in his hand.

McCray was the Senate majority leader and former chairman of the Senate Judiciary Committee. All new Supreme Court nominations from Bartlett would have to go through McCray to get a vote on the floor.

McCray, at seventy-two, had been in Congress for thirty-six years, first elected as a representative from the 11th District of North Carolina in the Blue Ridge Mountains area of the western part of the state.

Many in Congress considered McCray the closest thing they had ever seen to LBJ. He was tall, had a deep southern accent and was absolutely brutal in political affairs. McCray simply took no prisoners, politically speaking.

As powerful as McCray was—and there weren't many in Congress as powerful—he was surprisingly ignorant of the constant jokes about his appearance from various aides and staff members of other senators on the Hill. McCray had very bushy gray eyebrows that protruded at least an inch from his forehead. No better were his nose hairs, which stuck out obtrusively from both nostrils, along with the array of hair that grew from his ear lobes.

Political cartoonists had much delight in portraying his caricature with all the body hair but, strangely enough, McCray never attempted to alter or clean up his appearance, nor did anyone close to him dare try to convince him to do it.

Although there was mutual respect, Noyner and McCray were not originally the best of friends. Their relationship had been built as McCray frequently sought input from Noyner on Supreme Court issues, nominations and judicial appointments. Part of the reason Noyner agreed to go on this trip was to talk informally with McCray about Bartlett's expected nominations to the SCOTUS.

"Apologies for keeping everyone waiting. The traffic was brutal," replied Noyner, breathing heavily from climbing the steps to get in the plane.

"Would you like a drink?" asked the middle-aged, attractive stewardess.

"I'd love a Kentucky bourbon and water if you have it," he replied.

"We sure do. I'll have it up for you in a jiffy."

"Well, Judge, are you ready for some serious fishing?" asked McCray.

"I'll just be happy to be on the water. If I catch anything worth keeping, it will be a bonus." Noyner chuckled.

In addition to McCray, McCray's chief of staff, a legislative affairs aide, and a man Noyner didn't know were on the plane.

"Judge, please meet Nils Ottosson," McCray said. "He's with CIS, and this is one of their corporate aircraft," said McCray.

Ottosson reached to shake hands. "It's an honor to meet you, sir."

Noyner immediately didn't care for Ottosson; it was an instinctive dislike.

"Wow, the election business must be good," remarked Noyner, referring to the accouterments in the jet and the large government contract CIS had for electronic voting machines in the United States.

"Well, it's simply technology, sir," Ottosson told him. "And we are very good at it." He smirked.

"Apparently you are," answered Noyner in a slightly sarcastic tone.

Noyner's thoughts raced. He was now extremely uncomfortable being on the CIS aircraft. They had just shut the main cabin door. His mind drifted for a few seconds, recalling how he had made comments about the federal government awarding a contract for voting machines and software to a foreign firm. For a moment, Noyner thought about getting off the plane. He wondered to himself how it would look to the public for him to be a guest of CIS on their private plane after criticizing the federal contract that essentially paid for the plane.

"I know you guys have the federal election contract, but how are you doing in the States?" asked Senator McCray.

"Thanks for asking, Senator," Ottosson responded. "Currently, we are in forty-two of the fifty states in some way, shape or manner. In some states, it's only county or state elections, but in most we are joined at the hip with their state election commissions and secretaries of state."

"Your Honor, just so you know, CIS contributes equally to both parties," remarked the senator.

"Of course. You wouldn't want anyone to think the holder of the federal voting systems contract favored one party over the other, would you?" asked Noyner.

As the stewardess came back down the aisle with drinks, Ottosson's attention changed directions. Noyner leaned forward to speak to McCray in a quieter tone.

"Senator, I wish you had told me specifically whose plane this was ahead of time," said Noyner, looking slightly agitated.

"You didn't ask, Your Honor. I did mention it was a GOP donor, correct?" McCray said defensively.

"Yes, yes, you did," admitted Noyner.

Ottosson, overhearing Noyner, remarked, "Your Honor, I don't want you to feel uncomfortable. Just so you know, we don't have any pending contracts or tenders in front of the federal government. Our contracts are very long term and are already in place. There's nothing anyone on this plane could influence in pending legislation."

"Well, thank you for that. I feel better already," commented Noyner, smiling wryly.

Everyone laughed somewhat uneasily.

The conversations migrated to small talk and inconsequential subjects as the plane started the second engine and began to lurch forward down the runway.

It would be the last time Chief Justice Noyner would ever set foot in Washington, D.C.

CHAPTER 11

"The right of a nation to kill a tyrant in case of necessity can no more be doubted than to hang a robber, or kill a flea."

- *John Adams*
(1735-1826) Delegate to the Continental Congress
2nd US President

In just a little more than two-and-a-half hours from take-off, the group from the CIS private jet stepped onto the stern of a fifty-six-foot Hatteras fishing yacht, dubbed the *Ida Kay,* at a Fort Myers, Florida yacht club.

There to meet the group were the boat captain and three deckhands. The chartered boat was scheduled to be out for twenty-four hours, approximately seventy miles offshore in the Gulf to fish for tarpon, kingfish, red snapper, bonito, and ling. If they were lucky, they could stumble on some tuna, sailfish or blunt-nosed dolphin (mahi mahi).

The *Ida Kay* was well appointed with four private sleeping areas below deck and a small galley. The yacht was rigged for big game fishing, with a six-foot opening in the stern for dragging prize catches up on deck. The wheelhouse was elevated high above the deck, allowing for a great view of the Gulf while at sea.

"We are going to set sail in twenty minutes, gentlemen," said the captain after brief introductions. Senator McCray had used this charter company on several occasions before.

"Got some new deckhands, I see?" commented McCray to Captain Walsh.

"Two of them are brand new. Both came from another boat in Miami, but were highly recommended," said the captain. He went on to explain that his two experienced deckhands, after both had worked for him for years, were inexplicably no-shows as of the charter before this one.

"Your Honor, the stateroom below is yours. Feel free to make yourself comfortable. There is beer here on deck and just about anything you want in the galley. We have had some quite tasty snacks prepared and we will eat en route. The seas are a little choppy, but we should make it to the reefs I want to fish in about two to three hours."

"Thank you, captain. There's nothing like sleeping on a boat, in my opinion. The soundest sleep I ever get. If you don't mind, I'll probably just grab a bite and retire to my bunk. No need to wake me for dinner," said Noyner.

"Damn, Your Honor. Going to bed early, huh? Not even some scotch with old friends before you retire?" asked Senator McCray.

"I'm a bourbon drinker," shot back Noyner.

"Yes, Your Honor, please have at least one drink with us before you check out for the night," said Ottosson.

"Okay," Noyner conceded, "a nice glass of bourbon will help me sleep."

The captain motioned to one of the crew, who went down to the galley and fetched some snacks, glasses, ice and some small-batch Kentucky bourbon.

The crew members were busy stowing gear and making the guests comfortable. One of the two crewmen reached over to a small canvas bag with leather handles and a zipper that was sitting on the deck next to the luggage brought aboard. He snatched it up quickly and disappeared down the steps to the galley. Although he didn't think much of it at the time, Noyner wondered why the man only took the small bag below when so many other pieces of luggage remained topside.

The *Ida Kay* cruised slowly out of the harbor, passing Sanibel Island just at sunset, making a spectacular scene for the fishing party. Ottosson sat on the party deck in the rear enjoying the drinks, small talk, and a deep orange sunset.

Justice Noyner's one glass of bourbon turned into four as he and McCray delighted their small audience with anecdotes from past Supreme Court courtroom drama, politics, and the occasional off-color joke.

The *Ida Kay* was steadily plowing southwesterly through four- to five-foot seas in a steady up-and-down rhythm as Noyner stood and declared he was going down to his bunk.

Noyner noticed the entire time he was enjoying his bourbon with the others that one particular crew member was curiously fixated on him, enough to make him uneasy. He had become accustomed to this whenever he ate out with his wife or went to his favorite watering hole. However, every time Noyner glanced back, the crew member looked down and continued to work on the rods, reels and rigging.

At 4:00 a.m., the captain rang the bell that rousted his clients from slumber. Although they'd arrived an hour and half later than he expected, the captain had positioned the boat over the reef structure where he wanted to begin the day fishing. They were seventy-eight miles offshore from Sanibel Island.

Noyner, now well rested, was the first one on deck with the crew, anxious to get his day started catching fish.

"Good morning, Captain. Still a little choppy, I see," Noyner commented.

"Well, we are down to two- to three-foot chops as compared to last night. I'm sure you could tell the seas were up a bit last night. That's why it took so long for us to get out here. When we left, they were the same, but increased to four to six."

"I didn't notice; I slept like a baby."

"Glad to hear it. We have coffee and breakfast ready for you in the galley," the captain told him.

"I could smell the coffee and pastries," Noyner said.

"If you don't want pastries, our cook made some eggs, and there's oatmeal and other items that might meet your fancy."

"Thank you, I'll take a look. Coffee sounds great." Noyner was going down the galley steps as McCray, Ottosson and the others were grabbing coffee and pastries.

"Looks like a good day to wet a line, but a little choppy," remarked McCray.

Nodding his head while sipping hot coffee, Noyner said, "Indeed it does."

The crew was standing ready with baited rods as they headed topside,

"Let's start with some mullet, crab and pinfish. Tarpon love this stuff and we want your rig down pretty deep," suggested the head deck mate.

"Not much weight on these lines?" asked McCray.

"We like to free line, with just a little sinker on them to get them to sink slowly. This will work just fine," answered the other deckhand.

The two new deckhands were mostly quiet, and at times looked like they were somewhat out of place, just a step slower than the captain's regular deckhands. Noyner felt this a little unusual, as the captain was one of those boat captains that was always at the top of his game and didn't tolerate amateurs working as deckhands.

For the first few hours, the group pulled in three nice-sized tarpon, the largest by Ottosson weighing in at ninety pounds, a few kingfish and a couple of bonito. Noyner hadn't caught a tarpon yet.

By 10:00, the seas had picked up and the waves had increased to five to seven feet and the wind was beginning to gust.

"Gentlemen, we have about an hour left before I want to start heading in. I'm looking at the weather and we have some squalls developing to the west. If we pull out in an hour or so, we should beat them into shore," the captain told everyone on the back party deck.

"That should be all I need to get my tarpon," laughed Noyner.

"I'm done fishing. I'm going to grab some coffee and watch Your Honor get that tarpon!" remarked Ottosson, slightly annoying Noyner.

"I'm done, too. I may go down and grab a sandwich in the galley," McCray answered.

The minute McCray disappeared with his two staff members, Noyner's reel began singing.

"Tarpon!" yelled one of the deckhands. "It's a big one!"

"Here we go!" yelled back Noyner, happy he had finally got on to a tarpon.

"Judge, hang in there; the waves are picking up, too!" shouted the captain.

Well behind the boat, a two-hundred pound-plus tarpon leaped out of the Gulf, spinning acrobatically as it crashed back through the surface of the water. This battle was going to be a long one.

For the next hour, the crew focused on helping Noyner get the tarpon landed. Noyner had to transfer the rod to a deckhand on two occasions to take a breather. The waves made the deck slippery and hazardous and, with the frenzy of trying to land the big tarpon, the captain ordered the others to the galley or wheelhouse. McCray's two aides were up on the pilot's deck with the captain. Three of the four deckhands were on the deck. One of the new deckhands scurried past Ottosson on the ladder to the galley. He went down and came back up with the small blue canvas bag.

The only person that took notice was Ottosson.

"We're close, sir! Steady! Keep the rod tip up. John, get that gaff ready!" yelled a deckhand.

In all the excitement, commotion, and the rocking of the boat, nobody noticed one of the new deckhands who was in the corner of the deck against the bulkheads, mostly out of everyone's view.

The tarpon was slowly tiring, and Noyner was exhausted but excited. Two of the deckhands assisted Noyner with the rod, while another was ready at the stern to gaff the fish and bring it in. The captain was busy trying to keep the boat positioned bow first into the growing waves.

As the tarpon was near the stern, the deckhand who had been fiddling with the canvas pack stepped across the deck quickly. In one motion, he reached over and slightly grazed the forearm of Noyner with something. Noyner barely felt anything; his arm was drained of strength from fighting the big fish. He looked briefly confused at what the deckhand was trying to do, thinking he was somehow trying to help him with the reel.

"Got him!" screamed the deckhand at the stern, reaching out to gaff the tarpon.

"Oh," said Noyner. As he loosened his grip on the rod, it fell to the deck.

"It's okay, sir, we got him!" yelled another deckhand as he saw Noyner drop the reel.

Noyner turned to the deckhand behind him with a bewildered look.

"Sir, you okay? Do you want to sit down?" The deckhand noticed Noyner was suddenly ashen and void of color.

Without warning, Noyner's legs went wobbly and he dropped to the deck.

Thinking Noyner had slipped on the wet deck, the deckhand helping with the rod reached down to help him up.

"What the hell... are you okay, sir?" he shrieked.

Noyner was foaming at the mouth and suddenly began violently convulsing.

The deckhand at the rear was trying to hold onto the tarpon and keep Noyner from going overboard through the six-foot open gaffing section in the stern.

The captain, focused on steering the boat, turned to see something was wrong on the deck.

"What's wrong? What's wrong?" he yelled.

"Something's wrong with the judge!" screamed back one of the deckhands.

From the galley, McCray and the others stuck their heads out of the ladder hole, initially to get a look at the big tarpon, but then realized there was some other commotion going on.

"Oh, my God, what's wrong with Clarence?" shouted McCray.

Noyner was still convulsing wildly, and the crew could not gain control of him. Instead of a big game fish flopping around on the deck, it was Justice Noyner.

Another wave rocked the boat and, in conjunction with Noyner's wild contortions, it launched him off the deck onto the small platform deck on the stern. Two of the crew had fallen on the deck, and the gaffer let go of the tarpon and crawled back on the deck but was launched forward, unable to help Noyner.

The deckhand with the small blue canvas bag suddenly jumped down to the platform to assist, looking back to see where everyone was. The captain had turned his back to fight the next wave, and the deckhands trying to get their footing blocked the entrance to the galley. They could not see Noyner on the platform deck, which was two feet below the stern.

The deckhand looked right into Noyner's eyes as he was still convulsing, but not as violently. The deckhand put his foot on the judge's shoulder and, with a strong thrust of his leg, pushed him forcefully off the platform into the Gulf.

"Man overboard! Man overboard!" he yelled back to the crew, after allowing a few seconds to pass.

"Holy crap!" yelled the captain. "Throw him a ring! Throw him a ring!"

"What the hell is going on?" shouted McCray. A sinking feeling began to set in.

"I can't see him! I can't see him!" shrieked one of the hands.

"Turn to port! Turn to port!" another deckhand screamed to the captain, who couldn't leave the wheelhouse.

"Get the hell outta the way!" screamed the captain to McCray's aides who ventured on the deck to see if they could help.

Now all the crew but the captain were at the stern, some with life rings looking for signs of Noyner. Several rings were tossed into the Gulf in case Noyner could get to one but, even if he were in top shape and not having a medical emergency, it would have been difficult in the growing swells of the Gulf to see a ring or swim to it.

"Mayday, mayday, mayday!" shouted the captain into his microphone. "This is the *Ida Kay* fishing charter!" The captain yelled his coordinates to the U.S. Coast Guard.

"We can't see him!" yelled one of the crew.

"Damn it! We have the Supreme Court chief justice who has fallen overboard, having some kind of medical emergency! Get your birds in the air now!" the captain kept repeating into the mike.

"Nothing, sir, no sign of him!" a crew member yelled from the deck.

"Oh, my God... Oh, my God..." McCray was saying to himself as he tried to come fully up the ladder onto the deck.

"Stay below, Senator! Stay below!" ordered a deckhand to the senator. "It's too dangerous up here. Stay below!"

For the next forty-five minutes, the captain crisscrossed the area as the crew looked for Chief Justice Noyner, who had taken off his life jacket at a deckhand's suggestion during one of his breaks from fighting the tarpon.

The captain, realizing he may have lost a very high-profile client overboard, leaned over the rail of the wheelhouse on the port side and threw up. The swells were now eight to ten feet high, and the *Ida Kay* was way overdue to head back to shore and beat the squalls that were coming. A decision had to be made for the safety of the rest of the clients and the crew, and he knew what he had to do.

Nils Ottosson sat in the galley, strangely calm and silent, although nobody noticed as everyone was dealing with the horror of the moment in his own way.

"Gentlemen, we have a bad storm turning south, bearing down on us. For the safety of the rest of you and, as hard as it is to abandon our search, we are going to have to pull out!"

"No, sir! We have to find him!" McCray yelled up the ladder hole. "You don't see him? My God..."

"Senator, he appeared to be having some kind of medical emergency. He was fighting that fish very hard and appeared to have a stroke, heart attack, or seizure of some kind. With these waves and weather, I don't see how we find him," said the captain.

"Captain, the chief justice of the United States Supreme Court just went overboard! What if he is alive and trying to tread water?"

"Based on what we saw on the deck, Senator, he was really having some kind of very serious problem. I doubt he is alive at this point and we are all in danger if I don't pull out NOW!"

"Jesus…my God," said McCray as he backed down the ladder to sit in bewilderment on the blue padded bench that surrounded the galley table.

"The Coast Guard has launched a chopper and a search plane and they know who we lost. They will try to beat the weather to these coordinates before the storm, but even that looks dim."

The crew secured the deck and got into their positions as the captain got the thumbs up, then pushed both throttles to full speed as he turned back to the east for the long, sad ride back to shore.

Unbeknownst to the rest of the country, U.S. Supreme Court Chief Justice Clarence Noyner was floating somewhere in the Gulf of Mexico. He had just become the victim of the perfect assassination.

CHAPTER 12

"Government is in reality established by the few; and these few assume the consent of all the rest, without any such consent being actually given."

- Lysander Spooner
(1808-1887) Political theorist, activist

"**A**fter a two-day search, the U.S. Coast Guard recovered the body of Chief Justice Clarence Noyner of the United States Supreme Court," said the Fox News anchor in a "breaking news" alert on one of the big screens in Zach Turner's Bunker.

Zach and three others working in the Bunker stopped in dead silence. Nobody said a word during the news alert broadcast.

"Damn," said Zach, barely audible.

Then they all started to speak at once.

Holding both arms up, Zach said, "Hold up, hold up!"

"At the request of his family, Justice Noyner was cremated earlier today within hours of his remains reaching shore," continued the newscast.

"Are you kidding me? Are you serious?" yelled Will at the screen.

"Wow!" said another.

"Who does that? That's one of the most important men in our country and they don't order an autopsy? Are you flippin' serious?" screamed Zach at the screen, then turning to his men, who looked bewildered.

Will grabbed the remote to turn the sound down on the Fox screen and turned up CNN.

"They're all saying the same thing... Wow," Will said, his voice unbelieving.

"Guys, call your contacts right now. This may be an accident as they say, but I want to know what the chatter is. Do it now," ordered Zach.

Zach sat down and a sinking feeling came over him. The Supreme Court had several cases on its docket that were controversial and very close to Zach, including vital cases that involved gun control that could effectively gut the 2nd Amendment if decisions came down on the liberal side of things.

The death of Noyner now put the Court in a 4-4 deadlock, with one justice who was so moderate that he tended to be liberal in most decisions and was expected to be a gun regulation proponent.

President Bartlett was now poised to appoint a Supreme Court nominee that would be hard left. With Bartlett now in the White House and the conservative justices so old, Bartlett could swing the Supreme Court of the United States for generations to come. *Transformational* would be an understatement.

"Zach, Noyner was with Senator McCray and some guy named Ottosson from CIS. They flew down to Florida on the CIS corporate jet."

"CIS? What the hell is Noyner doing on their damned plane?"

"CIS is a major donor for McCray," replied Will, holding up a donor sheet pulled off a government campaign contributor website.

"Find out about this Ottosson guy. Who the hell is he?" bellowed Zach.

Holding the phone over the mic of his headset, another Turner employee yelled, "He's a lobbyist for CIS. Apparently some kind of playboy in D.C., too."

"This is already starting to smell," Zach stated. "It's not like Noyner to be on a lobbyist's jet. I don't get it."

"Bartlett is doing a statement from the Oval Office tonight at 8:00," said Will.

The eyes of the nation were on the East Room of the White House as everyone waited for Bartlett to stroll down the red carpet to the podium with the presidential seal.

This was the first opportunity for Bartlett to address the nation since her inauguration, and she was looking forward to the opportunity. Dressed in a powder blue pantsuit, she walked up to the podium, looking somewhat stiff.

"My fellow Americans, it's not lost on me that my first opportunity to address you as your president is on this very solemn day. We have lost Chief Justice Clarence Noyner of the Supreme Court to a terrible accident while he was fishing off the coast of Florida."

Bartlett tried to feign sadness and real emotion but, try as she might, it was hard for her to hide the fact she had been openly critical of Noyner for many years.

"I would like to thank the proud men and women of the U.S. Coast Guard who braved some very bad weather for two days in the Gulf of Mexico to finally locate and recover Chief Justice Noyner's body. My heart goes out to his immediate family and to his extended family at the Supreme Court."

Bartlett reached down under the podium for a tissue and dabbed her right eye, although no tears were visible.

"Justice Noyner and I had our differences for sure, but he was a principled man from Texas with very humble beginnings who became one of the great legal minds of our time."

She paused and looked around the room. A controlled environment, this was not a press conference where the president took questions.

"We have lost a great man, a great public servant, and an outstanding Supreme Court justice. We have lost a man known to many as *The Lion of the Law*. God bless his family and God bless America."

"No questions. No mention of an accident investigation, no mention of an inquiry and no mention of an autopsy. What the hell?" asked Will, looking around the group in Turner's Bunker who had stayed to watch the broadcast.

"It's the cremation that bothers me the most," said Zach. "Hell, the last two or three pop stars that died unexpectedly had autopsies ordered and here the chief justice of the Supreme Court dies, supposedly by accident, yet no autopsy and a very quick cremation?"

"Makes no sense to me, either. Why do it this fast?" Will agreed.

"You know, I could be thrown off the scent I'm getting on this if they had just done an autopsy. The immediate cremation just doesn't sit well with me." Zach looked both perplexed and suspicious.

"A couple of news commentators noted that his body was in the ocean for two full days. A lot could have happened out there to it," remarked one of the other men.

Zach stood up to pace a few steps back and forth while lighting a cigar. "I can understand under those conditions the family not wanting to do an open casket funeral; that makes perfect sense for that reason. But we all know autopsies are performed every day on remains likely in worse shape than the judge's."

Taking a cue from Zach, Will looked at the rest of the crew and said, "Keep digging, boys. We want details. What happened on that boat? Who else was on the boat? Why the CIS jet? Who knows anyone on McCray's staff?"

While Zach's crew was discussing their next steps, CNN was already profiling likely replacement nominations to the Supreme Court by President Bartlett.

CHAPTER 13

"What luck for the rulers that men do not think."

- Adolf Hitler
(1889-1945) German Nazi Dictator

Nils Ottosson walked into the vintage 1760-era bar King's Pub in Alexandria, Virginia around 6:00 p.m. He walked up the wooden stairs to the rear of the narrow second floor toward two men in suits sitting in the back smoking cigarettes.

"Gentlemen, nice to see you," said Ottosson, pulling a chair from the next table to sit with them as he looked around to verify that nobody else was up on the floor.

"We have already poured this for you," said the first guy in a Russian accent.

"Ahh, McCallen 25! Very fitting," replied Ottosson.

They raised their glasses to toast.

"To democracy! Great work, gentlemen!" congratulated Ottosson.

"To Florida and big game fishing!" laughed the Russian as they clinked glasses and downed the rare scotch in one gulp.

"I don't know how the fishing trip could have gone any better. I mean, you should have seen it. It was flawless. It was totally unsuspicious to everyone on the boat. Noyner flopped around the boat like a gaffed tarpon!" said Ottosson as the other two joined him in laughter.

They stopped laughing as a bar maid walked up the stairs to see if they wanted another round.

As soon as she left, Ottosson got serious and asked, "Do we have anything to worry about in Texas?"

"Texas was easy. A few bucks here and there, a few transcribed texts and, of course, a few married politicians with mistresses, not to mention the occasional married closet homo," one of the men, speaking with a heavy Russian accent, grinned. "And, if all else failed, promising the disappearance and dismemberment of a child to the parents always seemed to work."

"We have a few loose ends. Nothing to worry much over," said the second Russian.

Ottosson raised his eyebrows, concerned.

"Look, there are two or three who needed some additional coaxing. Those Texas politicians are a different breed. Remember, *everyone* has an Achilles heel. Hell, some just took cash. A few others we had to show some pictures of beheaded children, courtesy of our friends south of the border," the Russian said proudly.

"No loose ends, gentlemen. If you even think for one second that there is a remote chance any of your new found friends in Austin will get squeamish, then you know exactly what you will have to do."

"Not a problem. There are two we persuaded reluctantly. One's wife had already found out about his mistress, so that ship had sailed. He no longer has a vested interest in our business."

"Then deal with him," Ottosson ordered.

"We will. That state senator is due for an *accident*."

Again, the three raised their glasses in toast.

"Did the wire transfers reach your accounts?" asked Ottosson.

"It is a good day indeed," replied the first Russian as he nodded.

"Gentlemen, it's been a pleasure. Good luck to you both." Ottosson stood and shook both their hands before putting on his full-length wool coat.

As soon as Ottosson walked out the front door and began walking down the sidewalk on King Street, he pulled out his cell phone.

"Ottosson here. There is one task left in the Texas project. As soon as that last task is completed, eliminate our Russian problem," he said into the phone in a quiet tone while looking in every direction making sure nobody could hear him.

The next morning, the ABC affiliate in Austin reported on the 7:00 news broadcast that State Senator Jeffrey Milsap, the Senate president pro tempore, was killed in an apparent robbery attempt while walking to the parking garage near the Texas Capitol building the evening before. Even though Milsap was shot in the back of the head, execution style, reports were circulated that it was a botched robbery attempt.

CHAPTER 14

"Look at my arms, you will find no party handcuffs on them."

- Davy Crockett
Frontiersman, U.S. Congressman, Hero of The Alamo
(1786-1836)

"This body has been lying here awhile, Detective," said the Austin cop.

"The Texas Rangers are on their way," replied Austin Police Department detective Jason Edgar. "You ever met Pops Younger?"

"Nope, but I would love to," the cop said.

"You're going to get your chance. That's a Texas state senator there with a bullet through his head. Pops is en route. He'll handle this one personally, I guarantee it."

"Gotta text some buds," said the excited beat cop, looking down at her phone. "They're going to want to be here."

Three minutes later, a black Ford Excursion pulled up to the scene as officers let it through.

The rear door on the passenger side opened, and one foot clad in black hornback alligator boots hit the ground. Then came the next, and the law enforcement legend stepped out from the vehicle while he put his silver Stetson hat on in one motion.

Pops Younger strolled to the crime scene confidently as the throng of Austin beat cops, detectives and Texas state troopers all snapped to attention.

An aura seemed to surround Pops as he walked to the crime scene. The lawman had a distinctive, bold-legged gait that was probably as famous as that of John "The Duke" Wayne.

"How old is he really?" whispered one cop.

"Hell, he's gotta be a hundred!" answered another.

"He's taller than I thought," said someone else.

"That man is ten feet tall, I guarantee you that," said a trooper.

"I will never forget that scene on the Laredo bridge facing down the Mexican federales," said an EMT, referring to an indelible moment seen live worldwide as Pops became the epicenter of attention at one point during the *Texas Crisis*.

"That dude was legendary," offered another.

"Was? You mean *IS*. He's been a legend for fifty years at least," said a police sergeant.

As Pops approached the body after talking to two detectives, all the cops immediately became quiet, straining to listen to every word he uttered.

"I don't buy it. I don't buy it at all," said Pops. The scene of the state senator's murder was two blocks from the Texas Capitol building. It was as if Pops already knew that the accepted motive didn't make sense in the first few seconds. The crowd of police and Texas Rangers watched a body draped in a white sheet as it lay on a sidewalk leading into the Capitol garage, partially stained with blood in the area near the head. Police were keeping the press three blocks away from the scene.

Pops walked over to the sheet and pulled it back. He got down on his knees, along with another gentleman who was dressed in a badly wrinkled suit.

"The news channels are all assuming this was a robbery gone bad but, sir—his wallet, car keys and cell phone are still on him," said Edgar while he chewed gum, loudly smacking his lips with every other chew.

"Detective, how many robberies do you see where the victim is shot assassination-style in the back of the head and all the victim's valuables are still on the body?" asked Pops, who was visibly annoyed by the detective's loud gum-chewing.

"None, sir. You and I both know this ain't no robbery."

Pops glanced over at the detective. "Son, you trying to quit smoking or quit dipping?"

"No, sir. Why?"

"What the hell, son, are you in the seventh grade? I can't hear myself think over that incessant smacking. Get rid of that damned bubble gum."

The detective was about to snap back at Pops until he looked up to catch those steel-blue eyes staring a laser-like hole right through him, indicating the tall Ranger wasn't up for a debate on the issue. The detective tossed the gum into the bushes, but dared not say anything disrespectful to Pops.

"Ballistics will come back and tell us this was close range. From the looks of the entry and exit on the skull, looks like a 9 mm to me," noted Pops.

"We've already interviewed any folks that were in the area last night," said the cop. "Nothing. Hell, his body lay there on that damned sidewalk until someone called at about 5:00 a.m. The Capitol log shows he left about ten minutes to ten last night."

"I want everything on him taken into evidence. We can tell his kin they will get it back after the investigation," said Pops.

"They already know, sir. The local news has been broadcasting this since about 6:00. His kin already know, unfortunately through the news."

"Who called this in?" asked Pops.

"It was an anonymous tip," the detective answered.

"What was said *exactly*?" Pops focused intently on the detective.

"They informed the TV station that State Senator Milsap was killed during a robbery attempt. They also said whoever called it in had some kind of accent, but they didn't know what kind, except that it wasn't Spanish."

"Hell, they identified the victim on the call?" asked Pops incredulously.

"Yeah, they either saw it happen, I guess, or recognized the body." The detective shrugged.

Pops got up and pulled his hat down nearer to his eyes for a few seconds before calmly contradicting the detective. "The killer or killers called this in."

"Seriously? You think the perps called this in themselves?" asked the detective, curious as to how Pops came to this conclusion so quickly.

"This was an execution, son. This was no robbery," said Pops flatly as he motioned with a head nod to another Ranger, who knew instinctively Pops had as much information as he needed. The Rangers began walking back to the SUV.

The detective didn't even get a chance to ask another question. This wasn't his crime to investigate. The Texas Rangers, who operate strictly at the pleasure of the Texas governor, can take over any criminal investigation in the state at any point.

Many of the cops on the scene took their cell phones out to get a picture or movie of the legendary lawman as he strode past them. Within minutes, Twitter showed Pops' images at the scene of the murder.

"I want all the records off his cell phone and six months of call detail records. Also, get his office computer, home computer and laptop," Pops told the other Rangers in the vehicle as he got comfortable in the SUV.

Within minutes, Pops' images at the crime scene were broadcast nationally.

Twenty-four hours later, a vehicle with four Texas Rangers and a lieutenant from the Texas Department of Public Safety pulled up to the small, one-story ranch house on Pops' Hill Country ranch. Pops had a nice office at DPS headquarters in Austin, full of a lifetime of hunting trophies and collectible antique guns, but he was hardly ever there. Instead, he preferred to stay at his ranch forty-six miles west of Austin and conduct business there.

Pops was never much of an office guy. He preferred to be out in the field with his men and had a distinct distaste for the administrative responsibilities of his job. Over the years, the half-dozen Texas governors he served under had all given him carte blanche exception to any rules that required him to be at DPS headquarters eight hours a day.

Pops simply produced results, and he had the unwavering devotion of the Texas Rangers, DPS and law enforcement throughout Texas.

"Pops, take a look at these," said the highest-ranking Ranger as he laid out printed photographs taken from State Senator Milsap's phone.

"I'm guessing these pics ain't his wife?" asked Pops.

"No, sir, I'm afraid not."

"Okay, these are all different women. Do we know who they are?"

"A few of them are known to city. Most are *professionals*. We've already talked to two of them."

Pops reached into a cigar humidor on his desk, pulled out a cigar, and began to chew slightly on the end of it without lighting up.

"I want you to get their cell phone records, too, and do a cross-match on them," responded Pops.

"I'm sure they will all show what his phone does, sir, that they were communicating to Milsap for meeting places and sending these lewd photos back and forth to him."

"I deduced that already, Bob. What I want to know is who else they might have had in common. Who else were any of these gals talking to that might have also known Milsap? Also, interview every last one of them. Were all these gals pros?"

"We don't know for sure yet. We'll find out."

Pops leaned back into his leather chair, lit up the cigar he was chewing, and took a very deep draw on it, letting out a large cloud of cigar smoke.

"Wasn't Milsap one of the senators who changed his vote on the independence referendum at the last minute?"

"Yes, sir, he was. He ticked off quite a few politicians," shot back a lieutenant. "You think somebody got to him?"

"Well, if they did, he delivered for them in the vote. So why kill him now?" asked Pops. "I want to interview his wife."

"Yes, sir."

Pops felt his cell phone vibrate. He dug it out of his pocket and looked at caller I.D. to decide if he wanted to answer it.

"Younger," was his simple greeting.

"What's it look like, Pops?" asked Governor Brahman

"It ain't no robbery, Smitty, I can tell you that. Somebody simply walked up behind him and put a bullet in his brain. Smells to high Heaven."

"Damn, does his family know yet?"

"Probably. Hell, the news was reporting it live before the Austin PD ever got there."

"Execution?" asked the governor flatly.

"That's my bet right now," replied Pops after a few seconds to consider the governor's question.

"It couldn't be worse timing."

"How so, Smitty?"

"I'll have to call a special election to fill that seat. That will take at least forty-five days, which is way beyond when I was calling for a special session on the referendum," Brahman said.

Pops continued to chew on his cigar, rotating it a few times. "You expect the referendum vote to be that tight?"

"Possibly. Are you saying…"

"Smitty, I ain't prepared to say anything yet except how he was killed.

But, if you are telling me that vote could be delayed, that could be a possible motive."

"Right now, Pops, I wouldn't put anything past anyone," said Brahman.

"I'm on it. You know I'll find out who's responsible."

"I'd bet everything I own on it, Pops," Brahman told him. "You have the full authority and resources of the State of Texas behind you. Go get the scumbags responsible."

"You got it, sir," Pops said.

CHAPTER 15

"Political language is designed to make lies sound truthful and murder respectable, and to give the appearance of solidarity to pure wind."

- George Orwell
(1903-1950) British author

President Bartlett didn't wait until Chief Justice Noyner's funeral to throw a name into the hat for a new Supreme Court justice nominee. In a hastily prepared speech in the East Room just twenty-four hours after announcing the recovery of Noyner's remains, Bartlett introduced Shelly Ferguson-Haverton.

Haverton was a far left liberal activist judge from the 9th Circuit Court of Appeals and one of the most controversial district judges in American history. A Cal-Berkley and Harvard law professor prior to her appointment to the 9th Circuit Court by President Johnson, she was the complete and total opposite of Noyner.

Conservatives and Republicans pounced on the announcement.

"President Bartlett has used this unfortunate and tragic opportunity to name the most liberal and anti-2nd Amendment judge on record. I call on my colleagues in the Senate to stop this nomination by any means necessary, including filibuster," exclaimed Senator Perez from Texas while being interviewed on the steps of the Supreme Court.

The liberals, much more adept at messaging and managing public opinion than the GOP, launched into Ferguson-Haverton's qualifications, including the fact that Haverton would be the first gay person to be nominated to the Court.

"Judge Haverton believes in equal rights for all and in common-sense gun legislation," stated Bartlett, with Haverton and her female spouse standing next to her at the podium. "She believes, like most Americans, that all immigrants have rights and should be able to pursue the American dream. I urge the Senate to schedule hearings right away. We have seen in the past that the Supreme Court becomes dysfunctional without a full slate of nine sitting justices, effectively limiting decisions that would end in a 4-4 tie.

"Judge Haverton proudly represents the LGBT community and I'm especially delighted to nominate the first gay to the Supreme Court. Judge Haverton has an impeccable record on guaranteeing the constitutional rights of all citizens regardless of sexual orientation. I urge the Senate to take up a vote for her confirmation at the earliest possible time," beamed Bartlett proudly, turning to Haverton.

"I would like the judge to say a few words." Bartlett stepped aside so Haverton could position herself in front of the microphone as cameras clicked.

"Thank you, President Bartlett. It is an honor to be standing here in the White House and to be fortunate enough to be nominated for this highest honor. I promise the American people that I will follow the law, the Constitution, and will work to fulfill the promise of an *equal* America as designed by our Founders."

She paused as the small crowd clapped.

"Throughout my career, I have made tough decisions on important cases. No matter my personal or political beliefs, I applied the law, and that is exactly what I would do as a justice on the Supreme Court."

She stepped away from the microphone as President Bartlett returned to the podium.

"We will take just a few questions."

"Judge Haverton, how do you feel about being the most overturned district judge in U.S. history to be nominated to the Supreme Court?" asked a Fox News reporter.

Haverton never flinched, but President Bartlett was not amused and was visibly agitated. This wasn't an approved question, and it would not have been pre-approved by the White House press secretary.

"I've dealt with quite a few controversial cases and, in fact, some were eventually upheld in the Supreme Court. Even as a district judge, you don't always see eye to eye on the interpretation of law with the appellate courts, or even with the Supreme Court, especially if the Court is out of balance," Haverton deflected.

As she was answering that question, a Secret Service agent gently caught the right arm of the Fox News reporter, indicating he wasn't going to be allowed a follow-up to his question.

"Judge Haverton, do you feel every American should have unfettered access to firearms?" asked an MSNBC reporter.

"Unfortunately," the judge stated, "our Founders did not make the 2nd Amendment crystal clear, leaving it open to interpretation. Since it is likely I will hear cases related to this subject, I can't really elaborate any further on this subject."

"Judge, how do you feel about being the first gay to be nominated to the Supreme Court?" asked a New York Times reporter.

"It's long overdue. My personal experiences with civil rights in the LGBT community and in my own life gives me special insight into these issues."

"How would you rule on the *Texas Crisis* and whether a state has a right to offer an independence referendum to its voters?" blurted out a Dallas Morning News reporter, who was also not pre-approved to ask such a question.

President Bartlett stepped forward to make sure she answered this question instead of Judge Haverton.

"I will take that one," she cut in as she looked sternly at the reporter. "First of all, that is not a case that is before the Supreme Court. In fact, we have no crisis in Texas any longer. The Texas Legislature has not taken this up and we do not expect them to. This issue was settled in 1865 and again in 1870 in the Supreme Court. That is all, folks. Thank you very much."

Bartlett's smiles to the cameras turned to visible anger after she left the East Room and was out of the hearing of the press. She glared at Chief of Staff Weingold.

"Milt, how in the hell did those two questions get allowed into the briefing?"

"Madam President, I have no excuse; this should not have happened and I will get to the bottom of it. I'm so sorry."

"A career ended today for someone. I want you to tell me whose it is in the next hour."

"Yes, Madam President. I will fix this immediately." A steamed Weingold walked toward the West Wing, directly to the office of the Communications Director.

CHAPTER 16

"Democracy... while it lasts is more bloody than either aristocracy or monarchy. Remember, democracy never lasts long. It soon wastes, exhausts and murders itself. There is never a democracy that did not commit suicide."

- John Adams
(1735-1826) 2nd President of the United States
Signer of the Declaration of Independence & Founding Father

S enator Perez walked into the waiting room of his office in the Russell Senate Office Building, surprised to find Senate Majority Leader McCray talking to his chief of staff.

McCray rarely went to another senator's office; instead, he expected to be treated like royalty, with senators paying homage to him on his time, in *his* office.

"Mr. Leader, to what do I owe this special honor?" asked Perez, almost mockingly. McCray had never been a fan of Perez because of his outspoken opposition to establishment status quo positions that conflicted with Perez' Tea Party roots.

"Senator, we need to chat," said McCray. "Let's go into your office please."

Perez and his chief of staff escorted McCray to Perez' connecting office where he walked behind his desk and motioned to McCray. "Please sit, Mr. Leader. Can we get you some coffee?"

McCray turned to Perez' chief of staff and said, "No, thank you. That will be all." He motioned to Perez' subordinate, who was visibly irritated by McCray's boldness to dismiss him in such a cavalier manner.

"What can I help you with, sir?" asked Perez suspiciously.

"Senator, I know we've had our differences, but I come to you to personally ask for support for something that might seem controversial at first."

"Okay, you know me, Mr. Leader. I always listen, but I can't promise you and I will be on the same page," replied Perez, half-smiling.

"I'll get right to it, Senator. The Party has decided we are going to give Haverton a confirmation vote in the Senate."

"You can't be serious?" said a shocked and dismayed Senator Perez.

"I am. Hear me out. The Party does not want it to appear that we are not bringing a full vote to the floor simply because she is gay. The left will attack us unmercifully for it. Bartlett has assured me we can trade this vote for some other key items, including backing off on some of the 2nd Amendment initiatives she is contemplating."

"Mr. Leader, if that was truly the Party's concern, wouldn't they be more concerned with a senator going on record during an official vote? It seems the prudent thing would be to *not* allow a floor vote."

"The Party is concerned, and rightly so, that we could lose the Senate over this," replied McCray.

Perez rubbed his chin for a few seconds, and squinted, trying hard to think through the leader's position.

"Mr. Leader, you know as well as I do that some senators in purple states are going to be vulnerable. Certainly these senators will be under extreme scrutiny to vote aye. I'm sure you have tallied the numbers, but wouldn't this put Haverton on the Court for sure?"

"No, our initial research says we can have the votes and will narrowly escape that tragic scenario," assured McCray.

"How narrow?" asked Perez.

"Two votes, maybe three," answered McCray.

"Geez, Mr. Leader, we are talking about a vote that could alter the Court for decades. That's a very narrow margin for error, too narrow for my tastes. This is Noyner's seat!" said Perez, somewhat defiantly.

"Senator, I'm only asking that you allow the vote to come to the floor. We will only move forward if we are assured she doesn't win. This is all about theatrics, imaging and the greater good of the Party," reasoned McCray.

"Surely you don't need my vote just to get this to the floor?"

"I'm being pre-emptive, Senator. We all know how you like to filibuster!" chuckled McCray.

"What's the trade-off with Bartlett for putting the confirmation to a full Senate vote? Specifically." pressed Perez.

"She has agreed to table two executive orders she is contemplating that will evoke a huge battle."

"And those are?"

"She plans to circumvent Congress with a national registry database and orders to regulate private sales of firearms."

Perez started to laugh. "Both of which are unconstitutional and would be defeated in the courts."

"Senator, don't underestimate Bartlett. After the whole Texas thing, the polls show the rest of the country was horrified that Texas has its own militia and that some very good men were killed."

"I'm assuming you mean on both sides?" asked Perez.

"Of course, but why go through all this simply for a show vote? I've been doing this, as you know, for most of my adult life. We will whip this properly and construct the vote to fail. Simple as that."

"I don't know, Mr. Leader. I'd feel better with a larger margin of error."

"What is your number, Senator? How much of a vote cushion do you need?" asked McCray, scooting forward in his chair.

"I'm not sure, but two or three could be turned in a blink of an eye. Decades, sir… We are talking about overturning the conservative majority on the Court. The consequences would be devastating enough that the country would never recover."

"Senator, I'm fully aware of what is at stake. I'm also aware that we are now in our third presidential term in a row with a Democrat in the White House. I need you on board with this." Now irritated, McCray stated his position firmly in a patronizing manner, as if leaving Perez no choice.

"To me it makes a difference who the two or three are," Perez said. "The Senate is full of invertebrates, sir. I don't trust many of them."

"And they don't trust you, either, Senator. You need to trust me to handle this. It will go a long way toward repairing your standing in the Party and with your colleagues."

"And what do I tell my constituents back in Texas?"

"Whatever you like. The Party will help you with the messaging," promised McCray.

"What leads you to believe Bartlett wouldn't renege on her promise to squelch those executive orders?"

"She gave me her word," McCray said flatly.

"Oh, of course. Then that seals it!" laughed Perez.

McCray's body language changed all of a sudden as he stood up and placed both hands, palms downward, on Perez' desk.

"Senator, I will only ask this of you once. I highly suggest you think long and hard about it."

Perez leaned back in his swivel chair as they stared each other down for a few tense moments.

"Let me ask you a question, Mr. Leader. Why hasn't the Senate initiated an inquiry into why Noyner, as sitting chief justice, did not have an autopsy?"

Shaking his head slowly, McCray shot back incredulously, "Because, Senator, it was investigated and his death was an accident. Not all of us around here subscribe to every conspiracy theory that pops into the heads of the extreme right. Remember, sir, I was on that boat! I saw with my own eyes what happened!"

"I'll get with my staff on your request and get back to you through normal channels."

"I need your answer in forty-eight hours, Senator."

"Just so I'm clear on what exactly you are asking me," said Perez, "you are asking me to go back to my constituents in the reddest state in the country and tell them I'm voting aye for the most overturned liberal district judge in the country to replace one of the most conservative, highly respected chief justices in modern history, just because she is gay. I can't wait for the Party to tell me how to spin that!"

"It's for the greater good of the Party, Senator," argued McCray.

Perez looked at McCray, whose face had reddened since he stood up. "Mr. Leader, should I take this as some kind of political threat?"

"Senator, in life we can't always pick the moment, time and method of death. Just ask Chief Justice Noyner. But, in politics, we have the misfortune, or fortune, depending on how you look at it, to choose political suicide or not with a simple decision on a key vote."

McCray turned and began walking toward the closed office door.

"Mr. Leader, you are going to do what you are going to do with or without me. But it would seem to me that you expect this procedural vote to be close; otherwise, you wouldn't be here."

McCray turned back to Perez as he opened the door.

"There has never been a vote in the Senate with me as majority leader where I didn't know exactly what the outcome would be prior to allowing the vote to come to the floor."

"Of course, Mr. Leader, but this would be a transformational and colossal mistake if it went the other way. God help America if you're wrong."

"Yeah, yeah, yeah, not for you to worry about." McCray walked out.

CHAPTER 17

"In our country, the lie has become not just a moral category but a pillar of the State."

- Alexander Solzhenitsyn
(1918-2008) Russian novelist,
Soviet dissident, imprisoned for eight years
for criticizing Stalin in a personal letter,
Nobel Prize for Literature, 1970

National news crews lined the entrance to the Texas State Cemetery in east downtown Austin as the hearse pulled in carrying the casket of slain Texas State Senator Jeffrey Milsap.

The Texas State Cemetery is famous for burial sites of past Texas governors, senators, congressmen, and various heroes of Texas from the days of the Republic of Texas, the Confederacy, WWI, WWII, the Korean War, Vietnam War, and the war against terrorism.

Senator Milsap's family requested a private burial, although a few dignitaries and politicians were invited. News crews were kept hundreds of yards away from the gravesite ceremony.

"Governor Brahman and Texas Ranger Pops Younger are at the gravesite," said the local Austin ABC affiliate reporter. "Younger is the tall gentleman in the cowboy hat."

When the ceremony ended and the family had departed, Brahman and Younger strode to the assembled press area two blocks away and moved to the bank of microphones that had been set up prior to the funeral. The governor read from a prepared statement:

"Our condolences go out to the Milsap family," he said. "It's a sad day for all Texans.

"I will be brief and to the point. I have asked the Texas Rangers to lead the investigation into this senseless act. Texas Rangers Commandant Pops Younger will have a few words in a moment.

"The Milsap family has specifically asked me to make the following announcement. Tomorrow morning, according to Texas law, I will authorize a special election in Senate District 3 in East Texas to elect a candidate to serve out the remainder of Senator Milsap's term. The Milsap family believes the important work of the legislature and Senator Milsap's co-sponsored bills must go on without delay.

"God bless the Milsap family and God bless Texas. I would now like to introduce Pops Younger, who is leading this investigation."

"Governor, sir, what about the referendum vote?" yelled a reporter

Brahman, who was about to walk away from the bank of microphones, leaned back to them to answer. "Out of deference to Senator Milsap and his family, we will take this up after the District 3 election."

"But, sir, that leaves very little time in the current session…"

"I will call a special session if necessary. That is all," Brahman said as he motioned for Pops to go ahead.

"Good afternoon," Pops said. "As you are aware, the Travis County Medical Examiner has ruled Senator Milsap's death a homicide. The investigation is continuing. We do not have any news to report other than we are following up on current leads."

"Are there any suspects?" yelled another reporter.

"We cannot comment on that at this time, ma'am," answered Pops.

"Does that mean you don't have any suspects identified?"

"Ma'am, I'm not sure if I stuttered just now, but I'll tell you again, we are not prepared to name any suspects," Pops answered directly.

"Was he robbed, or was this an assassination?" asked an Austin-American Statesman reporter.

Pops glanced back at Brahman, as if asking him why Brahman put him in front of reporters to answer dumb questions.

"I will say once again, and for the last time today, we are not prepared to discuss any specific details of the case. It is still under investigation."

"We understand the senator had a girlfriend. Can you confirm or deny this?" asked the same reporter.

The veins in Pops' neck bulged as Brahman cringed.

"Son, his family just buried this man. Didn't your papa and momma teach you any manners? We are done here," said Pops flatly. He turned to Brahman and they walked away.

When they reached the governor's Suburban and got in, Brahman asked, "Is that true, Pops?"

"Smitty, that dude had girlfriends all over Austin. We are following up on all of them."

"Damn, just what we need, another scandal. Do you think a jealous boyfriend or husband may have done this?" Brahman asked.

"All his damned girlfriends we know about so far are the *professional* kind."

"Oh, great, even better. Does his family know?"

"I doubt it, but somebody knows. That damned reporter made sure everyone knows now," Pops answered.

"Do you think that has anything to do with his murder in any way?"

"Too early to tell, Smitty. But, when a man has secrets like that, he opens himself up to a lot of potential consequences. There's a motive out there; we just have to find it. And it may or may not have something to do with his bad habits."

"What's your gut say, Pops?" the governor asked.

Pops didn't answer right away as he turned to peer out the window. Then he said, "Looking at everything, Smitty, including the legislation he was working on, relationships with lobbyists and, of course, the pimps or jealous boyfriends of the girls, looks to me like a calculated assassination and not a crime of passion. We usually have physical clues in those cases. This was a professional hit."

"Did he owe money to anyone?"

"In fact, he had made twenty-six thousand dollars in cash deposits over the last three months into an account his wife wasn't a signer on. All the deposits were small and under the federal limits for reporting."

"This story keeps getting worse, Pops. I don't like the sound of any of it."

"I'm afraid it's just getting started," answered Pops.

CHAPTER 18

"[The founding fathers] conferred, as against the Government, the right to be left alone—the right most valued by civilized men."

- Justice Louis D. Brandeis (1856-1941)
U.S. Supreme Court Justice

Governor Brahman had just hung up the phone. He was sitting at his oversized walnut desk when an aide walked in.

"Governor, there are six men in the lobby with the U.S. Department of the Treasury demanding to see you. Three of them have guns…"

"What?" exclaimed a bewildered governor.

"DPS and two Rangers are with them asking them what they need, but they are demanding to see you personally," she said.

"Get Pops on the phone and see where he's at. If he's in Austin, get him over here right now. Make them wait about fifteen minutes just for the hell of it, then tell the guards to escort them up."

Fifteen minutes later, Brahman heard footsteps and chatter as the contingent of Treasury Department officials and his interior guards and staff made their way up the broadleaf pine floor steps to his office.

"Good morning, gentlemen, and to what do I owe this completely unexpected visit from Treasury?"

Appearing annoyed because he had to wait, the lead federal agent began, "Governor, my name is Sam Couch, U.S. Department of the Treasury, IRS. I'm here today, sir, to serve you a summons." He handed Brahman a document.

"Pardon me just a moment, sir, while I take a look at what *good news* you have handed me." Brahman reached for his reading glasses.

You are hereby summoned to produce all related 1040 personal income tax records for the period of 2007-2017 within 30 days of....

Brahman looked up at the agents. "So, gentlemen, if you want to audit me, why not just send a letter? You waltz in here without an appointment, interrupting the business of Texas to deliver this personally?"

"Sir, I'm just following orders."

"Whose orders specifically?" asked Brahman.

"My superiors," answered the agent sarcastically.

"And who might those be?" asked Brahman again.

"Well, sir, you can start at the Secretary of the Treasury and work your way down. Everything is in the summons. Consider yourself served." The agent turned his back to Brahman to head out of his office, having to wait until the others made way.

Just as Couch and the federal agents were exiting the governor's office, a black SUV pulled up and stopped right in front of the large plantation-like white columns.

Pops Younger grabbed his cowboy hat on the way out of the SUV, along with four other Texas Rangers. They quickly climbed the steps into the mansion.

Just as the federal agents were about to complete the journey down the steps, Pops and the Rangers met them at the foot of the stairs.

Somewhat startled by the sight of five Texas Rangers standing in their path, Couch and the feds stopped just a few steps above them.

"Who in the hell are you and what the hell do you want?" demanded Pops.

Couch knew exactly who was confronting him.

"Sir, we are federal agents here on official business with the governor. Now, if you will step aside, our business is done here and we will be on our way," answered Couch.

The Rangers didn't flinch or move one inch out of their way.

"I'm told you didn't have an appointment to see the governor," snarled Pops. "You best be on your way. I don't have much hankerin' for carpet-bagging federal agents, especially ones that are attached to the slime bucket some refer to as the IRS."

"Personally, sir, there's nothing more I would like than to mix it up with you *cowboys* who are personally responsible for the deaths of federal agents. However, since I'm a guest in this house, we will be on our way," shot back Couch.

Pops took a couple more chews on his tobacco, then fixed that famous steel-blue-eyed stare on Couch, replying, "Son, ain't you a typical Yankee? Comes into the governor's house uninvited, then considers himself an *invited* guest. Obviously you ain't the sharpest tool in the shed." Pops took a step to the side, opening a path for Couch to walk through.

Couch began to walk past Pops, then paused to stare back right in Pops' face.

"Boy, you keep eyeballin' me and I'll pluck each one of 'em out and feed 'em to the crows," laughed Pops.

"Old man, I'm sure we will cross paths again," blurted Couch, motioning his squad to leave.

"Damn, boy, I surely hope we do! Whenever that might be, wouldn't be soon enough!"

The federal agents stalked out the front door to their waiting cars as Pops, the Rangers and the DPS officers followed to make sure they left. Then Pops turned around and walked back into the mansion. He took a step to go up, then saw the governor coming down to meet him.

"You saw all that?" asked Pops.

"I did. I would have paid for an admission ticket to see it again," answered Brahman.

"That was one tightly wound little S.O.B.," Pops said to the laughter of the Rangers.

"I can't tell if the dumb ass didn't know how to size a suit. Damned thing fit too tight on him, if you ask me. Is that what they call a metrosexual?" asked Brahman as they continued to chuckle.

"A metro what?" asked Pops.

"Never mind; let's just say he was a little light in his footwork!" laughed Brahman.

"Sure wouldn't mind meetin' up with this smart ass again sometime soon, maybe under different circumstances," replied Pops.

"Now, Pops, be careful. Some might take that the wrong way," Brahman said as the laughter really started to roar.

It took a few seconds for Pops to figure out what the joke was but, when he did, he set them all straight, "I mean I'd wipe the floor with that scumbag Yankee's face!"

"Well, now I'm dealing with this," exclaimed Brahman, handing his summons to Pops.

"This ain't no coincidence, Smitty."

"You know, Pops, I didn't used to believe in many conspiracy theories, but Johnson's administration fixed that for me," Brahman stated.

"You know you can't trust a snake no matter what. It'll bite you. That's what a snake does. That's their damned nature, as it is the nature of the federal government to be inherently corrupt!" echoed Pops.

"Thanks for the entertainment today, Pops."

"You're certainly welcome, sir."

CHAPTER 19

"Crisis is the rallying cry of the tyrant."

- James Madison (1751-1836)
Father of the Constitution, 4th US President
Author of the 2nd Amendment

Nils Ottosson sat in his black Range Rover at the guard shack, located at the northwest gate on the corner of the White House grounds, waiting for clearance to enter.

Annoyed that he wasn't immediately let through, he asked the guard, "What the hell is taking so long? I have a meeting that starts in three minutes."

Equally annoyed at the impatience of the visitor, the uniformed Secret Service officer replied, "Sir, your clearance comes from the president's chief of staff. Apparently he has been in a meeting with the president."

"Yeah, that's the meeting I'm supposed to be in!" smirked Ottosson.

The guard just stared ahead icily, waiting for a response to come over his headset from inside the West Wing. Two more minutes passed.

"Well?" said Ottosson, putting his hands out palms up.

"Well, what?"

"I said I've got a meeting." Ottosson glared at the guard.

"Look, you asshat, you'll get in when you get cleared. You think you just waltz into the White House because *you* say so?"

There were now three other guards surrounding Ottosson's black Range Rover, all with fully automatic weapons hanging from straps on their shoulders.

The guard stopped and listened to his headset carefully before breaking into a broad grin.

"Mr. Otter?"

"It's Ottosson."

"Whatever. We have been informed that your meeting has been cancelled," smiled the guard.

"What?" Ottosson yelled.

"You will need to back up your vehicle and make a three-point turn and exit," said the guard, even though they could have let Ottosson inside the gate onto the White House grounds to make a U-turn out the other side of the gate through the exit side.

"You've got to be kidding me! I sat here for nearly twenty-five minutes."

"Take it up with the West Wing, sir."

"Son of a bitch! I will."

"Have a nice day," smirked the guard.

"Go f- yourself," Ottosson shot back almost under his breath, wanting to say it louder, but not fully convinced he wanted the guard to hear it.

Ottosson backed out and got on his cell phone as he turned the corner to go around Lafayette Park, then north on 16th Northwest.

Four cars behind Ottosson on 16th was a dark gray SUV with two people in the front seat.

"His meeting was not on the White House calendar," said Will Turnbow to Zach Turner, who was driving.

Without losing his focus on the target four cars in front of him, Zach replied, "Not surprised. I bet he's been here lots of times and no record of it in the logs."

The Range Rover swung to the left a few short blocks farther down the street and pulled into the valet parking in front of the Jefferson Hotel as Ottosson, still on his own cell phone, got out and headed into the lobby. The valet tried to speak with him. Ottosson glared at him and rudely walked right by him.

Zach pulled over to the right a block away. Without saying a word, Will got out quickly as Zach kept normal speed with the traffic and passed The Jefferson, then took a quick left two blocks farther down.

The Jefferson has one of the most iconic and quaint bars in all of D.C., known for years as a place for D.C. power brokers, congressmen and women, lobbyists and administration officials to cut backroom deals. The bar is also famous for scandalous trysts with senators and other high-ranking government officials. In the bar area are some private overstuffed alcoves where a private conversation, or more, is possible.

Will walked into the lobby and headed straight for the bar, passing by Ottosson, who was already sitting in one of the alcoves with a beautiful dark-haired woman.

Will walked to the far end of the bar so he could face the alcove, positioning himself on his chair so he could see the legs of the woman sitting with Ottosson.

A few minutes later, Zach walked in and took a seat at a small bar table. He also took a seat that could see the entrance of the alcove where Ottosson was sitting. The men didn't speak to each other, or give anyone any inkling that they knew each other. The bar was almost full, although it wasn't even 5:00 yet.

Zach glanced down at his phone to see a text from the Bunker.

"512," said the text.

"512," said Zach very softly into his watch, almost in a singular motion, as he took a sip of the bourbon the waitress had just delivered to him.

"5-1-2," came the casual soft reply on Zach's tiny unnoticeable earpiece, from a man with a full dark beard in a black suit who had just walked into the hotel. He carried a brown soft briefcase, and went straight to one of two elevators.

Exiting on the fifth floor, the bearded man went straight to Room 512, pulled out a room card key, and used it to enter Ottosson's room.

"Beard is in," he said into his watch as he quickly pulled on latex gloves.

He went straight to the room safe in the closet, placed a piece of electronics about the size of a mini-iPad on the door and, after a few entries, the small safe door unlocked.

Inside the safe was some money, which he quickly counted at more than ten thousand dollars in two-thousand dollar bundles with marked denomination bank straps and two cell phones. He plugged another device into both phones, taking thirty seconds to decode the passwords, then began downloading the contents of each in less than a minute. He placed them carefully back in the safe in the exact same spots he found them and closed the door.

Next, he went to the small desk where a laptop was sitting closed. He opened it and powered it up. Taking the same device used on the cell phones to decode their passwords, he plugged the device into a USB port on the laptop.

"Encrypted," he spoke into his watch softly.

"How long?" answered Zach again, the bourbon glass to his face.

"Not sure," came the reply.

Hearing the conversation on his tiny hidden earpiece, Will kept a keen eye on the alcove to make sure Ottosson remained occupied.

"Three minutes."

Suddenly Ottosson stood and walked out of the alcove.

Will threw a twenty on the bar for his drink and walked out of the bar, scanning for Ottosson. When he got to the elevators, Ottosson wasn't there. Will prayed he wouldn't have to kill the man.

"Two minutes," came the message from Room 512.

Will looked above the elevators where it indicated what floors the elevator cars were on. Thankfully, the old hotel only had a bank of two elevators. One was stopped on the tenth floor; the other car had just left the lobby and was headed up.

"Lost him. Elevator headed up now."

"Exit 512. Exit 512, abort!" said Zach nervously.

"I need one minute."

"You don't have a minute. Exit 512. Abort now."

Zach and Will held their breath as the elevator approached the fifth floor.

"Elevator just passed fifth floor, clear to continue."

Relieved for a moment, Will looked around. Where did Ottosson go, he thought?

Will walked back toward the bar.

"Beard is clear of 512."

"Wait at elevator," said Zach. He worried that others at the bar might think he was having a conversation with *himself* when he was speaking into the undetectable ear mic in his left ear. When he took a glance, all the patrons appeared to be consumed in their own conversations.

Will saw the men's restroom and walked in, finding Ottosson at a urinal as he walked up to one of the other two urinals.

Ottosson zipped up, washed his hands, exited the bathroom and headed back to the cozy alcove where the woman waited for him.

"Restroom," said Will softly, not sure if someone was in the stalls.

That was all Zach needed to hear. "All clear for 512."

"Confirmed, re-entering 512. Three minutes."

The waitress came over to Zach, standing in his path and obstructing his view of the alcove.

"Holding in lobby," came the reply from Will.

A few long minutes of silence followed.

"Exiting 512. All clear," finally came the word from the fifth floor.

The man with the beard and black suit waited for an elevator, then came down to the lobby where Will was sitting in a Victorian chair, pretending to read the days edition of the Washington Post.

Will watched as the bearded man went out the front doors with his briefcase slung over his shoulder and took a left heading north on the sidewalk. Waiting a few minutes, he neatly folded the newspaper, got up and walked out of the lobby, turning the opposite way and walking south in the direction of the White House.

"All clear. Rendezvous point."

Zach took his time, finishing the bourbon. He paid his bill and calmly walked out of the hotel and strolled several blocks to where he had found a parking spot on a side street. He got into his car and drove off, making numerous turns while watching his rearview mirror to be sure he wasn't followed. He then drove to a pre-designated pick-up point where Will got in the car at an intersection.

"That was close!" said Will, letting out a relieved sigh.

"Yeah, too bad we didn't have to kill the son of a bitch."

"What did we have to pay the girl?" asked Will.

"We paid her twelve hundred dollars last night. The dumb ass thinks he's getting lucky. She'll dump him about thirty minutes from now," said Zach, glancing at his watch.

"Let's hope we got something useful."

"This was too easy. Either he's got nothing useful to us or he thinks he's bulletproof."

"Did Beard say encrypted?"

"Yes, a laptop and two cell phones. Who the hell carries two cell phones unless he's hiding something."

"This guy's M.O. is he's a player. Maybe the two extra phones are how he keeps his affairs from his wife."

"Just remember, two hours ago this guy was about to enter the White House for a meeting that wasn't on the White House calendar. But he didn't get in, for whatever reason."

"We'll know tomorrow if he shows up on the log. People don't just show up and demand to be let in."

"He's too well-connected to be a nut case."

"We'll soon find out."

CHAPTER 20

"I want a government small enough to fit inside the Constitution."

- Harry Browne (1933-2006)
Libertarian candidate
for US President 1996 & 2000

Although months had passed since the *Texas Crisis,* it had roiled markets on a global scale. Oil prices skyrocketed and the stock market lost almost twelve percent of its value in three days.

There was some bounce-back in the markets once Bartlett was elected, with a small surge in the stock market that evaporated a week later. There was another surge right after her inauguration but, like the brief rally that occurred after Election Day, the small gains made after her inauguration quickly evaporated.

Politicians across the country continued to ignore the staggering debt that was nearly thirty-nine trillion dollars and instead focused the blame of the economic quagmire squarely on Texas. Governor Brahman had briefly shut down natural gas and oil pipelines from Texas to the rest of the country when the feds blocked access to Texas ports and interstate highways. Oil surged to over $100 per barrel as a result, but had dropped back down to eighty-five dollars per barrel.

Gasoline reached record levels with some Northeastern and West coast states paying over six dollars per gallon. Although the markets improved slightly, gas prices across the country remained high.

"Texas' treasonous acts dented the economy. It may take several more years to recover," said a Harvard economic professor on a CNN talk show.

"Should Texas be punished?" asked the female CNN host.

"Well, definitely. At a minimum, state leaders should be held accountable," retorted the economist.

"How do you punish an entire *state*? And, if so, you can't blame everyone in Texas for what happened, can you?" exclaimed the host.

"Well, Martha, the people of Texas elected their leaders. We should treat the State of Texas just like any other rogue state in the world. We punish other countries with economic sanctions. Why not Texas?" asked the economist.

"I'm not an expert on history, but have we ever imposed sanctions on a *state*? Wouldn't that be counterproductive to an economic recovery?" asked the host.

"I think there is precedent. The federal government put sanctions on many states in the South during reconstruction," the economist noted.

"And it took years and years for them to recover as a result of Reconstruction. It also can be argued that the feelings harbored in the South were more the result of Reconstruction than the war itself—and many of those feelings of ill-will still exist today, generations later."

"Rightly so. This is the same old South, the Confederacy that fought for slavery and was treasonous to the federal government," the man stated.

"I'm sure you are aware, Professor, that many people, especially in the South, do not believe slavery was the only issue."

"Yes, many illiterate and ignorant rednecks believe that to be the case, but that doesn't make them right," the professor said in a sanctimonious tone.

The host changed subjects and turned to a different guest.

"Congressman Phillips, you're a Democrat from California. Do you believe Texas is to blame for the current economic mess?"

"Well, the *Texas Crisis* certainly seemed to be the catalyst for the economic downturn we are saddled with currently. The fact they are still talking about a referendum to secede doesn't provide the markets any sense of stability, and we all know markets do not like instability."

"It's simply illegal," jumped in the professor.

"I would have to agree with the professor that this nonsense about an independence referendum is ludicrous. Essentially, Texas held the entire country hostage, demanding a president be impeached or they would secede. Who does that?" smirked the congressman.

Trying to appear fair to all sides of the issue, the host asked them both, "Gentlemen, Texas definitely had some grievances, but wouldn't you agree that dispatching federal agents into Texas that ultimately led to the death of their governor and his wife did nothing to help the crisis, indeed escalated its intensity?"

"We don't typically negotiate with *terrorists*," exclaimed the congressman.

"Let's be clear here. Are you saying that state leaders in Texas were, or are currently, terrorists?" she asked, looking perplexed.

"Dispatching thugs to arrest federal agents probably qualifies," added the professor sarcastically, referring to an order by the Texas governor for Texas lawman Pops Younger to arrest several FBI, ATF and Homeland Security agents.

"Professor, are you stating that the Texas Rangers are *thugs*?"

"Listen, Iran, North Korea and other rogue nations have official-sounding law enforcement outfits, too. Hitler had the SS. Stalin had the KGB. The fact is that these state officials took it upon themselves to arrest federal agents. How dare they?" questioned the congressman in a self-righteous voice.

"My goodness, gentlemen. Are we reduced to calling a very historic and respected law enforcement unit thugs and terrorists? The Texas Rangers have a very proud tradition. This is obviously going way off track here," she said. "I brought you both on the show to discuss the current economy, and instead you are both pointing fingers at Texas as the cause of the current economic troubles. Do you both really believe the Texas Rangers are thugs, which means Texas has thugs for state law enforcement?"

"They killed federal agents. They tried to secede, and are still trying," answered the congressman.

"But…" started the host.

Raising his voice significantly, the red-faced and visibly agitated professor interrupted, "If not for Texas' treasonous actions against the federal government, our economy would be humming along. The economy has gotten a bump typically after every election since the 1940s. The entire country knows Texas has put us all in this quagmire. It's not fair to the rest of the states and fellow Americans!"

"So what would you have Texas specifically do to help right the ship, Congressman?" the host asked as she turned from the professor to the congressman.

"For starters, drop any talk of an independence referendum, then issue a formal apology to the rest of the country, especially to the families of the federal agents who lost their lives during the crisis," answered the congressman.

"Congressman, there were also Texans who lost their lives."

The congressman continued, barely allowing the host to finish her statement, "What, would you have the rest of the country or the current administration apologize to *them*? They broke the law."

"Let's not forget the racist nature of secession!" added the professor.

"Professor, are you making the claim Texas would go back to a slave state?" she said half-jokingly.

"Texas has a history when it comes to reasons for secession. Texas was dragged kicking and screaming into the Voting Rights Act of 1965. Don't think they wouldn't turn back the clock to the Jim Crow days immediately if they were successful," claimed the professor.

"Gentlemen, we've run out of time. I appreciate you coming on the program today."

The camera now focused squarely on the CNN host, dropping the video feeds of the congressman and professor.

"Well, there you have it. We brought these two guests on to specifically address aspects of the economy and you saw what happened. Both our guests, an economics professor from Harvard and a sitting congressman, put the fault of the current economic downturn squarely on Texas and the recent crisis," she commented.

"Now, I'm sure some will vehemently argue that Texas' flirtation with secession has nothing to do with a return to slavery," she stated emphatically, ridiculing the professor. "But it is clear that many in the U.S. feel the country's current economic condition was directly impacted by Texas' decisions during the *Texas Crisis*. The crisis, thankfully eased somewhat by the new Bartlett administration, created a cloud that, unfortunately, still hangs over the economy. It is apparent that Texas' governor and legislature will still consider this secession legislation in a special session."

She paused for effect to make the following commentary.

"Maybe it's time for Texas leaders to rejoin their fellow Americans in their own hearts and minds in the union of states. For the state leadership to continue to foster the notion that secession is either plausible or possible does nothing but continue to hurt the economy and the rest of America."

CHAPTER 21

"We Americans have no commission from God to police the world."

- Benjamin Harrison
(1833-1901) 23rd US President

Kymbra Turner lumbered through the garage with four bags of groceries in her arms, almost dropping two of them trying to hit the garage door opener button on her way into the house. After setting the bags on her kitchen counter, she glanced through the kitchen window above the sink. With some alarm, she spotted four cars parked out front blocking her driveway. She thought it strange that she hadn't noticed them when she was unloading the groceries.

Suddenly, she heard loud pounding on the front door, followed by someone announcing they were agents from the Department of the Treasury. She immediately dialed Zach, who had just picked up Will at the rendezvous point after their clandestine operation at The Jefferson Hotel.

"Zach, some men are at the front door pounding on it, saying they are federal agents!"

"What? Damn it," said Zach, feeling highly ticked off and helpless at the same time.

"Go to the door, but do not open it! Do you hear me? I'll tell you what to say to them. Grab your Glock."

"Okay," she said, trying to concentrate on what Zach was telling her while the agents at the door kept demanding she open it. She reached into a small table in the foyer and pulled out her Glock handgun.

"My name is Kymbra. Please identify yourselves. I am fearful for my safety and will not open the door. I want a local sheriff or constable here before I will open my door. Do you have a warrant?" she yelled through the door.

"Ma'am, I have a summons that you must sign in person," came a voice from the other side of the door.

She repeated what Zach told her. "If you do not have a warrant, I am not required by law to open this door."

"Ma'am, I need your signature."

Zach covered his cell phone and turned to Will, "Call the sheriff's office, now! I have agents at my damned house and they are demanding Kymbra open the door!"

"Damn!" Will said as he dialed his main contact at the sheriff's office.

"I cannot let you in without a warrant!" she yelled back at the agent from behind the door.

"Tell me what's happening, baby. You may need to put me on the phone with them." stressed Zach.

"Ma'am, it's not going to make any difference anyway. We will lay this summons right here by your door. You can consider yourself served by the United States Treasury Department," stated the agent.

"They left some papers at the front door but they are still here in the yard, two of them on their cell phones, but there are six in total."

"See if you can give them my cell number."

"Sir, my husband wants to speak with you. Sir?" she yelled from inside the house.

The agent in charge heard her talking but couldn't make out what she was saying, so he stepped closer to the door.

"Ma'am, I heard you ask something but I didn't understand it," said the agent.

"My husband wants your cell phone number or wants you to call him on his," replied Kymbra.

"I'll bet he does!" snickered the agent. "But, ma'am, we are about done here, so tell your husband his instructions are in the summons." He began walking down the sidewalk toward the five other agents standing in the yard, all three now decked out in black paramilitary gear with fully automatic weapons.

Suddenly, the wail of a police siren could be heard getting closer in a hurry. A deputy sheriff's car careened around the corner with sirens and lights and sped up to the house, suddenly braking as the patrol car angled between two of the dark-colored government sedans.

"What the hell is going on here?" asked the young deputy, flinging open his door.

"We are serving a summons here," the head agent shot back at him. "Nothing to get excited about, Deputy."

"Then why are you demanding that the resident open her door? Do you have a warrant?" he asked.

"No, like I said, Deputy, we are serving a summons and would prefer to have her sign for it. She has a duty to respond to law enforcement requests at her front door," said the agent.

"Not without a warrant, she doesn't. You know that! Does she have her summons? What else is needed here?" demanded the deputy, who was obviously agitated that these agents frightened the wife of his good friend at her own home.

"It's right there by the front door."

"Okay, then you boys are done here."

"Careful, Deputy. We are serving a legal summons here. No need to get territorial," snarked the agent, speaking down to the deputy.

The agent stopped before he was about to say something else, as he heard two distinct sirens coming from different directions.

"The man of the house must have some friends in the department," said the agent as two more sheriff's cars pulled up from opposite directions.

"That would be an understatement. He does indeed," said the deputy.

"I'll make sure that is in my report," said the agent, opening a small binder and jotting down some notes.

"I want you to leave now but, before you leave, I want all of your names and badge numbers," the deputy told him.

"Well, Deputy…" the agent said, peering at the deputy's name tag, "Clarke, is it? My name is on that summons, along with the name of my immediate supervisor. You can go take a picture of it with your phone. And we aren't leaving until my superiors tell us to. As you can see, one of my men is on the phone with headquarters right now."

The deputy went over and took a photo of the summons, then pulled aside the other two deputies and had a private conversation with them while Kymbra continued to provide play by play to Zach on the phone fifteen hundred miles away.

The sheriff's deputies broke their huddle and approached the agents.

"You're done here unless you can produce a warrant. You served your summons. Now it's time to leave their private property and go on about your business."

"We just got word that we are done here for now. But I have a feeling we may be back at some point," said the lead agent sarcastically as the agents began walking back to their government sedans. The deputies waited until all the federal agents were gone before they got in their cars and left.

"Zach, they're leaving," Kymbra told him.

"Okay, open the door and grab the papers they left."

She cracked open the door and reached down to retrieve the documents. "It's a summons from the IRS. They're demanding documents for ten years to support our income tax returns," cried Kymbra into the phone.

"Geez, these sons of bitches never stop."

"Zach, I was just at the grocery store and my debit card and credit card wouldn't work. I had to write a check," she said. "Do you think there could be a connection?"

"That's impossible! We have money in all our accounts and I pay the credit cards off each month! Let me go online and see what's going on."

"Okay, baby, let me know. When are you coming home?"

"I need two more days," he told her. "Scan that summons and email it to me so I can get on it."

"Okay, Zach, I love you."

"Love you, too. Try not to worry. This is harassment and we'll get our attorney to get them to back off."

As soon as he hung up the phone, Zach powered up his laptop to check his bank accounts. He had done very well financially in the security business and wasn't too worried about his accounts.

He was fanatical about taking precautions from prying government eyes. Using his specially encrypted laptop and a proxy web browser, he logged into his bank accounts and all seemed normal. To make sure, he called the bank where Kymbra had the debit card account.

"What? How could that be? Damn it!" he said to himself after he hung up the phone with the bank.

"Will, they are jacking with me. Check your accounts," Zach told Will.

A few minutes later, Will returned and informed Zach, "The bank says my accounts are locked up due to an IRS lien. What the hell?"

"Me, too. Me, too," said Zach. He sat with his face in his hands, thinking of his next move. "Tell the entire team. If they don't have this same issue, they need to pull their money or move it offshore—now."

"No audit. No lien demand. No notice. Nothing," Will said with obvious disgust.

"Thank the National Defense Authorization Act. Congratulations. We are officially terrorists. No habeas corpus. Assumed guilty."

"Orchestrated *financial terrorism*. The government is terrible at most things, but that's not one of them. Thank God we followed your advice and have money offshore," Will said gratefully.

"Terror. That's what these scumbags at the IRS instill in everyday Americans just trying to get by. Look at my wife, scared senseless as they beat on the front door!" Zach threw an empty water bottle to the floor.

"Patrick Henry would have tarred and feathered a politician for even suggesting such an agency could exist."

"We have to find out who else is targeted. Let's start making phone calls and see if we are being singled out, or if this is some kind of grandiose scheme associated with the referendum," Zach ordered.

"I'm on it," Will told him.

"When will we have the Swede's data and files?" asked Zach, referring to the laptop and phones of Ottosson.

"Maybe by tonight but, if not, by first thing in the morning."

Zach stood up and leaned once to the right and once to the left, to stretch out a bad lower back.

It was a sign.

This was normally a routine Zach practiced just before each major covert operation he embarked on, whether as a Navy SEAL or a CIA agent. He then walked over to the hotel window and stared out at the Washington monument.

"The only thing a terrorist understands is terror. They want *terror*, we'll give them *terror*," he murmured to himself.

CHAPTER 22

"A Bill of Rights that means what the majority wants it to mean is worthless."

> *- Antonin Scalia (1936-2016)*
> *U.S. Supreme Court Justice*

The left-leaning mainstream media was on a public relations mission to make sure Shelly Ferguson-Haverton would get a U.S. Supreme Court confirmation vote in the Senate. The pressure put on moderate senators to elect the first LGBT judge to the Supreme Court was relentless.

Every major media outlet in the country was interviewing Senator McCray after he had scheduled a procedural vote for Haverton's full Senate confirmation hearing.

"I believe we should give this judge the opportunity to have an up-or-down vote in the Senate. The fact that we have our first LGBT nominee is historic in itself. Once we are past that issue, we can truly look at her record as a judge and vote her up or down. She deserves no less," pandered Senator McCray to the politically correct CNN host.

Most pundits believed the vote was a mere show vote and that the Republicans had no intention of confirming Haverton. Being labeled homophobic or anti-LGBT was almost as toxic to politicians as being accused of racism.

McCray had his ducks in a row and had his majority whip operate a war room scenario in McCray's spacious office. The procedural vote would give the GOP enough cover to placate the LBGT crowd and, instead of being cast as anti-LGBT for not bringing her vote to the floor, the GOP could focus instead on her lack of qualifications to sit on the nation's highest court.

The procedural vote went exactly as planned, despite three hold-out Republican senators who voted against allowing a full nomination vote. Senator Perez from Texas was one of the three nay votes.

"That son of a bitch. He can't play ball just one time, can he?" McCray said to his chief of staff as he walked with him after the procedural vote back to his Senate office.

"He's a showboat, nothing more," said a legislative aide.

"He will make a scene during the confirmation hearings, you can count on that," replied McCray disgustedly.

"All these Tea Party types do is throw up obstacles," the chief of staff replied. "Why can't he be more like the senior senator from Texas?"

There wasn't a free square inch of floor space in the large Senate Judiciary Committee meeting room in the Dirksen Senate Office Building as hundreds of cameras lined up to get a glimpse of the nomination procedural hearing of Circuit Judge Shelly Ferguson-Haverton for the Supreme Court.

Adding to the drama of the moment was that President Bartlett had not yet appointed the chief justice to fill the vacancy left by Chief Justice Noyner's death. Speculation swirled that Bartlett would break from tradition and appoint Haverton if she was confirmed by the Senate. Such a move would not be unprecedented, but highly unusual, as most chief justice appointments by past presidents were made from justices who had already served a period of time as an associate justice on the Supreme Court.

Cameras flashed and there was a buzz in the air as Haverton made her opening statement, "I present myself to this body in the hopes that my time on the bench and my standing as a double minority gives me special insight into everyday American issues. I believe in the rule of law, but also in the fair dispensation of justice under those laws. I believe it is our duty to uphold the civil liberties of all Americans and I wholeheartedly believe and commit to the premise that all men, women and transgenders are created equal."

Of the first four senators who questioned Haverton, two were Democrats and two were Republicans. The soft questioning from the Democrats was expected, but the questions from the two Republicans sounded like campaign speeches for her. Instead of asking her tough questions about past cases and even the fact that Haverton was the most overturned federal judge in the country, the Republican senators praised her courage.

Then it was Senator Perez' turn.

"I yield to the *junior* senator from Texas," said McCray, with the emphasis on *junior*.

"Thank you, Chairman McCray. Let me start by asking Judge Haverton what her thoughts are on being the most overturned federal judge in the country. Judge Haverton, what are we to make of this fact, and how can a federal judge who has interpreted the law and ultimately the Constitution so erroneously in the past be counted on to interpret it correctly going forward on the high court?" he pressed as the audience murmured in the background, as many in attendance were distressed with Perez' tone of questioning.

"Well, Senator, my views haven't always lined up with the extreme conservative faction of the Supreme Court. I actually take pride in that. Let's say we have had a difference of opinion on how to interpret those cases," she answered confidently.

"Judge Haverton, just last year you let stand a lawsuit brought on by the family of a man who was shot by the homeowner while burglarizing the home. Do you not believe that homeowner had a right to defend his family and property?" asked Perez.

"Senator, the testimony from that case was that the perpetrator was not a threat to persons in the house. He was shot as he was escaping from a window to *leave* the home," she offered.

"And he was armed, wasn't he?" returned Perez.

"He did not brandish a weapon or threaten the family. The homeowner could have let him leave; he was half-way out of the window."

"Ms. Haverton," continued Perez, intentionally not calling her Judge, "do you believe in the 2nd Amendment?"

"I do, but I probably do not agree with your interpretation."

"Did that homeowner have the right to defend his family?"

"Of course he did, but this man was not threatening his family."

"Are you saying a man that criminally trespasses in the dark of night, breaking into the home while this man's family was asleep, all the while being himself armed, was not threatening?"

"Senator, you are taking some of the facts of the case out of context."

"Okay, let's go with your theory then. First, does the homeowner have a right to own the weapon?"

"The weapon was not registered."

"But did he have a right to own it? Was he violating the law by owning the weapon?"

"It should have been registered."

"Ms. Haverton, was the homeowner arrested for having the weapon?"

"I don't recall. I believe he was taken in for questioning," she responded.

"Of course, which, in most jurisdictions, is probably common for a shooting incident involving a fatality, correct?"

"Different states have different laws on that."

"Were charges pressed against the homeowner?"

Haverton squirmed slightly as one of her lawyers leaned toward her and whispered in her ear.

"No, there were no charges filed. But you are referring to the criminal case, which I did not have before me. I had the civil case that ensued later."

"Yes, yes, I understand that, but let's get back to the central question here. Did the homeowner have the right to own the gun?"

"Under the current statutes, yes. But it was not registered."

"But that isn't the question here, is it?"

"Senator, that's a significant factor in the civil case that was brought. Did the man's family have a right to sue? I believe they did."

"Are you aware that the weapon used to defend that family by the father was a pistol his father had given him that was more than thirty years old?"

"I'm aware of the fact that he used an unregistered weapon to shoot a man in the back as he was leaving his house."

"So, Ms. Haverton, you really don't believe in the 2nd Amendment, do you?" Perez pressed. Haverton started to carefully measure her answers as she became increasingly annoyed with the senator.

"I believe there should be common-sense gun laws that ensure gun safety for all citizens."

"Let's get to the real question here. If you had the chance, you would support the repeal of the 2nd Amendment, wouldn't you?"

"You're asking me a hypothetical question about a future case and, without the facts, I can't answer it."

"The senator's time will expire in five minutes," McCray interrupted.

"Thank you, Mr. Chairman. Now, Ms. Haverton, how do you interpret the meaning of the 2nd Amendment? Does a citizen have a right under the Constitution to bear arms?"

Haverton and her lawyer were whispering back and forth, which agitated Perez because it ate into his time that McCray would gladly cut off from him the very second his allotted time was over.

"Ms. Haverton, this is a very straightforward question. I'll ask once again, does a citizen have a right under the Constitution to own a gun, or a hundred guns if he or she so chooses?"

"Senator, if you would like to cite a case that I had before me, I would be happy to provide my opinion on the interpretation of that case," she replied, avoiding the question.

"Ms. Haverton, this body and the American public have a right to know where you stand on the 2nd Amendment."

The crowd became more boisterous as Perez persisted, with some whistling loudly in their displeasure.

"Ms. Haverton, we need your answer," pressed Perez.

"Without the facts of a case to comment on, anything I say would be speculation."

"How in the hell do you speculate on the interpretation of one of the cornerstones of the Bill of Rights?"

"Order! Order!" roared the chairman as he banged his gavel twice. "Senator, you have one minute."

"Mr. Chairman, I ask for an extension of time as this nominee refused to answer a very important question."

"Your extension is denied, Senator. Finish up now," McCray said to Perez in a condescending tone.

"Ms. Haverton, if you were rewriting the Constitution, would it have a 2nd Amendment in it?"

Haverton thought for a few seconds and then shocked all in attendance, "Not *this* 2nd Amendment."

"And why is that, Ms. Haverton?" asked Perez, satisfied that he had pressed her enough to expose her.

"Because, in this day and time, guns have no place in a civilized society."

"Meaning that, in 1789, it was a different time and different circumstances? Is that what you mean, Ms. Haverton?" Perez leaned back in his chair.

"Totally different time, Senator, as no assault weapons existed in 1789."

"So, Ms. Haverton, what other amendments in the Bill of Rights are obsolete?"

"Time, time, Mr. Perez," shouted McCray as he banged his gavel again.

"Mr. Chairman, I ask that you allow Ms. Haverton to answer my last question and I will yield."

"Your time is expired, Senator," answered McCray without even looking in his direction.

Perez ignored the chairman, speaking loudly over the crowd that was noisier now than at any point during the hearing. "Ms. Haverton, Ms. Haverton, what else in the Bill of Rights would *you* do away with? I demand your answer!"

"Senator Perez, your time is expired!"

"Ms. Haverton, America wants to know what other radical views on the Constitution you have? I demand an answer! Which amendments would you eviscerate?" Perez shouted.

Haverton kept leaning over to her attorney, who was obviously telling her not to answer.

"Ms. Haverton?"

"Senator, I will not repeat myself again. Your time is expired!" yelled a red-faced McCray as he stood to hammer the gavel on the desk.

"Mr. Chairman, how inexcusable that you will not allow this nominee to answer this question and put on display for all to see her disdain for our Founding document and the Bill of Rights."

"Mr. Perez, you will either sit down and shut up or I will have the sergeant-at-arms remove you!"

"Shame on you, Chairman! Shame on all of you!" Perez pointed to the Senate Judiciary Committee members to his left and right who were all seated at the dais.

"Shame on you, Senator, for your actions to demean this honorable committee and a highly respected judge," said the Democratic senator from New York.

"Senator, tell it to your mistress!" came back Perez to the delight of the media.

Senator Perez packed up his briefcase, with three aides standing behind him, and left the chamber while the crowd buzzed.

"Ms. Haverton, on behalf of this committee, I offer my apologies for the behavior of the junior senator from Texas. You have conducted yourself admirably and honorably here today, and this type of outburst will not be tolerated."

"Thank you, Mr. Chairman."

"At this time, I move for a two-hour recess, at which time we will reconvene after lunch."

McCray was livid. Meeting with GOP leaders behind closed doors after the abrupt departure of Perez and the called recess, McCray announced, "Gentlemen, Perez made us look like we are attacking this nominee. We all know how sensitive the situation with this nominee is and how we need to avoid the perception of us not being all-inclusive. That son of a bitch thinks he can walk out of *my* hearing? I'll run him out on a rail!"

"My apologies on behalf of my counterpart," said Texas Senator Simpson.

"No need, Kevin. I'm going to call for a vote on this nominee as soon as possible."

"Are you sure, Mr. Leader?" asked Simpson, unsure of the strategy.

"We will be fair to this nominee despite Perez' antics and theatrics. After we are done this afternoon, I'm calling for the floor vote."

"That quickly?" asked a senator. "I haven't even met with her yet."

"Senator, you think she will change your vote?" asked McCray.

"You know, Mr. Leader, it's all about optics," said a senator from Virginia. "There's no need to mention I'm in a Blue state that Bartlett carried by twelve points. I need to have the optics that I met with her and did my due diligence before I vote against her."

"You don't have to remind me you're up for re-election, Senator. I can count," said McCray with finality. "Ask your questions this afternoon, Senator. I'm not letting this clown show continue. The longer this drags on, the more Perez gets face time on TV."

"Sir, I don't think Haverton has been thoroughly vetted yet. I'm not sure if one more afternoon of questioning is going to be enough," said another senator.

"End of discussion, gentlemen," McCray said.

They all succumbed to McCray and, along with the Democrats, rarely challenged Haverton on any substantive issues, including her poor record of being overturned at both the Appeals level and at the Supreme Court.

"Ms. Haverton, you have been a gracious and impressive guest of this committee today. We appreciate your responses during this full day of questioning," McCray told the judge. "Again, I would like to apologize to you for the badgering you endured this morning. I will recommend to this committee that a full floor vote on your nomination go forward as soon as possible."

Haverton was excused and McCray called for the vote. Shortly before the vote, Senator Perez came back to the chamber to sit in his seat. The drama playing out on the networks was making for great coverage.

McCray called the procedural vote for bringing Haverton's nomination to the full Senate. The vote passed easily, with the only nay vote coming from Texas Senator Perez.

Haverton was headed to a full Senate confirmation vote.

CHAPTER 23

"One man with courage is a majority."

- Thomas Jefferson
3rd US President, Delegate to Continental Congress,
Author of The Declaration of Independence, Founding Father

"Smitty, you ain't going to like this," said Pops as he walked purposefully into Governor Brahman's office. "Turn on the TV."

Brahman grabbed his remote and flipped rapidly through the channels to find breaking news, landing on the Fox News Channel.

The breaking news headline scrolling across the bottom said:

President Bartlett to issue a full and unconditional pardon to former Attorney General Jamail Tibbs

Shaking his head, Brahman said, "Bartlett was making all the right moves to quell this crisis. Who the hell is advising her?"

Brahman then yelled toward the door at his staff, "Get the damned president on the phone. Tell her it's me and that I'm pissed off!"

"Yes, sir, we will try," came the meek reply from outside the door.

"Well, sir, if you wanted the referendum re-ignited with the legislature, you should send her a thank you card," chuckled Pops. "She sure knows how to add kindlin' to the fire, don't she?"

"That fire finally reached a point that was manageable. Why now? Why not wait and allow for more time to pass?" thought Brahman aloud as he rubbed his chin.

"She's as cold and calculating as a damned West Texas rattler, Smitty. Hard for me to imagine there's not some agenda driving this."

"Let's listen to this," the governor said as he pointed the remote at the TV and turned up the volume.

President Bartlett was walking to a microphone set up outside at the White House Rose Garden.

"Prior to my election to become your president, our country was embroiled in an unfortunate crisis that eventually led to the deaths of citizens, military personnel, federal agents and even a governor and his wife. This was a sad and unfortunate chapter in our history. Now that this crisis has abated and the country has begun to heal, I am taking additional steps to return America to a sense of normalcy. Today, I have issued a full and unconditional pardon to former Attorney General Jamail Tibbs," stated the president to the small, specifically chosen pool of reporters.

"Madam President, will there be pardons for anyone else involved in the crisis, including officials in Texas?" yelled a pool reporter from MSNBC.

"There are no other pardons planned at this time," said the president flatly.

"What about the Joint Chiefs who were taken into custody?" asked a CBS reporter.

"The Joint Chiefs who were taken into custody are a military court matter, and I will not intervene there," she answered.

"Madam President, are there not active arrest warrants for several Texas Rangers and officials within Texas state government?" asked a reporter from Politico. "Is the Justice Department still going to pursue those warrants, or will you pardon them, too?"

"We are still in negotiations with Governor Brahman with regard to state officials that were acting under the direction of the former governor. We will continue to pursue an equitable outcome for all involved," answered the president with a noticeably uncomfortable change in her body language while she addressed this question.

After this, several advisors cut in and started to escort the president from the microphone back to the West Wing.

"Thank you for your time today," she said as she left. "We will continue to heal. God bless America."

"Is she single-handedly trying to get this referendum passed?" asked Brahman as he watched incredulously.

"I've seen a lot of things, but that is waving a giant red flag in front of a bull in full rut. What the hell is wrong with that woman?" Pops asked.

"There's a method to her madness but, God help me, I can't see it right now. Let's pull everyone in as soon as possible so we can issue a statement," announced Brahman as several aides and staff who were watching the press conference in other rooms began streaming into the governor's office.

Zach Turner was walking down the jetway as he departed his flight into Houston from D.C. when his phone began blowing up with text and voicemail messages.

"What the hell?" he said to himself, trying to scroll through the messages, looking up frequently to avoid other people walking in the terminal.

"Turner," he announced as he took a call from Will.

"Did you see the news?"

"Hey, Will, I'm just seeing some of it. My flight didn't have internet. What the hell is going on?"

"Damned Bartlett pardoned Tibbs. Said warrants are still open for Pops and other Texas officials. What the hell is her game here?"

"Hmmm, well, you know this is a calculated move. She knows something. Why else would she do this now? She obviously isn't worried about a referendum."

"Damned straight. She doesn't want another crisis. She knows very well this will incense Texans. What is her play here?"

"Something tells me we might get some answers when we see what role Ottosson has in all this. When will we get the contents of his laptop?"

"Beard is meeting us tonight."

"Was he able to defeat the encryption?"

"Yes," Will said.

"Did he give you any clue to its contents?" Zach asked.

"Said he was afraid to," Will told him. "Wanted us to see for ourselves."

"Beard, afraid? That'll be the day," Zach exclaimed.

"All he said is that we better have *every* priority protocol in place. He said that *twice!*"

As Zach got off the call, he felt a sickening sense that something ominous was brewing. As a Navy SEAL, and later a CIA operative, he had seen some of the worst of the United States government's underbelly.

He knew how far people would go to get power—and to keep it.

CHAPTER 24

"In U.S. politics, compassion means giving money and privileges to well organized interest groups at everyone else's expense."

- Paul Craig Roberts
(1939-) Economist, former Assistant Secretary of the Treasury in the Reagan Administration ("Father of Reaganomics")

Reaction from various Texas state politicians was predictable. Even the Democrats had a hard time explaining away how Bartlett could provide a pardon to the man responsible for ordering the raid that killed a very popular governor and his wife.

Instantly, there were demands among many state legislators for the governor to call a special session of the legislature immediately. They knew the governor had a minimum amount of days to call for the special election to replace murdered Senator Milsap, but most thought one vote in the state Senate was not critical for the ultimate passage or defeat of an independence referendum.

When Zach Turner pulled up to the Bunker at 5:45 a.m. for the 6:00 meeting with Beard and Will, their trucks were already there.

"Damn, boys, you must have good news," said Zach as he strolled in and dropped his backpack on the nearest table.

Beard had three laptops, with multiple large computer screens opened and USB cables going everywhere.

Beard looked at both of them with a dire face, "Guys, this is some crazy stuff, that's all I can tell you. We are sitting on a nuclear tinderbox of information."

"Okay, take us through it. Hang tight while I pour some coffee," replied Zach.

"I've got mine already. Ready to go," added Will.

"This first set of data is from one of Ottosson's cell phones. It shows text messages with three prepaid cell phones and I have only been able track down who bought one of them."

Beard pulled up messages on one of the screens.

The text message read:

Operation Walrus on track, set for Ft. Myers on rendezvous date
Replacement Crew Set

"Okay, what the hell does that mean?" asked Zach.

"Let's see if you'll begin to connect the dots when you see more related texts. This next one is the day after," answered Beard.

Walrus successful. Undetected. Perfect.

"Look at the date of this last text," said Beard flatly.

"Not sure if I see what you're seeing yet," Will stated.

"Okay, look at this one," responded Beard.

Tail #N56732 Back with McCray tonite on CIS, Pick Me up

"CIS? That's an aircraft tail number. Look it up," said Zach, somewhat frantic.

"Already did. That's a CIS private Falcon 900. I hacked into the private executive flight base operations (FBO) at Reagan. Here is the manifest for this flight. The same set of passengers, plus one, went to Fort Myers the day before, but came back less one passenger," noted Beard, who was eager to provide the important name that was missing on the return flight.

He pulled up the manifests for both flights on the screen.

"Oh, my God," Will said quietly.

Zach sat silently with little emotion. He knew where this was headed now, but waited for Beard to give him more.

"There's a ton of text messages on this particular date to these three phone numbers. They are all in this type of code referring to the *Walrus* moniker. But I think I need to show you this next, from the laptop in the hotel room." Beard pulled up a screen from one of the connections made to a laptop. "There was an awful lot of research on this laptop done on this particular chemical."

"Tetrodotoxin?" asked Will.

"Instant death, usually within minutes. Typically, an organic compound from a puffer fish, blue-ringed octopus or sea snake. He also had a lot of information about the presynaptic neurotoxins from the Inland Taipan, the deadliest snake in the world, as well as adrenaline. Apparently, he was in touch with black-market providers of the two poisons, one from Russia and another from Senegal."

"This is out of character for the Russians. They usually want to use polonium, a radioactive poison," offered Zach.

"So this isn't KGB?" asked Will.

"I have actual dosing instructions," said Beard. "This concoction was mixed with adrenaline to speed its absorption throughout the bloodstream."

Both Zach and Will now stood, both with hands on hips.

"Here it is. You can see here, they mix the two poisons with adrenaline. Look at how low of a dosage is needed, less than one-tenth of a milliliter," said Beard matter-of-factly.

"You've got to be kidding me. Holy crap!" exclaimed Will.

"How is it administered? You would have to inject someone, right?" asked Zach.

"Well, yes but look what the toxin was loaded in."

"An Epipen? Am I reading that correctly?" asked Will.

"It's an injector similar to an Epipen. I picked one up." He showed it to them. He then stuck it quickly into the fatty part of his bicep. "Look how quick that was. I didn't even feel it. I just jabbed it in and pressed the injector. Not even any blood and, honestly, I didn't feel a thing."

Both Zach and Will sat back down as the sheer immensity of the moment overtook them both.

"Okay, so if I had an Epipen injector loaded with this cocktail, I could essentially scratch someone or inject this tiny needle from the pen and that someone would have some very serious problems within minutes?" asked Zach.

"Probably within seconds," Beard said. "Those two toxins are the fastest acting natural toxins known to exist. The adrenaline would help the toxin move through their system quickly."

"And their immediate symptoms would be what?" asked Will.

"Cardiac arrest, partial paralysis, foaming of the mouth, loss of motor control, hyperventilation. A really bad scene," Beard told them.

"Enough to fall out of a boat into the Gulf of Mexico?" asked Will.

"Under the right circumstances, certainly," answered Beard.

"United States Supreme Court Justice Clarence Noyner was obviously *Walrus?*" said Will.

"The chief justice of the Supreme Court was *assassinated*," answered Zach.

"I've got more," claimed Beard.

"Geez, this isn't it?" asked Will.

"Not hardly," Beard replied.

"What else do you have?" asked Will.

"I wish I could say this was the worst."

"You can't be serious," Zach exclaimed. "His weakness is women. Who entrusted this guy to do something this diabolic?"

"Tip of the iceberg, sir."

"How so?" asked Zach. "Are there others? What is the immediate danger?"

"From what I can tell here, sir, our constitutional republic as we know it," answered Beard.

"This stays right here," Zach ordered. "Nobody knows this but us three. We will need to call our team in, but only the bare minimum staff we need for research and recon."

CHAPTER 25

"The natural progress of things is for liberty to yield and government to gain ground."

> *- Thomas Jefferson*
> *3rd US President, Delegate to Continental Congress*
> *Author of The Declaration of Independence, Founding Father*

In the late seventies, Congress enacted the Foreign Intelligence Surveillance Act, now known as FISA. Nixon effectively used the CIA and other agencies to spy on political rivals, so Congress enacted legislation where, at a minimum, a secret request for surveillance had to be made through a judge.

Congress, in its typical methodology, designated the act "Foreign," but its real purpose was for domestic spying. The act is thought by many constitutional scholars and personal privacy advocates to be unconstitutional because the entire process is secret and the party who may be "investigated" is given no right to object or participate, and the investigation is done in an *ex parte* manner (only one side is represented).

One basic tenet and restriction of the Constitution is to rein in the judicial branch of government, which may issue "edicts" when no case or controversy is before them. The FISA courts operate without a case or without probable cause or evidence, which led to the bulk collection of metadata on private American citizens. This secret court literally has no oversight on it in the traditional manner.

"Gentlemen, this next file you have in front of you will take some time to digest. I hate to forewarn you on what's in here because you will have to read it to believe it," said Beard.

Zach looked at Beard in disbelief as he dragged his chair closer. Beard pulled up a file on one of the big screens on the wall.

"Beard, you're gonna have to go through some pretty deep stuff to top the diabolical assassination of the chief justice of the U.S. Supreme Court," said Will.

"Unfortunately, *this* probably does," answered Beard. "Here's the first document. A committee memo from our esteemed senior senator from Texas, Kevin Simpson who, as you both know, is the ranking member of the Senate Intelligence Committee."

They both looked at the document, reading it slowly. Zach could not believe what he read. He stood up and walked closer to the screen.

"This is marked *Top Secret* and it is an internal emergency memo to the NSA advocating for the immediate surveillance of the people on the attached list for presentation to the FISA court," read Zach.

"Exactly. Now let me pull up the attachment," came back Beard.

"The attachment is a list of names. Holy crap! You've got to be kidding me!" yelled Will as he began reading names out loud.

"Okay, I don't know what the list represents, but I have a very good idea," Zach exclaimed.

"Help me connect the dots, Zach. They are all Texans and seem to all be Texas legislators," said Will, slightly confused.

"I had the same hunch, Zach. So I compared this list against the last independence referendum vote," said Beard.

"Let me guess," Zach said disgustedly.

"Yep, the majority of names on this list turned out to be no votes on the referendum. Look at the date of the memo," instructed Beard.

"This is fully two months before the vote," observed Will.

"Yeah, but that's plenty enough time to dig up dirt if any exists," stated Zach.

"What name stands out the most on this list?" asked Zach, already knowing the answer.

Will studied the list for a few minutes. Beard knew the answer but held back, waiting for Will to discover it.

"Damn, Jeffrey Milsap," Will said, referring to the recently murdered Texas state senator.

"I wish I could tell you that this was as bad as gets," announced Beard.

"I need to also tell you both there is one operation on these files that has references and mentions, but I have not been able to find many details. They refer to it as *Madison,* so who knows how bad or what that operation is?"

"Geez, Beard, how much worse could this get?" asked Will

"Much, much worse," replied Beard. "Before we go too much further, there is a detailed dossier with an incredible amount of detail on each person on the list. This includes phone conversations, text messages and even internet history and search criteria."

Very few of these legislators were considered clean, meaning irreproachable from an ethics standpoint. Several were closet gays, more than a few had mistresses or, like Milsap, sought the services of professional women. Many had porn site search histories. Several had drug or prescription drug issues or campaign finance irregularities. For the few clean ones, they were threatened with physical harm to their families. Others were simply paid."

"Extortion for a 'no' vote on the referendum. Simple as that?" asked Zach.

"Apparently so. I bounced this up against the referendum vote. Look here." Beard pointed to the screen.

"Seriously? One hundred percent?" asked an astonished Will.

"To the man or woman, one hundred percent," answered Beard.

"This makes total sense. There were votes that were head scratchers. Some of these guys were the loudest voices for independence who, when the vote went down, had puzzling justifications why they changed their votes," explained Zach.

"Let me pull up Milsap's file. Look at this!"

They both read, for a few minutes, accounts of multiple rendezvous with known prostitutes on a weekly basis. It also included a master scorecard of sorts that listed all the state senators and where they stood on the vote.

"He never got the chance to vote no," said Will.

"Read the next page on the scorecard document."

"Senator Milsap has refused to cooperate. The senator has lessened our leverage by coming clean with his wife about his transgressions and asking for her forgiveness. They wiretapped his phone and heard him tell his wife this was his last vote and he was going to retire and let the chips fall where they may. He was going to leave the state senate and focus on his family," said Beard, encapsulating the next three pages of notes.

"The state senate vote was expected to be very close, coming down to one or two votes," recalled Will.

"Look at the last entry," noted Beard.

"Milsap is noted as not scheduled to vote," read Will.

"He can't vote when he's dead," said Zach angrily.

"Them sons of bitches wiretapped all those senators for months," said Will as he studied the documents closely. "The administration turned the entire national security apparatus on to defeat this referendum. Who the hell is overseeing the FISA court?"

"While you try to wrap your heads around this, let me get to the major item I found," said Beard.

"The *major* item? This is getting progressively worse as we go. So far, we've got a Supreme Court chief justice and a Texas state senator assassinated, not to mention a dozen or so state legislators extorted to vote no," said Zach. Physically disgusted, he stood up and began to pace back and forth. "I'm not sure I'm ready to see what's next."

"Take a look at this one," Beard told them. "There is an extensive file with an extra layer of encryption that took me most of the night to break."

Zach read the file name on the screen, "*Operation Audacious?*"

"Assassinating Justice Noyner wasn't *audacious* enough?" Will chimed in.

"What the hell do these diagrams represent?" asked Zach as Beard pulled up schematic diagrams that detailed computer network connections.

"There are twenty-nine counties, representing forty-six polling places in eight states during the last election, overlaid against the major telecom carrier internet points of presence, or major gateways," instructed Beard.

"Let me guess. Those polling places have CIS voting systems in place," guessed Zach.

"You got it, Zach."

"Look at the list of counties. All of them would be considered key swing counties in battleground states," said Beard.

"Damnit, I have tried to tell people for years how insane it was to use a foreign-owned company for our election balloting systems," said Zach.

"Well, we knew CIS had sold balloting systems in forty-two states last time we looked," said Will.

"It's now up to forty-six states," replied Beard.

"Damn, Beard, I sure as hell don't like where this is going," said Zach.

"CIS operates a network operations center (NOC), in Falls Church, Virginia. All of these diagrams point to network connections established to and from that NOC to all ballot systems in the United States, in each polling place where they are using CIS voting booths, servers and software."

"Wait, I thought many states required the connections as part of the contract award to CIS to be connected directly to each state's secretary of state or state election headquarters," said Will.

"That's true; however, they offer every state a backup cloud solution to retrieve data in the event they lose a connection, lose data, or their state systems go down. This effectively gives CIS direct peering ability into the vote tallies for each polling place server, and even the balloting booths themselves," explained Beard.

"Who in their right mind would agree to that?" asked Will.

"I'm sure it's all done in the name of redundancy. Remember Florida during the hanging chad disaster? It makes for easy recount and provides for disaster recovery, right, Beard?" said Zach.

"Exactly, but it apparently also gives them the opportunity to intercept and change vote tallies before they hit the state systems," said Beard.

"Damn, remember election night? Bartlett was down in many of the key swing states, then made this miraculous comeback in each of them? 'The Comeback Kid,' my ass!" said Zach. He stood up, took his hat off, and rubbed his closely cropped head.

"Damn it. The freakin' election was hacked, of course!" roared Will.

"It was stolen, plain and simple, with the influence of a foreign entity. Who knows how deep this goes. Do any of these documents link this to any foreign government?" asked Zach.

"No, not directly. But what I will tell you is that CIS is entrenched on Capitol Hill just as we suspected. I did some more research on CIS and found out that one of their chief financiers is Alexander Isoltov, a Russian billionaire. And, if they can do this type of research on state legislators, imagine the dossiers they have at the highest levels of government," Beard added.

"Including..."

"Yes," interrupted Beard before Zach could finish his thought.

"The *Oval Office*," said Zach.

CHAPTER 26

"The fatal attraction of government is that it allows busybodies to impose decisions on others without paying any price themselves. That enables them to act as if there were no price, even when there are ruinous prices—paid by others."

- Thomas Sowell
(1930-) Writer and Economist

The day arrived for the full Senate confirmation vote on Circuit Judge Shelly Ferguson-Haverton. The news media had built such a buzz about the vote that all regular network programming was pre-empted to carry it live to the world.

The gallery above the Senate floor was full of dignitaries, politicians, gay rights activists, and media.

Senator Perez strolled down the hall of his Senate office building with his chief of staff and several aides before coming to the Capitol. Most expected Perez to attempt to filibuster the vote, but McCray's chief of staff had reached out to Perez' office to tell them that there was no need, that McCray had the votes in line to defeat the confirmation.

"Senator, you know McCray has never failed. He's assured us there is no need to filibuster," claimed Perez' chief of staff in hushed tones while strolling down the hallway.

"We talked about this," scowled the senator. "There is too much riding on this vote. I can't take the chance."

"Senator, the press will excoriate you," the chief of staff shot back.

"Of course they will... so what's new about that?" chuckled Perez.

"I just don't see the need, sir. McCray never fails to have his votes pre-determined. He will think you are simply grandstanding," was the chief of staff's reply.

As they entered the Capitol, the small Perez contingent approached the Hall of Statues just south of the Capitol rotunda where the bright lights from news cameras were everywhere. Standing in the center of the Hall was McCray with a large gaggle of live media staff from almost every major network, focused on McCray's every word. The Perez group had no choice but to walk through it or wait until McCray was done holding court.

McCray noticed Perez as he got closer, as did the press.

"Mr. Leader, some say Senator Perez from Texas plans to filibuster this vote," said an MSNBC reporter who was fully aware Senator Perez was in earshot distance.

"He certainly has that right; however, we don't think it serves the greater good and this nominee deserves to have an up-or-down vote," McCray answered, making sure he pointed his response directly to Perez.

"Does the nominee have the votes to pass?" asked another reporter.

"We don't know for sure but, even if this nominee does not pass, she will have had her day in the Senate and gone through the formal nominating process as has happened throughout our history," replied McCray in his notable monotone.

Several of the media left the large circle of reporters surrounding McCray and immediately put microphones into Senator Perez' face.

"Senator, do you plan to filibuster this nominee's confirmation vote?" asked CNN.

"Let's just say this nominee absolutely does not have the judicial credentials to have made it out of the Judiciary Committee. She is the most overturned nominee in U.S. history and for her to have gotten this far in the process is unfortunate. It has nothing to do with her sexual orientation. She is simply unqualified to sit on the nation's highest court," replied Perez, finishing his sentence by looking across the Hall directly at McCray.

"So, you will filibuster?" pressed the CNN reporter.

"I will do whatever is necessary to make sure this nominee doesn't get confirmed. If the majority leader presses with a vote, I will have no choice. My constituents in Texas expect me to fight this confirmation and I will do that."

Across the hall, a Politico reporter, hearing Perez' response, turned to

McCray and asked, "Mr. Leader, it appears as though the senator from Texas plans to filibuster this vote. Will you counter this filibuster in some way?"

"The senator can filibuster all he wants. All he would be doing is delaying a vote that is going to happen anyway. This is his modus operandi. He just wants to obstruct. This has been his history with the Tea Party and his single accomplishment during his short tenure in the Senate," answered McCray. "He must get some type of demented satisfaction in keeping his fellow senators up into the wee hours of the morning so he can read us all a Dr. Seuss children's book."

Reporters chuckled.

The time for the vote was at hand as the Senate sergeant-at-arms began corralling all the senators in the Hall to make their way into the full Senate chambers.

As McCray was leaving, he made a special point to walk in front of Perez and give him a wry wink.

"What the hell was that all about?" asked an aide to Perez.

"I guess he's trying to reassure me he has the votes to deny the confirmation," Perez surmised.

"I'm going now to talk to his staff. I'll be right back," announced his chief of staff. "Senator, if he really does have the votes, do we really need this filibuster?"

"I wish I could say no. I just don't know. It is very, very risky," lamented Perez.

The full Senate began debating the confirmation from the floor, with particularly impassioned speeches from the Democrats about Haverton's double minority status and noting that America had finally elected a woman for president and it was time to have a lesbian on the Supreme Court. The pleas and justifications were as if those facts alone made it imperative to confirm her.

The Republicans who came out against the confirmation focused on her record of being overturned. Not a single senator offered objections to her stance on the 2nd Amendment. McCray had successfully leaned on fellow Republicans not to yield any time to Perez. Even the Texas senior senator, Kevin Simpson, did not yield to Perez and offered little objection to the confirmation. It was as if the GOP senators, knowing the outcome, wanted to manage any damage control over attacking this nominee and being perceived as homophobic or anti-LGBT.

McCray had one wild card that he knew he must deal with. Perez' lone buddy in the Senate was Senator Mike Broussard from Louisiana. If Broussard got the floor, he would certainly yield part of his time to Perez, thus giving him the opportunity to filibuster. McCray had leaned on his Senate colleagues hard to try to prevent either senator from reaching the floor. In his view, a filibuster on the confirmation vote, followed by the double-whammy of rejecting her confirmation, would show the GOP in a very bad light. The media had successfully labeled the GOP as anti-immigrant, anti-Muslim, and anti-minority, and this was likely to be another hit on their image. He was determined not to let that happen.

"Damn, Broussard's got the floor!" a staff member whispered in the ear of McCray while he was in a sidebar with three other senators.

"I need to call the rules vote now!" said McCray.

As Senator Broussard was making his way to the podium on the floor, McCray stood up to the lectern at the head of the Senate and banged his gavel.

Senators and staff who were strewn across the floor in private conversations immediately took notice. This call to order was particularly unusual while the debate was still taking place and this special call to order would mean most of the senators opposed to the confirmation would not be heard.

Senator Broussard and his staff were incensed. Broussard still made his way to the floor podium and began his debate.

"Mr. Leader, I have not been given the time that was just yielded to me. I ask that the president of the Senate allow me to continue," said Broussard from the mic forcefully.

"My distinguished Senator from Louisiana, I have closed the debate. There will be no more debate as we move on to the next order of business." McCray slapped the gavel three more times loudly.

"Mr. Leader, I demand my time!"

"Sergeant-At-Arms, cut that microphone," said McCray quietly as he leaned from the lectern to shut down Broussard's requests, but the senator could still be heard on all the audio systems and was captured by the media.

The entire senate floor was abuzz, as was the gallery.

Once order had been restored, McCray stated, "I move this confirmation hearing return to regular order."

A senator from New York moved to second the motion.

"We will vote in ten minutes on the motion to move to regular order," announced McCray with another slap of his gavel.

It took a few minutes for fellow senators, the gallery and the press to realize what just happened. Throughout American history, a Senate confirmation of a Supreme Court justice needed two-thirds of the votes but this was eventually changed to sixty votes. When the Senate moves to regular order, all that is needed to pass is a simple majority of fifty-one votes.

The motion and vote on regular order passed easily. The drama intensified on the floor.

"My God, McCray better have whipped all the votes. This would be the wrong time in history to miscalculate his power in the Senate," Perez said to several senators standing near him.

Seeing their opportunity right before them, the Senate Democrats asked for a short recess, and the leadership, again trying to foster an image of inclusiveness, granted them an hour. Senator McCray would only agree to this delay if he were supremely confident he had enough votes with a few to spare.

"Look at those guys," Perez said to his staff while standing outside the Senate hall. "The Senate majority whip is being interviewed by the media instead of doing his job! He should be making the rounds with any undecided votes or those senators from blue states. What the hell is he doing?"

"Senator, McCray's staff is telling us they have sixty-one votes, maybe sixty-three. They told us not to worry," whispered Perez' chief of staff into his ear, but loud enough for the rest of the staff to hear.

"Then why the hell did he move to regular order if he had sixty-one votes to begin with?" shot back Perez.

"They were not going to give you the opportunity to filibuster, sir. It's as simple as that," said the staffer. "He would have to lose 11-13 votes in a one-hour recess. Is that even possible?"

"Look at the Dems. They are in full action mode." Perez pointed to Democratic senate staffers running through the halls with a sense of excitement and purpose.

MSNBC reported that President Bartlett, who was sitting in the Oval Office with staff watching the vote on television, immediately instructed her staff to take her directly to the Capitol. Once there, the President and her entourage went to individual senators' offices to lobby for Haverton.

Suddenly, this recess hour became a frenzy of activity.

Not since Ulysses S. Grant had a sitting U.S. president come to the Capitol during a Supreme Court confirmation vote. Grant was making sure a Reconstructionist nominatee made it to the Court, and he was successful.

"Senator, the sergeant-at-arms is calling us back in. Time for the full vote," said a female intern. "Senator?"

Perez, whose eyes were closed for a few seconds, opened them and looked at the intern, "I always say a prayer before I vote."

It took longer than usual for the full Senate to return to the floor. It seemed every senator wanted his chance in front of the media right before this vote and, coupled with the president in the building, this caused a forty-minute delay.

The vice-president hit the gavel, closed the debate formally, and called the vote for the Supreme Court nominee, Circuit Judge Shelly Ferguson-Haverton.

The move to regular order and the president's last-minute lobbying made for abundant fodder for the network television pundits. None of the analysts, however, were predicting the nominee would be confirmed, but there was quite a bit of speculation surrounding McCray's move, with some believing he didn't have sixty votes and others believing he wasn't going to let Senator Perez grab the spotlight with a filibuster.

The votes began to come in.

Alabama Senator Nix – "Nay"

Alabama Senator Crosston – "Nay"

Alaska Senator Hersey – "Yay"

Alaska Senator Norton – "Nay"

The votes were falling where most expected; however, Arizona Senator Hammock voted "Yay" in something of a surprise.

All votes were falling along party lines, except the lone Arizona senator until Florida.

Florida Senator Tilley – "Yay"

Florida Senator Merryman – "Yay"

"What the hell was that?" Perez stood, looking back at a few of his Senate colleagues on the floor.

"Oh, my goodness, two Republican senators from Florida who were expected to be Nay votes have flipped! We will have to keep our eye on this closely and relook at projections," exclaimed a CNN moderator.

Suddenly the vote slowed. Murmurs shot through the chamber.

"Georgia Senator Barnes? Georgia Senator Barnes, your vote please?" asked the vote tabulator from the podium.

A few seconds passed.

"Senator Barnes is an aye," came the voice of the eighty-one-year-old senator with a deep Georgia accent.

"What the hell is happening?" asked Senator Broussard as he came over to where Perez was standing.

Perez was intently focused, trying to see what was happening up front with the leadership.

"Look at McCray. The Florida votes have him stunned," Perez shot back as Broussard turned his attention to the activity in front of the chamber where the Senate leadership was huddled tightly.

Georgia, Senator Bloom – "Nay."

"Maybe some sanity has gained hold now," commented Broussard.

But the calm didn't last long.

Two Republican senators from Indiana voted aye for Haverton.

Then the lone Republican senator from Iowa voted aye.

The panic setting in on the GOP was palpable. The Democrats had used the recess to flip votes. Nine votes had already flipped and they hadn't gotten through half the roll call vote.

"We don't know if Senator McCray miscalculated the votes he had or if his dislike of Senator Perez clouded his judgment," stated the CNN anchor. "If two more votes flip from what we generally expected to be Nay votes, then his move to regular order will go down as one of the most significant miscalculations in American political history. And we just thought it was to block a potential Senator Perez filibuster," chuckled the anchor.

Missouri Senator Cargill – "Yay"

"There's another GOP flip. Wow, we still have four Democratic senators who are in primarily red states who haven't voted yet who were expected to vote against this nominee's confirmation," said the Fox News panel analyst.

Twenty minutes later, the Fox News set in their Washington, DC studios was in shock. Their expert panel was visibly stunned; even the Democratic guests on the show were surprised but getting happier by the minute.

The votes continued. Three of the four Democrats who were expected to reject the confirmation on Haverton's record of being overturned, flipped and voted for her.

"The vote roll call tally has a slight delay. This is just unbelievable; the events that have unfolded here today will be remembered for a long, long time, no matter how the vote turns out." The Fox News anchor swiveled in his chair to look at his five panelists. "We don't know if we have seen another Supreme Court confirmation like this in history. This looks like it's coming down to the wire. Looking at the rest of the votes, how does the panel see it?"

"I think this nominee is going to fall one to two votes short, so much closer than anyone expected but, in the end, she's not going to be confirmed," said the University of Virginia political professor.

"Too close to call," said the popular political blogger. "But I'm with the professor. I think McCray miscalculated some, but ultimately he will whip just enough votes to kill the confirmation. He's been in the Senate, what— forty years?"

"Here they go, back to the vote," said the anchor.

"Damn it!" said a red-faced Senator McCray, looking at his Senate whip while huddled at the front of the Senate chambers near the podium with John Nurvalt, the senator from Nevada. "Why is this that close?"

"I don't have an answer, Mr. Leader. I'm sure Bartlett changed some votes at the last minute."

"She ain't that damned good! Would those votes have flipped without the pause for regular order, John?" McCray asked.

"I don't think so, sir. I looked many of these folks right in their eyes. We had sixty-one votes; we both knew it."

"We are one vote flip away from confirming this nominee, John!"

"Sir, we are looking at our tally." Nurvalt looked down at his sheet. "If all goes according to plan, we should defeat her by one vote."

"Damn it, you better be right!" hammered McCray.

Texas Senator Simpson – "Ma'am, Texas would like to abstain until the end of the vote."

"What the hell is he doing?" screamed Perez.

"The senator from Texas abstains until the end of the vote," said the vice president.

"Mr. President, this Texas senator will not abstain. I vote Nay for confirming this unqualified judge to the Supreme Court," said Senator Perez.

Texas Senator Perez – "Nay"

The roll call of the senators continued with no surprises, casting their votes along party lines. Every Democratic senator who was expected to oppose the confirmation, didn't.

McCray and the Senate leadership were beside themselves.

Wyoming Senator Nelson – "Nay"

Wyoming Senator Landry – "Nay"

Before receiving the next and final vote, to everyone's surprise, the aye vote for confirmation was at forty-nine, with the nays at fifty, with only one vote left.

"It appears this nominee will not be confirmed by the narrowest of margins," said the ABC host. "The only vote left is Texas Senator Simpson. What we can't understand is why Senator Simpson temporarily abstained from the roll call vote, unless it was entirely for political theater. Did he know he would be thrust into the limelight at this juncture? His vote alone would effectively kill Haverton's confirmation. If he votes nay, which everybody expects, the vote would be fifty-one to forty-nine, and the confirmation dies. If he votes aye, and the vote is split fifty-fifty, it would mean the vice president, a Democrat, would cast the tie-breaking vote."

Circuit Judge Ferguson-Haverton was one vote from confirmation or going home after a narrow and acrimonious confirmation process.

"There seems to be a small huddle of senators around Texas Senator Simpson. It also looks like some choice words are being used. What in the world could be going on down on the floor?" asked the Fox News anchor. "Now you see the junior senator from Texas, Perez, walking over to Simpson. We know there is bad blood there. Let's watch the suspense as this nominee's confirmation hangs in the balance with Simpson's vote."

"Ken, what the hell are you doing?" asked Perez as he muscled his way into a tight circle of fellow senators.

Simpson didn't answer Perez, but continued conversations with several other senators.

"Order, order, order," came the call from the vice president as he swung the gavel down forcefully three times on the lectern.

"We have one final vote to tally. Texas Senator Simpson, are you prepared to cast your ballot, sir?"

"Yes, I am."

"On the motion before the Senate to confirm this nominee to the United States Supreme Court, how do you vote, sir?"

"After much deliberation, consultation and prayer... I vote aye."

The entire Senate chamber and gallery broke into chaos. Many senators threw papers in the air in celebration and some threw them in the air in disgust. The gallery above the chamber floor was abuzz. LGBT and gay rights protestors on the Capitol steps and in front of the Supreme Court sent up a roar from their crowds that could be heard for blocks in D.C.

Senator Perez made a beeline to Senate Majority Leader McCray, who had just exited the chamber.

"What the hell was that? Huh? Never lose, my ass!" Perez shouted at McCray.

The staffs of both McCray and Perez had to be separated before a fight broke out.

"Get out of my face, you imbecile. If you hadn't threatened a filibuster, I wouldn't have had to invoke regular order."

"You never had sixty votes, you tired old man. Bartlett outflanked you. Your leadership in this chamber is over!"

McCray's staff ushered him away to avoid the press. They knew they needed their boss to regain his composure before he talked to them. Perez, on the other hand, went straight to the media.

With dozens of cameras around him, Perez took a deep breath, "Ladies and gentlemen, this United States Senate has just filled the vacated seat of one of the most prolific legal minds and conservatives in our history, Chief Justice Noyner, with the most overturned, anti-Bill of Rights, radical progressive circuit judge in history. It is a sad day for America."

"Senator, what did you say to your fellow senator from Texas who cast the tying vote, allowing the vice president to break the tie and thus confirm?"

"I am literally disgusted by his vote. To think Texas contributed in any way to the confirmation of this radical judge is incomprehensible. I am shocked. I am saddened. I am mad as hell."

Perez went on to answer many more questions before news broke that President Bartlett had made a public statement congratulating Judge Haverton and making an important announcement at the same time.

"Senator, Senator," yelled a Huffington Post reporter. "Can you make a statement on the announcement the president just made?"

"Well, young lady, I've been out here with all of you so I didn't get to see or hear her announcement."

"She congratulated Judge Haverton on her confirmation, thanked the senators who she called brave for casting votes for her, then announced she will make Haverton the chief justice!" she beamed.

Perez looked at her quizzically for a few seconds. "Excuse me, did you just say the president is going to make her the *chief justice*?"

"Yes, Senator, apparently that is the prerogative of the sitting president."

"Yes, yes, I know the Constitution, but that is hardly the accepted norm. This radical judge hasn't sat one minute on the Court. For her to pass up much more qualified justices is a dereliction of her duty, in my opinion, if what you are telling me is true."

The Senate leadership was all in McCray's office. It was as if there was a funeral going on, hushed voices and guarded sentiment.

McCray sat at his large desk and put his head in his hands. He knew he had let his animosity for Senator Perez cloud his judgment, but his pride wouldn't let him admit it. Chief Justice Noyner had been a respected friend.

"Time to face the music," said McCray as he stood up to put his jacket back on.

"Sir, we have prepared this statement. Can you read and approve it? It's short," said his chief of staff.

"Yeah, yeah," McCray said as he read, "looks okay to me."

As the somber entourage walked out of McCray's office to go face the media, the majority leader's thoughts went back to his friend, Clarence Noyner, and how he felt so bad that he had let him down. With McCray presiding as the majority leader, with the Republicans holding a majority, an ultra-radical leftist had somehow been confirmed to take the place of the late U.S. Supreme Court Chief Justice Clarence Noyner.

The Supreme Court of the United States now swung to the left by a 5-4 margin. To make matters worse, Sally Ferguson-Haverton, the most radical liberal to ever sit on the Court, was now poised to be its next chief justice.

CHAPTER 27

"Liberty is not a cruise ship full of pampered passengers. Liberty is a man-of-war, and we are all crew."

- Kenneth W. Royce
Libertarian Author

Zach Turner was beside himself.

An American patriot, a member of Special Forces and former CIA operative, he thought he had seen everything. Until today. The files Beard revealed from Ottosson's devices were beyond belief. What the hell was he supposed to do with this information? Who would believe it?

Zach called in his top guys. He needed help. This was bigger than him. As he sat in the Bunker conference room, he looked around at his top lieutenant and best friend Will Turnbow and four other guys he had been willing to die for in past Special Forces and clandestine operations.

And then there was Beard. Although he didn't have the Special Forces chops of the others, Beard was a top-notch, analyst-turned-operative for the CIA that worked closely with Zach. They also trusted each other with their lives.

"Gentlemen, Beard has briefed Will and me on the Ottosson files. Before we go one step further, I want to make this perfectly clear. What we are about to show you will probably change your life as you know it. Just the mere revelation of this information will put you in immediate danger and, make no mistake about it, this includes your family and loved ones," he stated in the most serious tone he could muster.

"Damn, Zach, we've been in some pretty tight spots. Hard to believe we could be in more trouble than those three days in Kosovo!" laughed one of the men as he attempted to keep the conversation light-hearted, but referring to a time when the federal government, CIA and military abandoned Zach and his team, thinking they were dead.

"Zeke, that was downright bad news in Kosovo, no doubt about it. But this is here. This is our homeland. This is the good ole US of A. It's disturbing in its content and it is shocking in scale. It involves almost every level of government. The *Deep State* is alive and well, and it's more evil than even we imagined."

"Okay, Zach," said Luke, "you ain't scared nobody off, so let's have it." He looked around the room. Nobody made an effort to get up and leave.

"You should be scared off. The trouble is, I don't know what anyone else would do with this information, or what they *could* do with it. The *Deep State* is so entrenched that we wouldn't know who our enemies are at Langley, or anywhere else for that matter," replied Will.

"Gentlemen, what we do with this information from this point forward may be the most important decision we ever make in our lives. Beard is going to take us through it all. You're going to have a lot of questions; many we can't answer yet," he told them.

"Beard, as you know, ran the ops in D.C. that snagged this information from the CIS lobbyist known as Ottosson. The level of corruption runs all the way to the Oval Office. I would like input from all of you as to what, if any of this, we disclose and, more important, to whom. There are very few men outside of this room I completely trust, but deciding who and when to bring into the loop on this is extremely critical," stated Zach.

Beard stood up and clicked a remote to turn on the two big screens in the conference room. For the next three hours, Beard led Zach's team through the information, stopping to answer dozens of questions along the way.

When he finished, he said, "Well, there you have it, gentlemen."

The room remained silent for about fifteen to twenty seconds.

"This is much bigger than us, much bigger than what we can probably do to fix it," said Luke. "But we have to do *something*."

"Langley is out of the question," said Will, who was never coy about his distrust of his former employer. "Although there is a very small number of buddies there I can trust, the *Deep State* is so rooted there and in the Department of Justice and FBI that I can't see how we can bring them in."

"I agree," said Will. "I don't trust any of those bastards."

"Zach, you've got some good relationships with some high ranking military, including a Joint Chiefs major general," suggested Zeke..

"As you know, he was ousted by the Johnson administration right before the *Texas Crisis*, but he still has contacts. I'm just not sure what the military itself would do with this information. They would have to involve the FBI, NSA, CIA and other departments. Too risky," Zach replied.

"Whoever this goes to, I'm not sure if we offload everything. We need to test whomever we give the information to with bits and pieces. The enormity of it is simply too much. We have to do it incrementally. We are going to need help," stated Will with conviction.

"Will makes a great point. I've been thinking, where would we start?" asked Zach. "Who can we trust? What makes the most sense? Then I have an idea I want to run by everyone. There's an unsolved murder out there that we have proof of who committed it, right down to the man who pulled the trigger," Zach finished.

"State Senator Milsap!" exclaimed Luke.

"Yep, we have it all. But the motive of the murder brings in the much larger scheme here and really opens Pandora's Box," replied Will.

"Who would you share that information with, Zach?" asked Luke.

"The only law enforcement I trust is Texas Ranger Pops Younger," Zach said.

"I think you and Will are the only ones who really know him. Can you *really* trust him?" asked Luke, realizing that was probably a dumb question after he asked it.

"It's not like he's my best friend, guys, but I've been around him enough to know he thinks like us and he's trustworthy. I think we go at this carefully, but Pops is no dummy. I would be shocked if this doesn't lead him down the path we've already seen. And I'd much rather this information be held here in Texas than D.C.," Zach reasoned.

"He has resources we don't have," said Luke.

"And we have many resources he doesn't." Will referred to a very tight-knit group of operatives they'd cultivated over the years throughout the world.

"Well, I'm not making light of all the militia contacts and operators we have throughout the country, guys, but we have to find a way to activate our emergency network quietly and without panic of any kind. I have no idea where this is going to take us," said Zach.

"We have to tell our brothers at least something, Zach. These are guys we have bled with," Zeke stated.

"You know our brothers and they will want to take immediate actions to stop this, but the timing is critical and we better have the right friends in government and law enforcement on board before any of this becomes public or, for that matter, divulged in any way. Does everyone understand and agree to that?" Zach looked around the room at each of the men.

"Yes, sir," came back in unison from the group.

"I'm telling y'all, even a hint of some of this will put some of our brothers into immediate action of some kind. We will lose control of the response and put everyone in jeopardy, and I do mean *everyone.*"

"What is this op they keep referring to as *Madison?* We know nothing about it. That concerns me," added Luke.

"And it should concern all of us. We've got Ottosson under twenty-four-hour surveillance. We'll figure out this *Madison* thing but, with these guys, it's going to be tough to sleep knowing they have something planned we don't know about. It can't be good."

"Zach, I'll reach out to the Texas Rangers to get a meeting with Pops. I'll have to drop your name," said Will.

"Sure, but make sure you tell them we have evidence on the Milsap murder. I know Pops will remember me, but the evidence on the murder will surely get us in the door quickly," Zach replied.

"They've got the elections rigged, they extort, even murder politicians who don't vote their way. We have to focus on uncovering that ASAP. Hell, for all we know, there could be another assassination planned. What the hell else could they be up to, Zach?" asked Zeke.

"Whatever it is, we better find out before they implement it. America is at war with itself, gentlemen and, as we stand here today, we are the only ones aware that we're in a war!" said Zach in a determined tone.

CHAPTER 28

"Those who expect to reap the blessings of freedom must, like men, undergo the fatigue of supporting it."

Thomas Paine (1737-1809)
Founding Father, Author of "Common Sense," credited
with stoking the American Revolution & the single most
successful American title in history (proportionally)

Nils Ottosson walked down King Street in Alexandria, wearing a heavy wool coat, plaid scarf, and dark sunglasses. A cigarette hung loosely from the side of his mouth.

Three men stood outside a pub, dressed in too-skinny European suits incongruent for their body types. They spoke softly in heavily accented English. All were chain-smoking cigarettes until they spotted Ottosson walking down the street and, taking one last deep drag each, they quickly tossed the butts to the curb.

Ottosson walked right past them, not acknowledging the men as he strolled through the downstairs bar, which was already full of after-work happy hour revelers. The Swede moved straight through the bar and headed up the wooden steps to the second-floor bar, which was strictly a whiskey bar and had only a few patrons sitting on the bar stools.

The three Russian men waited a few minutes, then went in and up the same stairs and pulled up chairs to a corner table, furthest from the bar, with Ottosson.

"Gentlemen, it's good to see you. All is well?" asked Ottosson, looking at all three.

"Aw, yes, all is very well," said one of the Russians, who had a shaved head and looked like he could be the Russian version of a Special Forces operative or SEAL.

"Here's a toast to *Walrus*! Very good work, gentlemen. You are true professionals," boasted Ottosson, referring to the operation that assassinated Chief Justice Noyner. Two of the three men were on the boat with Ottosson that day as replacement crew.

"Do you have something for us, my friend?" asked the lead Russian.

Ottosson leaned over in his chair toward the Russian to let him see down into the deep pocket of his wool overcoat. Inside the pocket was a thick envelope full of cash.

"Oh, very nice. Very nice," the Russian responded.

Ottosson took off his coat and placed it over the chair behind him. "We have set the date for *Madison,* my friends. I trust you have all the pieces in place?" asked Ottosson.

"Yes, of course, but first we must drink a toast to our victories. Some good Russian vodka, yes?" laughed the Russian, wanting to celebrate before any more business took place.

Ottosson motioned to the bartender to get his attention, and he promptly came and took their order. "We don't have vodka upstairs but, for you, I'll run downstairs and grab our finest!" he said, knowing from Ottosson's frequent meetings in the same bar that he was an over-the-top tipper.

A few minutes later, all four were drinking toasts. "First, to the success of *Walrus* and to future success with *Madison!*"

"I would guess by now there are no suspicions about the outcome of the investigation surrounding *Walrus*?" the Russian asked.

"No, sir. In fact, America has already replaced him," chuckled Ottosson, which was followed by nervous snickers from the Russians.

"We have heard that. We are so happy for you. We are good? Yes?" asked the Russian.

"Yes, you are professionals! Very good to do business with!" Ottosson reaffirmed.

The group momentarily stopped talking as the bartender brought another round of vodka shots.

"Do we have a date and location for *Madison,* my friend?" the Russian wondered.

"Indeed, we do," said Ottosson in his Swedish accent. "September 7th."

"And where will we be required to be, my friend?" pressed the Russian.

"You will receive explicit instructions soon as there is quite a bit of prep work needed to pull this off," Ottosson stated as he leaned forward to speak more softly. "This is a more dangerous mission than *Walrus*, and it has to be executed properly. It is extremely perilous, my friends."

"Yes, Mr. Ottosson, we understand. And your people will pay more, yes?"

"This is worth millions of dollars to your team," Ottosson whispered.

"Standard terms, my friend? Yes? One-half when plan is approved and one-half when complete?" the Russian asked.

"Of course, and we will continue to pay the stipends you have been getting every month," assured Ottosson.

"This is good, my friend. This is very good!" The Russian raised his vodka glass for a toast as Ottosson motioned for another round.

Suddenly, one of the Russians, who hadn't spoken at any point, whispered something to the leader in Russian, glaring at Ottosson.

"It would seem we have had a friend join us. Mr. Ottosson, is he your friend?" asked the Russian. His entire tone, body language and facial expression changed. "Do not look at the bar, my friend. I just need to know if someone is with you."

"No, there is nobody with me. You know you *only* deal with me. What are you talking about?" Ottosson forced himself not to look obvious as he tried not to look toward the bar.

"Nobody?" asked the Russian again. "You are sure, my friend?"

"Trust me, Vasily, nobody!" Ottosson insisted.

"My friend, if you ever say my name again in public, I will kill you with an ice pick through your skull. Do you understand me, my friend?" snarled Vasily, who was just short of being fully enraged.

"Damn, yes! Yes, of course!" Ottosson stressed. He knew he was very close to a disastrous situation.

"There is a man at the bar who was not sitting there when we sat down, my friend. If he is not with you, why is he so interested in what we are doing over here?" questioned Vasily.

"He's not with me, I can assure you of that, my friend. Don't look now, but I think the guy you are worried about is leaving."

The conversation stopped for a few seconds as they waited for the man at the bar to pay his tab and walk out. Vasily motioned to his two friends, who waited until the stranger went down the stairs, then they got up, put their jackets on and strolled casually after him.

Vasily looked at Ottosson and announced, "We will find out who this man was that was looking at us suspiciously. Are you sure you were not followed?"

"No, I can assure you I wasn't followed, and there is nobody in my organization who knows who you are, only me!"

Ottosson was a lobbyist, politician, opportunist, playboy and a *wannabe* cloak-and-dagger agent, but by no means was he trained in counterintelligence. He would never know if he was being followed by an intelligence professional.

"Well, I must be getting up and on to other business, my friend." Ottosson was getting nervous and wanted to leave.

"No, my friend, you will sit here until my comrades come back," instructed Vasily, while forcefully putting his hand on Ottosson's shoulder to keep him from standing.

Ten minutes later, the other two Russians came walking up the steps, concerned looks on their faces. The three chatted in whispers in Russian. Ottosson was clueless about what happened.

"This man at the bar suddenly disappears? Vanishes like a ghost?" said Vasily, looking at Ottosson with obvious suspicion.

"They couldn't find him?" asked Ottosson.

"Nyet," came the Russian reply.

"Maybe somebody picked him up on the street, like he had a ride or something," reasoned Ottosson.

"That could be, my friend," Vasily said to Ottosson, his tone disbelieving while he coldly stared at Ottosson as if trying to look into his soul.

"I didn't get a good look at him," Ottosson said nervously. "What did he look like?"

"We got a very good look at him. We will know him if we see him again. It would not be good if we see him again when we are with you, my friend." Ottosson found Vasily's response chilling.

"Okay, gentlemen. It's time for me to go. We'll meet again in two weeks," Ottosson told them, trying desperately not to sound rattled because he realized if the same guy showed up at the next meeting, Vasily would kill him.

"Maybe we should pick a different place, my friends. I will let you know."

"Yes, my friend, maybe we should," replied Vasily, the same intense look in his eyes.

Ottosson got up, shook their hands, and left without his coat.

Vasily picked up the coat, left purposely behind with the cash in the pocket, and draped it over his right forearm as he walked out.

Three blocks away, a former CIA counterintelligence officer sent a coded text to Zach Turner from the passenger seat of the car that picked him up:

Ottosson & Russians rendezvous at King Street Pub/Alexandria - Had to ditch

CHAPTER 29

"The liberties of a people never were, nor ever will be, secure, when the transactions of their rulers may be concealed from them."

- Patrick Henry
Founding Father, Revolutionary Attorney (self-taught),
Orator, Five-Time Governor of Virginia,
famous for "Give Me Liberty or Give Me Death" speech

Zach was elated that Pops Younger agreed to meet with him. He was even happier when the meeting was scheduled for Pops' central Texas ranch instead of the dreary gray confines of the Texas Department of Safety headquarters building in Austin. Zach, Will and Beard left the outskirts of Houston early on a Friday morning for a noon meeting with Younger.

Zach had not seen or spoken to Pops since the governor's funeral during the height of the *Texas Crisis*, but Pops was understandably preoccupied then and didn't have much time for Zach.

Zach pulled into the Younger ranch and up to a pair of Texas Rangers waiting at the ranch gate.

"Are you Turner?" asked one of the Rangers when Zach rolled the driver's side window down.

"Yes, sir, and this here is Turnbow and Beard."

"You can go on up to the ranch house," replied the Ranger.

The asphalt road from the gate was a winding half-mile road lined by live oak and pecan trees. A couple of times, Zach had to beep his horn to move some large longhorn cattle off the ranch road.

"There he is," said Will. "He's on the front porch."

"Now that's a sight you don't see every day, do you, boys?" commented Zach, wryly smiling and indicating the unmistakable figure standing on the front porch that would make you think you were stepping back into the 1880s.

Pops wore a starched white pearl snap western-style shirt, cowboy-cut Wrangler jeans with a large silver belt buckle, and black alligator boots. He also wore his silver felt cowboy hat, and sported the thick, bushy handlebar mustache he was so famous for. That large mustache had made a worldwide comeback with twenty-somethings, baby-boomers and others sporting Pops' look. The trend could be credited to the video footage seen around the world of Pops shooting charging Mexican federales with his two ivory-handled Colt revolvers on the International Bridge in Laredo during the most intense days of the *Texas Crisis*. The YouTube video of that scene had over six million views.

His Rangers were dressed much like Pops, but wore their silver star Ranger badges on their left chest pockets. Pops didn't have to. Everyone knew he was *the law* just by looking at him.

"I've met the last three presidents before Bartlett, and I can tell you, I'm more anxious to meet Pops than I was of any of those dudes," offered Beard.

"Well, you won't be disappointed, Beard. He's a helluva guy," answered Will. "I haven't been around him as much as Zach, but damned if I didn't come away learning something from that man every time."

As Zach, Beard and Will exited the truck, Pops stepped off the porch to greet them. Despite his fame, Pops wasn't much for pomp and circumstance. Where many politicians or famous personalities would have waited for them to come pay homage to him, Pops went out of his way to greet people.

"Mr. Younger, this here is Will Turnbow and Beard," introduced Zach.

"Beard, huh? That's his entire name?" commented Pops. "I don't think your momma named you that, did she, son?"

"No, sir," said Beard, "but that's about all anybody has called me for years. Very nice to meet you, sir," said Beard.

"Mr. Younger…"

"Hell, call me Pops. Everybody else does," interrupted Pops as Will was about to re-introduce himself.

"We've met a couple of times, sir, but you probably don't remember," chuckled Will.

"No, sir, I do remember. Last time we met was at the Capitol right before the last referendum vote," Pops said.

"Damn, sir, you're right. I'm surprised you remember. There was a bunch of us in that group that day," answered Will, who was stunned Pops remembered him.

As they walked into the main ranch house, Zach whispered to Will, "Hey, Will, don't think Pops doesn't know *exactly* who he's meeting with. *Nothing* gets by Pops."

As they entered the main living area of the house, Zach was surprised at how much larger it was than it looked from the outside.

"Gentlemen, help yourselves." Pops pulled out a small wooden cigar box, flipped open the lid, and grabbed one for himself before he passed it around.

"Thank you, Pops," said Zach, taking a cigar before passing the box to the others.

Will remembered a saying attributed to Pops, in which he stated, "I don't know nobody that don't hunt, smoke cigars or drink bourbon, but not in any particular order and, if they do all three, chances are I like 'em."

Beard didn't smoke cigars, but he sure wasn't turning one down.

Pops introduced three other senior Texas Rangers that were going to sit in on the meeting.

"Pops, we have come across some sensitive information that could help with your murder case of Senator Milsap," offered Zach to start the meeting.

"Here, y'all need a cutter and torch?" One of the Rangers passed around the cigar cutter and lighter. It appeared that Pops couldn't start the meeting officially until they all had their cigars lit.

"Okay, son," he told Zach. "We know your background and we know some of the things you folks have been involved with in the past. Sounds like you have been in some tight spots. I speak for all the Rangers when I tell you we appreciate your service."

"Thank you, Pops, that means a lot coming from you," said Zach.

"What do you boys do now, exactly?" asked Pops with a piercing stare.

"Corporate security, sir," answered Zach.

"And my momma is the Queen of England," chuckled Pops as he looked at his Rangers, who were also laughing.

The three visitors were a little taken aback. Their militia participation and network was not widely known.

"You're right, sir. In addition to corporate security work, we have an active militia organization," Zach stated directly and without hesitation.

"Nothin' to worry about, son. We know the work you folks do. Truth is, I wish more folks would take that same kind of interest in things going on today. I know Governor Cooper and his wife were very fond of you, and that carries a lot of water for me."

"Thank you, sir."

"Now, before you show me what it is you have about the assassination of this state senator, explain to me how you boys got whatever information or evidence you got."

"We still have some strategically placed friends at the agency, sir. They brought us some information unrelated to this murder, and our subsequent research turned up additional evidence," said Zach.

"I see. And in what official capacity were you doing this investigation, son?"

"Nothing official, sir. It's just our interest as citizen patriots," answered Zach.

Zach and Beard were quickly determining in their own minds that Pops already knew the answer to almost any question he was going to ask them.

"And how do you finance your investigations, son?"

"Well, sir, you…"

"Oh, yes, corporate security, right?" interrupted Pops as he drew in a big toke from his cigar.

Zach sensed Pops was testing him.

"As I'm sure you are aware, Pops, we have patrons that support our cause."

"What is that *cause* exactly"?" asked one of the deputy Ranger commanders.

"We are committed to holding law enforcement, the military, and government officials to follow the Constitution, and to their constitutional oath to protect citizens from all enemies, both foreign and domestic," stated Will proudly.

"So you're a citizen militia then?" asked the Ranger.

"That's one aspect of our membership group, yes. I'm sure you're aware that, during the American Revolution, every community had a militia for the common good," Will pointed out.

"What's the name of your group?" the Ranger asked. "I can't say that you or your friends here have ever shown up on any of our lists."

"And what *list* might that be?" asked Zach, testing the Ranger right back.

"These boys are well within their rights to organize and hold government and law enforcement accountable, John," said Pops to his deputy commander. "These boys have never presented us with a problem."

"*Free Texas*," shot back Beard, who hadn't said a word so far after the initial introductions.

"*Free Texas…* from what exactly?" asked John.

"*Keep* it free. That's all," Zach interjected, attempting to shut down the direction of the conversation.

"Aren't we already free?" John asked.

Zach looked at Pops, a tiny bit irritated with this guy who was interrupting his conversation with Pops. "Pops, forgive me, but where was he during the whole *Texas Crisis*? Can he really sit there and ask if we are free after that whole damned federal incursion? How in the world…"

"Son, son… Calm down. John here is just old school law and order. He doesn't trust civilians to take matters of law into their own hands. He don't mean anything by it. Let's get back to the matters at hand. You said you have some evidence?"

"Beard here is going to fire up his laptop and show you some documents and communications we intercepted."

"Intercepted?" commented the deputy Ranger.

"Hold on, John, let them show us what they've got," snapped Pops.

"Beard is going to start walking you through what we have." Zach motioned to Beard as he set his laptop on a large mesquite coffee table and turned it to face Pops.

"Boys, tell me one thing. Do you have a name for the bald-headed Russian?" Pops asked.

Zach looked at Will and Beard. They were all dumbfounded that Pops already had this lead.

"Yes, sir, we do. His name is Vasily Volkov. He is from St. Petersburg, Russia. He came to the U.S. two years ago on a six-month temporary visa, although under a different name, and apparently never left," cited Beard matter-of-factly. "He's former KGB."

Pops and the Rangers were now equally dumbfounded that these three could easily espouse the name of the man they had been hunting as the lead suspect in the Milsap murder.

Pops took another drag on his cigar, then leaned forward. "Show me what ya have, boys," he said as he got closer to the laptop on the table.

"Beard, walk him through all the documents," instructed Zach.

For the next twenty minutes, Beard showed Pops and the Rangers everything they had on Volkov. The Rangers were astounded at the level of detail, the scope of the communications, and the accuracy of the information.

"I've got to ask, sir, how did you know you had a Russian for a prime suspect?" asked Zach.

"Some very shaky, after-the-fact eyewitness information that was just circumstantial. They didn't see the murder, but they did have interactions with someone that spoke with a deep Russian or Ukrainian accent with his description in the area both before and after the murder," answered Pops. "Now we just have to understand the motive and find this scumbag."

"Sir, we have a contact who just laid eyes on him yesterday in Alexandria, Virginia," said Zach.

Pops moved back into his chair slowly, reached for the lighter and relit his cigar, which had been unattended in the large ashtray as Beard led Pops' team through the evidence. What Beard hadn't done so far was connect the dots between CIS, Ottosson and Volkov.

"You boys aren't telling me something, right?" Pops squinted and locked down his steely blue eyes on Beard.

Beard looked nervously back at Zach.

"Pops, we believe Milsap was being extorted," said Zach.

"Milsap had a problem with the ladies. However, he wasn't wealthy and you don't get a bullet in the back of the head from a former KGB agent simply because someone saw an opportunity to bribe a few bucks from a cheating husband," said Pops.

"Well, no, sir," answered Zach.

"This is tied to the referendum vote, isn't it?" asked Pops.

Zach was ticked off at himself for underestimating Pops. Yes, they were telling Pops some things he didn't know or have, but they weren't that far ahead of him. He just hadn't made the CIS connection.

"Yes, sir, but it's a little more complicated than that," Zach said reluctantly.

"What the hell is a high-level Russian KGB agent doing in Texas, assassinating a middle-of-the pack state politician who's not wealthy? Who is willing to do a murder for hire to defeat this referendum? Boys, it's time to stop pussy-footin' around and tell me what you really have!" Pops ordered firmly.

Zach looked at Will and Beard.

"Sir, can I speak to you privately?" asked Zach.

Pops looked at his Rangers and said, "Gentlemen, go out to the kitchen and take these two boys with you and grab some chow. Mr. Turner and I are going to chat."

The rest of them got up and left the room.

Beard and Will turned back to look at Zach. The plan all along had been to only give Pops the information he needed on the Milsap murder, but Pops was even more intuitive than they had calculated. Would Zach tell Pops *everything*?

"Son, I get the distinct sense you are holding out on me," said Pops, letting out a huge billow of cigar smoke.

Zach had such immense respect and reverence for Pops that he was struggling internally to stick to the original plan.

"Sir, this is only the tip of the iceberg. What we uncovered is so large—and so unbelievable—that I have deep-seated concerns about who sees it because I have people in very vulnerable positions who could *die* if this gets out."

"Son, do you trust me?" asked Pops.

"Yes, sir, I honestly do. But I can't speak for anyone beyond you."

"Well, son, let's do this. How 'bout you share with me what you know and I'll commit to you right here and now, that information will not be shared with anyone unless you grant me permission? You have my word. Will that work for you?" asked Pops convincingly.

Zach pondered this for a few seconds. His thoughts immediately traveled to his network of operatives and their families but, if there was anyone he could trust outside of his inner circle, it would be Pops. As long as Pops kept the information, he decided he was comfortable.

"Sir, if you will commit to me that this information won't leave this room, I will share what I know," began Zach.

"You already have it, son."

"Sir, the same Vasily Volkov that murdered Senator Milsap was on the chartered fishing boat the day Chief Justice Noyner died."

"Son of a bitch!" exclaimed Pops.

"It was called *Operation Walrus*. They injected him somehow while he was on the deck of the boat with what's called a Russian cocktail that causes heart failure and seizures, then they shoved him overboard, where he likely drowned."

Pops sat silent for a few moments before saying, "This guy is apparently an assassin for hire. Who hired him? You're not telling me the Russian government had our chief justice murdered, are you?"

"He was working for a supposed lobbyist for the Swedish firm CIS. His name is Nils Ottosson."

"CIS? The damned foreign election systems firm those dumbasses in D.C. hired to run the elections?" asked Pops.

"Yes, sir," Zach confirmed. "They don't actually run them, but most of the states use their software and cloud applications for their election systems. And it gets worse, sir."

Pops put his cigar down in the ashtray and stood up. He took his cowboy hat off, rubbed his head, then put it back on as he stroked his mustache. Pops seemed to move and talk slowly to most people; however, despite his apparent age, his mind was sharp as a tack, and now it was working overtime.

"*No autopsy!* I said a hundred times, why in the hell aren't the feds doing an autopsy?" complained Pops.

"Same as me, sir. In fact, this is what originally got us suspicious, you know, with us being conspiracy theorists and all," Zach said half-jokingly, referring to the deputy Ranger who was questioning their motives earlier.

"Go on, son. I know you ain't done."

"The election, sir." Zach paused.

Pops turned back toward Zach with a look he had never seen from Pops.

"Damn it to hell! What is wrong with these lame-ass politicians? You are going to tell me now, I'm sure, that somehow this CIS was able to impact the last elections, aren't you?"

"Sir, they did more than impact it; they *manufactured* the results."

"Sons of bitches. I knew it," snarled Pops, referring to the improbable comeback Bartlett staged to win. "Son, you better show me everything you have."

"Let me get Beard, who can pull up all of these files and communications, sir." Zach began to walk toward the kitchen, then stopped and turned back to Pops.

"Sir, there is something very important. We've uncovered some kind of plot for an operation they have dubbed as *Madison*. So far, we don't have any data whatsoever on what, where or when this operation will happen," admitted Zach.

"*Madison*? If it involves these turds, it can't be good," Pops said, indicating that Zach should go get Beard.

A few minutes later, Beard, Will and Zach were briefing Pops with all the records and details.

"Should I ask you boys how you happened to get this information?" asked Pops, partly in jest, but also partly curious.

"Sir, I would attribute our ability to gain this intelligence cache to the fine training all three of us had at the CIA."

As they began to pore through the records, Pops' deputy commander came out of the kitchen wanting to take part in the discussion. The trio had arrived at the ranch near noon and it was getting close to 9:00 in the evening. The deputy really wanted to participate in whatever they were talking about.

Pops glanced up. "John, why don't you and the team go on home? I'm going to spend a little more time with these fine boys."

Zach knew Pops wasn't really asking.

"Are you sure, sir?" John asked, looking at the two open laptops and files spread all over the mesquite table, more than curious about what he was being left out of.

"Yeah, we'll be fine and, hell, Barbara's probably wondering where the hell you were for dinner," chuckled Pops to distract the Ranger, referring to the deputy's wife.

As the deputy commander and the other Rangers left, Pops' demeanor changed. He became more intense and began scrutinizing every piece of evidence the trio produced for him to review.

At half-past midnight, Pops pushed back from the table.

"We got us one helluva pickle, boys. Last year's crisis was the most challenging time I've seen in my lifetime, other than the Big War. This goes so far and so deep, I ain't sure if it's fixable." He got up and stretched. "I can see why you're holding on to this. It's the most dangerous information I've ever come across. It's pure evil at its core. I need to sleep on it. You boys stay here tonight," commanded Pops, like it wasn't even a question.

"Sir, we really need to get back to our families," said Will.

"Damn, son, you gotta stay here so we can work on this first thing in the morning. What the hell is more important in your life right now than saving this country?"

"Yes, sir."

"How many others know what we know tonight, boys? Exactly how many and who are they?" queried Pops.

"Just our crew, sir, four others. I trust them with my life," said Zach.

"And are they instructed not to share anything with anybody?"

"That is correct, sir, and they won't."

"Well, gentlemen, my house nanny will show you to your rooms. Thanks for sharing the information. Let's see if we can get some damned sleep, knowing we've got the fate of the entire western civilization in our hands. I know it won't do no good to tell you I wish I didn't know what you know."

"Honestly, sir, I'll speak for myself, but it helps us that we can share this with you," admitted Beard. "It's a load to carry."

"Well, I hope I wake up in the morning with you boys as a figment of my imagination and this as some kind of nightmare, because this is going to get bad... really, really bad." Pops said with finality as he strolled down the hall toward the master bedroom.

CHAPTER 30

"I think Americans raise eyebrows when you tell them that IRS agents are training with a type of weapon that has stand-off capability. It's not like they're carrying a sidearm, and they knock on someone's door and say, You're evading your taxes."

> *- Jeff Duncan (R)*
> *South Carolina Congressman*

President Bartlett and Chief of Staff Weingold walked out of the Oval Office together across the corridor headed into the Roosevelt Room. Already seated in the room were IRS Commissioner Ivan Stanislau, NSA Director Blake Herron, and Secretary of the Treasury Bethany Hobst.

Stanislau, an attorney by trade, was a crotchety, stubborn and inept career bureaucrat who had risen to the top of the IRS food chain as he mastered *Deep State* politics with ruthless aplomb. He considered himself an intellectual elitist, and he thoroughly enjoyed the unbridled power he held at the IRS to invoke fear in political enemies. His ability to consolidate power at the IRS kept him rising through the ranks, no matter which Party occupied the White House. Even his boss, Secretary Hobst, feared him.

He thought it strange, however, that they weren't in the Oval office with just these few people, as the Roosevelt Room with its stately formal conference table and chairs seated sixteen. On opposite ends of the table were paintings of both the Roosevelt presidents (Teddy and Franklin D.), who were principally responsible for the remodeling of the room during their administrations. It was typically reserved for cabinet meetings.

Everyone stood as President Bartlett walked in.

"Good morning, Madam President," everyone said.

The president jumped right in with no chit chat. "Milton is going to lead us through this meeting," she stated.

"First, per my instructions last week, I want to make sure this meeting is not on your calendars or your staff's calendars." Weingold peered over his glasses that rested half-way down his nose.

Everyone nodded.

"Okay. Now, first and foremost, this meeting didn't happen. It's not on the president's schedule nor mine, and it shouldn't be on yours. You will each come out separate entrances in an unmarked, blacked-out vehicle, just as you came in," he instructed.

President Bartlett stood.

"It was very nice seeing everyone here," she said, then she walked out the door and closed it behind her.

The meeting attendees were confused by her abrupt departure.

"I'm sure you're asking yourselves why the president didn't stay for this meeting, especially since she requested your presence and because we went to great lengths to protect anyone from outside eyes who may be prying now or at some later point," Weingold said.

"We understand," replied Director Herron, referring to the fact that the president likely needed *plausible deniability* that she was ever a part of this meeting.

Stanislau thought to himself how strange it was that she kicked off the meeting, yet needed deniability that she was ever a part of it. He figured to himself that she made an appearance simply to let all those attending know that this was *her* meeting, whether or not she was actively participating. It was *her* agenda that was going to be carried out by Weingold.

"First, let's get an update on the service of all the audit and collection summonses issued by your department, Secretary Hobst," said Weingold, looking at Hobst, knowing Stanislau would be the one doing the briefing.

"Mr. Weingold, Mr. Stanislau can update us all," she replied.

"Sure, thank you, Madam Secretary. We had a total of ninety-two summons that were issued and all but one was delivered," Stanislau stated.

"Who didn't get theirs?" asked Weingold.

"A state senator in Texas named Milsap. He was killed a few weeks ago. We didn't see any need to add this to his wife and family's misery," added Stanislau.

"That's not your decision nor Treasury's to make. Issue the summons to his wife, Mr. Stanislau," Weingold instructed in a very condescending tone. "What enforcement actions have taken place?"

"We have levied bank accounts or restricted access to funds for about half of them so far. I think the total number in levy status is about thirty-eight."

"Why have only slightly half had enforcement actions?" asked Weingold to Hobst again.

"Sir, there are some legalities and processes we must follow. Otherwise, we risk bringing the eyes of the Inspector General in, which nobody here wants. It will muddy the water and delay things," Hobst said.

"We have about forty-five days before the Texas governor can call for a special session. He has to fill the vacancy for the unfortunate state senator who died first. I need your assurance that the remaining enforcement actions will be carried out by then, Madam Secretary," stated Weingold.

Hobst looked again at Stanislau.

"It will be tight, sir, but we will make it happen," replied Stanislau.

"Now, Director Herron, can you update us all, please?"

"Data capture is going smoothly for the most part. We are sharing this information with Mr. Stanislau and the IRS to detect anything that might raise questions, concerns and opportunities. There are a handful of names on the list who are not providing us with electronic signatures, so our tracking of them has been inconsistent and void of much useful data," stated Herron.

"This is what I want to know," pressed Weingold. "I need to know what aberrations we have, if any. Are these legislators? Who are they?"

"No, sir, this group of about twelve is made up of former Special Forces and CIA operatives who are connected to a group called *Free Texas*. As far as we can tell, they are a Tea Party-aligned constitutional militia of some sort," Herron said.

"Ex-CIA?" Weingold asked, concerned.

"Yes, sir, CIA."

"Do we have outstanding warrants related to the *Texas Crisis* for them?"

"No, sir, we do not. They weren't identified positively in any of the actions at the time. These guys obviously learned their trade well at the CIA. We can't connect the dots yet, but it would be unlikely that they weren't in the thick of things at the time," noted Herron.

"I want warrants on them, too. Also, with the warrants, we can ramp up the surveillance on them as needed," said Weingold.

"In a case of national security, sir, I don't think you will need to get the standard warrants. I can get the FISA court to approve any level of surveillance needed. I'll get the FBI director on this today," Herron stated.

"Yes, that's right. This is definitely a case of national security. Of course. Do it. I'll give Justice a heads-up to provide you whatever cooperation you need," ordered Weingold.

"As I'm sure you're aware, sir, FISA court documents are sealed. There's no danger of a leak on this," Herron said.

"Look, before any of you are squeamish for one second about what we are doing here, this is a case of national security. We are operating under the premise that there are domestic terrorists that have infiltrated and control this ridiculous Texas independence movement that lead to the crisis resulting in the deaths of federal agents. These agents were law-abiding, career agents. Good men, every last one of them," Weingold claimed with surprising emotion for a normally stoic personality. "Right now, this president has manufactured a truce with their state government. If that referendum gets back on the legislative docket, this dust-up will start all over again. If it gets to a vote, we are to make sure it's defeated soundly, never to be brought up again."

"Sir, what if the referendum passes?" asked Herron.

"This president will do what Lincoln did when the South seceded. She will squash it with overwhelming force and punish them for years to come," said a resolute Weingold, whose face suddenly became red. "You must understand the end game here, folks. It is to avoid bloodshed, keep Texas in check, and continue this president's popularity so her agenda can be achieved. This meeting is over. Thank you for coming in."

CHAPTER 31

"To compel a man to furnish funds for the propagation of ideas he disbelieves and abhors is sinful and tyrannical."

- Thomas Jefferson
3rd US President, Delegate to Continental Congress,
Author of The Declaration of Independence, Founding Father

Six state legislators sat in a conference room next to Governor Brahman's office in Austin, patiently awaiting a meeting they requested the day before. The governor knew most of them well, as some of the legislators had been in office for twenty-plus years.

"Gentlemen, Senator Perez has agreed to join us by conference call. Let me patch him through." The governor reached across the conference table and pressed a button on the speaker phone.

"Good morning, gentlemen. Glad to be with you this morning," Senator Perez answered.

"Good morning, Senator," the governor replied, then immediately went into short introductions of each legislator in attendance.

"Senator Perez and Governor Brahman, every one of us has been harassed by the Internal Revenue Service in the last three months, some worse than others. We have had levies assessed without any audits or notices, and a few of us have had bank accounts frozen, including some of our businesses," said Harry Del Conte, a sixty-one-year-old veteran Republican legislator from Abilene.

"In fact, Governor, my business accounts were frozen, causing the employees' paychecks to bounce. Try explaining that to the employees whose own checks bounced when they paid their bills!" stated a legislator from Midland.

"Gentlemen, I'm right there with you. I have had the same problem, along with Pops Younger, the lieutenant governor, and other members of my staff," announced Brahman.

"As have I," echoed Senator Perez.

"What in the hell is going on? How can this be happening in America?" asked one legislator.

"There appears to be a common theme here. Either you were involved in the crisis or supported the referendum," said Perez.

"Well, we're not sure about that, Senator. Two of us in here did not vote for the referendum," stated a legislator from Galveston, referring to himself and another legislator from San Antonio.

"But you both indicated you would reconsider a second referendum?" asked the governor.

"Well, of course we would. An armed incursion by federal troops to stop a free election on a non-binding referendum resolution is overreach at its worst. It definitely changed our constituents' opinions on this whole matter, which means it changed ours," said the Galveston legislator.

"There you go," Senator Perez replied.

"So are you saying the federal government is targeting us for our position on the crisis, or for our position on a future referendum?" asked the Galveston legislator.

"Yes," stated Perez bluntly.

"So they are either punishing us, or trying to influence the next vote?"

"Bingo. It doesn't take a rocket scientist to put the pieces together. We know the carry-overs in the Bartlett administration are essentially the same folks we dealt with in manager positions in the Johnson administration. The *Deep State* is alive and well," the senator admitted. "I have taken this information to the Senate Oversight Committee and to the Senate Judiciary Committee. I've also tried to arrange a meeting with the Inspector General's office, but so far to no avail."

"Senator, what are the two committees' actions on your information"?" asked Governor Brahman.

"Well, as you all are well aware, the Senate majority leader and I are not on each other's Christmas card list!" Perez chuckled. "He is on a mission to make me completely ineffective in any committee assignments, and the ranking members who do listen to me admit that taking any action on bills or investigations I ask them to take up get quashed due to reprisals on their political careers from McCray."

"What about Simpson? What can he do?" asked another legislator, referring to the senior senator from Texas.

"He's not a friend of this office, nor of Texas, that's for sure," the governor stated.

"We've called his office repeatedly but never hear back from him. From what we understand, he isn't talking to any of us who supported the referendum," revealed Del Conte. "Washington changed him. He's not the same guy. This is really a shame, especially since he sits on Oversight."

"Can we use the press?" asked another legislator.

"We could, but I think this needs to be a multi-layered approach," Brahman remarked. "We need to have Senator Perez work whatever angles he can through the Inspector General's office, but we need each of your local congressmen to assist the senator. There is strength in numbers."

"Governor Brahman is correct; we need your congressmen to get on board," affirmed Perez.

"Next, we should align our tax and legal experts so they are all on the same page. It seems like there are several common actions the IRS is taking. Have any of you met with anyone from the IRS yet, or have your legal and tax folks been working through this?" asked the governor.

"I have," said a legislator from East Texas. "Strangest meeting. They actually sent a revenue officer who carried a sidearm to my district office. During the course of our conversation, he asked for a list of donors, and wanted to talk about upcoming legislation. I asked why he couldn't get the donor list through the Texas Election Commission from our quarterly election finance filings, but he said they weren't current enough, so we produced them for him."

"Wow, seriously? Did he specifically ask how you would vote in a new independence referendum?" asked the governor.

"Actually, he did. I told him I would have to see the legislation before I could comment, but he continued to press. I would say only a quarter of the meeting dealt with my finances. It was strange as hell."

"Did he offer any deal or agree to make the audit or levies go away?" asked Perez.

"No, but he did say we could revisit it after our next legislative session, which we all know is months away. Instead, he indicated the governor was going to likely call a special session, and we could continue to discuss my case after that session was over," revealed the legislator.

"There you go! They aren't really trying to hide the fact that they're attempting to extort us," exclaimed Del Conte.

"Amazing. This is banana republic kind of stuff," said the legislator from Galveston.

"It is. As long as we have an IRS that can punish political enemies, it will remain effective. How much time has each of you had dealing with this crap over the last few weeks?" asked Perez.

Most agreed it had occupied almost one hundred percent of their days and led to sleepless nights and undue hardships.

"I would advise that nobody meet them without legal representation but, if you can avoid meeting with them altogether, that would be better," suggested Perez. "Expect your largest donors to be hit, too, and those you have personal relationships with I would call immediately. If some of these folks are influential business owners or community leaders, we'll need their help to bring pressure to bear. I have already done this with mine. I have regulators of every kind all over my top twenty supporters."

The group agreed to start having weekly conference calls and include their tax and legal advisors for parts of those calls. They also agreed to bring their largest donors into the loop.

"This is another sad day for America," lamented the Midland legislator. "Turning the IRS loose on what the administration perceives as political enemies is beyond the pale."

The governor and senator said their good-byes, and Brahman reached over the table to disconnect the call. The call wouldn't hang up, and it took him several tries before the line disconnected.

At the same time, two analysts with the NSA who had been listening in to the conversation realized they were the reason Brahman couldn't disconnect the call and disconnected it from their end.

The NSA had wiretaps on Senator Perez' and Governor Brahman's offices, homes and cell phones, granted to them from the FISA court.

CHAPTER 32

"As long as it served his purpose, Mr. Lincoln boldly advocated the right of Secession."

- Belle Boyd (1844-1900)
Actress & Confederate Spy
Recipient of the "Southern Cross of Honor"

Nils Ottosson strolled down the main hallway of the Hart Senate Office Building near the Capitol in Washington, D.C. with various Senate interns and CIS staff in tow.

Ottosson, in his official capacity as the chief lobbyist for CIS, had just concluded meetings with senators from Missouri, Indiana, Minnesota and Kentucky. These four states represented CIS' newest state customers for CIS' election balloting system, and Ottosson was there to brief the four senators on its implementation plan. CIS now had its election balloting systems in forty-six states, with two more states likely to ink new contracts in Nevada and Montana. Texas and Oklahoma were the only two states that had not approved implementing the CIS systems.

Two years before, President Johnson had threatened to federalize the election systems by executive order in all fifty states, primarily using the 1965 Voting Rights Act for justification. The left had used the initiatives by the GOP in dozens of states for voter ID laws to threaten the centralization of election laws and take over what had primarily been under the control of each individual state.

President Johnson, knowing that his executive order would be challenged in the courts and likely land in the Supreme Court with its conservative majority in the hands of Chief Justice Noyner, pulled it back just before implementing it. Several bills introduced in Congress to federalize the state election systems were being championed by proponents' racism accusations against voter ID laws, largely being implemented in traditionally red states. Some of those bills had made it out of committee. The handwriting was on the wall.

The *Texas Crisis* only added to the push by the left to federalize the election balloting process. The referendum vote would likely have never materialized under federal control. The left and government officials always claimed the original referendum vote was rigged to benefit the Texas nationalist agenda. Under this new executive order, the election results were required to be certified by the Federal Election Commission. The feds maintained that the CIS balloting system was the only way to assure such certification.

Now that the Court was firmly in the control of progressives, and with newly confirmed, Bartlett-handpicked Supreme Court Justice Sally Ferguson-Haverton as chief justice, any fear of an executive order being overturned at the Supreme Court level evaporated.

Later in the same afternoon, the White House Press Secretary issued this press release:

"In line with the best practices that have been identified by the Federal Election Commission, and with these latest four state governments that have signed on to use the same balloting systems as forty-two other states, President Bartlett is announcing an executive order that will bring the outlying states into alignment, thereby insuring equality, fairness and accuracy in all of our democratic elections."

The states of Texas and Oklahoma were quick to respond. Within two hours, the attorneys general of both states issued a joint response:

"The attempt to federalize our states' election apparatus and thereby control the free elections in each of our states is unconstitutional and both Texas and Oklahoma will initiate immediate lawsuits to place a temporary restraining order on this incomprehensible federal overreach."

With elections only months away, political analysts and legal experts fully expected this legal battle to be fast-tracked, meaning the Supreme Court could get the case before all of the lower courts chimed in with their opinions, thus likely cutting two years or more out of the process.

If Texas and Oklahoma prevailed, it would not invalidate the individual states' decision to contract the balloting systems with CIS, but it would keep the election process at the state level.

A federal judge in Dallas issued a temporary restraining order in favor of Texas within four hours. The restraining order was issued to cover any elections through the November election cycle, meaning the district court in Dallas would not hear the case until *after* the November elections. The United States attorney general immediately issued a fast-track appeal to the Supreme Court.

This high drama was lost on the average American citizen, more concerned about their next three-day weekend, but to conservative Constitutional scholars, states' rights advocates, Tea Party groups, and even moderate Republicans, the prospect of federal control of all elections was a watershed moment in American history. It was definitely not what the Founders intended.

Texas' public referendum vote had passed during the peak of the crisis; however, the Texas Constitution required a vote by the legislature to authorize any binding referendum. When the legislature took it up formally, multiple forces converged to narrowly defeat it. Governor Brahman had promised another vote was forthcoming.

The special election in Texas Legislative District 3 to replace State Senator Milsap was two weeks away. A firebrand Texas nationalist was leading the polling by a wide margin over six other candidates to replace Milsap in the special election. The regular session of the legislature was going to be out of session by that time, and the governor had less than forty-eight hours to bring the legislature back into special session. The Texas Legislature only meets every two years, but Texas governors can call special sessions to extend a current session if a critical vote is needed.

News broke the next day that the U.S. attorney general had requested an emergency appeal of the restraining order from the Dallas District Court judge to the 5th Circuit Court of Appeals, who refused to hear the case or the motion to quash the restraining order until all issues referred to in the order were settled in district court.

Within hours, despite the 5th Circuit decision not to take the case, the news broke that the Supreme Court *would* hear the case. This was extraordinary, and had only happened a few times in history. The next Monday at 9:00 a.m., all parties would be in front of the U.S. Supreme Court and the new chief justice. The Court did not allow live cameras but requests to attend the hearing numbered in the thousands, with only a few dozen seats available.

This would be the first official case for Chief Justice Haverton.

During one exchange between the Texas state attorney general and the chief justice, Haverton asked, "Under the Voting Rights Act of 1965, which Texas and most Southern states are still bound to, does Texas object to having an effective balloting system? Does Texas object to reports that institutional discrimination still exists at polling places?"

"Chief Justice Haverton, this executive order is unconstitutional on its face. The federal government has no constitutional authority to take over state elections or to force Texas, Oklahoma or any other state to comply with a mandate to use a particular balloting system. This is, in fact, a de facto way to federalize state elections," argued the Texas state attorney general.

"Does this executive order tell Texas when to have elections?"

"No, Chief Justice, it does not."

"Does this executive order tell Texas where to have polling locations?"

"No, it does not..."

"Does this executive order do anything that discourages a voter from casting his or her ballot?"

"Chief Justice, that's arguable, particularly if a citizen has less confidence in the federal balloting process versus the states'."

"My belief is, if in 1965 when the Voting Rights Act was written and implemented and if this type of balloting system was available at the time, it surely would have been made part of the Act," Haverton replied.

"Chief Justice, this case will be fully heard in due course. We are asking the Court to uphold the temporary restraining order not to implement the executive order until full arguments are held. The executive order also dictates both states to expend funds not approved by our state legislatures."

"The Court fully appreciates your concerns," Chief Justice Haverton stated, "but, in the interest of fairness, the Court has to look at each state's voting discrimination history and adherence to the Act. The recent voter ID law enactments are especially troublesome. The Court will recess and issue its decision in due time."

"Thank you, Chief Justice. We implore the Court, due to the fact that the upcoming elections will be held before this case is heard, to allow the restraining order to remain intact, if it please the Court. Also, to force Texas and Oklahoma to change decades of precedence on how we run our state elections without those states' day in court is un-American."

"What's *un-American* is discriminating against your citizens to alter the outcome of certain elections. What's *un-American* is encouraging citizens to participate in a *treasonous* and illegal vote. The Supreme Court of the United States is adjourned," said Haverton sternly as she slammed down the gavel.

At 4:00 p.m. the next day, the Supreme Court ruled.

In a 5-4 decision, the Court overturned the temporary restraining order, allowing the executive order to stand until trial by the district court. The Court also ruled that Texas and Oklahoma must adhere to the executive order and prove to the Federal Elections Commission that the CIS balloting system was implemented.

CHAPTER 33

"History is the version of past events that people have decided to agree upon."

Napoleon Bonaparte (1769-1821)
French Emperor

Pops Younger spent the entire next day with Zach, Will and Beard. They pored over the documents, files and transmissions Beard had decoded from Ottosson's devices. Pops was deeply impressed with the professionalism and work ethic of the *Free Texas* trio.

The four of them were so deeply entrenched into the examination of the records and files that none of them were paying close attention to anything going on outside of Pops' ranch. They were still wearing the same clothes they came to the ranch in the day before.

Will had stepped outside the ranch house with a cup of coffee to stretch his legs and to take a peek at a couple of Pops' longhorn cattle that were rubbing their faces and immense horns on the split rail fencing. While checking his phone, he saw a breaking news alert come across regarding the executive order that was issued the day before.

"Holy crap..." he exclaimed, tossing the coffee from his cup and running back into the ranch house.

"Guys, check the news. Bartlett issued an executive order stating Texas *has* to use the CIS balloting system! A Dallas judge issued a restraining order, and the attorney general got it fast-tracked to the Supreme Court. They are in session this morning!"

"You can't be serious," said Beard. They all started looking at their phones, trying to digest what was happening.

Pops immediately got on the phone with the governor's office.

Zach was initially worried that Pops would start to divulge the information they presented, but was relieved that Pops seemed to be listening and not speaking much on his call with Governor Brahman.

As soon as he ended the call, Pops picked up a new cigar, sat in his chair and lit it, drawing a deep toke on the large stogie.

"What's the angle here, gentlemen? What is Bartlett trying to accomplish?" asked Zach.

"Well, son, you probably can already figure this out. Want to try?" asked Pops.

"Bartlett is hedging her bets. They got rid of Noyner, so now they control the Supreme Court. She can issue any executive order she wants. Congress is impotent, and she owns the Court. They want this balloting system in before the next elections, but especially before any referendum vote," guessed Zach.

"Well, yes," said Pops calmly before taking another toke on his cigar, then stroking his bushy mustache, "but our esteemed lady president appears to be *complicit* in the murder of a Supreme Court chief justice. Hell, Louis L'Amour couldn't have written a cheap dime-store novel anyone would have taken seriously with this plot."

"It would appear so, but I think we all know how much more serious this is. We are talking about the gutting of the Constitution, literally," Zach shot back.

"Okay, it's official," announced Will as he looked up from his phone. "The Supreme Court has ruled and will not uphold the restraining order."

"Damn," said Zach and Beard.

Everyone's attention now turned to Pops, who stood and walked over to one of the panoramic windows that looked out over his ranch. It was clear he was thinking. As Beard looked at Pops' silhouette in contrast to the light shining through the window, he couldn't help but go back to the image he remembered seeing in a textbook as a child. It was the picture of John F. Kennedy looking out a window at the Oval Office at the height of the Cuban Missile Crisis. Kennedy looked alone, like he had the weight of the world on his shoulders.

The silence was deafening, and it seemed to go on forever. Zach couldn't stand it.

"This just keeps getting worse by the day," he stated.

"Boys, we've got to tell the governor. He has to know what we know. Those bastards are destroying it all. They've got to be stopped," said Pops firmly.

"I'd be open to that, Pops, as long as we have some assurance it's a tightly controlled dissemination of the evidence to a very trusted circle of people," Zach replied. "I've got brothers at Langley and elsewhere who this administration would love to unmask and eliminate."

Pops turned from the window slowly, then peered at the three with those piercing eyes, "Boys, these folks are scumbags of the worst kind. They won't think twice about putting a bullet in your eye. All three of you are in *serious* danger. Hell, I suppose your families are, too. You better git them to high ground." That was Pops' way of saying to move them to a safer place.

It wasn't until just that moment that the enormity of what was happening actually hit Zach, Will and Beard. Zach looked at both of them. "This is what we and our teams have prepared for for years," he said, loud enough for Pops to hear. "It ain't what we wanted, but damned if it hasn't come true."

"The question is, will anyone else really care? Hell, I know people in Texas will care, and care a lot about this. But the rest of the country? Doubtful," Will lamented.

"We will definitely be in the minority. You could show people the facts and they still will refuse to believe it," said Beard.

"Boys, this country has *been* gone for a while. Texas was and is the last hope. But I gotta tell y'all, I thought I would be out there six foot under that giant pecan tree you see over there full of worms before this would have ever gotten this bad. *America is a rotting corpse and it's beginning to stink to high heaven.*"

"Well, it's now infected Texas. The question is, can this disease be reversed or should we amputate ourselves from the rotting corpse?" asked Zach.

"Damned if I know how to answer that, son," said a distressed Pops, "but I do know that, just like an ol' sawbones on the battlefield, there comes a time when there ain't no more pussyfootin' around. Ya gotta take that leg or arm, or the soldier dies."

CHAPTER 34

"Purveyors of political correctness will, in the final analysis, not even allow others their judgments... They celebrate "difference," but they will not allow people truly to be different—to think differently, and to say what they think."

- Mark Berley
Author

Pops Younger and Zach Turner waited in Governor Brahman's office for fifteen minutes. Pops never sat down in one of the big burnt-orange, oversized leather stuffed chairs or couch. Pops stood in front of the framed *1789* flag, contemplating it, almost paying homage to the events it represented.

"It's my first time to see it," said Zach as he walked over to stand next to Pops. "Amanda Flores was a hero. So was Chuck Dixon. I'm just in awe to be standing near it."

"Damn near brings me to tears every time I'm in here to see the gov. I'm going to tell him this needs to be displayed where more Texans can see it."

"It's probably all the dried-up blood on the flag that keeps it from being displayed publicly. We'll have to ask the governor," said Zach.

"Damned folks oughta see it takes blood to maintain liberty," shot back Pops. "Those folks gave their lives for a *non-binding* referendum."

"I wonder what they would do today if they knew what we know?" Zach thought out loud.

"Same thing; just wouldn't be a non-binding vote. Wouldn't be a damn thing symbolic about it. It would be the real deal," said Pops.

"Do you think that's where this is headed?" asked Zach.

Before Pops could answer, Governor Brahman, Lieutenant Governor Tommy Wilson, and Texas Attorney General Bradley Drummond came through the door. They all walked over to the large conference table on the other side of the office and took seats.

"Dang it, Pops. I'm so sorry we kept you waiting," apologized the governor, who knew Pops would never keep him waiting if the roles were reversed. "This damned IRS thing is outta control. I understand they went after you, too." The governor peered at Pops quizzically.

"Damned straight. I got suits all over the damned place trying to clean this mess up. They're after all of us, it seems," answered Pops.

"Let's get settled in here, gentlemen. I'm almost hesitant to ask about the details of your request to meet, Pops. I can only remember one other time you said something was urgent, and it wasn't good news."

"No, Smitty, it wasn't," Pops responded.

"Pops called me the night the governor and his wife were killed. Dark days, very dark days." The governor loosened his tie.

"Sir, I think you know Zach Turner." Pops motioned to Zach.

"Yes, we've met on a few occasions. Nice to see you again, Zach. Let me introduce Lieutenant Governor Tommy Wilson and Attorney General Bradley Drummond.

After the introductions, Governor Brahman turned to Pops. "Okay, Pops, let me have it. What news do you have?"

"Sir, Zach here brought me a bunch of evidence that him and his boys have been gathering…"

"His boys?" asked Drummond. "Excuse me, everyone, but maybe I'm not up to speed on Mr. Turner and his organization. Can you enlighten me, Mr. Turner, so that I can put whatever you tell us about into some kind of context?"

"Sure. First, I'm former Special Forces, Navy Seal to be exact. After thirteen years, I was recruited by the CIA and went to work for them as an operative. About five years ago, I left the agency due to what I would describe as irreconcilable philosophical differences. I came back to my hometown in Katy, Texas and founded a corporate security firm." Zach took a look around at the other men, then continued, "I also started an organization called *Free Texas*, which focuses on issues concerning Texas' sovereignty and adherence to the Constitution."

"So, you're a militia?" asked Drummond.

"That's a fairly broad term," Zach stated. "Let's just say we have a network of like-minded individuals who maintain preparedness for any kind of disaster, natural or *political*."

"How many in your group are ex-CIA?" asked Drummond.

"I'm not at liberty to say, sir," replied Zach, making sure he didn't tell them he had his own people still embedded at the CIA.

"If Pops vouches for this man, he's my friend, too," Brahman said flatly. "Can you describe this evidence Pops was referring to when he called me?" He looked over at Zach.

"With all due respect, sir, this information is highly sensitive and, if it gets in the wrong hands, could have dire consequences. It would be my preference, sir, with no disrespect to either the lieutenant governor or the attorney general, if you, Pops, and I discussed the nature of the data I have before we decide to share it with others."

"I understand, but I do want you to know I trust these two gentlemen as well."

"I'm sure you do, sir," smiled Zach. "And I mean no disrespect at all, but can we present it to you before we decide who else needs to know?" asked Zach.

The body language of the other two officials changed noticeably. Who in the heck was this guy, telling the governor who the information could or could not be shared with?

"Pops, you've seen this information. Your call," deferred the governor.

"When you see this, Smitty, you will likely want these folks involved sooner than later but, since this young man and his team risked their butts to get this info, I say we respect his wishes," advised Pops.

"Gentlemen," the governor said, looking at Wilson and Drummond as they began to get up. "We will get back to you soon. Thank you for coming in."

Wilson and Drummond excused themselves and left the room, displeasure and disapproval following in their wake. They were not happy.

Once they settled back at the table, Zach asked if it was okay if he brought Beard and Will into the meeting. The governor, at first hesitant after dismissing his top two state officials, agreed to bring Zach's colleagues in to present the information.

For the next two hours, the trio from *Free Texas* led the governor through the same evidence presented to Pops. For the most part, Pops didn't add anything to the conversation unless asked. The governor lit a cigar, but was so engrossed in the information that he never smoked it, and it went out on its own sitting in the large ashtray.

"My God, I knew we had some serious problems in the federal government, but this is beyond the pale. What we could be seeing here is our Republic in its final death throes. What in the hell do we do with this?" asked the governor.

"It should be as clear as the Guadalupe River what the hell these IRS dipshits are up to," said Pops.

"Crystal," replied Zach. "It's their stock in trade. It's called intimidation, and they are doing it to those who voted for the referendum."

"Chief Justice Noyner and that poor State Senator Milsap and his family. Damn."

"Smitty, this reference to *Madison* really has the hairs up on my neck. Hard to imagine they are cookin' up somethin' worse, but these damned folk are downright evil. My gut tells me it has something to do with your called session."

Beard had been sitting silently listening to Pops, the governor and Zach, only answering questions as they came up.

"*Madison.* Of course..." said Beard thoughtfully.

Everyone stopped talking and focused on Beard.

"What? You figured out their next operation?" asked Zach.

"Not exactly, but I have a hunch," explained Beard.

"What do you have?" asked Will, now curious himself.

"Yes, do tell. Even a hunch at this point is more than anything else we have," said the governor.

"James *Madison*," replied Beard.

"The Founder?" asked the governor. "Okay, what could it mean?"

"It's only a hunch," Beard reiterated.

Everyone just sat looking at Beard for a few seconds, trying to connect the dots.

"Oh, my God. Of course!" exclaimed Will.

"Damn it!" cursed Zach.

"What? What does it mean?" pressed Governor Brahman.

"James *Madison* is the author of the 2nd Amendment," stated Beard.

CHAPTER 35

"The liberties of our country, the freedom of our civil Constitution, are worth defending at all hazards; and it is our duty to defend them against all attacks."

- Samuel Adams (1722-1803)
Founding Father, Organizer of the Boston Tea Party

The next morning, Governor Brahman walked into his regular staff meeting with a sense of purpose. He scheduled this one an hour earlier than usual, starting at 7:00 a.m.

The governor's schedule for the day was packed. After the thirty-minute meeting, he was to go straight to the airport for a short flight to San Antonio to speak to a GOP women's conference, then turn right back around and fly back to Austin to meet with Pops Younger, Tommy Wilson, and Bradley Drummond to reveal some of the information passed on by the *Free Texas* trio.

As the governor's vehicle pulled up to the Texas Department of Public Safety Aviation terminal at the Austin airport, the King Air 400 twin turboprop was already running its propellers and poised to roll down the tarmac when the governor's entourage boarded. Traveling with the governor was Lieutenant Governor Wilson. The flight to San Antonio was a short one, only twenty minutes or less from take-off to touch down.

Wilson had sensed something ominous in the meeting with Pops that Wilson was asked to leave. He called the governor the night before Brahman's San Antonio trip and asked to join him so he could get some one-on-one time with the governor to discuss what he learned in his meeting.

The gleaming King Air, adorned with the State Seal of Texas on the tail, rocketed down the runway and caught air quickly, climbing rapidly.

As it flew over the road at the end of the south runway, the flight attendant looked down to see the cars parked at a small parking lot made for aviation enthusiasts.

Six cars were parked watching planes taking off, including a plain white panel van. The two occupants sitting in the front seat looked up.

"Bye, bye governor," said Vasily Volkov to his comrade as he put the van in drive and slowly left the parking lot.

Fourteen minutes into the flight, at an altitude of eighty-eight hundred feet, a red warning light began flashing in the cockpit.

"Low on fuel? Hmmm… Got to be a malfunction. We are full of fuel," said the co-pilot.

"Reset the indicator," instructed the pilot.

"It won't reset. I watched them load the fuel. It's got to be an indicator malfunction," said the co-pilot, confident no real issue existed.

Suddenly, an engine warning light came on for the starboard engine.

"Starboard engine not getting fuel. I don't like this; should we put her down?" asked the co-pilot, now with some fear creeping into his voice.

"RPM is not dropping; makes me think it's the electronics," shot back the pilot.

The passengers had no clue this type of activity was going on in the cockpit. The governor and lieutenant governor were deep into their conversation, and the flight attendant had just freshened their coffees.

"There it goes! Starboard engine RPM just dropped. We are losing the starboard engine!" yelled the co-pilot.

The King Air yawed toward the engine still under power. As the plane surged to the left engine, it was enough to jolt everyone in their seats.

The flight attendant opened the cockpit door.

"Do we have a problem, captain?" she asked.

"We've lost the starboard engine, but port engine is running fine. We are only about seven minutes or so from landing. Tell them we will hold course and should land as scheduled," the pilot reassured her, but noted the co-pilot's uncertain expression.

The highly trained, experienced pilot began his emergency procedures like clockwork, with no emotion visible.

"Feather the dead engine props," commanded the pilot, trying to limit the windmilling effect wind speed had on the propellers. The propellers were causing a terrific drag on the aircraft, pulling the plane in a right-hand direction.

"Props feathered," replied the co-pilot.

"Banking five degrees port," announced the pilot, following the first rule in a twin-engine single failure, which was to raise the dead, meaning tipping the wing on the dead engine side to create more lift on the left wing.

"Cut fuel to starboard," the pilot said.

"Starboard fuel shut off," repeated the co-pilot.

The very second the fuel to the dead engine was cut, the remaining engine on the port side shot up in RPM.

"What the hell?" the pilot exclaimed, fighting the yawing effect with his stick and pedals.

The pilot knew that part of the protocol when losing an engine when not in take-off mode was to point the nose downward to gain airspeed, but that also reduced the margin for error. It was a "damned if you do, damned if you don't" scenario.

"San Antonio, this is Governor One," the pilot radioed the San Antonio tower. "We have lost our starboard engine. Requesting clear flight path to land and permission to lower to eighteen hundred feet."

"Governor One, permission granted to lower to eighteen hundred feet. We will clear airspace for you immediately. Please stand by. Do we need emergency equipment on runway?"

"We should be okay. Port engine spiking in RPM intermittently. Lowering to eighteen hundred feet now," returned the pilot as he began a fairly rapid descent.

"Go tell the governor where we are and what we are doing," said the pilot.

"You got it?" asked the co-pilot.

"I've got it. I don't understand the RPM spikes, but we are only twenty-four miles out," the pilot re-assured him.

The co-pilot unsnapped out of his seat and climbed over the controls console to open the cockpit door.

When he got into the cabin, the co-pilot told the governor, "Governor, we lost the right engine but the left engine is fine. The back-and-forth effect you are feeling is the pilot adjusting the yaw effect caused by having power coming from only one side. We are about twenty miles from the airport and we are cleared to land," the co-pilot stated, appearing confident.

"Do we need to be concerned?" asked Wilson.

"Well, we would rather have *both* engines," chuckled the co-pilot, trying to lighten the situation. "But one engine will get us there."

"I may need a flight bag," Brahman told the flight attendant. He was getting motion sickness from the yawing effect of the plane.

"No problem, sir. I'll fetch one," she said.

In the meantime, the plain white van that had been parked at the end of the Austin runway was making its way south on Interstate 35 toward San Antonio, driving at posted speeds. The pair in the front seats was listening to a police scanner.

The co-pilot went back to the cockpit, closing the door behind him and crawling back over the controls console and was almost strapped in before multiple warning lights went off and the RPM on the port engine suddenly surged.

"Damn it!" said the pilot as he tried to look at his gauges, but he was busy fighting the stick and pedals. With the sudden surge in power, the King Air was literally trying to turn itself on its axis, twisting violently to the left, counterclockwise.

The co-pilot didn't even bother to strap himself into his seat.

"RPM is redlining, sir!" he yelled. "Twenty-six hundred feet, dropping too fast, sir!".

"I'm fighting this damned thing. What the hell is going on with this engine?" the pilot grimaced as he struggled with the stick.

The pilot, who had remained calm from the beginning, now had real fear on his face, and the co-pilot could see it.

The pilot had to make a split-second decision to cut the engine to keep the aircraft from turning upside down and beginning a deadly spiral.

"Cut the engine! Cut the engine!" he yelled to the co-pilot as he fought with the stick and rudder pedals.

"It's not shutting down!"

"Try again. Keep trying! Keep trying!"

"My switch is not working!"

"Hit mine! Hit mine NOW!"

"Damn, it won't shut off either!"

The King Air turboprop aircraft slowly started to roll over on its left wing.

"San Antonio tower, this is Governor One. Mayday! Mayday! Mayday! We have lost control of the aircraft!"

In the cabin, the flight attendant felt a sensation she had never experienced in her ten-year career—fear.

"Oh, my God!" she shrieked, grabbing the armrests of her chair.

"Oh, no, this ain't good..." exclaimed Governor Brahman.

"God, please help us!" Wilson murmured under his breath as he also grasped the arm rests on his chair.

The King Air rolled to a ninety-degree angle as the pilots fought to cut off the engine and keep it from rolling further. Meanwhile, the plane was losing altitude. Had the pilots been able to cut the engine, they still would have had a major problem keeping airspeed to prevent the aircraft dropping from the sky. Their only hope would be to glide into some type of emergency landing, but there simply wasn't enough altitude had they succeeded.

The King Air rolled to one hundred ten degrees and the engine cut off on its own. Now, almost completely inverted, the nose dropped and began an intense spiral from twelve hundred feet.

"Governor One, Governor One, do you read?" shouted the San Antonio tower.

"God forgive me," said the pilot to himself.

Thirteen miles from the San Antonio airport runway, the King Air, in steep descent and traveling at a speed of more than 320 miles per hour, slammed into a hillside nose first right outside the small bedroom community of Selma, Texas.

A ball of fire rose up from the ground several hundred feet and could be seen in the Texas hill country sky for miles. Despite the fuel warnings on the aircraft, the King Air had plenty of fuel.

Within minutes, the chatter on the police scanner in the van traveling south on Interstate 35 increased rapidly. The two occupants looked at each other and smiled.

The special concoction they were able to load into the aircraft fuel supply was only a little more than a gallon but, in thirty minutes and under pressure, it caused the jet fuel to gel and clump. The clumping had the same effect as a clogged artery when it caused a heart attack.

The pair had solicited help from an employee of a contract jet services firm that contracted with the Department of Public Safety for aircraft maintenance. The employee had managed to get Volkov access to the King Air, and uploading the fuel additive was a simple procedure. With Volkov wearing the bright blue jumpsuit of the aircraft maintenance firm, nobody knew the difference.

Volkov picked up one of four cell phones in a cardboard box on the floor between the two front seats and dialed a number.

"The eagle has landed," Volkov said in broken English.

"You confirmed it?" asked the voice on the phone.

"*Watch the news*. You'll get your confirmation," answered Volkov, ending the call and handing the phone to his passenger to destroy.

In Washington, D.C., Nils Ottosson ended the call.

Two hours later, the pair knocked on the front door of the apartment the maintenance worker lived at in South Austin with his young wife and four-year-old son.

When the pair of Russians left the apartment, their silenced pistols were hidden inside their shirts, which were tucked neatly into their jeans.

Inside the apartment were the three dead members of the young family. The maintenance worker had a gunshot upward in his mouth through his brain. The wife and mother had been shot in the back of the head with a single bullet, along with the four-year-old boy.

The Russians' only ties to the King Air were now dead, and the chances investigators could trace the jet fuel coagulant from a fiery crash scene were remote.

CHAPTER 36

"To oppose corruption in government is the highest form of patriotism."
- G. Edward Griffin
American Author

E very morning at 5:00 a.m., Pops Younger saddled up *Pecos*, his big bay
quarter horse, and rode the fence lines of his Hill Country ranch west
of Austin.

It was a habit he continued for the forty years he owned the ranch. He
never took a cell phone and claimed he did it to "knock out the cobwebs"
every morning. It didn't matter if it was one hundred degrees or freezing
rain; Pops never missed his ride.

Today, instead of taking one trip around the outside fence lines of the
sprawling ranch, Pops did it twice. The weight of the evidence he was shown
by Zach Turner was heavy on his mind. Although he didn't intentionally
decide to be gone this long, he was so heavy in thought that he rode right
past his turn-off to head back to the ranch house. The only other time that
had happened to him was twenty-five years earlier when his wife Betsy died.

As Pops headed down the rocky back road, he turned the corner where
the house, several hundred yards away, would be in sight. He immediately
noticed at least a half dozen black Department of Public Safety SUVs parked
in front of his barn.

"Here he comes," said a trooper, pointing to Pops, with his signature
Stetson, riding on his big bay, coming toward them at a slow trot, kicking up
dust clouds behind him.

"God, I love that man!" said another.

Pops rode right up to the group milling around the vehicles.

"I hope y'all ain't here for breakfast. I ran outta bacon this morning," joked Pops. "I trust y'all ain't here to share some kind of good news with me, are ya?"

Dick Dyson, Pops' second in command, spoke up first.

"No, Pops, we've got some awful news," Dick told him. "

"Well, spit it out," ordered Pops as he climbed down off the horse.

"There ain't no good way to say it, sir. The governor's plane went down a short time ago on his way to San Antone. *There are no survivors*. The pilot indicated they had some engine problems, then next thing you know the San Antone tower got a Mayday."

Pops looked off into the hills, completely silent. He reached into the left upper pocket on his pearl snap shirt and pulled out a half-smoked cigar and began chewing on it. The silence was deafening.

"Who else was on that plane?"

"The lieutenant governor, a flight attendant and two pilots," Dyson replied.

Pops was still holding the reins of the big bay. He motioned for one of his Hispanic ranch hands to come get it.

"Smitty. Damn it to hell. Does his wife and kin know yet?"

"It hasn't been made public yet, except the crash site is hard to keep quiet. Everyone in the air traffic community knew it was Governor One, but nobody has confirmed the governor was on board to any news agency."

"I need to git to the governor's mansion. Need to see Louise," said Pops, referring to Brahman's wife of forty-six years.

"Do you need to freshen up or change clothes, Pops?" asked Dyson.

"How I smell will be the last thing on Louise's mind. Let's just git over there now."

Within minutes, a caravan of SUVs and black state trooper cruisers with lights flashing were headed east to Austin out of Johnson City. The forty-minute drive was enough travel time for the news to break before Pops could reach Louise. News agencies everywhere had picked up the story that Governor One went down with no survivors; however, no state agency would confirm it. A local Austin report, however, was able to get a Department of Public Safety airport hangar employee to state the governor and lieutenant governor were on the flight manifest.

Zach Turner was driving his large diesel pickup truck west on Interstate 10, headed to the Bunker, when he got a call from Will Turnbow.

"Zach, have you heard?"

"Heard what?" Zach asked.

"The governor's plane just crashed south of Austin!"

"What? How? Are there survivors? Who was on the plane? Please tell me Pops wasn't on the flight!"

"Pops was not on it," Will confirmed. "There were no survivors. It's unconfirmed officially, but our team had the governor and lieutenant governor on the flight manifest. He was doing a GOP women's speech this morning before heading back to meet us in Austin this afternoon."

"How did it go down?" asked Zach, still unable to grasp the gravity of the subject.

"The San Antonio tower got a mayday from the pilot reporting engine trouble. Apparently one engine went out, but they should have been okay. They went down only about twelve miles from the airport," reported Will.

"My God, what the hell is happening?" Zach wondered out loud.

"I know where you're probably going with this, Zach," Will told him. "We won't leave any stone unturned. We have lots of friends at DPS, and you know Pops will be all over this."

"Two Texas governors in less than eighteen months," Zach mused. "This better have been a real accident. You know I don't believe in coincidences any more."

"I'm with you, Zach. This is absolutely horrible. I wish I could say there is no way the federal government was not behind this," Will said.

"Who's next in line, the Speaker?" asked Zach.

"I believe so, Zach, and Strasburg is no real friend of ours," said Will regretfully. Under the Texas Constitution, the lieutenant governor succeeds the governor in death but, since the lieutenant governor was also on the plane, the next in line is the Speaker of the House.

Speaker Jim Strasburg was not a friend of the hard right. A "rehabilitated" Democrat, Strasburg flipped political parties when he saw the handwriting on the wall twenty years earlier. He was not an outspoken public opponent of the independence referendum, but privately he was against it. A purely political animal, Strasburg tended to check the political winds on a daily basis, and his centrist approach got enough Democrats to vote for him in the legislature to vault him to the Speaker's position, which wielded great power in Texas politics.

"No, he's not, and he will be in way over his head dealing with the feds. He's definitely someone I don't trust with the evidence we have. We are really going to have to discuss this with Pops. This is horrible." Zach sounded depressed.

By the time Pops' contingent arrived at the governor's mansion, the press had already caught wind of the tragedy and had descended onto the street in front of the mansion.

"Damned scalawags," Pops muttered under his breath as state troopers directed satellite trucks to make way for the group of SUVs in Pops' party.

Once inside the mansion, the scene was exactly as Pops expected, with Smitty's wife Louise bearing the burden of the sudden tragic news surrounded mostly by staff. It was only a couple of hours after the crash, and no family had made it to Austin yet.

Nobody had ever seen Pops cry, but when he got up from the couch after consoling Louise, he wiped a tear from his left eye.

Pops went way back in years with Smitty. Smitty was a long-time hunting buddy and Pops was a true friend of the entire Brahman family. He had been to all the weddings of Smitty's five kids.

Now two of Pops' best friends, who had each risen in Texas politics to be governor, had died tragically only eighteen months apart. Popular Texas Governor Brent Cooper and his wife were killed in the failed raid by the feds at the Swingin' T ranch in the Hill Country during the pinnacle of the *Texas Crisis*.

One of Pops' greatest attributes was his gut instinct about things. Call it a "hunch," but there were too many occasions where Pops' ability to solve crimes went beyond sound investigation protocols. Pops just had the innate ability to see things nobody else could.

As he walked out toward the large solarium in the back of the mansion, he couldn't ignore the deep-down gut feeling he had.

"This wasn't no accident," he resolutely said to himself, incensed that he may have lost *both* of his dear friends as a result of criminal administrations.

CHAPTER 37

"The two enemies of the people are criminals and government, so let us tie the second down with the chains of the Constitution so the second will not become the legalized version of the first."

> *- Thomas Jefferson*
> *3rd US President, Delegate to Continental Congress*
> *Author of The Declaration of Independence, Founding Father*

Zach Turner finally reached Pops' second in command by cell phone. Pops had just left the governor's mansion and was headed south to the crash site with Department of Public Safety officials and a contingent of fellow Texas Rangers. Understandably, Pops would not be able to keep his meeting with the trio from *Free Texas* that afternoon.

After Zach hung up, he sent out a coded message to his team, scheduling an emergency meeting at the Bunker for later that afternoon. This type of emergency meeting meant that anyone on Zach's team that could reach the Bunker in the next six hours should be there.

Zach was struggling with the fact that he had not fully divulged the evidence Beard had gathered with the rank-and-file members of his security team and the nationwide network of operatives he had cultivated. In the same way that Pops' gut instinct told him the crash was no accident, Zach sensed the Russian connection with Ottosson was fully capable of such a dastardly operation.

"Zach, we've got some very restless natives," Will said on a phone call to Zach.

"We are all restless. The crash…"

"Not just the crash, Zach," interrupted Will.

"Okay, then what?" asked Zach.

"The IRS levy actions are having an impact. I'm hearing there are some who want immediate action, even retribution," Will relayed.

"How bad is it? We told them to move money immediately, didn't we?"

"It's apparently pretty bad," Will told him. "Some didn't act right away; others had already had their accounts levied before they could do anything. It seems the IRS is going to extra steps to target our folks. They all know they're targets due to the referendum but, Lord, Zach, once they know what *we* know, I'm not sure if we can contain all of them from acting on their own."

"You know at some point we have to tell them. If we don't, we stand to lose trust with them all in the end for not keeping them informed," stated Zach.

The beauty of Turner's organization was the breadth, scope and talent the group possessed globally. Although only three dozen security specialists were on the payroll of Zach's security firm, the rest of the organization accepted Zach as the undisputed leader. It was an amazing collection of current and former operatives—SEALS, Green Berets, Army Rangers, mercenaries, self-proclaimed patriots, and a highly organized, tightly knit collection of regional volunteer militias.

The national news was covering the crash nonstop. All members of the *Free Texas* organization could easily connect the dots of an emergency meeting. An emergency meeting called just a couple of hours after the governor's plane crashed? That was a coincidence, and this group didn't believe in coincidences.

Although the meeting wasn't scheduled to begin until 5:00, *Free Texas* members and Zach's security employees began streaming into the Bunker site as early as 2:00. Zach expected his full roster of security employees, except four who were on assignment escorting corporate executives in various places around the world.

The mood of the group that assembled at the Bunker was not festive, even though many had not seen each other since the *Texas Crisis* broke out. Almost immediately, they began comparing the horror stories of their IRS dealings over the last few weeks.

For a group of high-testosterone, Type A personalities with notable black ops skills to start sharing their hatred for the IRS, coupled with the news that another Texas governor was dead—even if by accident—created a volatile environment, especially for those on the extreme anti-government side of things. Beard, who was the first of the fully knowledgeable trio to arrive at the Bunker, sent Zach an advance coded text message that he needed to be prepared to defuse the volatility of the group.

Although Zach's first instinct was to head straight to the Bunker, he needed to go home first and see to Kymbra and his son. The news of the governor's death just the day after she knew her husband met with him rocked her. Zach hadn't been home much over the last few weeks, especially after they lifted Ottosson's files in the D.C. operation.

"Baby, I don't know exactly what is going on or why, but I know that you know. Are you okay? This stuff is really scaring me," Kymbra pleaded.

"Darlin', I won't lie to you. There are some seriously evil folks out there and we know for the most part who they are. But, listen to me... I'm safe. You're safe. Our son is safe."

Kymbra was very skeptical, mostly because the level of Zach's intensity and distraction over the last few weeks was like nothing she had ever seen from him. They hadn't met yet when he was in Kosovo, so she never saw him in that frame of mind, but she did witness how intense he was during the *Texas Crisis*.

"Zach, you haven't left the country, so are you telling me the enemies are domestic?" Kymbra pressed.

"Some, but not all," Zach deflected.

Kymbra could tell he didn't want to talk about it anymore, and she didn't force the conversation further. She moved to embrace him.

As they sometimes did, Zach and Kymbra put their heads together and rubbed noses. That small innocent gesture quickly turned into a heated moment. Seizing the opportunity they had with their son in school and not due home for another hour, they passionately undressed each other and made love on the kitchen floor.

For a brief while, Zach had no thoughts of Ottosson or the tragic death of Governor Brahman. It was only him and Kymbra for a brief period. Afterward, they both lay on their backs on the kitchen floor. They began to laugh at a moment that reminded them of their early years together.

Thirty minutes later, Zach was back in his pickup truck en route to the Bunker, with a slight edge taken off his intensity. He thought to himself that this meeting might be the most important one they had ever had there, including one in which the group voted to participate in the militia action in Austin during the crisis.

Zach arrived at the Bunker a full two hours before the special meeting. It had been a while since he had seen many of his crew, and he was surprised at how many drove in from Oklahoma, Arkansas and Louisiana. He even learned some had jumped on a plane and were scheduled to land in Houston just in time to make the meeting.

As Zach was shaking hands and carrying on with fellow operatives, he caught a glance from Will. He saw serious concern in Will's eyes.

He slowly made his way over to his friend through the small crowd.

"How concerned should I be?" he said, leaning toward Will and asking quietly.

"I would say *very* concerned," Will answered. "We have a very big decision to make."

He was referring to the dangerous dilemma they faced in telling the group about the Ottosson evidence, or holding some or all of it back from them. If he chose *not* to tell them, he risked losing their trust, which would mean the end of the *Free Texas* organization and could jeopardize his network of operatives. If he chose to tell them everything, he would have a very hard time containing some of the group whose choices could threaten the entire organization.

This quandary was not lost on Beard, either. He noticed the two talking in the corner of the building and came over to them.

"Zach, if you want my opinion on what you are about to do, I don't see a good outcome either way. I've prepared as if you are going to spill it all, but you know I can hold back any or all of it. I'll respect whatever decision you make," Beard whispered.

With less than an hour before the meeting started, Zach still hadn't made up his mind. His mind drifted to Pops. He needed to know what Pops knew about the crash and to get his advice. He took his cell out of his pocket and called the number he had for Pops.

Pops had just left the crash scene. Federal investigators from the National Transportation Safety Board had arrived. He made sure his crew had seen the site and evidence and left six Texas Rangers to assist, but also to watch the federal investigators for any investigative irregularities they might witness.

"Dick Dyson," came the voice on the cell phone number Zach dialed.

"This is Zach Turner. Can I speak to Pops?"

"This is who?" questioned Dyson, even though he knew exactly who Turner was.

"This is Zach Turner. I'm sure you remember me. I just spent the evening with Pops a few days ago," replied Zach in an irritable tone.

"Son, Pops is in the middle of this crash investigation. I don't think he can be bothered."

"I'm sure if you tell him it's urgent, he will want to speak to me."

A few seconds of uncomfortable silence followed.

"Hello? Hello? You there?" Zach asked.

"Yeah, yeah, hang tight. Let me see if I can run him down. You may have to wait a bit," Dyson replied.

Zach paced back and forth for what seemed like an eternity. He knew Pops didn't like to carry a cell phone and, when he did carry one, he only used it for outbound calls *he* wanted to make.

"Younger here," finally came the voice over the phone.

"Pops, I'm sorry to bother you during this bad time. I really need to know whether you think the crash was an accident," Zach said.

"Well, we ain't got all the evidence in yet. It's way too early to be calling the game," returned Pops.

"Pops, this is me you're talking to. I've kept government secrets that will go to my grave with me. I've got some decisions to make with my people and it would help if you told me what you think," Zach pleaded.

"I guess it depends on what you would do with that kinda info. It could be the kind of information that'll get people killed, and it ain't nothin' that can be spread all over," Pops answered.

"It's nothing I'm going to share, but it will help me make a decision I have to make," Zach replied.

"Son, I'm assuming you ain't going to go off half-cocked? You're too damned smart for that," Pops pressed.

"Thank you for saying so, Pops. I'm actually trying to straddle the fence between what I share with my people. I've got some folks that could cook off in a hurry, but I stand to lose a lot of trust and relationships I've built over the years by withholding too much."

"Damn, son, that's a helluva predicament. I'll tell you this and you can do with it what you think is right, but it ain't a lot at this point. You simply cannot jeopardize my investigation."

"Okay, Pops, I'll take whatever you can give me."

"First, there ain't no evidence this was anything but an accident. I've listened to the tower communications and they were having a devil of a time with their right engine. Their fuel indicators were also acting up. What? Hold on a minute," Pops yelled to someone else away from the phone. "Son, I'll be right back. You hang on here," he said. Zach heard some commotion around Pops.

"Yes, sir," Zach replied.

Dyson was trying to get Pops' attention.

"Damn, I'm on the phone, boys. What the hell has lit fire to your tails?"

"Austin police are reporting a double murder-suicide in south Austin at an apartment complex. Looks like a guy shot his wife and son, then shot himself. His name is Endio Hernandez," Dyson told him.

"Well? Then get some of the team out there!" Pops shot back, looking visibly annoyed.

"Pops, he worked as an aircraft maintenance contractor for the Aviation Department in the hangar. *He touches that King Air almost every day.* There's a suicide note," Dyson reported to Pops.

"Son of a bitch. They got a time of death?" asked Pops. "How was it reported?"

"A relative found them in the apartment about thirty minutes ago."

"Nobody called in shots fired at the complex?" Pops asked.

"Not that we are aware of," Dyson answered.

"How could it be nobody hears three shots in an apartment building? Also, I need to know time of death right away!" demanded Pops.

He motioned for them to stop talking to him as he picked up his cell phone and took a few steps away from Dyson. He dialed Zach.

"Son, we've got some new developments here. I've got no proof of anything yet, but what I will tell you is that I'm not treating this as an accident until someone proves to me it ain't one. There's just too damned much going on for us to accept that conclusion. Hell, I owe it to Smitty. That's about all I can tell you for now."

"Thank you, sir, thank you very much. I will tell you I stopped believing in coincidences with *anything* involving our government many years ago. Again, thank you, sir."

"I'm sure we'll be talkin' soon 'nuf," Pops said, ending the call.

Just then, Will walked out of the Bunker and approached Zach.

"Did you reach him?"

"I did. Apparently, some kind of development in the crash investigation happened while I was talking to him. He couldn't say anything officially, but he's not convinced that plane went down by some mechanical failure or pilot error."

"So do you have what you need?" asked Will carefully.

Zach stared out across the Katy prairie and began stretching and adjusting his neck and shoulders. Will had seen that routine a hundred times when a mission became clear to his friend, and he needed to get his mind right.

"So we're good to go?" asked Will.

"Start the meeting. I'll be right in."

CHAPTER 38

"A freedom fighter learns the hard way that it is the oppressor who defines the nature of the struggle, and the oppressed is often left no recourse but to use methods that mirror those of the oppressor. At a point, one can only fight fire with fire."

- Nelson Mandela (1918-2013)
South African anti-apartheid revolutionary,
imprisoned for 27 years

Zach walked into the meeting room. Despite the short notice, the room was packed. All who entered the room deposited their cell phones in a cardboard box sitting on a table next to the door. No recording devices of any kind were allowed, and the staff of Turner Invincible Security made sure of it.

Nobody, however, was ever asked to check his or her weapons at the door. Zach didn't believe in making *anyone* disarm.

The collection of members of *Free Texas*, Zach's security staff, and black ops in the room was an interesting mix. It consisted of *Free Texas* members who had never been in any Special Forces to highly trained and highly motivated black ops professionals. Rarely was this collection of Zach's members and acquaintances ever in one place, and it was on purpose.

"Good afternoon, everyone. Thanks for coming on short notice," Zach opened the meeting. "It's great to see so many of you I haven't seen in months. Since it's rare we get to meet like this, let's open this up in style." Zach turned toward a Texas flag hanging on the wall.

Everyone stood, took off any hats, and placed their right hands over their hearts as they said the pledge to the Texas flag:

"Honor the Texas flag; I pledge allegiance to thee, Texas, one state under God, one and indivisible."

A short invocation was led by one of the group, and most sat down. There weren't enough chairs to go around, but people found places on the floor, or on tables or desks.

"Ladies and gentlemen," started Zach, "I know we need to address the crash that killed our governor. I promise we will get to that. But first, I know many of you are going through some extreme hardships over this IRS crap. We need to address anyone who's having severe issues so that your brothers can assist in any way. I know most of you have had some type of levy on funds in your accounts. I need to know if any of you have had property, other than your bank accounts, frozen or levied and have no access to cash with which to operate."

About a dozen hands went up. Zach was surprised at the number.

"What happened? Don't you have money put away?" Zach asked those in the group that raised their hands.

"Zach, I was in the Far East when this went down, " said one operative. "I couldn't get to my accounts fast enough and my cash reserves were too low. It's my own damned fault. I know we preach this, but the timing was just bad as I was about to replenish those cash reserves from the job I'm doing for Langley in Singapore."

"Ladies and gentlemen, let me reiterate that your bug-out bags must include cash and that you must be able to access six months of emergency cash somewhere offsite within easy reach. What you're seeing today could be just the beginning of a scenario that worsens in a hurry."

That got everyone's attention. Then *it* began.

"These sons of bitches keep messing with us. I, for one, am damned tired of it. We've got guys here that can't feed their families. We've obviously been targeted—again! It's way past time for these lowlife bloodsuckers to get theirs!" shouted Henry "Hank" Lofton, to the echoes of many who agreed.

Lofton was a career SEAL, retiring after twenty-two years. He was then recruited by the CIA. Lofton detested the CIA, claiming several of his buddies over the years were killed in operations where the CIA's intelligence was bad or the CIA failed to provide support. Although a well-respected SEAL commander, his outspoken and politically incorrect verbal tirades at various congressmen, congresswomen, and bureaucrats forced him to retire.

Lofton was a huge guy who still lifted weights several hours daily and, despite being in his forties, looked every bit a black ops guy, with short-cropped hair, closely trimmed beard and bulging veins in his temples that got more pronounced when he was angry.

Zach had been on many missions with Lofton and respected him immensely, but Lofton always saw himself as Zach's equal.

"Hank, you're damned right. But I'm going to ask you and everyone else here to hold onto your thoughts as we lay out some other facts we've uncovered. I'll tell you it won't make you feel any better and you'll likely be angrier than you are right now. But we could potentially be at that *crossroads* event we've always talked about," Zach told them.

The entire group knew what he meant by the term *"crossroads."* In every revolutionary or independence movement in history, there comes a crossroads event where people have to choose sides. That choice, if it's the wrong choice, could literally put the chooser's life, liberty, family, business, and fortune at ultimate risk.

"All right, Zach, I'll listen, but I'll be damned if I'm going to put up with this anymore. I'm about ready to put a bullet in the eye of the IRS."

Many clapped and cheered. It took a few minutes for the group to settle back down.

"First, let's start with the governor's plane crash. I just got off the phone with Pops Younger about an hour ago. So far, no evidence this was anything but an accident," Zach began as the group jeered and hissed.

"Okay, okay. Now listen up, Pops is very suspicious. I'm very suspicious. Many of you... hell, most of you know our government is totally capable of something like this. That goes without saying."

Lofton leaned forward in his seat. "What, are they going to try to kill us all? I say bring it!"

"This administration is too smart for that. They want to cut the head off the snake. They can control the masses from there," said another guy.

"Okay, hang on now," said Zach, motioning with his hands to lower voices. "We all know we are targets and have been for some time. They have also targeted state legislators, and even the governor and Pops Younger were served with IRS summonses. We are not alone."

"They ain't going to stop this from going to referendum. If we find out they had anything to do with killing Brahman, there will be hell to pay!" said Lofton loudly.

"Hank, I agree. We just have to wait and see what we turn up," Zach stated. "Okay, we need to move on. I have more information to share." Zach glanced over to Beard and Will, standing back in the far corner. Neither of them knew what Zach was about to divulge.

"Let me reiterate that the information I am about to share is considered top secret in this organization. I don't have to tell anyone here that any leaks of any kind can damage all of us, damage our mission, and put lives in jeopardy," Zach said.

"Hear, hear!" yelled a few in the room, with most everyone nodding agreement.

"First, let me tell you that information has come to us, credible information, that the death of Chief Justice Noyner was likely not an accident."

"Goddamn it! I knew it!" Lofton yelped as he stood and turned to others sitting behind him. "Why in the hell didn't they do an autopsy? Who did it, Zach?" Lofton turned back to face Zach.

Beard and Will winced noticeably. They knew once Zach put evidence out to the group, there was no turning back.

"I'm not prepared to make that call yet. All I can tell you at this point is we have a Russian operative involved, a Swede, and some very highly placed officials in the federal government. I will have more on this to you as we confirm it."

Lofton slammed his hand on the back of the chair in front of him "Bullshit, Zach! You know more than you're telling us!"

"Of course I do," said Zach, surprising everyone. "But what I have hasn't been fully vetted."

Lofton turned to look back at Beard and Will for any hint of dishonesty. Beard felt his stare, and continued to look straight ahead at Zach to avoid eye contact.

"Now, we can all look at the motives behind something so bold that the *entire* face of the Supreme Court has changed in a matter of months!"

"Yeah, we got a damned lesbian on the Supreme Court now!" shouted another from the group.

"Worse than that, we have an unapologetic, anti-2nd Amendment chief justice," shot back someone in the back of the room.

"Next, we have information that ties some of the players in the Noyner case to our federal election systems," Zach added.

"What the hell does that mean, Zach? Come on. How are they tied?" demanded Lofton.

Zach couldn't figure out how, gracefully, to get out of being boxed into this corner by Lofton.

"One of the operatives on the boat has ties to CIS. In fact, Justice Noyner flew down to Florida on their corporate jet and their main D.C. lobbyist was on the boat, too."

"Holy shit, you can't be serious," Lofton remarked, still standing. Lofton turned again to those sitting behind him and said, "I told you CIS stunk to high heaven. Why in the hell would the U.S. government outsource our elections systems?" Again he turned back to Zach.

"We haven't nailed down all the connections yet. We can tell you, however, that there are definite links between CIS and a Russian operative. We have identified this operative as Vasily Volkov."

"I know this man. He's KGB, but even too hardcore for them. He won the Hero of the Soviet Union medal, which is akin to our Congressional Medal of Honor, for his military heroics in the Chechen War, but the KGB quietly expelled him. He's ruthless. He's cunning. He is one of the most dangerous operatives we ever dealt with. He's meticulous. He has a scorched-earth approach to everything and everyone. He will eliminate anyone in his way, and will not take any chances that someone can tie him to an operation. He will murder women and children if he thinks there's a chance he is compromised," offered one of Zach's ex-CIA operatives.

"How the hell is this guy tied to CIS?" asked Lofton.

"He's for hire, and he commands big bucks," answered Beard out of nowhere.

"And CIS has plenty of big bucks, but what the hell does a software company need Volkov for?" asked Lofton.

"There's obviously a bigger plan here, Zach. Do you know what it is?" asked someone else from the group.

"We do not. We have intercepted communications that refer to an operation known as *Madison*, but we have yet to put any details to that operation. We don't know the date, plan, or mission of *Madison*. I would say that is among our highest priorities for intel at the moment."

"Madison? Like James Madison, Madison, Wisconsin? What the hell could that mean?" asked Lofton.

"There's nothing we can link it to yet," answered Beard.

"Well, we've got a murdered chief justice and the IRS has declared war on us. I say it's time to shoot back!" yelled Lofton, getting a smattering of applause.

"Hank, we all feel exactly the same as you. But what action do you recommend we take at this time? We need to know what *Madison* is," said Zach calmly.

"Well, damn, Zach, I don't need any explanation on what the IRS is doing to this team. I say we need to put the fear of God into them in the meantime. It won't jeopardize whatever the hell is going on with this Russian and CIS," shot back Lofton.

"Hank, we don't know if there is a connection."

"Do we just sit back and continue to take this crap from the administration? You know there's no way these turkeys are doing this without orders from on high. We are *enemies of the state*, and we all know it."

"As hard as that might seem, that is *exactly* what we need to do until we know what *Madison* is," Zach stated firmly.

The atmosphere in the room got uneasy. Zach's group always knew the potential existed for Lofton to challenge Zach for leadership of the group.

"You may not know until it's already happened, whatever *it* is. Hell, for all we know, it could be a dirty bomb," challenged Lofton.

The body language of the entire group in the room became uncomfortable. Nobody had ever openly challenged Zach.

"Our focus needs to be on finding Volkov and determining what *Madison* is," said Zach adamantly.

"Yeah, Zach. I agree with that, except the IRS is hitting us on our flank. This is simply harassment. I can't see how this is connected to CIS or this Russian. I'm tired of my team being a target," Lofton argued.

"I'm open to suggestions from anyone on the team, but anything we do to counter the IRS other than what we are doing with tax attorneys, FOIA requests and pressure from our friends in Congress and elsewhere will bring undue attention while we try to find Volkov and determine what *Madison* is," insisted Zach, looking to his left as he watched Will leave the room with one of his security staff.

"Unless you can produce some evidence that ties them together, Zach, we are going to respond," said Lofton.

"Hank, the wrong response could get us all killed. You know that."

"It's not in my nature, nor is it for many others in here to get attacked and not respond," answered Lofton.

"You're not getting shot at, Hank," Zach countered. "It's a huge problem, I agree. But we have a larger mission here. A mission you took an oath on to be part of the group. I'm asking you not to react yet. The time will come when the IRS will pay for this."

"I appreciate that, Zach. It's just not in my nature to sit back and let the enemy constantly nip at my heels. We will respond appropriately. I'll give you two weeks to come up with a link between this Russian and the IRS harassment. Absent that, the IRS is going to get a response," Lofton said defiantly. He got up and motioned with his head to some others sitting with him.

"That's unfortunate, Hank. If you take any action outside of this group, you put us all in potential danger," said Zach flatly, glancing around the room at those who stayed.

Eight others got up with Lofton to leave the meeting. This was the first time ever that the group was split on a major decision, or where Zach's leadership was questioned openly.

In a tense moment, the group made room for Lofton and his allies to leave the room.

Will came back into the room and handed Zach a note.

The note said, "Aircraft mechanic who worked on Governor One was found dead in his apartment with his wife and son. There was a suicide note, apologizing for the crash."

"Who's this from?" Zach asked Will.

"A reliable source in the Austin police department," Will answered.

"Is it public yet?" asked Zach.

"No, but Pops is aware," Will added.

The room settled back down as Lofton and the others left. That group was outside at their trucks. The rest were waiting to see how Zach would react.

With the underlying knowledge of what CIS, Volkov and the administration had been up to at this point, Zach was determined not to let his group splinter.

"They are still our brothers. I think they are making a mistake and I don't agree with it. Let's all work together to see if we can find a link or get them enough information to not put us all at another level of danger," reasoned Zach.

"We're with you, Zach!" came the chorus from several in the room.

"I'll be back," Zach told Will and Beard as he turned to walk out the door, taking his cell phone out of his pocket.

Outside, he dialed the same number he used to reach Pops earlier in the day.

"Dyson here."

"Commander, this is Zach Turner. Is Pops available at the moment?"

"I doubt it, but I'll find out," replied Dyson, slightly irritated that someone not attached to law enforcement had such easy access to Pops.

"Younger," came the raspy voice a short time later.

"Pops, we found out a little more about this Volkov dude. Turns out several of our operatives have dealt with him in the past. He is a calculating, smart and elusive former Russian Special Forces and KGB operative. Turns out he was even too hardcore for the KGB, if you can believe that. They kicked him out."

"Bad hombre?" asked Pops.

"The worst. Listen, sir, I got word about the double-murder/suicide and the note."

"You've got some good sources, son," Pops chuckled. "Where are they, in Austin PD?"

"Yes, sir, among other places."

"So why are you asking about the note, son?"

"Is it authentic? Did this mechanic purposely sabotage the aircraft?" asked Zach.

"The note was an apology. Says he worked on the fuel system two days before the accident. Appears to be authentic, but we won't know for a few days. You got some kinda hunch or info you need to share with me?"

"What bothers me is Volkov. He is totally capable of putting that aircraft down."

"Nothin' from the mechanic's family indicated he was in a bad way. Doesn't make sense to any of them. Checking all his financial records; maybe somethin' will show up," answered Pops.

"I'll keep you posted if we get any new news," offered Zach. "But I've got to tell you, I've got a deep-down gut feeling Volkov is somehow involved.

"Makes no sense taking out his kid and his wife, too, even if he did screw something up," remarked Pops.

"I know you were good friends with the governor," said Zach. "He was a good man. I'm so sorry you lost another friend."

"Thank you, son. Smitty was a good man. If that son-of-a-bitch Volkov is responsible, I'll hunt him down to the ends of the earth."

CHAPTER 39

"We must learn that passively to accept an unjust system is to cooperate with that system, and thereby to become a participant in its evil."

> *- Martin Luther King, Jr. (1929 – 1968)*
> *Christian Pastor and Civil Rights Icon*

Ten hours after the crash that killed the governor and lieutenant governor, Texas Supreme Court Chief Justice Timothy Devlin stood in his black robe in the Texas State Senate chamber at the main podium, awaiting the arrival of Speaker of the House Jim Strasburg.

The Senate chamber was packed to capacity, as was the gallery above it. News crews filled the back of the chamber, and the world was about to witness the order of succession.

Under the Texas Constitution, the next in line to become acting governor was the president pro tempore of the Senate. Senator Jeffrey Milsap had been the president pro tempore but, when he was murdered under mysterious circumstances, Strasburg was next in line. It was doubtful that anyone in the media mentioned to the world that three people in higher office would need to die for Strasburg to ascend to the governorship.

The time arrived, and Strasburg entered the chamber wearing a dark blue suit, red tie, his silver-gray hair longer than most of his House colleagues. At the prompting of Chief Justice Devlin, Strasburg pledged, with his left hand raised and his right hand on a Bible, "I solemnly swear to uphold the Constitution of the United States of America and the Texas Constitution."

Normally, a swearing-in ceremony for a new Texas governor carries much pomp and circumstance. Today, the mood in the chamber was somber.

Both the governor and the lieutenant governor had been popular, especially with those in the state legislature.

Pops Younger stood on the podium deck, feeling the moment was surreal. He had never been a fan of Strasburg, claiming he had the "spine of a jellyfish," based on Strasburg's penchant for taking conflicting stances on difficult issues. Pops also battled Strasburg, who had tried his best to technically defund the Texas Rangers through massive budget cuts, when he was a Democrat.

Trust was not easily dispensed by Pops, and Strasburg had earned none from him.

As the throng of elected officials and bureaucrats crowded around Strasburg to shake his hand and offer somewhat conciliatory congratulations, Pops couldn't stomach the entire scene. He had just lost one of his dearest friends in Governor "Smitty" Brahman, and months before lost an even closer friend, Governor Brent Cooper. Although Strasburg would only be acting governor, the chance for him to become the incumbent governor in the next election was very strong.

One could always tell when Pops was sizing someone up. He stood on the podium deck, eyes squinted and completely focused on Strasburg and how he was acting with others. As he watched Strasburg interact, he began to get a gut-wrenching sense that something was wrong with what he was watching, but he couldn't put his finger on it.

Strasburg, who had his back to Pops, suddenly turned around and found himself face to face with Pops.

"Well, hello, Mr. Younger," said Strasburg.. He reached out to shake hands with Pops. Pops did not take the acting governor's hand.

"Am I supposed to call you governor now?" asked Pops.

Several people around them stopped their conversations to watch this one proceed.

"Sir, I realize you were close to the governor. You have my condolences." Strasburg continued to hold his right hand out to Pops.

"He was a good man, as solid as central Texas granite. Men like Smitty and Coop don't grow on trees," replied Pops. "How the hell are you going to fill their boots?"

"Yes, they were indeed," Strasburg said in a patronizing voice. "And, Mr. Younger, I know you still hold that budget issue from twenty years ago against me, but that was a long time ago and now we must work together for all of Texas, especially in this perilous environment." Many others paused to take in the conversation.

"It ain't just that, Strasburg. You flip-flop on issues more than a beached Pecos perch," said Pops with a half-smile.

"Legislating is a tough business, Mr. Younger. Sometimes you have to compromise to move issues and legislation forward. Part of governing is strategic compromise," chuckled Strasburg.

"I've never met a man of any substance who was just as good riding *backward* in his saddle as he was facing forward," Pops retorted.

"Well, sir, I'm not sure what that means, but I look forward to working with you." Strasburg began to direct his attention elsewhere as his aides tried to remove him from this conversation by placing their hands on him, gently prodding him to leave the podium deck. As he was about to go, Pops grabbed his hand for a handshake, surprising Strasburg.

Pops firmly pulled Strasburg closer to him, and Strasburg's painted-on smile suddenly vanished. Pops looked him straight in the eyes and leaned toward his left ear.

In a soft, but firm tone, Pops whispered, "Texas will be watching you closely, Strasburg, *and so will I.*"

"Thank you, Mr. Younger. Thank you." Strasburg let himself be steered away feebly to the next conversation by his staff, but he was visibly shaken.

CHAPTER 40

"A people armed and free forms a barrier against the enterprises of ambition and is a bulwark for the nation against foreign invasion and domestic oppression."

- *James Madison (1751-1836)*
Father of the Constitution, 4th US President
Author of the 2nd Amendment

Pops Younger, the Texas Rangers, National Transportation Safety Board, and the FBI were all in Austin the next day for their investigation into the plane crash.

"Mr. Younger, we appreciate your help, but the NTSB will lead the investigation into the crash itself. The FBI will stand by as a matter of routine if anything turns up in the investigation that would further warrant our involvement," announced lead regional FBI director Michael Jarvis.

"Son, I appreciate y'all's efforts in finding the cause of this crash, but my job here is different. You see, I'm treating this crash as if it was a *criminal* act *unless* you find overwhelming evidence that this here engine failed, or a sprocket broke, or some wingnut flew off," said Pops with uncompromising authority. "Now, I know you boys and—excuse me, ladies—have a meeting set up to speak to this mechanic's relatives. The Texas Rangers will be in those meetings, also."

"Mr. Younger, this plane crash is under federal jurisdiction," insisted Jarvis.

Pops stared at Jarvis and asked, "Where did that there plane crash?"

A little confused by the obvious answer, Jarvis replied, "Just south of

Selma, Texas, sir, but you know that."

"And who was on that plane, son?" asked Pops.

"The governor, lieutenant governor, a flight attendant and two pilots."

"Governor and lieutenant governor of…?" Pops prompted.

"Well, Texas, sir," came the bewildered reply.

Pops then glared at Jarvis. "There's a recurring theme here, seems to me. That recurring theme is Texas." Pops stood up from the uncomfortable wooden chair he was sitting in, and placed his hat on his head as he appeared ready to leave.

"Sir…"

"That's a Texas governor, a State of Texas aircraft, and a crash site in Texas. Now you boys and gals can argue with me 'til the cows come home, but I'm tellin' y'all here and now that the Texas Rangers will be part of this investigation until you can identify the exact reason that plane went down and when you have convinced *me*. Now, you are burnin' daylight. Let's git on with this!" said Pops, never giving them the chance to argue about it.

An hour later, several family members came into Austin Police headquarters for the crash investigation team to take their statements. For the NTSB, their first impressions, based on air traffic control conversations and initial review of the flight data safety recorder, pointed to the crash being either a mechanical failure or pilot error.

To Pops, the FBI seemed somewhat indifferent and they weren't going to add a ton of resources to this investigation unless the NTSB turned up something concrete that linked the crash to foul play or the interview of the mechanic's family shed some new light on the coincidental double-murder suicide the day of the crash.

Pops sat in interviews with five family members of the mechanic. Three were siblings and the other two were in-laws. Pops let the FBI conduct the interviews.

Throughout the interviews, Pops did not hear anyone mention or claim that mechanic Endio Hernandez was anything but a good husband and father with no symptoms of depression or mental illness whatsoever. There was simply no hint at what caused him to murder his wife and child.

Pops kept looking at the suicide note, which read:

"I am so sorry the failures of my work on the governor's aircraft caused it to crash. I am so ashamed that I have brought this disgrace to my family and my family name. The pain is too great for us to endure." - Endio Hernandez

Something wasn't right about the note, but Pops couldn't figure it out.

"Did this go to your handwriting analysis experts?" Pops asked the FBI investigator.

"We have some other samples of his writing we took from the apartment," the man told him. "From my perspective, it's legitimately his writing."

"Son, you didn't answer my question," noted Pops.

"No, we haven't. But, if you would like me to, I will," the man answered.

"If you don't mind, son, I've got a local expert on this kinda thing right here a couple miles away at the University of Texas."

"We have our own people, Mr. Younger; this would have to go to FBI headquarters."

"And how long would those boys up there in D.C. take to get a good gander at this?" Pops held it up in its plastic evidence sleeve.

"Probably a few weeks."

"I'll tell ya, I ain't willing to wait that long and, besides, I trust my guy down here as he has helped me solve many cases over the years." Pops opened his briefcase, tossed the documents in, and shut it.

"Sir, I'm sorry, but that evidence has to remain with the FBI," the agent protested.

"Well, son, I'll have it back to you in a day or two, then you can send it to those boys in D.C." Pops seemed completely indifferent to the investigator's claim to the evidence.

"...and besides, you folks don't think there is any direct evidence that changes your mind about whether this was an accident or not," added Pops.

"Mr. Younger, I know we are in Texas and you and your state leadership think everything is a conspiracy to somehow punish Texas, but the FBI has rules. And those rules state that letter and those other handwritten items from Hernandez are evidence that will remain in the hands of the FBI and are not leaving this room."

Pops chuckled. "Ya wanna arm wrestle for it?"

"Seriously, Mr. Younger, my job and my department is at stake if I let that evidence leave the room."

"Well, sonny, you might just want to find another line of work then."

"Mr. Younger, I'd like to remind you there is still an active federal warrant for your arrest. We haven't forgotten about the federal agents killed down here. It's by the grace of God and President Bartlett that you're not in handcuffs this very minute."

Suddenly, the room got intense. Three FBI agents and two Texas Rangers were in the room. The stenographer who was recording the interviews hurriedly stepped outside.

Pops walked his six-foot, two-inch frame up and stood directly in front of the five-foot, nine-inch FBI investigator. "I'll tell you what, boy. I'm gonna take this here suicide note and those samples and walk them over to the university myself, with these two fine Rangers escorting me and the evidence," Pops said without the blink of an eye.

A few moments of dead silence fell on the room. Pops reached over on the table and picked up the coffee cup the lead investigator was drinking from. He spit tobacco juice in it and then sat it right back down in the same place.

"Now," he said, "if you ain't gonna try and arrest me, then get the hell outta the way so we can do our jobs!" Pops focused his deadly, steel-blue eyes on the investigator without so much as blinking.

The investigator tried to swallow his own saliva but didn't realize his mouth and throat had become dry. He coughed meekly and moved to the side so Pops and the Rangers could exit the room with the evidence.

"Didn't think so," said Pops to the FBI agents in the room as he and the Rangers departed.

In the hall outside the interrogation room, a small crowd gathered as word got out that Pops and the feds were getting sideways on the crash investigation. About a dozen police officers and administrators of the Austin PD got to see Pops get in the lead investigator's face and leave with evidence the FBI insisted they should keep.

It was another story to add to the many legends of Pops already making their way through the police department. Pops had defied the feds… again.

Within four hours after Pops and his Rangers delivered the handwriting samples and the suicide letter to the University of Texas professor, they received word to come back to the archaeology department. Pops and his team wasted no time taking the short drive back to the University of Texas.

Professor James Buckley, PhD, was a world-renowned handwriting expert, weighing in on historical documents especially important to history. If someone was trying to buy or sell a document, for instance, by George

Washington, having Professor Buckley make a definitive certification on the document's authenticity would typically make a huge difference in the value. Buckley was summoned all over the world for his expert testimony in both criminal and civil cases when a handwriting expert was needed.

"Thank you for taking a look at this so quickly. Whatya think, Professor? Is it authentic?" asked Pops.

"From everything I've examined, it's definitely the same handwriting. I would testify in a court of law that the same person wrote the samples and the suicide note," claimed the professor.

"Then that would blow away any theory that someone else wrote the note, wouldn't it?" asked one of Pops' Rangers.

Before Pops could answer, the professor chimed in, "Yes, but I've noticed something else."

"What's that?" asked Pops, pulling his chair closer to the table with all the documents spread out.

"Look at the angles of the writing in the suicide note compared to the other handwriting examples," the professor suggested.

"Okay, not sure what I'm looking for."

"The angle of the cursive writing on the suicide note is directly opposite of the angles of the other samples. See here." The professor compared the note with the other documents. "There are other subtle details in the note. Some letters are not completely finished, as you see in the other examples. Also, there is some of what we call slashing, wherein the letters of words are carried beyond the normal shape, size and alignment of what we see in all of these other examples," the professor added.

"What does that tell you, Professor? You're saying this is his handwriting, but what does this slashing mean?"

"First, when we see this type of difference, it could mean a few different things. It could mean the author of the suicide note was in an awkward position while writing. Think of when you have put a piece a paper up on the wall to sign something when you have nowhere else to get a surface to sign it on."

"Okay," Pops said. "What else?"

"That might explain the difference in the angle of the writing, but it wouldn't necessarily explain the slashing. What we have seen is that a handwriting example like this has a tremendous amount of *stress or duress* associated with it."

"*Stress or duress*? This boy was about to kill his own wife and kid, then commit suicide, if you believe the crime scene. If he already had made that decision, wouldn't he be a little stressed by that?" Pops wondered out loud.

"He would, I'm sure," the professor agreed. "But, in the thousands of suicide notes I have seen in my career, by far the majority of them are written very calmly if they weren't under the influence of a narcotic. I've heard countless relatives even claim a note wasn't their loved one's handwriting because, in many cases, the handwriting was better than the person had ever written in his or her life."

"Could he have written it after he killed his wife and kid? Surely that would have stressed him?" asked another Ranger.

"That's a possibility. But what convinces me he didn't write the letter *after* he killed them is that he didn't specifically mention them in the letter, nor did he express his regrets for what he had just done," instructed the professor.

"Is that what you see in these cases?" asked Pops.

"Yes, so this suicide letter is not typical in my experience when you have a double murder of your immediate family, then a suicide," advised the professor.

"Could it mean someone could have *made* him write the note?" asked Pops.

"Certainly. That would account for the anomalies I see in his note compared to the provided examples," answered the professor.

"What are you thinking here, Pops?" asked one of the Rangers.

"I've talked to those family members," Pops stated. "Not a one of them thought this kid had a screw loose. This kid had put himself through aviation school, and his family said he adored that child."

"We've also interviewed his co-workers. There's nothing there, either. They all said he was a stand-up guy," said one of the other Rangers. "He also isn't the only aircraft mechanic who touched that plane. There's six more people that routinely touched it, including at least two more that worked the plane after he did. The NTSB is poring over the maintenance logs"

"I hope this was helpful," said the professor.

"It was, and we owe you a big thank you," answered Pops.

"Not a problem. But, off the record, Mr. Younger, I get the sense you think there is something else in play here," said the inquisitive professor.

"Let's just say I got a hunch. It's like we are seeing some smoke signals over the horizon and we ain't figured out what they mean," said Pops.

Just then, one of the Rangers stepped out to take an urgent call for Pops.

The remaining participants made a little small talk for a couple of minutes before the Ranger stepped back in.

"Excuse me, sir, I think you might want to take this."

Pops got up and stepped out of the room. "Younger here."

"Sir, this is Ranger Tyler down at the state aviation hangar. We have been reviewing all the security tapes and you aren't going to believe what we found!"

"What ya got?" Pops asked.

"We have a maintenance man on camera the morning of the flight that nobody can identify. He's dressed the part. Here's the crazy part. He matches the description of State Senator Milsap's killer to a tee," Ranger Tyler claimed.

"Was that the only day this unidentified figure was at the hangar?" Pops was curious.

"We went back two days prior to the flight and haven't seen him on any other videos yet. These videos re-loop every seventy-two hours so, if he's not on them, we won't know if he was ever there before. We've interviewed almost everyone; some say they saw him but thought he was a contractor."

"Did anyone speak with him at any time?" asked Pops.

"We have one and only one so far who talked to him when he asked for a rivet gun," said Ranger Tyler. "And get this; he said he had an accent—a *Russian* accent."

CHAPTER 41

"And they are ignorant that the purpose of the sword is to save every man from slavery."

- *Marcus Annaeus Lucanus (A.D. 39-65)*
Roman Poet

Zach Turner's cell phone rang as he was driving his jacked-up pickup truck down an asphalt-paved farm road near the Bunker. When he glanced at caller ID, he noticed it was Pops. "Turner," he answered.

"Pops here," came the voice over the phone.

"Any news, sir?" asked Zach.

"We've got security video from the state aviation hangar," Pops told him. "We have a figure on tape that nobody who works at the state aviation hangar can positively identify."

"What's he look like?" asked Zach.

"This character is wearing a ball cap. There's not much to distinguish him except that nobody had ever seen him there before, and it's the only tape we have of him. He was there the day of the crash."

"Whoa, that's interesting. How can I help?" asked Zach.

"Need you to look at the tape right away," Pops told him.

"You think I may be able to help identify this guy?" asked Zach, a little confused why Pops would think he might be able to help by looking at the tape.

"That morning, this turkey talked to a fellow mechanic and borrowed a tool."

"What kind of tool?" Zach asked.

"A rivet gun."

"Hmm… okay, that's interesting." Zach thought for a minute. "You have a guy that doesn't belong there. Pardon me for asking, Pops, but how is it you think I might be able to help you in the identification of this mechanic?"

"His co-worker, who had never met him or seen him before, said he spoke with a *Russian* accent."

It took a few seconds for Pops' last statement to sink in with Zach. "*Russian*? He's sure it was Russian?"

"Well, he ain't no linguistics expert, but he said he sounded Russian. He also said he guessed this turkey was bald under his ball cap."

"Damn! Really?" Now Zach was really excited.

"When can you high-tail it on over here?" Pops asked him.

"I'll come now. I've got someone who may be able to help us," Zach told Pops. "The problem is, he's in D.C. on assignment for me but, if we can video conference him in, we can have him look at the tape."

"Sounds like a plan, son. Appreciate your help."

"No worries, Pops. Come to your ranch?" Zach asked.

"No, sir, we will meet you at Austin Police Department headquarters." Pops went on to give Zach further details about the location of the meeting.

Three hours later, Pops, several Texas Rangers, Turner, Beard and Turnbow were in an interrogation room in downtown Austin police headquarters.

"Shut them blinds," Pops instructed one of his Rangers. He didn't want anyone seeing the video they were about to put up on the big screen in the conference room. "And lock the door, too, but wait till this young man leaves to do something more important than show an old fart how to hook this technology up."

"Sir, I've got the video conference all linked up and ready. Just call me back in if you need further assistance," said the young IT administrator employed by the city of Austin.

Within a few minutes, a link appeared on the big screen. Everyone was expecting to see an image from Washington, D.C. of the mystery man who was joining the live video conference. Everyone could see that he was online, but he blocked the web camera on his laptop.

"My operative in D.C. will be incognito for this meeting, gentlemen. I hope you understand," stated Zach.

Pops looked at him, a crooked grin on his face. "I love all this cloak-

and-dagger crap y'all bring to the table. Never can be too careful when you got the feds staring right down your unmentionables." Everyone chuckled at Pops' humor.

Zach introduced everyone in the room before mentioning the D.C. operative. "Gentlemen, I would introduce this fine gentlemen in D.C. by name if I could. All I can tell you is he's highly placed in international and national security operations. He is here to tell us if he can identify this unknown actor in the aviation hangar video. I can vouch for him personally, as can these other men." Zach nodded toward Beard and Will.

"Okay, we have less than four minutes of total footage of this unknown mechanic," said Texas Ranger Commander Dyson, who was leading the walk-through of the security tapes. "Here he is walking from the locker room to the hangar floor. Notice he has on the contractor overalls and a cap."

"Wait, can you back it up for about ten seconds?" came the voice from D.C. "Can it zoom?" There was a slight pause. "Okay, okay, that's good, I got it. What else do you have?" asked the D.C. operative.

"I've got two more clips," Dyson noted. "Here he is underneath the governor's King Air."

Again, the operative asked, "Wait, can you pause that scene about five seconds back?"

"There you go. Is this what you needed?" asked Dyson, fiddling with the controls of the web meeting application.

"We can't see exactly what he is doing under that right wing of the aircraft and I'm no mechanic, but I am a pilot and I can reasonably tell you that he is likely accessing the fuel tanks or fuel lines in that general area of the wing," noted the operative.

Pops and Zach glanced at each other, and Pops nodded affirmatively.

"Can you identify him?" pressed Dyson.

"No, not yet. That's a fairly lousy security camera system in that hangar," said the operative.

"Geez, I would agree," chimed in Beard, who was a technology expert. "These are state-owned aircraft and the security cameras look like they were installed in 1995."

"Here's the last clip," said Dyson. "It's only about twenty seconds, but it's him leaving the hangar. It's about an hour before the governor arrived."

"Wait! Wait! Back it up!" yelled the operative.

Pops tilted his cowboy hat back slightly on his head as he stepped closer to the screen. Everyone remained silent as Dyson ran the last segment back and forth in slow motion.

"There's that son of a bitch, Zach. That's him. No doubt in my mind."

"Are you sure?" asked Zach, who had a good idea who they were looking at, based on the Russian accent alone.

"That's him. *There's that son of a bitch*. I guarantee it."

"King Street Pub?" asked Zach.

"Yeah, that and Crimea, Chechnya and Georgia. It's him."

"Okay, gentlemen, can you enlighten us please?" asked Pops patiently.

"Go ahead," Zach told his operative. "Pops won't be surprised."

"Gentlemen, that man is Vasily Volkov. He is the most dangerous Russian operative in history. He is a cold-blooded, extremely intelligent and ruthless former KGB operative. The Russians lost control of him years ago after awarding him their highest military honors. He is bad news; always leaves havoc behind. Interpol, the CIA, and almost every Western security apparatus has him as their number one target for apprehension *or elimination*. He works for the highest bidder. Strictly mercenary stuff now." The operative finished his report.

"What the hell is he doing here?" asked Dyson.

"I think we know, based on his location under the wing of that aircraft," commented Will.

"But why? How the hell does someone simply walk into the Department of Public Safety's aviation hangar, put on a pair of contractor overalls, and mess with the governor's aircraft no less, without anyone asking him any questions? Unbelievable!" exclaimed Dyson.

"This man is a master. I can guarantee he had his bases already covered. Volkov has killed women and children if it meant completion of his mission or to cover his trail," said the operative. "He typically leaves no witnesses, so anyone who met or saw him in that hangar that is still alive is extremely lucky, but no less in immediate danger."

"How do we find this bastard?" asked Dyson.

"We've had operatives all over the world looking for him for years. He doesn't make mistakes."

"You've seen this man, yes?" Pops asked the voice on the phone.

"Yes, sir, I have."

"How long ago?" Pops persisted.

"Very recently. Weeks," said the operative.

"Here in Texas?"

"No, sir, in the U.S.," the operative responded.

"Did you not have the opportunity to take this turd out then?" asked Dyson.

"Yes, possibly. However, there was a larger mission at stake and to do so at the time would have jeopardized the larger mission."

Pops looked at Zach with a raised eyebrow. *Was there something Zach wasn't telling him?*

"Sir, there is a larger mission, and I'll ask you to hold on that question until we are done here. However, that mission is part of the files we shared with you," answered Zach quickly, realizing he could lose Pops' trust.

"Damn it, Pops, at some point you are going to have to bring us into the know here. This is frustrating as hell, doing these investigations, being blocked by the feds on one hand and by these militia guys, who aren't associated with any law enforcement, on the other hand!" ranted Dyson, who had no qualms about expressing his displeasure with Turner's group.

"We're getting close; just hang with me," Pops said. Dyson nodded reluctantly.

"Who could be paying this guy to tamper with the governor of Texas' aircraft?" asked another Ranger.

Pops and Turner looked at each other. Zach didn't want to answer, and he surely didn't want Beard or Will to answer.

"We have some leads on that. We are still working them," noted Pops. "Is there anything else you can tell us at this time?" Pops asked the operative.

"Yes, but it's highly sensitive," he answered.

"Gentlemen, let's take a short break. I'd like to meet with Mr. Turner alone right now, with his friend here on the phone," commanded Pops. Everyone else got up to leave the room.

As soon as the room cleared, Pops sat down directly across from Zach at the conference table. He looked concerned.

"At some point, son, we will need your testimony. Hell, we may need it to get warrants at some point," Pops told the operative.

"That could be a problem, sir. I am literally entrenched in the *Deep State* in D.C. and Langley. I would have to agree with it. It will blow my cover, not to mention that Zach will lose an extremely valuable inside source. It would also put me and my family in very real jeopardy," answered the operative.

"I understand. We will cross that bridge when we git there." Pops stood up, took his hat off, and scratched his head.

"I've got one more thing to bring up," said the operative. "I'm sure the NTSB will run a chemical fuel analysis from the crash site if they can get any molecular data from the ground or aircraft remains. Ask them to provide you a copy, then re-contact me."

"Roger that," said Zach.

"Hang on here a second. What is it you think that report could turn up?" asked Pops.

"Could be many things. But if I was going to take a plane down, tainting the fuel mixture could be the easiest and least detectable way to do it," answered the operative. "Volkov is resourceful and inventive. If he is responsible, and there's no reason for me to think otherwise now that I know he was in the hangar and around this aircraft an hour before take-off, I would be looking at the fuel analysis."

"Okay. What are we looking for exactly?" pressed Pops.

"Look for unusual amounts of diethylene glycol monomethyl ether," answered the operative.

"What the hell is that?" asked Pops.

"Isn't that essentially a de-icer?" asked Zach.

"It is. It will typically suppress the freezing point of any water at high altitudes that might be in the aviation fuel but, used in the wrong quantities or introducing product that has been expired or mixed with a variety of other fuel additives, will produce microbes that actually do the opposite; it coagulates the fuel. Essentially, the aircraft engines have a heart attack. They fail."

"We don't see him loading any fuel in the video footage," mentioned Pops.

"Are there security cameras at the jet fuel loading area on the tarmac? You might want to look at those," suggested the operative.

"We will find out," answered Pops.

"If all he had to do was to introduce this additive into the jet fuel, why would he be under the aircraft wings?" asked Zach.

"Not sure. My guess would be to work on the fuel lines," the operative told them. "He could adjust them to run leaner. The combination of a leaner fuel burn plus a coagulant could cause stalls in the engines that would be hard or nearly impossible to restart while airborne, and that King Air, on a short flight like that, probably wasn't more than fifteen thousand feet."

"This is valuable information. How long would it take the lab reports to come back from NTSB?" asked Zach.

"Weeks, if not months. You may want to talk to the NTSB and get them pointed in that direction to get it done sooner," the operative suggested.

Pops pulled a cigar from his pearl snap shirt pocket, bit the end off of it, and spit the tobacco end of the cigar into the metal trash can from five feet away.

"Mute that damn thing for a second." Pops motioned to Beard, who shut off the mic to the web application.

"This is also the hombre that killed that state senator..." Pops thought out loud. "We have to ask why a former KGB agent is murdering a Texas state senator and why he would want to take down the governor. This guy is involved in the murder of Chief Justice Noyner of the United States Supreme Court! Jesus, *what the hell is going on here*?" Pops looked squarely at Zach as if he knew Turner wasn't telling him something.

"Sir, you and I both know this goes to the highest levels of government."

"Son, right now there ain't nobody I can trust as far as I can throw them. Hell, this information we are sitting on today wouldn't make a good dime store novel 'cuz nobody would believe it's this rotten through and through," lamented Pops.

"It sometimes makes you wish you weren't in the know," Zach said wryly. "Most people are worried about their upcoming Labor Day weekend and how their favorite football team is going to fare. Who ever said ignorance is bliss is probably right."

"I'm about to circle the wagons and put every Texas Ranger I've got on finding this bad-ass Russian dude. If he's in Texas, they'll find him," Pops assured Zach.

"The CIA has been looking for him for years," replied Zach before he realized how stupid that sounded.

"Turn it back on." Pops motioned Beard to bring the operative back on live.

"Anything else we should know?" asked Pops.

"I would strongly caution everyone regarding Volkov," the operative warned. "This guy is a criminal at the highest level. He's motivated by money, but I will tell you his motivation to make money is not nearly as intense as his hate for the West, especially the United States, and his effectiveness is well documented with bodies strewn across the globe directly at his hands.

He is *most* dangerous when cornered."

"Like every snake, he'll come out of his hole sooner or later," answered Pops.

"Volkov doesn't make mistakes, sir," shot back the operative.

"*He already did,*" Pops responded.

"How so?" asked the operative.

"He plied his trade in *Texas,*" said Pops matter-of-factly.

CHAPTER 42

"The best we can hope for concerning the people at large is that they be properly armed."

- Alexander Hamilton (1757-1804)
American statesman, Secretary of the Treasury

Politically, the deaths of the governor and lieutenant governor had the same effect as a complete reshuffle of a deck of cards that had been tossed into the air, only to be spread out unceremoniously on the floor to be picked up in random order. The loss of two governors and two lieutenant governors in two years had the effect of reshaping the entire Texas body politic.

As Speaker Strasburg ascended to the office of governor, the leadership of the state legislature roiled with the changes in subcommittee chairmanships and memberships to important committees. Although Strasburg was hardly a conservative, many considered him a moderate.

What was most noticeable was that the pro-independence faction had gained substantial popularity among the electorate, but that wave of political feeling was not being represented in committee chairs and assignments coming out of Strasburg's minions. Austin was becoming as highly polarized as Washington, D.C.

The opposing forces were not so much Democrat versus Republican or even conservative versus liberal as they were the pro-independence faction versus the status quo of politics as usual. Very few in the media realized it was taking shape much like the original American colonies when there were conflicts between Tories and rebels. Loyalties and alignment with leaders on both sides of the argument were becoming increasingly entrenched.

Beard and Will had been planning another inconspicuous rendezvous with Ottosson, but were about to find out it wasn't necessary. It had been several months since they had accessed his devices and emails, and it was time to do it again. This mission was to try to uncover any more detail they could find on whatever *Madison* was, as well as clues for the whereabouts of Volkov.

Intelligence from Zach's operatives had tracked Ottosson on a trip back to Sweden to CIS' world headquarters with a stop in Amsterdam.

A message came into the Bunker, indicating operatives had mined some new and important intelligence from Ottosson. While in Amsterdam, Ottosson got coked up and spent two days with professional prostitutes in the red-light district. Apparently, Zach's operatives in Europe had an even easier time accessing Ottosson's devices while he was in a coke-laden tryst with multiple prostitutes.

Zach's company had developed its own proprietary encoded communications systems that were reshaped every thirty days. This was especially important because of the *Deep State's* intrusion into all things electronic of the average citizen under the guise of *"national security."*

Beard was decoding several messages that burst through to the communications hub in the Bunker. Zach, Will and several others waited anxiously for him to decipher and translate the information.

Beard read off the first deciphered message:

CIS donor list lifted. Major donations funneled to Senator Simpson, Speaker Strasburg and others through PACs via dummy corporations and non-existent American citizens.

"Holy crap," exclaimed Will.

"We shouldn't be surprised. Illegal campaign contributions from a foreign source. Wonderful. I guess now we really know why Simpson and Strasburg opposed the referendum," said Zach.

"Here comes the next one," said Beard before they could fully digest the first.

Madison *on track for September target date. Appears BIG. No other details except $150k distributed to the Bear for advance groundwork.*

"Who the hell is the bear," asked Will.

"Volkov is Russian…. the Russian bear?" offered Beard.

"That's got to be it!" agreed Zach.

"The team is also saying here that Ottosson's encryption methodology changed. These items are more than ten days old. They are working on breaking the encryption to get the rest," claimed Beard. "Wait, one more coming through..." he said excitedly.

"Lone star eagle grounded successfully."

"Damn!" Will was astounded.

"Well, there it is, confirmation." Zach was talking about both his and Pops' assertion that Ottosson and Volkov were behind the governor's aircraft crash. "I've got to get this news to Pops."

"Wait, there's one more!" interrupted Beard. "What... What the hell does this mean?"

Source indicates rogue militia faction actions are imminent. No interception planned. Plays right into plans for Madison.

Suddenly Zach stood up. "Son of a bitch! Are you freakin' kidding me? Get Lofton on the phone, NOW!" he shouted.

Within minutes, Beard had Hank Lofton on speakerphone.

"Hank, you've got a mole," said Zach immediately, without saying hello.

"What the hell are you talking about, Zach?" asked Lofton.

"Hank, do you have some type of operation you are about to launch?" pressed Zach.

There was a pause and silence on the other end.

"Hank, you there?"

"Yeah, I'm here. Why are you asking me that?" queried Lofton.

"Because we intercepted intelligence on Ottosson. They know you have something planned."

"What! No way!" objected Lofton.

"Well, do you? They think you do."

"Did the intelligence specifically mention us or what the operation was?" asked Lofton, trying to discredit the intelligence.

"No, only that something from our rogue militia was imminent," answered Zach.

"Well, that ain't rocket science. The mole could be yours, Zach. I told you in our meeting we aren't standing pat and letting the IRS steal our hard-earned money and ruining our lives," countered Lofton.

"Hank, whatever you have planned plays into *Madison* somehow."

"Zach, how could that be? Do we even know what *Madison* is?"

"Not yet, but the messages *specifically* credited your operation with aiding in their objective, whatever it is. So, Hank, I'll ask you again. What do you have planned?" Zach demanded.

"I can't..."

"Cut the crap, Hank!" Zach yelled, frantic. "Whatever it is likely puts us all in jeopardy. Now, exactly what is it?"

"Listen, Zach, you had your chance at the Bunker with us all there to unite us to take action on this IRS scandal. If you had, we'd all be planning this response together. All I can tell you is we *are* going to respond. Now that it appears *you* have a mole, I'm not at liberty to discuss it unless you're offering your team's help in meeting our objectives."

"Hank, I'm asking you as a friend to stand down, at least until we figure out what *Madison* is. Will you do that, Hank?" pleaded Zach in the most civil way he knew how.

"Zach, I appreciate your concern, but our operation is already in motion. My team is suffering undue hardship. Unless you are willing to bring your team on board with this response, we don't have a lot to discuss. Now, if you figure out what this *Madison* operation is, call me; otherwise you'll be hearing about ours soon enough," said Lofton flatly.

"Hank, my team also has these damned levies, audits and harassment. But we are mindful of the bigger picture."

"Not to the extent ours is. I've got team members who are borrowing money to feed their families. A couple have had assets seized. The damned tax attorneys can't seem to get anything rectified. Hell, even personal bankruptcy is too late as some of them are coming under criminal indictment," Lofton exclaimed. "It's all a bunch of lies, a hit job, and you know it, Zach!"

"If your people had followed protocol months ago, they couldn't touch your money. My team has gotten hit the same, but they followed our established protocols to protect cash and assets. Yours didn't."

"Circumstances, Zach. Some of them have circumstances why protocol wasn't followed to the letter. What am I going to do, abandon them?"

"No, of course not," Zach said sympathetically. "Are you going to tell me what your plans are so we can at least try to minimize any exposure we have? Surely you could use our intelligence apparatus."

"I have my own intelligence apparatus, Zach, you know that."

"Hank, I'm going to let you think about this for twenty-four hours. These turds are saying that your operation will enable or help *Madison*.

Doesn't that concern you?" Zach was frustrated.

"Sure it does, Zach, but I have no idea how reliable that intelligence is. And what am I supposed to do in the meantime? Hell, you might not figure out what *Madison* is until after it has happened."

"Hank, I'm begging you to stand down for now," Zach said.

"I appreciate your concern. Call me when you have new information." Click.

"The son of a bitch hung up on me!" shouted Zach.

"Damn. He doesn't believe us?" asked Beard.

"No, that ain't it. He's determined to run his own show. He's hell bent on leading his own operation to pay back the IRS. What do y'all think he's going to do?" asked Will.

"He doesn't have the technology experience on that team to do anything covert in their systems, although he may have some common contacts with us that could," said Beard.

"No, I don't think so," Zach stated. "Our contacts aren't going to initiate any kind of large-scale effort against a governmental agency without a lot more behind them than Lofton's team. When you decide to act on the IRS, NSA, FBI, ATF or the military complex, you are playing with fire."

"Zach, what type of response is he talking about?" asked Will. "What could make the IRS stand down?"

"He would have to use covert technology in my opinion, but I don't think he has the means or desire. He wants his pound of flesh," Zach lamented.

"If he goes that route, he's going to bring them down on all our heads!" yelled Beard.

"Yep, and he can't see it because his hatred is getting in the way of his judgment. There's other ways to respond. Let's hope he has something more tactical in mind," Zach said hopefully.

"He doesn't care or doesn't believe our intel on *Madison*?" asked Beard.

"Deep down, he cares. But he knows we really don't have much to go on. We really need to uncover something, anything that could sway him to stop. But I have a feeling we don't have much time," Zach said ominously. "Let's get on the phone and break the latest news to Pops."

Meanwhile, Lofton got on his cell phone with his chief lieutenants. "This is Lofton. Circumstances indicate that we might be compromised. Operation Payback is officially moved up seventy-two hours."

CHAPTER 43

"The Union was formed by the voluntary agreement of the states; and these, in uniting together, have not forfeited their nationality, nor have they been reduced to the condition of one and the same people. If one of the states chooses to withdraw from the compact, it would be difficult to disapprove its right of doing so, and the Federal Government would have no means of maintaining its claims directly either by force or right."

- Alexis de Tocqueville (1805-1859)
French historian
Source: Democracy in America, 1835

The massive regional Internal Revenue Service complex that sits on I-35 South in Austin is a dark gray concrete monstrosity that has few windows and zero architectural soul.

Almost twenty-four hundred government employees work at the sprawling complex, which is due for eventual closure since this is one of the major sites that still processes paper tax returns, which are becoming less prevalent in today's society. The complex hosts three eight-hour shifts of government employees Monday through Friday and one shift on Saturdays during the peak of tax season.

Shift changes occurred at 7:30 each morning, causing a minor traffic jam as employees tried to leave the complex while others were coming in. It was a typical government operation with very little forethought or planning, and the Texas Department of Transportation was forced to put a red light on the frontage road to allow cars to exit the parking lots.

On a bright August morning, nothing was unusual or different from a normal shift change at the complex.

At 8:01 a.m., a phone call came into IRS headquarters, announcing that the facility had one hour to evacuate the building because a bomb had been planted. At the same time, a call came into the Austin Police Department, as well as two local television broadcast stations, giving the same information.

The FBI and ATF were immediately notified. Police cruisers, SWAT, and bomb squad trucks from the police department rushed to the scene. The news hit the broadcast airwaves.

Within moments, the Texas Rangers were also notified, and Pops Younger was immediately aware of the situation but, for now, Austin police would be the lead law enforcement agency, dispatching their own bomb squad.

Bomb threats had come into the IRS facility before, and the employees were trained on these types of drills regularly. The employees emptying the building did not seem to be alarmed in any way; in fact, some of them were celebrating what might end up being a paid day off.

What the TV stations were not disclosing to the public was that the callers had indicated to them and to the IRS that the bombs would go off at exactly 9:45 a.m., urging them to get personnel off the premises promptly.

At the same exact time, the same phone calls were made to IRS offices in Houston, Dallas, and San Antonio with the exact same instructions. The FBI and ATF were slow to communicate between cities, and it was not immediately obvious to them that they were dealing with some type of coordinated threat.

The chief security officer at the IRS in Austin was not worried. He believed this was another hoax and considered it wasn't a stretch to think it was an IRS employee who just wanted a paid day off. He wasn't in any hurry to get employees out; in fact, he instructed a few of his subordinates to stay behind and not evacuate.

The scene in the parking lot was more tangled than normal, as police kept open a turn lane so the bomb squad could get in easily. There were ten minutes left until the threatened detonation of the bombs, yet there were still dozens of people in the parking lot making their casual way to their vehicles. Cars were jammed in line trying to get out of the parking lot.

The Austin bomb squad was going through the building, trying to find anything that looked remotely like a bomb. With only a little more than an hour's threat notification and a massive complex to cover, they knew they likely had to get lucky to identify the threat, if it was real at all.

The scene was similar in the other IRS offices in Texas that were also threatened, although none had as many employees to evacuate as Austin.

"Zach, you seeing this news break?" asked Will via cell phone.

"No, what's happening?" Zach asked.

"There's apparently bomb threats at multiple IRS offices in Texas. They are all being evacuated. It's a coordinated threat."

"Geez, this has got to be Lofton," Zach muttered. "Let's pray it's only a threat."

"We'll know, I guess," Will stated. "They have bomb squads on scene at each one. Surely he's just jacking with them."

"God, let's hope so," answered Zach.

In Austin, almost all the cars in the parking lots were gone, but a few remained parked. Austin police asked the IRS security officers why so many cars were still there. The officer believed some employees left with others, figuring they would be called back.

The building was finally cleared, and the IRS security chief remained with the Austin police bomb squad on the perimeter of the parking lot waiting for the 9:45 a.m. mark. There were no employees left in the building.

At 9:45 a.m., the sergeant in charge of SWAT looked at his watch and asked the IRS security chief and bomb squad leader if they had the same time. They all confirmed it was 9:45 or very close.

"Nothing. A big fat nothing," chuckled the sergeant.

Suddenly—Kaboom! Kaboom! Kaboom! Kaboom! Kaboom! Kaboom!

Six cars in the parking lot exploded in sequence, a few seconds from each other. The initial blast knocked the IRS security chief on his back, and he landed with a thud on the parking lot pavement, which knocked the breath out of him. Police, bomb squad technicians, and IRS security personnel were all knocked to the ground. A small number of windows still existing on the structure were instantly shattered.

At nearly the same moment, the same scene played itself out at all the other locations that were threatened, although none of those locations had more than two explosions each.

The drama played out on live TV as Austin stations broadcast remotely from near the IRS complex. The stations, not thinking the threat was credible, had dispatched rookie crews who just got the scoop of their young careers.

"Damn it, Lofton!" yelled Zach, thinking about calling Lofton, but deciding against it. He didn't want anything that could be discoverable in the event Lofton was responsible.

Reports coming about the explosions did not confirm any fatalities or serious injuries, although some police got hit by shattered glass and debris—nothing serious from any site so far that couldn't be treated at the scene.

Like clockwork, media outlets in the affected cities got anonymous faxes that read:

Today's events are the direct result and fault of the IRS, Congress and the courts.

The criminal IRS has continued to operate without proper governmental oversight, terrorizing citizens who must comply with a repressive tax code they don't understand.

The IRS has now been weaponized by this administration to harass and terrorize those who make their enemy list.

Despite our Bill of Rights, the courts and the IRS allow our due process rights and our privacy rights under the Fourth Amendment to be eviscerated. We demand immediate action from Congress or by presidential executive order to immediately rescind the elements of tax law that violate the U.S. Constitution.

If the IRS continues to terrorize us, we will have no choice but to continue to terrorize those who would carry out unconstitutional enforcement actions against American citizens. This is your last warning. If we do not see immediate action and resulting reform, like ordinary citizens who get no due process, IRS employees won't either.

No IRS employee is safe—ever.

Concerned Citizens Willing to Take Action Now

All the TV stations were broadcasting the exact memo. Politicians were immediately chiming in, as the ATF and FBI were now swarming over the exploded cars for clues to the perpetrators. The IRS announced all of the affected locations were going to be closed until further notice while they reassessed security at the locations.

"This is a domestic terrorist attack," claimed U.S. Senator Kevin Simpson from Texas. "No matter how much someone disagrees with a current law or the tax code as written, the process for change is in our democratic system and this crime will not go unpunished!"

"That dumb ass Simpson still thinks this is a democracy instead of a constitutional republic," laughed Hank Lofton as he sat and drank beer with several on his team. They had gathered at a deer lease in an undisclosed location to watch the coverage of the event—their event.

"Do you think they got the message?" asked one of Lofton's team members.

"Hell, no, but it sure will slow down whatever enforcement actions they have going on in the near term," answered Lofton as he lit up a cigar. "I want to congratulate everyone here. Exactly as planned. No injuries, but maximum terror! I can't wait to see the faces of IRS employees the next time they are allowed to come to work in each of those buildings." They all laughed out loud, clanking beers together and slapping high fives.

"We are going to become extremely disruptive to their operations, same as they have us. They will rue the day they messed with us. Maximum pressure, maximum terror. If this doesn't drive the change that's needed, then we'll make it hard for them to operate, at least in Texas."

Pops Younger's Texas Rangers' office made contact with acting Texas Governor Strasburg, requesting a late afternoon meeting with police, FBI and ATF at Austin Police headquarters. Little did he know this was already planned, and Strasburg's meeting time was intentionally thirty minutes later than the time scheduled to start. In a cramped conference room, about twenty federal ATF and FBI agents crammed in to meet over the bombings. The meeting and debriefing were well underway when Pops and four Texas Rangers opened the door. It was immediately obvious to Pops the meeting had started without him.

"Did I get the time wrong?" asked Pops, pulling a fancy pocket watch out of his starched jeans.

Many of the agents and some of the detectives in the room had never seen Pops in person. There he was, bold as life itself with his Stetson, alligator cowboy boots and famous handlebar mustache. Any time Pops walked into a room, his presence commanded attention.

"Three-thirty?" asked acting Governor Strasburg.

"No, sir, we were told 4:00 p.m.," said a visibly annoyed Pops.

"Well, we've already started," Strasburg stated. "The FBI has taken jurisdiction of this bombing because it was on federal property." He nodded to Michael Jarvis, the lead regional FBI director from Dallas.

"We will, of course, provide any support needed," responded Pops.

"We don't need *any* help from the Texas Rangers," said Jarvis harshly.

"Son, I'm here at the request of our governor and the people of Texas. I don't give a rat's ass if you like it or not," retorted Pops sharply.

"You boys are responsible for the death of some of my friends, good people, during the *Texas Crisis* and you aren't impeding this investigation one iota," claimed Jarvis

"Are we here to solve this crime or are you Yankees just here to whine about bad judgment resulting in unconstitutional orders that got your own damned people kilt?" responded Pops, stepping closer to the front of the room.

"Since this is probably one of your yokels, I'm sure we can solve this without you," snarled Jarvis as the room became very tense.

Pops reached over to the table where a cup of coffee sat in front of Jarvis, spit his tobacco juice into the cup, then set it back down. The FBI agents jumped up and the four Texas Rangers each took a step forward.

"Listen, calm down, calm down," said Austin Chief of Police Dan Watson. "We understand there's bad blood here, but we all have to work together to solve this."

"Pops, we are going to let the feds handle this. I appreciate you coming down. We will call you as necessary," said Strasburg, dismissing Younger.

Pops squinted his eyes and glared at the governor. He knew Strasburg had set him up to embarrass him by making a late entrance, only to be dismissed in front of federal agents.

"Chief, good to see you." Silence settled over the room. Pops nodded to Watson as he began to make his way to the door. Dyson, Pops' second in command, was livid. He had never seen Pops disrespected in such a manner.

"Chief," Dyson tipped his hat as he walked out, then said, just loud enough for everyone to hear, "Tread carefully, my Yankee friends."

CHAPTER 44

"We have no government armed in power capable of contending with human passions unbridled by morality and religion. Our Constitution was made only for a religious and moral people. It is wholly inadequate for the government of any other."

- John Adams (1735-1826)
Founding Father, 2nd US President

President Bartlett entered the White House briefing room to a throng of reporters the day after the bombings of Texas IRS offices.

Political pundits and policy hacks were again all over the people of Texas, blaming an anti-government culture that emanated from the state, resulting in instances such as the *Texas Crisis* and the latest bombings of government facilities.

"Good morning," President Bartlett said, nodding to the crowd of media reps. "I am saddened and horrified that I am in this room this morning addressing a domestic terrorist incident in Texas. Although no one was seriously injured, it has disrupted operations of the Treasury Department, preventing employees from doing their constitutionally protected jobs in Texas." She paused, then continued, "The FBI is leading this investigation and, rest assured, the perpetrators of this act of terror will be apprehended and face the full force of American justice. Now I will take your questions."

"Madam President, are these bombings in any way related to the *Texas Crisis*, including those not arrested or held accountable for the death of federal agents?" asked a CNN White House correspondent.

"We don't yet know who the perpetrators were. As soon as we do, we will announce the identities of the suspects, after they are apprehended, for obvious reasons," Bartlett said firmly.

The CNN reporter pressed, "But why weren't the others ever arrested?"

"The focus today is the recent bombings of IRS offices." Bartlett scowled at the reporter. "We have answered those questions before and I will refer you back to those statements. Next?"

"Madam President, is the focus of the investigation on militia groups or those who were connected to the independence referendum vote in Texas?" asked a correspondent from MSNBC.

"The FBI is looking at all possibilities. Nobody and no organization, at this time, has been ruled out. Yes, Jim?" the president acknowledged a reporter from the BBC.

"Were these pipe bombs? Can you tell us how sophisticated the bombs were?"

"No, I cannot at this time. The FBI crime labs are still doing their research. We do know that the timing is such that whoever planted these bombs was no stranger to explosives or timing devices. The timing of the bombings themselves take considerable expertise for them to go off in synchronization as they did.

"Yes, Brittany. Brittany, right there," said the president, pointing to a Politico reporter.

"Will you or will Congress be addressing any of the threats that were made? They said no IRS employees are safe if you do not act," she stated.

"We don't succumb to terrorist demands and we don't negotiate with terrorists," said Bartlett flatly.

"But, Madam President, how do you tell the IRS employees to show up to work now that their lives have been threatened?" Brittany followed up.

"Security is being significantly increased at IRS locations in Texas. I can't, for obvious reasons, disclose all the details, but I would like to assure the hard-working government servants at the IRS that we do take this seriously and we will fully protect them. That's all I have for you for now. We will keep you abreast of any developments," concluded the president as she walked off the small platform to more shouted questions..

Meanwhile, Turner, Beard and Turnbow were at the Bunker debating whether to reach out to Lofton to see if they could arrange a private meeting. Understandably, there was serious hesitation because it was more than likely that Lofton's team was responsible for the bombings. Any contact with Lofton after the fact could link them to the conspiracy.

In the middle of the heated discussions, Zach's phone rang.

"Turner here," he answered, knowing by caller ID Pops was calling him.

"Son, this is Younger."

"Hello, Pops. Hell of a last twenty-four hours for you, I bet?" asked Zach.

"Just got one question, son, and I know you'll answer it for me."

Zach cringed. He knew what Pops was going to ask him.

"Any of your folks connected to the people that did these bombings?" asked Pops.

"Sir, this wasn't one of our operations," Zach said.

"I don't think I asked you that. I know it ain't. I'm asking if you know who could have done this?"

"I don't have any direct evidence, sir," Zach responded hesitantly.

"The IRS has been a royal pain in the ass to all of us. But you've got an idea, don't you?" pressed Pops.

"I do, but I'd ask you to let me follow up on it and let you know."

"Son, I need you to be very careful," Pops told him. "You need to bring me into this as soon as possible. If you get linked to whatever group is doing this, I don't know how much I can protect you."

"Sir, I completely understand and I sincerely appreciate that."

"If the feds get out ahead of us on this, everything will escalate again." said Pops, a clear warning in his voice.

"I understand, sir. I definitely understand," Zach said. "Good-bye, Pops." He ended the call.

"You don't want to tell him, do you?" asked Will.

"We don't know for sure. But this is one of our guys. I don't know if I can turn over one of us," Zach said miserably, feeling like he was caught between the proverbial "rock and a hard place."

"The minute, the very nanosecond he stopped listening to you and doing his own thing, he became *not* one of us," replied Will.

"If he did do it, and I think all three of us believe he is behind it, we will be guilty by association, you both know that," said Zach.

"We've got Pops' trust right now. Sure would hate to jeopardize that," admitted Beard.

"He knows we likely know. He also knows we are trying to sort through this," Will concluded. "We need absolute confirmation Lofton did this before we offer anything to anyone."

"Put feelers out to his crew, without implicating us in the conspiracy. I'm not exactly sure how to do that, except that we have to let Pops know we know, once we *really* know it," instructed Zach.

"Look, another statement!" Beard pointed to one of the TV screens in the Bunker.

"Turn it up!" yelled Zach.

The ABC affiliate in Austin was reading from a fax, supposedly from the same source that provided the faxed statement after the bombings. It read:

President Bartlett has chosen to ignore our demands for accountability by the IRS for unlawful seizures, harassment and the terrorization of lawful U.S. citizens.

Therefore, we provide this warning to IRS employees in Texas. When you go to work tomorrow, next week or next month, it may be your last day.

To Congressmen and Congresswomen who do not immediately authorize new legislation to curtail the IRS' authority and to pass laws allowing due process as in every other accusation under the Fourth Amendment, worrying if you will be re-elected will be the last thing you will need to worry about.

Time is short. Life is precious.

Do the right thing. Do it now!

Concerned Citizens Willing to Take Action Now

"This is not going to end well, not at all…" said Beard.

"We are going to have to tell Pops we have an idea about who it is but stress we have no way to confirm without further implicating ourselves," said Will.

"Damn it, Hank," cursed Zach, even though Lofton wasn't there to hear it. "There's other ways to rid ourselves of the IRS vermin."

"How far will he go, Zach? You know him better than we do," asked Will.

"The dude is dead serious," Zach stated. "He's obviously been pushed to his limit. I'm not sure how to stop him at this point. He's got the full force of the federal government looking for him right now; he just doesn't know it yet. If he was sloppy in any way, they will tie those bombs to him and they will look to take him out."

"You have to make the call, Zach, tough as it is," said Will regretfully.

He meant that Special Forces soldiers create very unique bonds. You don't rat on your comrades—ever.

"This is gut-wrenching. Do we have an ounce of doubt that he's responsible?" asked Zach, looking for any angle to get out of making that call to Pops.

"Look at it this way," Will told him with a very stark reality check. "We are going to be tied to him, no matter what. You have a duty to protect those with us. If he makes good on his threats and starts killing IRS employees, it will be that much tougher on the rest of us. Your security business will be toast."

"Damn, it may be anyway," Zach said sadly.

"We will survive, Zach, you know we always do," said Beard. "Here's your phone."

Zach snatched the phone from Beard and looked at it for a moment, then reluctantly dialed Pops' number.

For the first time ever when he called, Pops actually answered himself.

"Younger," said Pops.

"Sir, this is Turner. I've got you on speaker with Turnbow and Beard."

"What took you so long, son?" asked Pops.

"We've been discussing it. This is very hard to do," Zach said with conviction.

"Listen, you've got some pal or some pals that have gone off the reservation. I understand. I also know you ain't involved. Now, you boys know your buddies are way better off if I get to 'em before the feds," reasoned Pops.

"You're right, sir. First, we don't have anything confirmed. We've been hesitant to make contact for obvious reasons," Zach told Pops.

"You've got good instincts, son. Go ahead. Tell me what you know and why you think you know who may be behind this."

Zach walked Pops through the last meeting with Lofton and the others. Pops asked a ton of questions, including names, backgrounds and specialties Lofton's crew might have. At least two in Lofton's group were demolition experts who would know how to construct the bomb sequences.

As difficult as it was for all three, they laid all their cards on the table for Pops to make his own evaluation.

"It seems these folks are fully capable. I have to admit I enjoy seeing the IRS squirm as much as you boys, but you know we are likely headed down a road that may offer a way out from under those bastards without bloodshed if the damned federal government gets out of our way," Pops said.

"The only people we trust in D.C. are part of our organization," confirmed Zach, which was seconded by Beard and Will.

"Boys, as you know from the evidence you've gathered, these bastards are ruthless and this *Deep State*, as you describe it, is so tangled that it's like a pit of vipers. You can't tell where one snake starts and where another snake ends. That being said, I want y'all to know I've got your backs, but I've got to act on the information you have provided me. You certainly know that as sure as the sun is comin' up tomorrow, right?"

"We understand, sir, and we appreciate it," replied Zach. "Is there anything else we can do at this juncture?"

"Keep using your sources and find that damned Russian!" suggested Pops.

CHAPTER 45

"Since when have we Americans been expected to bow submissively to authority and speak with awe and reverence to those who represent us?"

- Justice William O. Douglas (1898-1980)
U. S. Supreme Court Justice

The late August morning sky was gray and cloudy in Austin, with a stiff breeze from the southwest that reflected the general gloom in Texas. The world was about to witness the second funeral of a sitting Texas governor in less than two years.

In a scene eerily reminiscent of John F. Kennedy's funeral procession down Pennsylvania Avenue in 1963, two horse-drawn wagons carried the caskets of Governor Brahman and Lieutenant Governor Wilson, both draped with the Lone Star flag, northward up Congress Avenue to lie in repose at the state capitol. Behind the carriages were the families of both men, followed by the entire contingent of Texas Rangers.

The rest of the world was watching Texas' version of royalty. Pops Younger, mounted on *Pecos*, led one hundred sixty-two Texas Rangers. The Rangers all wore crisp white western pearl snap shirts, Wrangler jeans and straw cowboy hats. The modern-day Texas Ranger looked every bit like their 1880s version. It was the first time anyone could remember the full command of the Texas Rangers on horseback and together in one place. The rest of the world was mesmerized by the scene they witnessed on television.

"And there they are, arguably the most recognized law enforcement unit in the world, with no doubt the richest history and tradition," said the Fox News analyst covering the funeral live. "The Texas Rangers serve at the pleasure of the governor of Texas and my goodness, what a tribute to Governor Brahman and Lieutenant Governor Wilson!. Buckingham Palace has nothing on the pomp and circumstance of these Texans. And, of course, there, on his horse *Pecos*, is the most famous Texas Ranger in modern history, Pops Younger. Wow, what a sight!"

"What strikes me is the silence. There are nearly one hundred thousand mourners or more here by some accounts, but other than the sound of those Lone Star flags popping in the wind and the clopping of the hoofs of the Texas Rangers' horses on the pavement, nobody says a word. Incredibly solemn. It's hard to describe and I'm actually down here on Congress," said a correspondent from C-Span.

Lone Star flags lined Congress Avenue with thousands of Texas mourners waiting for a glimpse of the carriages carrying the two Texas leaders and the Texas Rangers. It was quite a sight to see in person, but the rest of the world was seeing their version of what most outsiders think Texas is all about, cowboy hats and horses.

As the procession crossed East 5th Avenue, the clouds parted and sun peered through, seemingly called on to light up the procession as it traveled slowly north. The crowd remained silent. A lone bugler standing on the east side of Congress began playing "Texas, My Texas," the Texas state song:

Slowly, like the wave at a sporting event, the crowd began singing the song all Texans learn in elementary school. Crowds who could barely hear the bugler from both ends of Congress Avenue began singing when the sounds of the song reached them:

Texas, Our Texas! All hail the mighty State!

Texas, Our Texas! So wonderful so great!

boldest and grandest, withstanding ev'ry test

O Empire wide and glorious, you stand supremely blest.

Texas, O Texas! your freeborn single star,

Sends out its radiance to nations near and far,

Emblem of Freedom! it sets our hearts aglow,

With thoughts of San Jacinto and glorious Alamo.

Texas, dear Texas! From tyrant grip now free,

Shine forth in splendor your star of destiny

Mother of heroes, we come your children true.

Proclaiming our allegiance, our faith, our love for you.

God bless you Texas! And keep you brave and strong,

That you may grow in power and worth, throughout the ages long.

As the chorus grew along the length of the procession, some TV commentators noted they could see tears streaming down many faces in the crowd, even on many of the Texas Rangers as they rode by.

As the procession reached the state Capitol building, a throng of state employees and politicians awaited on a hastily built grandstand at the south Capitol steps. Once the procession entered the Capitol grounds under an ornamental iron gate, the entrance split into two paved narrow roads with a green belt in between. The carriages carrying the caskets, followed by family members and clergy of the Brahman and Wilson families, took the path to the right. The Texas Rangers and the state troopers walking behind them took the left path.

The procession passed the Confederate Soldiers monument and the monument dedicated to the heroes of The Alamo, which sat in the greenbelt area. CNN and MSNBC couldn't help adding their own editorial comments about how Texas still allowed Confederate memorials on the Capitol grounds. They went on to criticize other statues on the Capitol grounds, including Terry's Texas Rangers Confederate Cavalry statue, Hood's Brigade statue and the monument to the Ten Commandments.

"Yes, indeed, Texas is different than the rest of the country," snarked a CNN political analyst in his attempt to mock the state.

As the Texas Rangers dismounted, eleven pre-selected Rangers went to the carriages to act as pallbearers. Pops Younger went to the families; he took off his cowboy hat and went down the line comforting each of them. At the end of the line, acting Governor Strasburg stepped down off the grandstand to make sure he got in the photo op with Pops.

The Rangers were waiting for Pops, the final pallbearer, to make his way through the line of mourners to assist with the caskets. Once Pops got through the throng of family members, he turned to them, nodded and put his cowboy hat back on. Strasburg was right behind and waited for Pops to acknowledge him with the hundreds of video cameras on the spectacle.

Pops looked at him as Strasburg stuck out his hand to shake Pops' hand. Pops took a step closer to him and locked onto Strasburg's hand to pull him in closer. To most, this seemed like an intimate moment of both sharing their grief over the magnitude of the moment.

Strasburg looked at Pops' steel-blue eyes now inches from his face.

"If I find out you had even the slightest involvement in this, I'll kill you myself with my bare hands," Pops murmured.

Strasburg, visibly shaken by Pops' threat, moved away and somehow managed to smile for the cameras.

CHAPTER 46

"We are rapidly entering the age of no privacy, where everyone is open to surveillance at all times; where there are no secrets from government.

- Justice William O. Douglas (1898-1980)
U. S. Supreme Court Justice

N ils Ottosson arrived back in Washington, D.C. after a visit with his employer's leadership at corporate headquarters in Stockholm, which was preceded by two days of debauchery in Amsterdam.

Ottosson was not happy. He was previously a regular in meetings with Bartlett's chief of staff and various other cabinet members, but he hadn't been invited back in months. What was obvious to others wasn't so obvious to him.

His womanizing was a liability, but the administration and politicos in the Democratic Party put up with it simply because his lobbying efforts were so effective. His relationships with members of Congress was surprisingly strong. His ability to maneuver various statehouses to get the CIS voting systems in place and past huge hurdles was admired by many.

The effort to federalize the elections had long been a plank in the Democratic platform. Losing presidential elections where their candidate won the popular vote, only to get trounced in the Electoral College, was a volatile and painful talking point for them.

The Democrats had a simple formula for permanent change. First, the flow of illegal immigrants who were granted amnesty over time by either Party continued to tip the scale of the popular vote to the Democrats. If the Electoral College was eviscerated and replaced by a popular vote in presidential elections, Democrats would almost assuredly win every time. The federalization of elections was simply an outgrowth of the government's plan to become the centralized authority. This process was begun by Lincoln and had grown more powerful and centralized with every administration.

Democrats successfully used the race card, citing supposed voter suppression efforts and mythical violations of the Voting Rights Act of 1965 to shift public opinion from state to federal control, with oversight of every federal and state election. The CIS election system was the tool they needed to put their plan in play, and the relationship had become a mutual lovefest between CIS, the Democrats and even powerful moderate and establishment Republicans. CIS had craftily found loopholes and established corporate subsidiaries in the United States to be major political contributors to their campaigns.

Ottosson had become a very powerful lobbyist, and CIS gave him carte blanche on which candidates to fund. There were very few politicians in Washington, D.C. who wouldn't immediately allow Ottosson an audience. CIS had given him over two hundred million dollars to spread among Congress and to state politicians, simply to get their election systems and software in place and, with this war chest, he was very effective.

The Bartlett administration, however, knew that a relationship with Ottosson carried substantial risks, with the main risk being that he was a heavy drinking womanizer, philanderer and occasional drug user. Besides his relationships with those at the very top of the political food chain in Washington, Ottosson was known to have relationships that were too cozy with known underworld figures, international criminals and general lowlifes. His relatability with people from all walks of life was his greatest attribute, but the wallet he wielded for CIS to influence politicians opened doors, even to the Oval Office.

Chief of Staff Weingold scheduled a meeting with Ottosson in a hotel room of the Hay-Adams Hotel, which was one block from the White House and whose rooms overlooked Lafayette Park and the White House. Weingold did not enter through the front lobby of the hotel, but had arranged to be taken in a rear door and up the service elevator by the Secret Service to a large suite. Ottosson was instructed to take the same route. This irritated the Swede; he very much liked to be seen, especially with one of the most powerful political brokers in the country.

"Good morning, Nils," said Weingold as he welcomed him into the suite, peering at the Swede over eyeglasses pulled halfway down his nose.

"Nice tie," replied Ottosson in his Swedish accent, noting the red bow tie with blue polka dots accenting Weingold's bold gray plaid three-piece suit.

"Well, you look pretty comfortable," noted Weingold half-sarcastically, referring to Ottosson's casual warm-up suit and tennis shoes. "I have breakfast waiting for us here. Please sit down and let's get to it."

They sat down to a formally arranged table with a lavish breakfast spread as aides and Secret Service quietly exited the suite.

"Please give me an update on how the CIS efforts are going in all your remaining target states," said Weingold.

For the next thirty minutes, Ottosson walked through the remaining obstacles to get CIS systems in place in the remaining states, purposely leaving Texas for last.

"So, tell me, what are your specific struggles in Texas?" Weingold asked.

"Texas is a different animal altogether, as you know, Mr. Weingold. The *Texas Crisis,* as your folks like to call it, has made my job there much harder."

"Yes, we know. However, haven't *recent* developments there increased your likelihood of success?" pressed Weingold.

Ottosson chuckled as he bit off a large piece of bacon. He took a few seconds before answering. "You mean the dead governor? Sure. Strasburg is definitely our friend, correct?" he said coyly.

"He's a Republican," Weingold leaned back and took a sip of coffee, "but he is our friend."

Weingold leaned back in toward the table from his chair, becoming somewhat more serious, "So tell me, Nils, is there anything the president should know that might come out about this unfortunate plane crash?" he asked.

Ottosson smiled, taking another bite of bacon. "You mean the accident?"

"Of course, the *accident,*" emphasized Weingold.

"Well, sir, you have the ability to pick up the phone and know exactly what the NTSB has," Ottosson stated matter-of-factly.

Weingold didn't appreciate the answer.

"I do know exactly what they have, Mr. Ottosson, so far. What I'm asking you, is there something they might discover that is not yet known to them or to anyone else?"

"If you're asking me if I am covering our tracks, why don't you just ask that?" reasoned Ottosson.

Weingold peered around the room and then looked at the ceiling suspiciously.

"Wait, surely your teams *cleaned* this room. Are you worried about *me* wearing a wire? Why aren't we in the West Wing, sir?" pressed Ottosson.

Weingold was not amused and was hesitant to answer such a direct question. "Yes, we take precautions, Mr. Ottosson, but let me remind you who I represent."

"I know full well who you represent, Weingold, and I get just a little irritated that I have to somehow speak in code when you and others know *exactly* what we are talking about. If you don't mind, let's cut the façade and get this meeting done."

Weingold stared at Ottosson for a few seconds, somewhat stunned by his candor, then answered, "I would have loved to have met in the West Wing, Nils, but your exploits, such as the recent one you had in Amsterdam, preclude our ability to host you there."

Ottosson became visibly enraged. "You have people tailing *me*? What the hell I do in my personal life is *my* business!"

"It's also *our* business, Mr. Ottosson, as long as *we* are in that business together," Weingold said calmly.

"Are you threatening me?" Ottosson demanded.

"Not at all. You just seem quite disturbed that we're not in the White House today."

"The last time I was invited to the White House for a meeting, you had them turn me away at the gate," Ottosson snarled.

"Yes, that was unfortunate but necessary," Weingold said. "My apologies."

Ottosson stared at Weingold, waiting to hear a reason or logical excuse why he was turned away and embarrassed at the White House gates. "Well?" asked Ottosson as he raised both hands, waiting for an answer to the implied question.

"Your personal life is potentially a liability to the president. We need you to finish this project without any scandal or bad press," instructed Weingold. "Now that that is understood, can we go back to my original question on the *accident*?"

Ottosson rubbed his chin and thought for a moment. "I'll answer you if you agree to take the surveillance off me."

"Mr. Ottosson, you're a key player in our overall strategy for this country," Weingold told him. "You, and everyone else associated, have to realize that not one single piece of this strategy can be revealed, not to *anyone*. You know as well as anyone the stakes involved. The surveillance is really for *your* safety, and it will be over when the project is over."

"You need to call off the dogs, Mr. Weingold. I have a certain lifestyle, but it doesn't impede my work. I'm getting incredible things done for you and this president. So don't you dare threaten me!"

Weingold was fully cognizant that Ottosson had single-handedly changed the election system with his CIS war chest and his lobbying efforts at both the congressional and state levels. He also knew the job wasn't quite done; he needed Ottosson until their goals were completed. "Okay, I get it," he said. "Just remember that anything you do reflects on the president. Please, I'm asking you to limit your indiscretions."

Ignoring the last request, Ottosson continued, "Can we get back to the business at hand?"

Weingold didn't immediately respond as he stood and went to pour himself some coffee from the cart that had been rolled into the suite.

"Fine, Mr. Ottosson. Now, tell me about the last remaining project we have at hand. Is it set? Do you have all your pieces in place?"

"*Madison* has had the most advanced planning I have ever been involved in. I'm going to ask one last time. Mr. Weingold. Are you and President Bartlett absolutely sure you want go through with this?"

Ottosson purposely referenced the president in this question. Never before, in any conversations regarding *Madison* did anyone, not even Ottosson, utter the president's name in reference to this operation. Weingold glared at Ottosson for even mentioning the president in the same breath as *Madison*.

"Well, excuse me," said Ottosson sarcastically, knowing full well that, if Weingold knew the details about Ottosson, Bartlett would surely know.

"I wanted to have this face-to-face meeting with you so that I can be assured no detail has been too small to ignore, that no additional resources are needed, and that this will come off exactly as planned and as you have laid it out for me," pressed Weingold.

"So that you can be assured? You mean so *Bartlett* can be assured!" chuckled Ottosson.

Weingold was getting exasperated. He wondered why Ottosson was so intent on bringing the president into the discussions; it made him very uncomfortable. He had not had the Secret Service agents pat the Swede down for a wire or recording device, but he sure was going to have it done before Ottosson left the suite.

"The president isn't part of these discussions. I'm not going to state it again," said Weingold.

"Fine. Just know that *Madison* is scheduled, is on track, and will be executed as planned, just in case *anyone else* besides you wants to know."

"That's great. These nut jobs in Texas who are setting off bombs at IRS offices play right into the narrative. I am worried, however, that the FBI or ATF will make arrests before *Madison* goes down. Those guys are the perfect patsies," worried Weingold.

"We can't change the *Madison* date. Can't even think about it at this point. You have to remember what *Madison* is designed around and its effect. If anyone had the power to slow down an investigation or pause arrests, who would that be other than you?" Ottosson laughed out loud, incredulous that Weingold would even suggest a date change to *Madison* when one phone call to the FBI director could delay the IRS bombing investigation. "My suggestion to you, sir, is to have the Oval Office get daily briefings on that investigation. You have been granted the perfect opportunity. Don't waste it." Ottosson smirked at the consternation on Weingold's face.

"We won't," said Weingold, standing to shake Ottosson's hand, indicating the meeting was over. "Hang on for just a minute. I'll be right back." Weingold left the room.

Two Secret Service agents entered the room and stood by the door. Ottosson was not amused.

"Where the hell did he go?"

"Mr. Weingold had to leave. We will escort you out the same way you came in. However, we are going to pat you down and scan you before you leave this room," said one of the agents.

"Are you serious?" Ottosson sneered and raised his arms. "Go ahead."

As one agent physically patted down Ottosson, the other disappeared into another room and came back with an electronic wand, similar to the wand the TSA uses at airports, but much more sophisticated. This wand was designed to pick up any listening devices or electronics on the human body or clothes.

Ottosson was not happy about this apparent mistrust by Weingold, but he made small talk with the agents as they scanned him.

"That damned thing won't make me impotent, will it, gentlemen?" laughed Ottosson, but the agents did not respond with in-kind laughter.

As they scanned down his legs, Ottosson worried the agents would notice a bead of sweat forming on his right temple.

The agent looked Ottosson in the eyes, then noticed he was beginning to perspire slightly, a sure sign of stress, maybe more.

"You seem a little nervous about getting checked for a wire, Mr. Ottosson."

"Ha, no. I'm just no fan of these gadgets you guys are using near my family jewels. I've heard they cause cancer."

"I doubt you have anything to worry about," answered the agent.

"I hope not," said Ottosson as he was led through the door and down the service elevator with the same agents and whisked away in the same unmarked SUV he had arrived in.

As Ottosson sat in the backseat of the SUV, he let out a deep breath. The Secret Service agents did not detect the high-tech listening device, made of ceramic and carbon and the size of a thumbtack, sewn into the toe of each of his shoes. The device had been given to him by Vasily Volkov, who told him, "Don't ever go into a high-level meeting or any other government function without recording it. If you can do it without being detected, the information you get could save your life someday… but it could also get you killed."

CHAPTER 47

"Crisis is the rallying cry of the tyrant."

- James Madison (1751-1836)
Father of the Constitution, 4th US President
Author of the 2nd Amendment

Texans typically don't see a break from the summer heat until well into October. But, on this mid-September Saturday, a small cool front swept in, bringing temperatures down, lowering humidity levels, and giving most of the state relief from the searing ninety-degree heat. By Texas standards, temperatures in the mid-eighties were a welcome relief.

The break in temperature was perfect for the massive annual Children's Literacy Festival that had grown into the largest of its kind in America. Originally founded to encourage literacy awareness, the festival had morphed into a combination of concerts, food trucks, vendors, and arts and crafts in a carnival-like atmosphere, all geared toward children.

The festival had been moved several times to accommodate the growth of the two-day event. It now occupied a sixty-acre site south of downtown Dallas, where families could park their cars in a field and walk to the event. Organizers believed attendance at this year's event would easily eclipse the record attendance from the previous year.

Families began streaming into the festival early on Saturday morning when the gates opened at 8:00 a.m. The line of cars waiting to get in created a traffic jam on the frontage roads off Interstate 20.

Among the vehicles already parked in the vendor parking was an unmarked white cargo van. The four occupants of the van had already entered the festival to work in different food trucks.

Mindful of security concerns, the organizers had erected metal scanners and bag checks at four different entrances to the festival. Even the vendors and their workers and volunteers for the event were required to enter through a specific entrance with a scanner. All four of the occupants of the white van passed through security the opening morning with no problem. None of them carried anything but a cell phone and keys to their food trucks. In the days before, the vendors had brought their food trucks and trailers onsite and set them up, stocked them with supplies, and were ready for the onslaught of the crowds wanting to taste their fare.

Vasily Volkov took a set of keys out of his pocket and opened a food truck he had purchased for the event. Volkov's food truck was called Cajun Delight, indicating that the truck offered food from southern Louisiana, very popular in Texas.

Volkov's three crew members worked to get the food ready for the event, boiling crawfish and preparing redfish, red beans and rice, seafood gumbo, and other Cajun dishes. To anyone observing the food truck, Volkov's crew conducted themselves in the same way as any other of the one hundred or so food trucks on the festival property.

As the gates opened and families began streaming in, the food trucks began to get busy as families got hungry while they enjoyed the rides, music, attractions and artisans. The festival had launched without a hitch and, by mid-afternoon, estimates were that the crowd onsite would swell to more than thirty thousand. The festival had hired off-duty sheriff's deputies and constables, but most of the security inside the festival came from a contract security company and were commonly referred to as *rent-a-cops*.

At each entrance point, a large sign with black letters on white backgrounds indicated the festival was a *"gun-free zone"* and that any firearms were prohibited, including prohibition of firearms carried by those who lawfully held a concealed carry permit in Texas.

Wherever one looked, families with children of all ages, including some in baby strollers, could be seen enjoying the beautiful weather. There were balloons, stuffed animals, ice cream, funnel cakes and soft drinks. Music blared from four different stages around the grounds, and cartoon characters roamed the grounds to greet children and have their pictures taken.

Of course, politicians couldn't miss the opportunity to be seen at the official kick-off of the event on the main stage, and several websites broadcast uninterrupted footage of the event from cameras strategically placed throughout the grounds.

Volkov's crew in Cajun Delight was busy serving up food to customers, and two lines formed with at least ten people in each line almost constantly, as it was very popular.

"Maybe I should be Cajun chef?" joked Volkov in his deep Russian accent to his crew, who laughed out loud. Most of the food being served in his truck was bought from another source, just reheated in the food truck.

All the food trucks cooked their food with propane gas, and they all used various sizes of propane tanks, either on the ground right beside the rear of the trucks or on racks welded to the back to hold the tanks, some as large as one-hundred pound capacity.

At exactly 3:00 p.m., Volkov looked back at his crew and announced to the people in line that they had run out of food, to the groan of those who had been standing in line. He pulled down the shades of the two large open windows where food was served and money collected and already pre-printed on the shades, it said, *Sorry, Cajun Delight is Temporarily Out of Food! Check Back with us Later*!

Volkov and his crew had rehearsed the next few minutes dozens of times. One of the crew opened the back door and took the latch off a welded platform holding four one-hundred pound propane canisters and swung the platform close to the door. Two others hustled two of the canisters into the food truck, then swung the platform back out and shut the door.

The canisters had a precision cut, barely visible to the naked eye, near the top, machined for screw-on and screw-off. The crew frantically unscrewed the tops off both canisters.

Volkov reached down into the first canister and pulled out four sets of black overalls that had a State of Texas patch on both shoulders, with a skull and crossbones below it. Light-weight carbon fiber bullet-proof panels were sewn into the fabric on front and back. Each crew member removed his tennis shoes and hurriedly put the overalls on over his work clothes. Then they put on black tennis shoes that were also stored in the canister. Next, four ammo belts at the bottom of the first canister were pulled out, each carrying six magazines holding dozens of .223 rounds of ammunition each.

Volkov switched to the other canister, only to be interrupted by someone knocking at the back door, asking when they would have food again. Volkov yelled that it would be a while, hoping to chase the would-be patron away.

Volkov unscrewed the next canister, carefully removing the first of four fully automatic flat-black rifles. These rifles, sometimes known to gun enthusiasts as *"bullpups,"* had the unique feature of the firing mechanisms being engineered behind the trigger and made part of the gun stock. This made the rifles extremely compact, easily storable, and very maneuverable in tight quarters.

Once all the bullpups were out of the canister, Volkov put his hand fist out to the others waist-high and they bumped fists in unison. He reached to a phone below the counter and dialed a number. Through three other resources, Volkov got an instant update on police presence at the gates.

"Volkov, we will either die today, or we will all be rich beyond our imagination! Screw these Americans!"

Next, each man pulled a costume out of a large cardboard box that would normally carry hamburger buns. They slid these over their overalls. Each costume had a thin black hood that covered most of their faces and all of their heads. The costumes had Velcro attachments that went down the side, which made it easy to rip them off. They hauled medium-sized canvas duffle bags from the corner of the truck. The bags were adorned with stickers of cartoon characters and were half-full of candy. Moving the candy around, they stuffed their rifles into the space vacated by the goodies. Each duffel bag had a strap that went over the carrier's head so the bag was affixed to their bodies, chest high.

Each of the men wore masks of well-known cartoon figures on their heads, ready to pull down over their faces. Except for the different cartoon characters, the four looked identical. Volkov had gone so far as to specifically recruit three other former special operatives, two from Russia and one from Venezuela, who were almost identical in body build and height.

"Synchronize now," instructed Volkov.

The four looked at their watches to sync times.

"Good luck, men! Let's go!"

The door of the Cajun Delight was opened slowly and the men, in full cartoon-character costumes with large duffel bags of candy, stepped down the four metal steps to the truck and walked in four separate directions.

The four cartoon characters spread out on the sprawling festival grounds and, for the next forty-five minutes, they met kids, handing out candy and getting pictures taken with literally dozens of youngsters by their parents. The crowds, especially the parents, were really enjoying how well these cartoon characters interracted with the children.

Volkov had just finished giving some children more candy when he looked at his watch and walked a short distance to the port-a-can area. The festival had set up four separate areas for port-a-cans, including two that were handicapped-accessible. Dozens of festival-goers were lined up at each location.

Volkov calmly walked into an unoccupied handicapped port-a-can, much larger and with more room than the standard port-a-cans, and locked the door. He took his costume and mask off, shoving them back into the canvas bag. Then he pulled the black, thin ski mask over his head, revealing only his eyes. He cocked his rifle to load the first shell and looked at his watch again. He waited two minutes for the top of the hour as he squinted, trying to look through the crack in the door at the crowd went about its business.

At exactly 4:00 p.m., Volkov launched *Madison*.

Opening the door slightly, he looked around for anyone who might be focused on the bank of port-a-cans. All he saw were several dozen people waiting for their turn on the cans.

Aiming the tip of the rifle muzzle barely out the door, Volkov held the trigger down for brief spurts of .223 bullets, spraying through the people standing in line at the cans. Although the rifle had a suppressor, it couldn't disguise the sound of gunfire completely. With the vortex of sounds from four stages and the noise of the carnival rides, nobody outside the immediate area could connect the muffled rat-a-tat-tat of the bullpup rifle with live fire.

Creating a grisly scene, Volkov mowed down everyone standing in the vicinity of the port-a-cans, including some who started to run as people started dropping around them. His goal was to eliminate as many witnesses as possible who saw him step out of the port-a-can. He then turned and showered all the port-a-cans with rounds, instantly killing anyone in the cans doing their business at the worst possible time in their lives.

The screams of the wounded echoed throughout the grounds, sounding eerily like the screams of people on the daring carnival rides. The only thing that would make festival-goers think something was amiss was the unthinkable carnage on the ground around them.

Volkov was indiscriminate. He shot everyone in sight, including children, even putting rounds into baby strollers. Next, he calmly walked out of the port-a-can area with his rifle. He moved around the bank of port-a-cans to the opposite side. Again, he began spraying automatic .223 fire into anyone and everyone. Soon, the crowds began to realize what was happening as blood, guts and the wailing of the wounded began to panic everyone near him. People started running in all directions, with the heaviest concentration sprinting toward the nearest exits.

At first, police were confused about reports coming over their radios, initially thinking a carnival ride had malfunctioned and some people had gotten hurt.

Volkov walked fast in a designated direction, methodically shooting at anything that moved and even at the wounded writhing on the ground. He changed magazines effortlessly, never losing a step and with very few seconds lost to reload. He continued to be indiscriminate, spraying bullets on carnival rides, into food seating areas, and even food trucks. He made a special effort to spray Cajun Delight with bullets as he passed the unmanned food truck, making sure not to hit the tire or the propane tanks that actually contained propane.

Two hundred yards away, one of Volkov's crew was crouched and waiting in another handicapped port-a-can. He had just followed the exact same steps to create the same carnage Volkov was dealing out.

Volkov was down to his last magazine, which was his plan. As he took his last shots, he timed it perfectly to reach the bank of port-a-cans, where his crew member waited, within three very long minutes. Volkov ducked into the can just behind the corner port-a-can holding his crew member, stepped inside, and banged with his fist twice on the back plastic wall. His crew member exited immediately, taking up where Volkov left off, spraying anything that moved, walking briskly in the direction of the next bank of port-a-cans.

Now police and security were beginning to realize the gravity of the situation but, with the chaos that ensued and the brisk movement of Volkov, it was hard to distinguish any accurate location or description.

Once Volkov heard the gunfire resume, he immediately peeled his overalls and mask off and stuck them down into the gross muck of the port-a-can, making sure the overalls, gun and mask were underneath the concoction of chemicals, human urine, and feces. The gun was collapsible and Volkov had no problem sinking it to the bottom of the deposit well in the port-a-can.

Volkov exited the port-a-can wearing his Cajun Delight work clothes and began running as if in panic mode to blend into the crowd back toward his food truck. Numerous times while running, Volkov had to jump over dozens of victims he had killed or wounded on his rampage.

The crew member who had taken up the baton from Volkov had reached the next bank of port-a-cans right on schedule, within three minutes, duplicating Volkov's march of death through the festival in exactly the same method, with exactly the same brutality and disregard for children, adults, elderly or wounded. Two bangs with his fist on the back of the handicapped port-a-can and the next crew member was off and shooting as he buried his clothes and weapon in the slop of feces, exactly as Volkov had.

Finally, the rotation reached the fourth crew member and, within a minute of leaving his port-a-can, he encountered two sheriff's deputies who returned fire but missed him. The deputies, armed only with handguns, were no match for the Russian special ops criminal armed with what amounted to a machine gun. He mowed them down with two short bursts. A man in his mid-forties, crouched behind a metal trash can, opened fire on the crew member from a long distance with a small caliber handgun. He had obviously ignored the weapons ban notice at the entrance. The Russian sprayed the trash can with a burst of armor-piercing .223 rounds that launched the can in the air and knocked the man with the handgun back five yards as the rounds exploded into his chest.

When the fourth and final crew member discarded his clothes and weapon in the same manner, he also ran back to the Cajun Delight.

All four fled the festival through an exit with thousands of others and met at their van as prearranged. The chaos and stampede of people hampered the dozens of police trying to make sense out of the pandemonium.

Reports on the radio indicated there was one shooter, wearing a ski mask, dressed in black overalls with a patch showing an outline of Texas with a skull and crossbones below it. Volkov's plan essentially was like a cattle drive, pushing the crowd to the next shooter, making it much easier to target their victims.

It was cold, calculated, and effective, and it was completely over in twelve minutes, hardly enough time for the police to get organized and mount an effective response in the face of thirty thousand frantic festival-goers running panic-stricken in every direction. They were dealing with wounded and an overwhelming crime scene they couldn't possibly contain.

Police cars, SWAT, and ATF crews reached the festival grounds within ten minutes. Police helicopters appeared overhead, and the police were treating the festival as if an active shooter was still at large. Dozens of ambulances were held at the entrance because they believed an active shooter was still on the premises. Authorities had no idea it was actually four shooters, as they all operated in the same manner, dressed exactly the same, had the same height and build, resulting in the same description by witnesses, and wreaked their despicable butchery in the exact same manner.

Soon, the gleeful sounds of the carnival rides, music and laughter were replaced by the wailing of festival-goers who had seen the unspeakable deaths of their own family members and others, especially children. Slowly, SWAT and people inched their way through the festival acreage, creeping behind every tent, trash can, food truck and vendor booth, not knowing where the shooter was. Brave EMT personnel started to attend to the casualties behind the line of police as they advanced through the festival.

The local ABC affiliate in Dallas was the first to break into regular programming during a college football game with the desk anchor stating, "There has been a mass shooting at the Children's Literacy Festival in south Dallas. Initial reports are…wait a minute… I need to make sure this is correct." She looked over to her producer. "Yes, I'm told this is correct, that there are likely hundreds, yes, hundreds of dead. Oh, my God!" She looked at the producer again. "We will break in as this story develops. We are told there is still an active shooter and this is a scene in progress."

Dallas Chief of Police Harold Birmingham ordered the scene contained, meaning the police would not allow anyone to leave the premises. They closed the interstate from both directions and moved the survivors off the festival property. Some were standing on the frontage road, and even on the interstate. Live helicopter news crews captured the incredible scene on live television.

Initial reports of the bloodshed that came in from police and EMT radios were indescribable. The inordinate number of children killed, coupled with the horrific and traumatic fatal wounds from the armor-piercing rounds, caused many police to stop in their tracks, drop to their knees, and cry. EMTs were overwhelmed, as many were screaming into their radios for more medical assistance and trauma supplies. The stress on police, SWAT, and the ATF was visible in their faces.

Officials tried to separate the crowd into two groups, but the hysteria was so bad that it was a difficult challenge. They tried to separate those people missing relatives and likely still in the festival from those whose families or groups were intact. One combat veteran turned police officer said it was more chaotic than a battlefield scene. Police made people in the crowd hold their hands up because of the possibility that the shooter was mixed into the immense crowd.

The news media, which arrived before the police, could contain the scene and keep them at a distance, mixed with grieving family members, broadcasting the horrific heartbreak and utter panic to the world.

One by one, officials came to each person in the crowd to get names and to ascertain if they had anyone of interest to interview further while the search for the shooter continued, tent by tent, booth by booth and ride by ride. At least four food trucks were on fire, and police believed their propane tanks could explode and endanger the SWAT teams. Fire trucks were slowly making their way through the frontage roads, which had turned into parking lots. Hundreds of officers and SWAT units from nearby communities poured in to assist, with many parking two miles away and hustling on foot to get to the scene.

A sheriff's deputy approached Volkov, who was sitting on the freeway, along with his three crew members, with their hands in the air.

"Your name?" asked the female deputy sheriff.

"Nicoli Orlov," he told her.

"Do you have ID?" she asked.

"It's on my food truck that terrorist shot up! See my truck," he said, pointing to his shirt with Cajun Delight embroidered on it. "He shot my truck. We are lucky we do not die." Volkov motioned toward the fairgrounds. "When can I get my truck?" he asked. "When can I get my truck?"

The deputy seemed disinterested, not noting anything special about this food vendor except that he was a foreigner. She moved on to another person, skipping the crew members entirely. She didn't have a single ounce of suspicion about the crew of the Cajun Delight food truck.

Several hours passed, and bottled water made its way in to relieve the crowd still being held. It soon became clear that hundreds or even several thousand festival-goers had gotten completely off the property, fleeing for safety and possibly allowing the shooter to escape.

At nearly 9:00 p.m., almost five hours after the first shots were fired, the police announced the festival had been fully cleared without finding the shooter, and efforts were focused on identification and recovery of bodies and searching for any wounded or hiding survivors.

A corporate VIP tent that had been set up at one of the festival entrances had been turned into a makeshift morgue, but it soon became obvious that the huge tent was not big enough.

The mayor, who had arrived by helicopter an hour after the shooting began, pulled Chief Birmingham to the side and away from other authorities.

"I know it is really bad, but exactly how bad is it, Chief?" asked the mayor.

"Man, it's horrible. Right now, the body count is over six hundred, sir and we aren't nearly done. The worst part of it is that at least half or more are kids."

"God help us all," said the mayor sorrowfully.

Eventually, as the night wore on, the city brought in buses to take the crowd to three different sites. Officials told the survivors that the passenger cars still at the festival were impounded until the investigation was complete and that it might be weeks before they got them back.

As the news and graphic images, cell phone videos taken by survivors, and other details of the carnage began going viral, the outrage throughout the country built quickly and with extreme intensity.

President Bartlett issued a statement condemning the gun culture, the NRA, and claimed that Congress had not done enough to protect the public from gun violence.

By midnight, the death toll had reached an incredible eight hundred sixty-four dead, including four hundred seventy-three children, the youngest being four months old, shot in his baby stroller. Hospitals throughout the Metroplex had quickly been overwhelmed with level one trauma patients, and medical personnel were caring for another three hundred eight wounded, with more than eighty of those in critical condition. Air ambulances and Life Flight helicopters ran shuttles to other hospitals in Fort Worth and some all the way to Houston.

Volkov and his crew members finally boarded a bus after 11:00 p.m., which took them to a mall parking lot in Arlington where taxis and relatives were waiting to pick up survivors. Each bus had a SWAT member on board who watched the passengers carefully, looking for any clue the shooter might be on their bus.

Volkov and his three crew members stepped off the bus and got in line for a taxi, finally getting one and crowding in. Twenty minutes later, the taxi dropped them off at an apartment complex in Fort Worth. When the taxi was out of sight, the foursome walked three blocks to an office building where they had parked an SUV. Volkov entered the door code, unlocked the SUV, picked up the key fob beneath the front seat, started the vehicle, and pulled out of the parking lot.

Finally, the four let out a deep breath almost in unison, but nobody spoke. Even these hard-core special ops criminals had never conducted an operation where they indiscriminately killed children.

An hour and a half later, the crew reached the county airport in Waxahachie, which was not manned and had no tower. A fueled Cessna 206 was parked and ready to go. Volkov and the crew climbed in and turned on a switch that sent a signal to the airport to light up the runway, then fired up the Cessna and lined up into the wind to head south to Houston.

A little over an hour later, the Cessna, piloted by Volkov, landed at a similar county airport near Houston. By mid-morning, Volkov and one other were on a flight to London, with the other two on a flight to Paris.

Less than twenty-four hours after Volkov fired the first shot in what was the worst mass shooting in American history, all four perpetrators were out of the United States, and authorities had no clues as to the identity of the shooter.

CHAPTER 48

"Oppressors can tyrannize only when they achieve a standing army, an enslaved press, and a disarmed populace."

- James Madison (1751-1836)
Father of the Constitution, 4th US President
Author of the 2nd Amendment

Ottosson stayed close to the news on Saturday afternoon, choosing to stay in his swanky apartment in Alexandria, Virginia, with two television sets on different stations and his iPad, streaming Fox News.

He saw his first news report on the festival in Dallas at 5:40 p.m. local time on ABC. He and Volkov decided mutually to cease communications immediately before and forever after *Madison*.

"Damn, they actually pulled it off," he said to himself. He still worried they would be caught or killed, which would provide clues for authorities to follow up on. The dread of anything being tied back to him regarding this incredibly huge event suddenly became real. He had to keep reassuring himself that Volkov was the ultimate professional.

Throughout the night, Ottosson couldn't sleep as he strained for any news that would indicate the authorities had clues. The plan had always been for communications to go dark at all levels right before and forever after the seismic event that unfolded in Dallas.

Even Ottosson had a hard time digesting the horrible video scenes of carnage that came in showing bloodied children mangled by high-powered bullets.

At 6:00 a.m. the next morning, Ottosson was on his encrypted laptop, keying in wire transfer approvals to two Swiss bank accounts for two million dollars each, one in the Cayman Islands for one million dollars, another one million dollars to the Bank of China for Volkov. These were merely deposits. Other money transfers were guaranteed over the next few months and coming years, as long as the unspeakable crime was never pinned to him or any links to the administration or CIS. Volkov and his team would have enough to retire comfortably for the rest of their lives.

Madison was the worst example of the most brutal and ghastly outgrowth of the *Deep State*.

Meanwhile, President Bartlett met with her cabinet in an urgently called meeting to address the shooting and to consider recommendations on next steps by her staff and cabinet. They decided Bartlett would make a statement live from the Oval Office to the nation that evening regarding the mass shooting.

Immediately after her cabinet meeting, a private meeting was set up in the Oval Office for the president to meet with Chief Justice Haverton and Bartlett's chief of staff, Milton Weingold.

Weingold and President Bartlett met privately while waiting for Haverton.

"Madam President, in this horrific tragedy we have the opportunity to historically change the direction of this country."

"We have a very angry public, Milton. There's always opportunity to make significant strides when the mob is this angry," the president said.

"Yes, indeed. I agree. What was the saying in the Johnson administration? There's always opportunity in chaos?"

"This has to be the turning point on guns and the 2nd Amendment in this country. It should be the death blow," Bartlett told him. "We won't even have to go through the constitutional amendment process to effectively repeal it. The public will be so angry they will accept executive orders and woe be the legislator that has to answer to those pictures of dead kids."

"I would predict you are going to get carte blanche on this, Madam President. The country is outraged. Hell, even in Texas, they're sick of it," boasted Weingold.

"This guy had some kind of Texas patch?" asked Bartlett.

"Yes, and we expect to start leaking reports this morning, tying this event to the IRS bombings. This will start to splinter their independence movement as we tie these radical acts to the groups promoting it. It will discredit them fully, and it won't take long."

"So can you assure me there won't be another *Texas Crisis?*" Bartlett asked seriously, leaning toward Weingold, her arms resting on her folded legs.

"I'm very confident but, after all, these are *Texans* we're talking about." They both chuckled. "It also helps that we now have our man Strasburg in place. He should be able to control things in Austin to some extent."

"Let's hope so," added Bartlett.

"By the way, they named this latest operation *Madison*, Madam President," announced Weingold.

"Really? That's interesting. Why?" she asked.

"After James Madison, the father of the 2nd Amendment. They thought it would be fitting to name this operation after him, considering it should be the death blow to the 2nd Amendment that he was primarily responsible for creating in the first place," Weingold informed her.

"I like it. How fitting," the president agreed.

Weingold's phone rang, and he answered it.

"Sir," announced one of the guards at the gate, "the chief justice has arrived. Shall we let her in?"

"Yes, please," Weingold said.

There was a short wait as Chief Justice Haverton was escorted to the Oval Office. After pleasantries were exchanged, the three sat on the two couches in the room.

"Thank you, Sally, for coming over on short notice. Unfortunately, this tragedy in Dallas gives us a unique opportunity to forever change the gun laws in this country, which I know is a real issue for you," stated the president.

"Of course. Thank you for inviting me, Madam President, and good afternoon to you also, Milton. I would love to hear your approach, especially in light of what happened in Dallas," replied Haverton

"I want to be very direct here, Your Honor. We feel now is the time and the country is ready for some deliberate, swift, and sweeping executive orders to implement immediate common-sense gun control. But we want to do it in a way that you would advise so that the court challenges that would surely follow would be unbeatable in the Supreme Court," said Weingold.

"Your Honor, we also think Congress might actually act for once in the face of this horrible tragedy. Can you lead us through the elements of the legislation that are likely to make it through the Court now that you are our chief justice?" asked President Bartlett.

It was highly unusual and ethically questionable for the president and her chief of staff to be meeting privately with the sitting chief justice in the Oval Office to ask these types of questions. Many previous presidents had discussions with chief justices, but it was usually conducted quietly to at least give some nod to the separation of powers.

But Chief Justice Haverton didn't seem to have an issue with the invitation, especially in light of the circumstances that just occurred in Dallas. After all, she was the president's hand-picked choice to replace Chief Justice Noyner, and she was anxious to reward Bartlett because she went out on a limb and named her chief justice ahead of several other justices who had been on the Court for years.

For the next two hours, President Bartlett, Chief Justice Haverton and Milton Weingold went through a detailed discussion of how to effectively neuter the 2nd Amendment without repealing it.

That evening, the president made her live statement from the Oval Office to address the country regarding the Dallas tragedy. The cameras opened with her sitting at her desk in the Oval Office in a bright blue wool pantsuit with an American Flag brooch on the right collar, looking as if she could cry at any moment:

"My fellow Americans, my heart and the heart of every American breaks for the survivors that are still lying in hospitals recovering from this senseless tragedy and the families of those who lost their husbands, sons, mothers, daughters, aunts, uncles, nephews, nieces, brothers and sisters. We pray that you may find some kind of peace through this very difficult time.

"While this is not the time to politicize issues around gun control and the unique experience that is mass shootings in these United States, I do believe this is a watershed moment. How many more times do we have to see children slain in the streets and, in this particular case, while they were enjoying a children's literacy festival?

"It's time we valued life over guns. It's time Congress actually acts and it's time we ignore the special interests of the gun lobby that perpetuate the myth that someone's right to own a gun trumps the right of these children to live a full life.

"In the next few days, you will see me issue new and sweeping executive orders to curb this type of violence. I urge you to contact your congressman or congresswoman to tell them to stand with me and pass any and all legislation that stops this madness, once and for all.

"There are no more excuses. It's time America joined the rest of the civilized world and rid ourselves of the type of assault weapons that can evoke this type of carnage.

"To those families affected by this tragedy in Dallas, you have my solemn promise that you have the support of this Office, the full resources of the federal government, and our commitment to bring those responsible to justice.

"I ask that America pray for these families. Americans have always been a people that responds to tragedy and takes action. America will remember those fallen, especially the children who lost their precious lives on a bright fall day.

"God Bless those affected families, and God bless America."

The talking heads on most of the news channels praised President Bartlett for her resolute and steadfast determination to change America's course regarding guns.

"This is truly a watershed moment, as the president stated. I believe you will see very real action, and woe be unto those in Congress who don't see the immediate and lasting public opinion on this subject. The gun lobby has to be shaking in their boots tonight because they can't hide behind the terrible images of dead children at a literacy fair in Texas," claimed the CNN analyst.

CHAPTER 49

"You seem... to consider the judges as the ultimate arbiters of all constitutional questions; a very dangerous doctrine indeed, and one which would place us under the despotism of an oligarchy. Our judges are as honest as other men, and not more so. They have, with others, the same passions for party, for power, and the privilege of their corps.... Their power [is] the more dangerous as they are in office for life, and not responsible, as the other functionaries are, to the elective control."

- Thomas Jefferson
3rd US President, Delegate to Continental Congress,
Author of The Declaration of Independence, Founding Father

The Texas Rangers based in the Dallas area arrived on the scene in Dallas within an hour after the shooting had stopped.

Pops Younger had seriously considered boarding a plane in Austin with interim-Governor Strasburg, at his invitation, to get to the fairgrounds as soon as possible. Strasburg wanted to make a statement from the scene and wanted Pops with him, as any photo op with him would do wonders for his political career in Texas.

"I'll be damned if I'm getting on a state-owned bird right now," Pops confided to his second-in-command Dyson.

"It would be good for you and Strasburg to mend fences," answered Dyson. "But I understand why anyone wouldn't want to fly right now."

"There ain't no mendin' fences with a weasel," Pops flatly replied. "Hell, though, we're probably as safe as ever flying with that son of a bitch."

"Sure sounds like that *Free Texas* crew has been getting into that noggin of yours," snapped Dyson, "all them damned conspiracy theories and such!"

Pops knew that at some point he was going to have to trust some others with the information Zach Turner had shared and, although he trusted Dyson, he knew anyone that had the same information was likely in mortal danger. He was extremely hesitant to share anything for fear that the information would get back to someone in the *Deep State*.

Three SUVs containing Pops, Dyson and six other Rangers left Austin and began their caravan to Dallas north on I-35. It was a two-and-a-half-hour trip, and Pops had decided he would begin to fill Dyson in on the intelligence that Turner's group had revealed, but he would do it in small doses. Pops asked Dyson to drive with him as passenger, and the other Rangers would ride in the other two SUVs so he could privately discuss with Dyson what he knew.

Dyson drove in silence for the first hour as Pops began to divulge the irrefutable evidence that Turner, Beard and Turnbow had presented. Eventually this led to a conversation about the governor's plane crash and, although he still didn't have the smoking gun he needed, it was becoming easier to connect the dots to Volkov, which directly implicated Ottosson, CIS and the *Deep State* in the administration. Pops' guess was that the suicide letter by the aircraft maintenance worker was a sham, likely penned by him while Volkov held a gun to the head of his wife and children before he killed all three of them.

"You ain't said much," Pops said, trying to gauge Dyson's response.

"Damn, Pops," Dyson blurted, "in the span of the last hour and a half, you've laid out a conspiracy theory that the chief justice of the Supreme Court was assassinated, our governor's aircraft was taken down, and a state senator was bribed, then killed. And, to top that off, the Russian operative behind these murders is tied to a government lobbyist for a foreign firm that controls the software of almost all the elections held in the United States! Of course, the current administration is involved knee deep in this and the president likely knows? I gotta ask you, Pops, am I understanding all of this correctly?"

"That about sums it up, Dick," Pops said flatly.

"Geez, Pops, besides the fact ain't nobody going to believe it, even if it were true, where the hell do we go with it?"

Dyson's cell phone rang, interrupting their conversation as a Ranger from one of the other SUVs was calling.

"Commander, you may want to turn your radio to a news station right away," the Ranger said urgently.

"Roger," answered Dyson. "Williams says to turn the radio to news; something is breaking…"

Pops turned the knobs trying to find a news station, then flipped it through several AM radio stations to find what the Ranger was referring to before finding one. They listened for a few seconds, then the news anchor dropped a bomb:

"Unnamed sources within the FBI today are reporting that key evidence has been acquired that links the mass shooting in Dallas and the recent IRS bombings to an anti-government militia in Texas with ties to various Tea Party groups and the failed Texas independence movement. The sources stated that two weapons registered to members of that group have been found at the site of the worst mass shooting in history, which claimed the lives of hundreds of children at a festival in Dallas. We expect a formal statement confirming this information later today."

"Please tell me that ain't *your* boy, Pops?" asked Dyson.

"No way in hell, but he does have some gung-ho types he can't control." Pops fished out his cell phone and began slowly dialing out, as if it was the first time he had ever used a cell phone. He dialed a number that had been saved in his phone by someone else

"Turner here. Hello, sir, I guess you have heard the FBI leak?"

"Son, you are about to have a ten-ton shit basket land on your head. Now, I know you ain't got a damn thing to do with this, but I also know you gotta tightly screwed Rambo-type that's off your reservation. Is he capable of this festival mess?" asked Pops.

"Ain't no way in hell, sir," Zach told him. "Yes, he's capable of planning and executing any type of operation that's put in front of him, but I will tell you he is a true patriot through and through. We haven't always agreed on methods, but I'd stake my life on the fact that he didn't go to Dallas and start shooting up those kids. No way. Didn't happen, sir. I've not been in contact with him since the bombings, sir, honest to God."

"Is he capable of the bombings?" Pops asked directly.

"Capable? Yes, hell, we are all capable," answered Zach, referring to many in his *Free Texas* group, "but I have no knowledge of an advance plan of any kind for those bombings."

"Are you sayin' he ain't tied to the bombings whatsoever?" said Pops.

"I'm saying I don't have any direct knowledge, sir. Was he angry at the IRS for disrupting his life and those of some close to him? Absolutely. Is he capable of planning a series of bombs that would instill fear into the IRS employees to even show up for work? Hell, yes! He's also capable of planting those bombs in a manner so nobody got hurt or killed."

"We all hate those SOBs, son, but that ain't the way to approach it. Hell, they are attackin' all of us. Anyone associated with Governor Cooper, from the very start of the independence push," Pops reasoned. "I guess it comes with the territory and folks underestimated how pissed off the rest of the country would be if we took our marbles and went home without them."

"I understand, sir."

"Now, with this new news coming to light, I need to be as straight with you as a Comanche arrow, son. If you are tied to any of this, the evidence you brought me is as good as a dog turd in the sun. Ain't nobody going to see anything but those bombings and those dead kids," pressured Pops.

"As God is my witness, sir, we did not have a thing to do with either event. I can't vouch for Hank Lofton in regard to the IRS bombings. The last time we were together, he was very angry. He and several of his closest buddies have, for all intents and purposes, left our group. But do I think he would shoot innocent civilians like what happened in Dallas, including children? Hell, no. He has children of his own. I don't buy it for one second, sir."

"Okay, son, I believe you. That don't mean *they* will," Pops said, referring to the feds.

"None of my people were even at the festival, sir. I guess they might come question us. Wouldn't be the first time. Even if they arrest us, they got nothing."

Dyson was shaking his head, listening to the conversation and, knowing Pops for almost thirty-five years, knew what he was about to say next.

"That ain't what they are going to do, son. Damn, you should know this more than anyone. Right now, those boys in D.C. want some skins on the wall for that turkey shoot. They ain't going to ask questions. They are going to come to get you and your buddies. And, if you resist, they kill you all, then they have their suspects," said Pops plainly. "Haven't we learned this over the last two years?"

Zach's mind was racing. He knew Pops was right, but every now and then he caught himself thinking life could be normal and he wouldn't be worried about how his political beliefs and push for Texas independence could have warped into the dilemma he now faced.

"If we hunker down and hide, then we look guilty. Do you believe they have any real evidence, sir?"

"They don't need it," Pops said seriously. "They need scapegoats."

"You know they will manufacture evidence, Pops. Whatever they produce that may look like it ties to us on the surface, please do not believe it," begged Zach.

"If you'd told me that ten or fifteen years ago, I would have dismissed it as hogwash. Damned if I know how our government got this screwed up, but I'll tell you what." Pops looked directly at Dyson, who was listening intently. "All these pieces link together—Chief Justice Noyner, the plane crash, and Milsap. God help us all if the government, by God, was involved in this mass shooting."

"No way. I think they are capable of many things, but killing kids for political ideology, no way," muttered Dyson under his breath so only Pops could hear him.

"Sir, the things I have seen while I was in the CIA that our country would do in the name of patriotism or some sort of perverted American interest, would make your heart hurt." His response indicated Zach had heard Dyson's comment. "It's why I got out. The Constitution means nothing to the *Deep State*."

"I'm not sure what to tell you to do at this fork in the road, son. I'll go on up to Dallas and see what we're dealing with. In the meantime, distance yourself from your Rambo dude."

"Already have, sir, already have."

CHAPTER 50

"The right to revolt has deep sources in our history."

> *- Justice William O. Douglas (1898-1980)*
> *U. S. Supreme Court Justice*

B eard rushed into Zach's office in the Bunker.

"Jesus, Zach—look at this. This is a message we intercepted from Ottosson to CIS off one of his encrypted phones," urged Beard.

Madison underway...

"*Madison* underway? What the hell?" Zach exclaimed.

"Look at the time, date stamp!" said Beard.

"You've got to be kidding me!" Zach noted the message was sent approximately fifteen minutes after the first reported shots were fired from the Dallas Literacy Festival. "Do you have messages yet that tie Ottosson to Volkov?"

"No, we don't know how they are communicating. We're tailing Ottosson 24/7 and he hasn't met with Volkov since Alexandria," answered Beard.

"Why in God's Holy Name would CIS be involved in such a dastardly event? It makes no sense to me."

"Boss, it's *Madison... Madison!*" Beard emphasized, becoming instantly animated and referring to his earlier reference to the Founder. "The entire nation is in a *frenzy* over repealing the 2nd Amendment! They murdered Noyner and flipped the Court. We've now got a new chief justice who is openly anti-2nd Amendment. The president is crafting a series of executive orders. Ottosson was a regular at the White House. We've got dead children and families on TV and *we* could be a very convenient scapegoat!"

Zach was stunned. Will walked into the office just as the conversation started, and also read the message from Ottosson.

"Zach, think about it in this context, too. If they can link us to this somehow, it will absolutely be a death blow to the Texas independence movement because they will make us look like far-out, far-right lunatics who would kill children and bomb the IRS. The support the movement has today in Texas would likely evaporate!"

Zach stood, cracked his neck and shoulders and stared out the window in a distant gaze at the Katy prairie. "I've clearly underestimated the *Deep State*. I've got to get a call into Pops as soon as possible"

"Do you want me to see if I can reach him for you?" asked Will.

"Yes, but one more thing," stressed Zach. "We have to implement *Ghost*."

Will was surprised at the suggestion, but Beard wasn't.

"I totally agree," said Beard. "It makes sense when you think about it."

"Worldwide?" asked Zach. "It would be the first time to call *Ghost* worldwide…" He turned back to the others. "Before we do that, I need one more piece of the puzzle. I need our people in Europe. Get them on the satellite," he told Beard, despite the fact that it was nearly midnight in Brussels, where his primary European operative was stationed.

Ten minutes later, Beard had the Brussels contact on their encrypted satellite phones.

"Any leads on Volkov?" asked Zach after apologies for the late hour. "He's completely off the radar. He's got to be out of the country."

"Zach, I just got this information in the last couple of hours. I was waiting for one more piece before I messaged the team. Two of Volkov's known accomplices have turned up dead, one in Brazil and the other in the UK. We've lost track of the other one, which is likely an indication of his fate, too," said the operative. "To me it appears Volkov is erasing evidence. It's a scorched-earth philosophy he has always had. No witnesses, not a scintilla of evidence or possible links to him."

"How in the hell does he get people to sign on with him?" Zach wondered. "They've got to know his history."

"Volkov is a charismatic killer," the operative explained. "He has the innate ability to convince guys who should know better that he is their best friend. It also helps that he pays his people exorbitant amounts of money.

His jobs are so dirty that he commands a king's ransom, but he gets it. When he is done with his accomplices, they either completely disappear, never to be heard from again, or he sends his own kind of message."

"Bodies were found? If that's the case, he's sending a message," said Zach.

"The guy in Brazil was decapitated. His head was put in a microwave."

"Geez."

"In London, that body was found with his genitals in his mouth." the operative said.

"Are you sure these are the men we identified in Alexandria?"

"Affirmative," confirmed the Brussels guy.

"So, this is a message, but to whom?" Zach asked.

"Maybe the third dude is in hiding and it's a message to him?"

"Volkov ain't going to leave loose ends," Zach stated firmly. "He'll get this guy. He always does. I'm sure if the guy is alive, he's gone completely underground."

"Hmm, we'll have to figure it out."

Thoughtful, Zach thanked the operative. "I appreciate the info. Please contact me if you get any additional information."

"Man, you've got a shit storm there back in Texas. Good luck!"

"Thanks, we need it, but your info is invaluable," Zach told him. "Appreciate it as always!"

Zach hung up his satellite phone and sat down at a table with his team.

Will walked back in. "I haven't reached Pops yet."

"Implement *Ghost* now…" Zach said calmly.

Zach asked for the rest of the crew to be brought into the conference room, and for the entire team to get on an encrypted satellite conference call in two hours.

Two hours later, Zach had his entire team worldwide on the conference call, with some participating in the wee hours of the morning, based on where they were located.

"Let me be very clear," Zach announced. "It's our belief here that Lofton and his team are behind the IRS bombings. Although it's not an understatement to say that we enjoy seeing IRS employees fearful about going to work, what this has done has brought increased federal scrutiny on us, and you can bet your britches that we're about to have the full weight, power and vengeance of the United States government drop squarely on our heads. Although I do not have any proof, I'm sure we can thank Hank and his team for this, as he has handed them a very convenient reason to launch on us."

"Please tell us, Zach, that Hank is not involved in Dallas," said the operative from Brussels.

"We have no reason to be believe that is the case. In fact, we just received evidence that this is a massive conspiracy orchestrated by the *Deep State*, and it has Volkov's fingerprints all over it. We know he has gone completely underground, and two of his trusted associates have turned up dead and mutilated," said Zach.

"Is Volkov still the lead suspect on the plane crash?" asked another.

"The feds *officially* don't believe the crash was anything but an accident. Texas Ranger Pops Younger, who has turned out to be a very good friend of this organization, is convinced Volkov orchestrated that crash and the double-murder suicide of the mechanic and his family. Beard theorizes Volkov got to the fuel tanks and added a coagulant to the fuel that stalled the engines, leading to the crash. It sure appears that way, but the NTSB is focused on pilot error."

"Wait a minute, slow down. Are you telling us the federal government is somehow involved in the murder of those children?" pressed a U.S. operative. "I know they are capable of unspeakable crimes, but are you telling us *our* federal government is complicit in this mass shooting?"

"We have intercepted a text from Ottosson going to CIS that the code name they were using for some kind of operation was underway. It was sent fifteen minutes after the shooting started. The code name was *Madison*."

Almost in unison, groans came from several operatives on the call. They all knew the significance of *Madison* regarding the 2nd Amendment.

"How far does this go, Zach?" asked another.

"We have to assume, and we believe it goes all the way to the White House."

"Jesus, Zach, and now they're trying to pin the IRS bombings and *this* on us? What the hell are we going to do? This is going to get serious fast," stated another operative.

"If they are coming after us, which plan are we implementing?" asked an operative in D.C.

"By midnight tonight Central Time, I am implementing *Ghost*," Zach announced. "I don't suggest you wait that long."

There was a momentary silence on the phone.

Ghost was an operational term that, when implemented, mandated that all operatives were to go completely underground. It meant tightly controlled communications on a limited basis, on highly secure platforms only. It also meant operatives with families were to go to predesignated safe houses off the grid and known only to the individual operatives.

Zach implemented this silo approach to secrecy because of the high probability of torture being used. No matter how badly an operative was tortured and eventually broken, the operative wouldn't have the knowledge to disclose his compatriots' whereabouts.

To this group, *Ghost* meant total disruption of operatives' family lives if they had spouses, kids in schools, and some semblance of a normal life, for an undetermined amount of time. Zach's team was made up of ultimate preppers and, if there was any group of individuals who could instantly vanish and not only survive but thrive, this was it.

"Zach, do you believe this is absolutely necessary? You know many of us have wives and children. You know what this ultimately means to us?" asked the D.C. operative.

"Team, this is Will Turnbow. I hate to say it, but you can partly thank Lofton for this. Y'all know Zach. We have never had to do a worldwide *Ghost*. If Zach is calling for it, rest assured your lives and the lives of your families are in jeopardy."

"Do we have specific intelligence that the feds' actions are imminent and in what timeframe?" asked another. "Are we implementing *Ghost* strictly based on what CNN is reporting and on this text?"

Will was annoyed that anyone would think Zach would implement *Ghost* without extreme prejudice.

"That CNN report was based on an actual leak; it was not supposed to be released. We believe they are moving on us as we speak," Will stated unequivocally.

"So there is no separate specific intelligence that supports the CNN report?" the same operative pressed.

"Beard and his team have successfully hacked the CIS data centers in four locations. He is breaking down encryption protocols, but it may take several days. I don't believe we can afford to take that chance, based on what we know at this point."

"Zach, it's time to grab that son-of-a-bitch Ottosson. A little rendering of him will reveal a lot," suggested another operative, suggesting kidnapping Ottosson, taking him to another country, and using advanced interrogation techniques to gain intelligence.

"In due time. He's somewhat of a useful idiot to us right now. Sending that text about *Madison* was about as amateur as you get," Zach told them. "Let's all remember he's not CIA, MI6 or Mossad. He's a damned lobbyist and a semi-accomplished wealthy criminal who thinks he can operate at our level. Like every criminal, he'll make mistakes."

"Besides, even if you had Ottosson, he's likely not being told the plans the FBI, ATF and Homeland have for us," added Will.

"That's absolutely true," agreed another operative.

"There's a *Deep State* master plan here, gentlemen, and we are getting closer to figuring it out every day. It's also possible that this cancer runs so deep and is so evil that we really never comprehended how embedded it is in our political systems and government bureaucracies. It is beyond anything we originally envisioned," Zach stated.

"Are we all on board?" asked Will.

"*Ghost* it is," said the D.C. operative.

"Affirmative. *Ghost* is implemented for all operatives," said Zach.

CHAPTER 51

"I have no reason to suppose, that he, who would take away my liberty, would not, when he had me in his power, take away everything else."

- John Locke (1632-1704)
English philosopher and political theorist

D yson handed the cell phone to Pops. "It's your buddy Turner."
Pops took the phone and walked a few steps for privacy.

"Younger here."

"Pops, I'll make this very short and to the point. I know you are at the mass shooting site. That shooting is tied to Ottosson and Volkov. It was *Madison*, named after James Madison who penned the 2nd Amendment. That damned shooting was a *Deep State* operation, sir," stated Zach firmly.

"You are sure of this? You have proof?"

"We have an Ottosson text message intercepted fifteen minutes after the shooting that *Operation Madison* had begun."

Pops was silent for a few seconds as he tried to digest what Turner was telling him.

"My Jesus… The world is going to hell in a handbasket right in front of us," lamented Pops.

"Sir, not sure if you are hearing the news reports, but they are trying to tie this on us, this and the IRS bombings. We are about to go underground. You won't be able to reach me through normal channels. I'll have to reach to you from time to time as I have opportunities."

"Son, I may need you and I have to have a way to get hold of you."

"Give me twenty-four hours, sir, and I'll have another method. I'll be in touch soon. Give 'em hell up there."

As Zach hung up, Pops stood silent for a few minutes as Dyson watched from a distance.

"What the hell was that about?" asked Dyson, who knew full well by Pops' reaction that he just learned something important and likely to do with the mass shooting.

"Dick, this shooting wasn't no crazy nut job. This was a cold and calculate assassination of these kids for political purposes."

"No way? Are you serious?"

"Let's get in there. Those boys in that tent are over their damned heads."

Pops Younger stood in a packed circus-sized tent on the site of the mass shooting in Dallas with dozens of other law enforcement officers from the FBI, ATF, Homeland Security, Dallas police and various other agencies that Pops didn't even recognize. The media was kept out of the tent.

Pops was the most experienced law enforcement official in the tent, yet nobody solicited his opinions on solving the largest mass shooting of its kind in American history.

That morning, the Dallas police chief stopped them all in their tracks as the discussions became heated on what evidence existed that there was more than one shooter. Nobody had found a weapon up to that point. Law enforcement had combed every vendor tent, trailer and trash can to find any evidence of who was responsible.

Pops breathed a sigh of relief as he realized the news report he had heard on the way to the Dallas shooting site had no basis in fact. He wondered who the "unnamed source" was that had provided misleading information to gullible media.

"We have literally searched every square inch of this site, and there is no weapon," claimed the FBI regional director, who somehow had inherited de facto control over the investigation despite the fact it was Dallas police jurisdiction, and the chief wasn't happy about it.

"I've heard theory after theory. We have no weapon, and no lead on the shooter," claimed the FBI regional director.

"He obviously got his weapon off the grounds somehow," offered another agent.

"From what I understand, in the chaos that ensued, anything was possible. We have positive ID on one shooter and the description was the same from all witnesses so far. He had to have gotten out with the weapon," offered the ATF lead agent.

Frustrated with the progress of the investigation so far, the Dallas police chief looked around the tent and found Pops standing in the background, easy to spot with his tall lean stature and wearing his signature Stetson cowboy hat.

"Pops, can you come up here a minute and tell us what you think?"

A couple of groans came from federal agents, one even saying under his breath, "Gee, now we get to hear the hick with the cowboy hat," barely audible, but loud enough for those immediately around him to hear.

Pops moseyed up to the front of the tent.

"Ladies and gentlemen, this is Pops Younger, commandant of the Texas Rangers. Proud to have you here, Pops," he said, as several dozen Texas-based law enforcement types starting clapping. The federal agents, still sore about their tangles with Pops and the Rangers during the *Texas Crisis,* were not amused.

"Pops, have you walked the grounds? What did you notice?" asked the chief.

"I did," Pops said plainly.

"You got a theory, Pops?"

"How many rounds we got?" asked Pops, referring to number of shots fired.

"We are still gathering casings, but it's got to be several thousand rounds. These were .223 rounds, likely an AR-15," answered the ATF lead.

"How long did the shootings last?" asked Pops.

"No more than fifteen minutes, according to the sheriff's deputies who were onsite," answered the chief.

"You got ballistics back?" asked Pops.

The officers in the room looked around as if nobody knew who was in charge of ordering ballistics.

"The FBI crime lab is on it, should have results in a day or two," the director answered.

"There was some sensitivity to extracting bullets from bodies until remains were identified," said the ATF agent, but it was suddenly obvious that this basic step in solving a crime was temporarily overlooked.

"I'd check those reports carefully; you're likely to have more than one shooter," Pops claimed to an immediate uproar of resistance.

"What the do you base that on, sir?" asked a Homeland Security official.

"Thousands of rounds from one AR-15 in fifteen minutes? That barrel must of lit up like a Christmas tree. I ain't no gun expert, but I'm sure you boys can tell me if all makes of AR-15s could endure that rate of fire without jamming or becoming too hot to hold. Hell, I don't know; I'm asking you?" chuckled Pops as if he knew something they didn't.

Nobody knew the answer to the question.

"Are you done collecting shell casings?" asked Pops.

"I think so," said the chief, turning to the FBI director. "Are we?"

"Yes, we think we have all the shell casings marked and collected."

"Have you compared the number of shell casings to the discarded magazines? Does it match up, or is it even close?" asked Pops.

The FBI director looked panicked. He turned to his team as his second in command huddled with some other agents as they took out their pens and paper notebooks. Another agent punched out numbers on his calculator app on his iPhone. He then looked back at the director and shook his head.

"Mind sharing with the rest of us what you boys just ciphered up?" asked Pops.

"Ciphered? What the hell is that?" asked a federal agent from Connecticut to another agent standing next to him.

"Must be Texas talk for calculating is my guess," he answered.

"I think we must be off here in our count. We need some time to review the numbers and go back out to the fairgrounds and count the marking flags," said the lead ATF agent.

"My bet is you ain't going to match up," answered Pops, to quizzical looks from dozens of faces.

"What's your theory, Pops?" asked the Dallas chief.

"Wasn't just one shooter," Pops said flatly.

An uproar went up from the feds. Pops reached over to one of the tables and grabbed a red plastic cup that obviously belonged to one of the FBI agents. He spit tobacco juice in it, totally oblivious to the feds, who were essentially mocking him.

"I don't follow, Pops," said the chief.

"You want my boys to search the fairgrounds? Has anything, and I mean anything, left the fairgrounds yet?" asked Pops.

"Sure, if you want to, go ahead. Nothing has left. We do have a request, however, from the port-a-can company to take out their units. They have about three hundred here and they have a contract to set them up at the State

Fair of Texas at the Cotton Bowl in three weeks. They need time to dump, clean and re-deliver them. They have about six trucks waiting at the gate for entry when we give them the okay. They are also getting fairly rank," reported the chief.

Pops rubbed his mustache and looked down at his cowboy boots, deep in thought.

"We've already looked in each and every can, Mr. Younger," said the FBI agent.

"You boys then won't mind if mine take a look? What about all the vendor and food trailers?" asked Pops, as the FBI lead was starting to become irritated that Pops was asking him how well they did their job.

"Go right ahead, cowboy," he snarled sarcastically. "If you don't mind, my team is going to follow yours just to make sure our crime scene remains intact."

Pops walked out with his Rangers, followed by a couple of dozen federal agents, the police chief, and several detectives. One detective turned to another, "Wow, we actually get to see Pops Younger work a crime scene! You don't get to see this every day!"

"Show me where the first shots were reported, if you will?" asked Pops politely.

"It's quite a walk, sir. They were first reported in the northwest corner of the fairgrounds."

"Okay, let's go," answered Pops.

The large contingent walked to where the first shots were reported. Everywhere they looked, they could see small evidence flags marking spots where shell casings were found. Pops and the Rangers surveyed the area, walking carefully around the markings, pointing to certain areas and talking among themselves.

Pops walked over to the corner bank of port-a-cans.

"There's a heavy concentration of casings here, next to this handicapped can," he noted to the chief as he stood next to the can and looked in front of it and behind it.

"Quite a few shots fired from this location but, if he was hiding behind the can to shoot, the casings would be back here instead of in front of it," Pops noted.

Nobody said a thing, except Dyson, who was standing next to Pops. "These shots were in front of the can."

"Did your boys look in these cans?" he asked the FBI director.

"Of course, we did," the director answered indignantly.

Pops reached over and slowly opened the door to the port-a-can, careful not to step in. He peered into the smelly unit, slowly taking everything in. Several others stepped back due to the smell.

Then, to the surprise of everyone, Pops stepped into the port-a-can, asking Dyson to hold the door.

"Got us one right here, boys." He turned to the FBI director. "Your boys must have missed these," he smirked.

"Missed what? What the hell are you talking about?" The FBI lead stuck his head in the can.

"There's a casing in the urinal right there." Pops pointed. "There's another one right there, too," he said, pointing to the slop below in the toilet. A shell casing could barely be seen poking out of the mixture of feces, urine, toilet paper and chemicals. Pops stepped out so the FBI director could get a clearer view.

Pops took a deep breath once he got out.

"Son of a bitch, you guys missed these. How the hell did they get in here?" he asked his team, absolutely disgusted that it took Pops less than twenty minutes to find evidence his team didn't find.

"How the hell did casings get in there?" asked a detective.

"The shooter was taking shots from inside the can. I'll bet there's more shell casings in that crap," said Pops.

"How the hell do we find them? Nobody is going fishing in that stuff!" said the chief.

Dyson instructed another Ranger to go speak to the port-a-can vendor to find out how they were dumped and if there was a way to screen each can when dumped. Several FBI and ATF agents followed them back to the big tent used as the investigation headquarters.

Pops then walked around the entire bank of cans before asking where the next set was. They all walked several hundred yards, past hundreds of casing markers to the next bank of cans, only to once again find a concentration around a corner handicapped access port-a-can.

Pops opened the door, and again found three casings in this one.

The FBI director was livid and didn't hide his anger from his agents.

This time, Pops stayed in the can, staring into the abyss for what seemed like too long to everyone who was watching him from outside the door.

"Fetch me a stick," he said.

"A stick?" asked the chief. "You going fishing in there, Pops?" he chuckled.

"Somethin' like that," Pops answered.

Nobody knew what to get Pops, but another ranger pulled a three-foot-long wooden tomato stake, that had been used to anchor a vendor tent, out of the ground. He took it over to Pops.

Pops took the stake and slowly stuck it down the toilet and began to slowly stir the murky concoction, then stopped.

"I need something with some kinda hook on it," Pops yelled out.

"What the hell has he got?" asked another detective.

"I don't know yet," answered Pops. "I need something with a hook of some type."

Now everyone was curious what the hell this Texas Ranger was doing, stirring the nasty concoction in the toilet of a port-a-can.

"You thinking what I'm thinking, Dick?" Pops asked Dyson in a low voice.

"I hope you're right, Pops, or these boys here will be laughing at us all the way back to D.C."

Pops walked back out of the can and reached for a cigar from the front of his pearl snap western shirt, bit the end off, and lit it up.

"I need something to kill that damn smell," he said to no one in particular.

"We've got somebody getting something for you that might work," said the chief. "Give him a few minutes and he'll be here with it. Had to go back to his patrol car."

Ten minutes later, a Dallas police officer showed up with an iron tool used to unlock a locked car. It was thicker than a coat hanger and much stiffer, with a small hook on the end used to open door handles or door locks once a wedge was placed on the window to allow the officer to breach the window and fish for the handle inside.

"That just might do the trick," said Pops, as he took it from the officer, looked it up and down and took his hat off and handed it to Dyson. "Don't need any unnecessary accidents," he said, referring to the possibility of his Stetson dropping into the toilet.

Pops took the tool and stuck it down into the toilet, carefully using it to feel around. He had felt something out of place with the wooden stake; now he wanted to pull out whatever it was he felt.

Minutes went by. Nothing. Pops held a handkerchief over his mouth and nose to try to stifle the smell.

"There we go," he said, as a crowd gathered around the door opening.

Slowly, Pops maneuvered the tool. It was obvious he had hooked *something*, but what?

"Back up! Back up!" Pops yelled. "Make a hole!"

Dyson began to back everyone up.

As Pops slowly pulled up out of the port-a-can toilet with the tool, a dark object began to appear. He pulled it completely from the toilet, then swung around, careful to back out slowly, as the dark object was dripping with the rancid concoction from the toilet.

As he backed out of the can, he could hear gasps.

"Are you freakin' kidding me?" said the police chief.

Pops held up a bull pup AR-15 with collapsible stock and pistol grip and let it fall onto the grass.

"I'll be damned," said the FBI director.

Several Dallas police began clapping.

"How the hell did you know that was in there?" the ATF lead agent asked.

"Son, I go where the evidence leads me. Shell casings were *inside* the can. Nobody saw anyone leave with a weapon. Where would be the perfect place to hide it? Where nobody else will look."

"So, are you saying our shooter calmly walked out with the crowd?" asked the chief.

"Or your *shooters* calmly walked out," replied Pops. "If the other cans show this concentration of casings, it means shots were fired from inside the cans. Now, if you boys are telling me all these rounds were shot in fifteen minutes, how the hell could a shooter get that far in that short of time, calmly and methodically walking through the fairgrounds as your witnesses have declared? But, more important, why would he bother to get into a can and shoot from *inside* it once the melee started?"

"And, if this is where the shooting started, why is the gun in the place where it began instead of where it ended?" Dyson added.

"Damn, Pops. That makes sense!" said the chief.

Pops took three steps toward the FBI director.

"Here you go. I know this is your crime scene, so you might want to get your boys to go fishing in the other couple of hundred cans." He handed the director the car unlocking tool that was covered in fecal muck almost to the top.

The FBI director's face turned beet-red.

"Now, you educated types will likely want to fish every can but, if you have more of these handicapped cans on the ends of the rows with a heavy concentration of shell casings on the ground outside of them, that's where I would start. You may find the weapons of the *other* shooters," said Pops as he put his hat on after Dyson handed it back to him, then reached into his back pocket to take a pinch of snuff.

Later that day, after fishing all of the cans, the FBI found three more identical weapons in the exact cans Pops predicted.

"Damn, Pops was right!" exclaimed the chief after learning his agents pulled out three more weapons from the handicapped port-a-cans.

"Whose mind works like that anyhow?" asked the FBI director, trying to brush off Pops' law enforcement brilliance. "How could you think someone would literally hide a gun down a toilet?" He made sure Pops could overhear their conversation.

"Son, one thing I've learned from the bad guys is that I can't deduce a damned thing about how a criminal mind works. Every crime I've been involved with throughout my time as a Texas Ranger that wasn't solved by a confession was solved through *evidence*. Your boys miscounting those shell casings, as compared to the number of recovered magazines, didn't make no sense to me. Neither did that many shots in that short of a timeframe by one shooter. Simple as Sunday afternoon's apple pie."

"Spare me the Texas country colloquialisms, cowboy," snarled the director. "You got a theory on the shooters and their motive?"

"I do, in fact. But I ain't ready to share it just yet. Let's just say this was a major political statement for now," answered Pops.

"Political statement? How is killing children a political statement?" asked the director.

"When it serves a greater *evil* cause," Pops stated as he calmly walked out of the tent.

CHAPTER 52

"Positive laws are tyrannical. One's individual rights—whether they be life, liberty, or property—must be sacrificed by the state in order to fulfill the positive rights of another."

> *- Mark Da Vee*
> *Political Commentator, Blogger & Author*

Senator Kevin Simpson walked into the closed-door meeting of the Senate Intelligence Committee. Guards were posted at the two separate doors that were the only entry and exit into the meeting.

Simpson, a former federal prosecutor from Dallas, chaired the committee and had garnered a lot of favor from the D.C. elite because of his unpopular stance in Texas in opposition to the independence referendum. He spoke out against it, loudly and often. He was a favorite of the establishment.

Simpson was up for election in eighteen months but had only recently gotten a Republican primary challenger. A hard-core Texas nationalist was gaining momentum and his donations from individual donors were surprisingly strong. Simpson, a four-term senator with an eight-million dollar campaign war chest, would be hard to beat, even though his popularity was at an all-time low in Texas.

"I call this meeting of the United States Senate Intelligence Committee to order," said Simpson as he struck the gavel in front of him.

"I second," said a senator from Kansas.

"Fellow Senators, we have a short agenda today. We welcome the presence of FBI Director Nelson, who will answer any questions the committee may pose on the matters at hand. On our docket is Top Secret information from the NSA regarding current FISA court actions with respect to domestic terrorism. I will ask our colleague, Senator Hill, to summarize the report."

"Senator Simpson, before we begin, let us all express our sincere condolences for the tragic mass shooting that took place in Dallas," said Senator Rockley from Oregon.

In mutual agreement, all the senators lowered their heads for a moment of silence.

"My fellow senators," said Senator Hill after the pause, "today we have an update from the NSA on known and existing militia groups and their relationship with the Texas independence movement and various Tea Party organizations the FBI has linked to this horrible mass shooting. What you have in front of you is a summary of the initial findings. To be clear and to get to the point quickly, it appears guns were staged at various locations within the fairgrounds so that the shooter could shoot one gun, dispose of it and then pick up another and begin shooting again as he made his way through the fairgrounds. The ATF and FBI found four guns in total and forty magazines disposed of at random as the shooter emptied them. This was a carefully orchestrated and methodical attack for maximum carnage.

"The FBI has traced these weapons by serial numbers to members of these various groups, including the paramilitary pro-independence group, *Free Texas*, whose identities are linked to multiple militias and Tea Party organizations. These folks are far-right freaks. I move that this committee adopt a resolution re-authorizing FISA court warrants that allow for unrestricted surveillance."

"I second," said a senator from California.

"Hold up, hold up, I've got a few questions, please, before we just ramrod this through," said Senator Galvin from Kentucky, who was widely known to be somewhat Libertarian and extremely protective of any incursion into American civil liberties.

"I recognize the objection from the senator from Kentucky," said Simpson. "Please state your objections for the record."

"For the record? Is this committee stating that this top-secret meeting that required security clearance is on the record? That would be good. I'm all for it. Just want to be clear," stated Galvin.

"It's on the record for the committee, but it won't be shared outside of the committee," answered Simpson.

"Well, it may be subpoenaed someday, so I'm happy to be on the record. First, the resolution says this is a re-authorization of existing FISA warrants? I have no record of this committee being involved in those original FISA requests. When were those original FISA warrants issued and when did this committee see them? I have never missed a committee meeting, and I have no record of this request."

"Senator Galvin, we were not privy to the original FISA warrants. The FBI and the administration obtained those warrants in their normal course of business and obviously did not need our input or oversight to obtain them," stated Simpson

"I would ask the chairman then, if that is the case, why it is this committee is asking for a resolution for the continuance of an *existing* FISA court warrant?" pressed Galvin

"I would offer to the committee that, in light of the tragedy in Dallas, the FBI is requesting extraordinary surveillance authorizations on those suspected to be involved with the IRS bombings and mass shooting. I think this committee owes the FBI our full support," Simpson said pompously, followed by "hear, hear" from several other senators.

"I would ask FBI Director Nelson to explain what is extraordinary about these FISA warrants. The FBI didn't need our permission before. How many times have these existing warrants been renewed?" Galvin pointed his questions at Nelson, who was sitting at a table by himself facing the twenty-two committee members.

"Senator, these FISA court warrants are now on their sixth ninety-day renewal cycle," answered Nelson.

"Sixth? These warrants that last ninety days have been renewed five previous times?"

"Yes, Senator."

"Then please explain to the committee why, after five previous renewals of these warrants by the FISA court, you are sitting here in this meeting asking for this committee's blessing? I don't get it." Galvin paused as he glanced to other senators on the committee, who were not asking what seemed to him to be an obvious question.

"We are asking the court to expand the number of suspects under surveillance, Senator Galvin. That's about the extent of it."

"I still don't get it, Mr. Nelson. Mr. Chairman, there is nothing on this printed summary brief that would indicate Mr. Nelson's explanation as to why this is extraordinary. Mr. Nelson, can you help me, or any other senator on this committee, fully understand why you felt you would like to have this committee's blessing to expand this FISA warrant after you have renewed it five previous times without it?"

"As I stated, Senator, we are asking the FISA court to expand the surveillance in light of the IRS bombings and the mass shooting," Nelson responded.

"Okay, I must really be dense. Let's start with this. How many people were on the original FISA Warrant"?" Galvin asked.

"Two hundred sixty-four, Senator."

"Wow. Really? And the suspected crime was what?"

"It was national security interests related to the *Texas Crisis*," answered Nelson.

"How many people are on this FISA court warrant you have before us today?" demanded Galvin.

Director Nelson looked at the chairman, hesitant to answer.

"Senator, I'm not sure I'm at liberty to say."

"What? Then what the hell are we all doing here today? There is obviously something extraordinary in this request for our blessing. Mr. Chairman, I am trying to get to the root of why you have called this hearing."

"The senator from Kentucky has two minutes left," interrupted Simpson.

"Okay, then let's try this again, Director. What is the exact reason you are asking us for a top-secret resolution for a FISA court warrant that you have already renewed five previous times? I would like a very direct answer, sir!" demanded Galvin.

"My presence here was requested by the president," Nelson stated, to the obvious discomfort of several on the committee.

"For the record, I will ask our stenographer to delete that comment," Simpson instructed.

Galvin, who was extremely annoyed with Simpson's request, had to think fast and pick his argument. The chairman had only allowed him a few minutes and challenging Simpson about a strike of a comment on the record would likely leave him little time for the director.

"We can debate that strike later, Mr. Chairman. Now, Director, exactly why would President Bartlett ask you to come down here and get what really amounts to political cover to request a blessing on a five-time renewed FISA court warrant? Is it because the sixth renewal is the magic number? I need your direct answer right now, Director."

Nelson reached for his water and took a gulp.

"I'm waiting, Director."

"The senator from Kentucky has one minute."

"Yeah, yeah. Director, what is your answer before this committee?" demanded Galvin as he slid to the front of his chair to get closer to the mic, and thus louder in the committee room, for emphasis.

"Senator, beside the fact that this is the sixth renewal request of this FISA warrant, we have been unsuccessful in the surveillance of several key suspects, which is why this has been renewed so many times."

"*Bull crap, Director*! I'm sure the FBI has to renew FISA warrants all the time because you haven't uncovered enough evidence in a surveillance that would lead to an indictment in hundreds of cases. What are the special circumstances that are so important to the president, who has directed you to be here before us."

"The senator from Kentucky has thirty seconds."

"Director?"

"We are asking the FISA court to greatly expand the surveillance."

"In what terms, Director? In scope? In methods? Expand how?"

"Yes, methods for sure, but specifically number of suspects," Nelson finally responded.

"Okay, now we are getting somewhere. Your last warrant was two hundred sixty-four. What is your current request to expand the number of suspects?"

"Uhh-um," the Director cleared his throat. "Twenty thousand, two hundred eleven suspects."

"Excuse me? Can you please repeat that number? I don't think this committee heard it correctly."

"Twenty thousand, two hundred eleven, Senator."

Galvin was incredulous, "You absolutely *cannot* be serious, Director. You are sitting here asking this committee to bless a FISA court warrant to surveil twenty-one thousand Americans? Are you insane? Is the president insane?"

"Order. Order. Order. Mr. Galvin, your time is up." said Simpson.

"Mr. Chairman, I asked the director who exactly makes up the twenty-one thousand individuals and what suspected crimes does he have that justifies a surveillance warrant on each of them?" demanded Galvin.

"The senator from Kentucky, your time is up," stated Simpson as he brought his gavel down.

Galvin, now standing, directed his vitriol toward Simpson. "Mr. Chairman, I ask that any senator on this committee yield their time to me to continue this extremely important questioning, or to continue this same line of questions to Director Nelson!"

"The chair recognizes your request, and we will proceed," continued Simpson.

One by one, as the floor was yielded to senator after senator, not one senator yielded time back to Galvin, who was becoming increasingly frustrated. If a senator asked Director Nelson a question, it was either a question everyone already knew the answer to or a line of questions that did not follow the same track that Galvin took. Most of the senators didn't even ask a question, taking an opportunity to laud law enforcement for the response to the Dallas mass shooting or, in the case of the Democratic senators, to sing the praises of the hard-working average Internal Revenue Service employees who were now terrorized over the bombings.

Down to the very last senator, a Republican from Wyoming, Simpson declared, "The floor is yielded to the senator from Wyoming, Senator Kettering."

"Mr. Chairman, let me state that I, like the good senator from Kentucky, have grave concerns over the scope and size of this FISA warrant request. Therefore, in the interest of time, I yield the remainder of my time to the senator from Kentucky."

Simpson was incensed that Kettering broke from the rest of the Republicans to allow Galvin to press his line of questioning. Simpson had assured Chief of Staff Weingold that this hearing would be a formality and that he would keep tight controls. It was important to the president that, at any point now or in the future, this FISA warrant was not considered an executive branch overreach, was legal and that Congress, and specifically the Senate, had agreed to the extraordinary FISA requests and were fully on board.

"Thank you, Senator Kettering. I'll get right to it. Mr. Nelson, who are the twenty-one thousand people on this list? I have no attachment with names. How does this committee know who it is you are surveilling?"

"Senator, that list is considered Top Secret and we did not make a copy of it for this hearing." Nelson said.

"Why not, Mr. Nelson? Every person on this committee has Top Secret clearance. Surely, as the FBI director, you are aware of that."

"Senator, yes, we are aware but are mindful that copies of that list could get out."

"So you are saying members of this committee would not hold those documents and would distribute those willy-nilly, despite the fact that we have clearance and are entrusted with sensitive intelligence documents on a regular basis? I don't buy it, Director!"

Director Nelson didn't offer any other explanation, but just sat there waiting for the next question.

"Mr. Chairman, I respectfully ask for a two-hour recess so that the FBI director can march back over to his office and produce a list of the twenty-one thousand Americans he plans to surveil for review by this committee."

"The senator's request is denied," stated Simpson flatly. "It is this committee's opinion that we have government employees at the IRS in immediate danger, that the suspect in the mass shooting of children is still at large, and that any unnecessary delays jeopardize the lives of IRS employees and the administration of justice for those children killed. I will, however, change my mind and offer a procedural vote for a recess."

Simpson took a quick voice vote and Galvin was easily defeated for the recess, with only Kettering voting for recess with him.

"The senator from Wyoming had two minutes remaining."

"I yield the remainder of my time to the senator from Kentucky," said Kettering again.

"Mr. Nelson. Again, I will ask you, who are the twenty-one thousand Americans you are asking the FISA court to allow unfettered surveillance activities on?" Galvin demanded.

"Senator, these are people the agency, the NSA and Homeland Security believe have ties to organizations that likely participated in the IRS bombings and in the mass shooting in Dallas."

"Mr. Nelson, that is a huge number. Are you telling me that you have substantial evidence of a conspiracy that seeks to kill IRS agents and children, so large that you need unrestricted warrants on twenty-one thousand people?"

"Senator, what our information tells us is that these anti-government groups are so pervasive that they have a sophisticated network of militias that is much larger than most of us realize," answered the director.

"Let me ask you a few questions about these people on your list," pressed Galvin. "Are there any Tea Party groups represented on this list?"

"I'm not sure, Senator. Based on our information, I would expect so."

"That's very interesting, Director, in that you are probably aware I am very active in Tea Party groups, and I would *never* consider them anti-government unless that designation is in your agency's mind and that of this and past administrations. Is asking your government to follow the U.S. Constitution somehow *anti-government*? Am I on your list, Director?"

"I do not believe you are on that list, Senator."

"Are there any other people who hold political office on that list, Director?"

"Yes, Senator. Unfortunately," Nelson responded.

"How many are Democrats? How many are Republicans?"

"Senator, I do not know the answer to that question as we sit here today."

"Would you guess that there are more Republicans than Democrats on this list for surveillance?"

"Probably, Senator, but I do not have those kinds of numbers here today."

"Is there a geographic area or state where most of these people reside?"

"Yes, Senator, Texas," replied Nelson. "That would be the predominant geographic representation, based on the fact the IRS bombings were in Texas and the mass shooting occurred there."

"Are there existing law enforcement members on that list?" Galvin asked.

"I believe there are, Senator."

"Mr. Nelson, are you aware of any FISA court warrant in American history that has ever asked the court to allow the unrestricted lifting of the protection of the Fourth Amendment to the United States Constitution for such a large number of citizens?"

"Senator, I'm not an expert on the historical significance of any particular warrant."

"Mr. Nelson, have you... have you specifically had a direct conversation with the president of the United States about this FISA court request or regarding the people on the list you are asking to be allowed to surveil?"

The director paused carefully before answering, "I have not had those personal conversations, Senator."

"Time is up, Senator Galvin." Simpson struck the gavel on the table.

"One last question if you will, Mr. Chairman," pushed Galvin.

"The Chair has the floor, Senator..."

"Mr. Nelson, to your knowledge, has your boss... has the attorney general had those specific conversations with the president? Has she seen and approved this list?"

"Mr. Nelson, this committee has closed questioning. Do not answer the senator's question."

Galvin continued, despite Simpson's closure of questioning. "Mr. Nelson, did the president of the United States direct your agency to seek this FISA court warrant on twenty-one thousand Americans? I demand your answer!"

"Time is up, Senator! Mr. Nelson, thank you for your appearance here today. You are respectfully dismissed. The committee will strike the last line of questioning from the record from the time Mr. Kettering yielded his time to Mr. Galvin."

As Director Nelson was packing up his briefcase to leave the witness table, Galvin shouted out: "Director, do you think it's patriotic to spy on twenty-one thousand fellow citizens?"

Nelson turned toward Galvin, picking up his briefcase, "I think it would be unpatriotic *not* to."

CHAPTER 53

"When liberty comes with hands dabbled in blood it is hard to shake hands with her."

- Oscar Wilde (1854-1900)
Irish Poet and Playwright

The *Free Texas* team had been busy preparing the Bunker headquarters for *Ghost*. In this scenario, Beard and his team were virtually destroying any connection to their operatives around the world and making sure no clues were left behind in the event of a complete takeover of the Bunker by the feds. The objective was to erase any and all evidence, data or files that the feds could use against them.

Beard had been busy on the encrypted satellite phone with his counterparts in London, Brussels and Pune, India. He was shouting out directions to those around him, while totally immersed in conversations on the sat phones and two computer screens.

Zach knew Beard was on to something but wasn't sure what. When Beard got like this, Zach and Will knew to back off and let his intelligence skills bear fruit. Zach was getting more nervous with every minute that passed. He was sure the feds were going to launch on them at any moment as the convenient scapegoats for the IRS bombings and the mass shooting in Dallas.

Beard rushed into Zach's office with his laptop opened, careful not to drop it.

"Damn, Beard. We should be scattering to the wind right now. What is so important that you're keeping us here longer than necessary?" asked Zach.

"Boss, we've been working on a hacking protocol on CIS' software and their data centers. We're in!"

"Beard, you're the man! Are you serious?" shrieked Will, who for a moment forgot they were almost in *Ghost* mode and really needed to exit the Bunker.

"It wasn't just me; we had six team members working on this since we were able to defeat the encryption on Ottosson's laptops. Once we figured out how they encrypt, it gave us clues as to how they protect and encrypt all the data on their network and in their data centers, and we've learned their security styles. The A-team is damn good!" claimed Beard, who was referring to a small group of hackers who had either cut a deal with the U.S. government in the past to avoid prosecution or jail time, or hackers that Turner had flipped from foreign subversives.

"These guys are all-stars. Damn, I'm impressed. Worth every penny we pay them. Let me have it! What are you finding?" pressed Zach.

"It's very interesting, but too early to draw any conclusions. We have several directions we could go, but we need some time and some direction," requested Beard.

"Damn it, Beard, we really don't have the time, but I've been extremely suspicious of Bartlett's miraculous presidential election comeback. While we are in *Ghost,* I want you to poke around on the feeds coming in on the comeback swing dates. See what you can find there, but before you do that, I want to know everyone on CIS' payroll worldwide. Can you crack their human resources files?"

"We cracked their data centers so now the front door is open. We've just got to unlock other doors as we get to them," claimed Beard.

"Are we talking hours, days or weeks?"

"Likely days, but the team has been in high gear for several weeks. They are exhausted."

"Keep pushing them, Beard. We are potentially entering a very perilous time. CIS is deeply entrenched into the *Deep State.* If we can identify any politicians that are being paid, or where political contributions were funneled to disguise foreign campaign contributions, we can make those public to re-direct some of the heat back on them."

"Roger that, boss. I'm on it."

In the meantime, Turner's security firm had a messaging protocol that went out to all employees, operatives and members. It signaled the entire apparatus of Turner Invincible Security (TIS) and the *Free Texas* movement with immediate orders to go underground and stay that way until further notice.

Kymbra Turner had gotten the emergency text message at the same time everyone else did. Zach was still at the Bunker, having just declared *Ghost*. There was no need for Kymbra to talk to him; she knew exactly what to do. Everyone in TIS and the *Free Texas* movement had rehearsed *Ghost* in annual drills.

Kymbra grabbed three bug-out bags, one for her, one for Zach, and one for their six-year-old son, Colt. Less than four minutes after receiving the text, Kymbra had tossed their bags into a 1972 Torino they had stored in the garage, fired it up and backed out of the driveway, leaving her more modern SUV in the driveway. A 1972 Torino doesn't have electronic ignition. Most serious preppers have a vehicle they can reach that can't be affected by an electromagnetic impulse bomb that will fry almost all modern-day electronics. The Torino's points and condensers wouldn't be affected by an EMP.

Kymbra drove straight to her son's school, which was only two miles from their home. Kymbra's heart dropped when she turned the corner within one block of Oak Grove Elementary School to find dozens of police cars and numerous dark-colored and unmarked SUVs. When she pulled up to the parking lot, she was stopped by police in full military black ops-style gear, complete with helmets, bulletproof vests and automatic weapons.

"I'm here to pick up my son. What's going on?" Kymbra asked.

Her first thought was another mass shooting incident with all of the police squad cars everywhere.

"Kymbra Turner?" asked the officer.

"Who's asking? Is everything all right here? Is my son safe?"

"Identification, please, ma'am" said the officer.

"And who are you? Where's the local sheriff?" she asked.

"Ma'am, are you Kymbra Turner?" he asked again.

"Yes, and who is asking? I'm here to pick up my son."

"Your son is safe. We have him. I need you to step out of the car, ma'am. Turn your ignition off and stick your hands out of the window."

"I'm asking YOU, again, who the hell are you?"

Now there were six other federal agents surrounding the Torino, guns drawn and pointing at her.

"I'm not going to tell you again. Shut the car off and stick your hands out the window," shouted the officer.

Kymbra slowly reached down to the ignition and turned the key off, then stuck her hands out the window, at which time two other officers came over and placed handcuffs on her outstretched arms.

"What the hell is going on here? Where is my son?" pressed Kymbra, becoming more panicked by the moment.

"Ma'am, keep your arms out of the window. We are going to slowly open the door and remove you from the vehicle."

"Remove me? The hell you are. I'll get out myself."

"Ma'am, sit still and follow our directions explicitly!" warned another officer.

The officers slowly opened the driver's door and removed her handcuffed arms slowly as the door swung open. They then unlocked the handcuffs and roughly removed one handcuff from her right wrist and then jerked her arms behind her and re-handcuffed her with her arms behind her back. Another officer came up from behind her and attached ankle cuffs and a chain to both feet.

"What the hell is going on here?" she demanded. "Where is my son?"

"Ma'am, we are placing you under arrest," answered a man in a gray suit and blue tie who had just walked up to the car.

"Arrest for what? What about my son?" she screamed.

"Kymbra Turner, you are hereby placed under arrest for conspiracy against the United States, for placing bombs at federal facilities and for eight hundred sixty-four counts of murder," said the man in the suit.

"Y'all are out of your mind. Where is my son?" she yelled back at him.

"Ma'am, your son has been picked up by Child Protective Services."

"What? What the hell is wrong with you people?"

"Child Protective Services will determine if it is safe to leave a six-year-old boy with a family that bombs federal facilities and murders hundreds of children," said the man in the suit sarcastically.

Kymbra glared at the man.

"I'd wipe that look off your face, ma'am. You're in some deep shit, ma'am. Your husband would be well served to turn himself in."

"You took our son. You will be lucky if my husband doesn't kill you before you put your head on your pillow tonight."

"Ma'am, you can add charges of *threatening* a federal agent to your list of crimes. If you want to talk, you can tell us where to find your husband and maybe you'll get to see your son again before you go to prison for a very, very long time, or worse."

"Look what we have here sir," mentioned another federal agent who was searching the Torino. "Looks to me like bug-out bags."

"Where were you headed, Ms. Turner?" asked the man in the suit.

"I want an attorney, right now. I demand to know where my son is being held!" she yelled.

"I already told you, CPS has your son. He is safe."

"I want an attorney."

"Finish searching the vehicle and impound it. Take Ms. Turner and put her in the van."

Kymbra looked around her, intently looking for sheriff's deputies who were friends of Zach's, but there were no local law enforcement vehicles on the school property. It was evident they hadn't been alerted. A small contingent of teachers and school staff were standing underneath the American and Texas flags on a concrete circle, watching her arrest.

"You think Zach is going to make a mistake just because you are harassing me? You are sadly mistaken. Zach didn't have a damn thing to do with either the IRS bombings or Dallas. Are you people insane? You think you can get to him by arresting me and kidnapping our son? All this is going to get you is DEAD!"

"Ma'am, dead is exactly how your husband is likely to end up, if it were up to me. In fact, we're counting on it!" said the man in the gray suit.

"What are there, fifty federal agents out there to arrest one woman?" asked the school principal. "Was that really necessary?"

"It must be serious," added another teacher.

"Don't know much about them. They really kept to themselves. I think her husband owns some kind of security company," replied one teacher.

"The word is he was heavily involved in the *Texas Crisis*," added another.

Kymbra Turner was marched in shackles to the black unmarked van and loaded into the back. Four agents got in the back with her. The van quickly drove out of the parking lot with four other unmarked SUVs.

Several agents remained. They continued to search the Torino and had a wrecker on stand-by come and put a tow hook on it. Within minutes, the highly-organized plan to snatch Kymbra Turner was over.

At the same time, a caravan of federal agents arrived at the Turner home, while a full contingent of FBI, Homeland Security and ATF agents were descending on the Bunker from three different directions.

CHAPTER 54

"The duty of a patriot is to protect his country from its government."

- Edward Abbey (1927-1989)
Author

When the federal agents arrived at Turner Invincible Security headquarters, commonly known as the Bunker, it was deserted.

"They knew we were coming," said an FBI agent.

"These guys are black ops we're dealing with here. These aren't your normal criminals. Turner and his followers are highly trained, thanks to our government," noted a Homeland Security commander.

"Sir, we can't find a way into this facility," noted an ATF agent.

"Blow the door," said the commander.

A few minutes later, the door exploded and teams of FBI and ATF in full gear entered the building. Once they got inside, they found nothing but tables, chairs and a few other pieces of furniture. No files, no paper of any kind, and definitely no computers. Even big screen TVs were taken down off the walls.

"Look at this. It appears they have fast take-down capabilities. These fasteners allow a quick release once you unplug cables. I bet they cleaned this place out in less than thirty minutes," said another FBI agent as he indicated points in the concrete walls where it was apparent a widescreen monitor had hung minutes before.

"Did we jump the gun with his wife?" asked the lead ATF agent.

"No, that operation was simultaneous. We just got the message she is in cuffs and in their custody. There's no way she tipped him off."

"Then he knew we were coming for him anyway," the FBI agent noted.

"He definitely knew. Now we've grabbed his wife and kid. He's going to look at that as a kidnapping. Don't be surprised if this escalates," lamented the commander.

Zach and Kymbra Turner had always had an action plan if *Ghost* was implemented, the same as all of Turner's operatives. They were to meet at a pre-determined location and no communication was supposed to take place. They had practiced this scenario at least a half-dozen times in the past when Zach had sent her the code via text that indicated the emergency.

A little over an hour after Zach had abandoned the Bunker, he turned onto a dusty county road on the Texas coastal plains about fifteen miles from Shiner, Texas. He drove three miles before turning into a non-descript farm entrance with a locked gate. He got out, unlocked the gate, and pulled through, then re-locked it again. He drove another half-mile up the farmhouse road and, as the farmhouse and barn came into view, he was a little concerned Kymbra hadn't beaten him there. The code was sent to her before they started packing up the Bunker. He reasoned to himself that she must have been a little delayed picking up Colt from school, and he fought the urge to try to contact her on her secure phone.

He opened the door to the barn and pulled his Jeep into a horse stall. He then used a rake and cleared some hay off the floor of another stall, revealing a door that opened up to an underground safe room. He went to the back of his Jeep and unloaded some supplies he had managed to get from the Bunker and took them down the steps to the safe room.

The safe room was actually two rooms and was outfitted with high-tech electrical gear, computers, about thirty guns of all calibers, plenty of ammo and emergency food supplies. Zach had disguised a satellite dish in the roof beams so that he could get satellite reception. He had a full generator placed underground, with buried propane tanks about twenty-five yards away. The exhaust from the generator was hidden in a stand of small trees, with a very high-tech look-a-like four-inch tree trunk that filtered exhaust, muffled the sound, and made it nearly undetectable.

Turner had purchased the eighty-acre farm five years prior under a fictitious name and identity. To the neighbors, the family that owned this farm was the Kingsburys from Galveston. A neighboring ranch hand took care of the twenty-two cattle, chickens and various other farm animals the Turners kept on the ranch. He also tended to the five acres that were planted with various crops and herbs. Turner paid him modestly, but the ranch hand got free eggs and any crops from the small garden that Kymbra didn't can. He had no idea about the safe room or exactly what Turner did or who he was.

After keeping himself busy for about two hours, Turner started to get nervous that Kymbra hadn't shown up. He couldn't wait any longer. He got on his satellite phone and dialed the number to Kymbra's sat phone that was stashed in the bug-out bag.

Two rings later, a man answered.

"Kymbra Turner's phone," came the man's voice.

"Who the hell is this?" demanded Zach.

"This is FBI agent Milson. I assume this is Zach Turner?"

"Where the hell is my wife? Put her on the phone NOW!"

"She's been taken into custody," the agent answered.

"She was picking up my son from school…"

"Yes, he's fine. We have him, too."

"What the hell do you mean you have him, too?"

"Child Protective Services has him and he is fine."

"You sons of bitches. My wife and son have nothing to do with anything. What the hell is wrong with you people?"

"I've been informed that if you turn yourself in to authorities, we will let Kymbra out on bail. But this offer is only extended for twenty-four hours."

"You've kidnapped my wife and son!"

"She's being held on conspiracy charges," Milson said flatly.

"You're full of crap! And my son?" screamed Zach into the phone.

"CPS has the authority on that one, Turner. I don't think they are apt to put a child back into a home where the parents are involved in bombing government buildings," snickered agent Milson.

"You're a dead man, Milson."

"Threatening a federal agent? Just add that to the list of charges. But, hell, compared to *treason,* what difference does it make? You've got twenty-four hours, Turner. Turn yourself in to any law enforcement authority, wherever you are, and have them contact me once you've done it."

"What assurances do I have that Kymbra will be released? The deal has to be that she is released and re-united with my son, or nothing."

"You're not really in a good bargaining position, Mr. Turner. The clock starts as soon as we hang up. This is a one-time offer. If you don't take us up on it, there will be no deals later. Understood?"

Zach wanted to say something but bit his tongue as his mind raced for a few seconds.

"I need to speak to her right now; do you hear me?"

"Mr. Turner, she isn't with me. She is in a jail cell. You're not really in a bargaining position to start making those kinds of demands."

A few seconds of silence ensued.

"Mr. Turner, are you there?"

"You'll be hearing back from me. Keep this line open, you son of a bitch," Zach said in a very firm and determined manner.

Turner walked into the shade of the barn and began pacing. He then walked back out and starting dialing a familiar number.

"Pops' Younger's phone," Dyson answered unceremoniously.

"Dyson, this is Zach Turner. I need to speak to Pops. It's an emergency," Zach pleaded.

"Hang tight. We are still up here at this circus in Dallas. I'll go see if he will take your call."

"Tell him to hurry, please."

Dyson walked into the police tent on the fairgrounds and walked up to Pops, "I've got Zach Turner on your phone. Says it's an emergency. He sounds a little flustered."

Pops took the phone and walked out of the tent, away from anyone that could listen in. Dyson followed him for a few steps but kept his distance.

"Younger here."

"Pops, sorry to bother you. The feds have picked up my wife Kymbra and they even grabbed my son out of school. They are demanding I turn myself in for the IRS bombings or they say they are going to press conspiracy charges on her. Hell, they gave my son to Child Protective Services!"

"How did they reach you? Where are you at?" asked Pops.

"I'm about two-and-a-half hours from Houston. I called Kymbra and they picked it up. She was leaving Houston with my son, and I assume they took him out of school before she could get him. I want to kill the sons of bitches, Pops. What should I do?"

Pops took his time before answering. "Son, I know you had nothing to do with those bombings. They've got you by the short-hairs. Why don't I come down to Houston and negotiate the release of your wife and son, or exchange, whatever the hell they're gonna call it. Do you have an attorney?"

"Yes, of course. I'll call him next."

"One piece of advice I'd give to both you and your attorney is that turning yourself in also includes an agreement not to remove you from Texas and that all hearings be conducted here."

"I'm sure he will want to talk to you, Pops. I sincerely appreciate your help."

"We can't trust those scalawags, son. I'll see you in Houston in a few hours."

After Zach got off the phone with Pops and his attorney, he sent coded messages to his team worldwide, letting them know the feds had picked up his family and he was going to turn himself in. All the operatives knew the leadership of the group in Turner's absence fell to Will.

At 6:00 p.m. that evening, with everything pre-arranged between the feds, Texas Rangers and Zach's attorney, two SUVs pulled up to the Mickey Leland Federal Building to a throng of news cameras. The feds had leaked to the media that the IRS bomber was turning himself in.

"Apparently, the Texas Rangers have brokered this surrender by the nationalist and white supremacist Zach Turner. There you see the legendary Texas Ranger Pops Younger exiting the vehicle, followed by bombing suspect Turner. Awaiting them at the door of the federal building is a throng of federal agents," announced the CNN analyst on the live broadcast.

FBI agent Milson approached Pops and Turner, ordering Turner to turn around so he could handcuff him right on the sidewalk.

"Son, I told you boys he is surrendering. You can put the cuffs on him in the building but not out here in the street. We ain't putting on no damn show for the cameras," said Pops sternly to the agent.

"This man is wanted for treason and for the attempted murder of hundreds of federal workers. He's going to wear handcuffs. Back off, old man," said Milson.

Pops took a step in between them.

"We seem to have some kind of problem on the sidewalk right outside the door. It appears there is a heated argument between the Texas Ranger and the FBI. We can't tell what is being said, but tempers are flaring down there," continued the CNN analyst.

"Son, this man is in MY custody," Pops shouted at Milson. "You ain't cuffing him out here. Now get the hell outta the way!"

"He's on federal property now and out of your jurisdiction, cowboy," snarled Milson as he reached over Pops' shoulder to grab Zach's arm and slap cuffs on his wrist.

Pops grabbed Milson's forearm, surprising the agent with his amazing grip and strength, which gave him immediate pause.

Pops then got an inch from Milson's face, affording him the look with his steel blue eyes that had backed down so many criminals in his career, "You're in Texas, boy. Federal property don't start until he walks through that door right there. Now git them cuffs back in your pocket before I stuff 'em down your throat!"

Milson removed his arm and turned to the remainder of the federal agents crowded on the sidewalk, embarrassed that Pops stood him down. "Get his sorry ass in the building and don't cuff him. Shackle his ass!"

"Thanks, Pops," Zach said.

"You watch yourself in there. This will get straightened out in time. I'll make sure we get your wife and son," said Pops as they marched Zach into the building. They made sure they stopped him right inside the door and shackled him in leg, waist and wrist cuffs like a common criminal, while the cameras peered through the first floor's twelve-foot glass windows to get a visual of the alleged IRS bomber doing the perp walk.

The Texas Rangers drove around to the back of the federal building, where the feds were to bring Kymbra and Colt. The feds made the Rangers wait an hour on purpose to transfer them.

"Mr. Younger, I hope you realize and know in your heart Zach had no part in those bombings," Kymbra told Pops as she put a seat belt on Colt in the SUV.

"Ma'am, I know that. This is so much bigger than that, if you can believe it. They want a scapegoat for the *Texas Crisis,* and they want to discredit the independence movement. Don't be surprised if they try to connect your husband to the shooting in Dallas. We won't let them succeed at it, if I've got a damn thing to do with it."

CHAPTER 55

"Congress has doubled the IRS budget over the past 10 years—making that agency one of the fastest growing non-entitlement programs. It has increased its employment by 20 percent. The IRS's powers to investigate and examine taxpayers transcend those of any other law enforcement agency. Virtually all of the constitutional rights regarding search and seizure, due process, and jury trial simply do not apply to the IRS."

- Daniel Pilla
Founder and director of the Tax Freedom Institute

W ill got a message from Turner on the same afternoon Zach spoke with Pops and turned himself in. He was now in charge. They had waited an hour too late to implement *Ghost,* allowing the feds to grab Zach's family and use him as a public relations prop.

Will had gotten approval from Zach right after the mass shooting and prior to implementing *Ghost* to grab Ottosson and get whatever information they could out of him. It was time. Ottosson could be the perfect bargaining chip to secure Zach's release.

Empowered by the arrest of Turner, the *Deep State* became even bolder. Governor Strasburg and Senator Simpson called a hastily prepared press conference after Zach's arrest to seize on the momentum created by the supposed IRS bombing crime being solved.

On the steps of the Texas Capitol building, Governor Strasburg stepped to the microphone. "We are deeply saddened that someone attached to the Texas independence movement is also allegedly involved with these horrific IRS bombings and that federal officials have some belief that this

Free Texas movement is somehow connected to the tragic mass shooting in Dallas. Because of this development and the fact that I am hearing from so many Texans and elected officials, we will not be calling a special session of the state legislature to take this issue up. We believe the public sentiment for this extreme action is waning and it is in everyone's best interest to let this investigation take its due course before deciding to have any kind of referendum that would not honor those victims in Dallas," said Strasburg as he conflated the vote for independence, which was more popular than ever with Texans, with dishonoring the child victims of the shooting.

After he was done, he took two steps backward and Senator Simpson stepped to the mic to make his statement.

"Ladies and gentlemen, fellow Texans and fellow Americans, I applaud the governor's decision to cancel any plans for a special session of the legislature while this investigation progresses. We have heard from the Justice Department that Mr. Turner and his militia group are now being investigated for possible links to the horrific tragedy in Dallas. Texas needs to heal. It has lost two governors and two lieutenant governors in two years. The emotions from these types of tragedies fueled the fire of the independence movement. Most of you know my objection to this effort. I have never hidden my disdain for any illegal effort to separate Texas from the Union. This movement has bred the environment for these types of militia and white supremacy groups to grow and thrive. I believe, as does the governor, that we honor those child victims by postponing any plans for a special session to take up such a volatile issue. The governor and I will take a few questions."

Will watched the press conference from his iPhone. He was incensed that the governor and the senator would have the gall to tie Zach to the mass shooting or the bombings. He immediately dispatched codes to Beard and several operatives in D.C. and on the east coast to implement the standing order they had established to nab Ottosson. The plan was already in place; now it just needed to be executed.

Ottosson was not hard to find. Turner's operatives had been maintaining twenty-four-hour surveillance with the hopes Ottosson would lead them to Volkov again. Despite the fact that surveillance was in place, Ottosson could be found starting his womanizing efforts every evening at the bar of The Jefferson Hotel just blocks from the White House.

Will's plan was to use Ottosson's penchant for women against him.

A very good-looking female operative was already stationed at the bar as bait for Ottosson. A few casual but suggestive looks, coupled with free-flowing alcohol and some flirtatious chatter, would likely be all it took to get Ottosson out of the bar and into a situation where the team could acquire him.

Finally, thirty minutes later than normal, Ottosson showed up at his usual spot. It didn't take long at all for him to spot the female operative at the bar. She wore a tight pencil dress, and dark flowing hair cascaded down her back. Ottosson zeroed in on her after his first two dirty martinis.

The thirty-two-year-old female operative was excellent at playing coy with Ottosson, flattering him yet giving the impression she was unattainable. This encouraged Ottosson even more as he bragged about his importance to Congress and the administration, as well as his newly obtained wealth.

By 11:00 p.m., Ottosson had had nearly ten martinis and was feeling no pain when he suggested that the female operative retire with him from the bar to his swanky brownstone in Georgetown. She agreed to leave with him, on the condition they go to her loft in Alexandria, and that he wouldn't drive drunk. She would summon Uber on her iPhone. There was no way Ottosson could resist her. She asked him to meet her outside the women's restroom and then they would leave.

Ottosson went to the men's bathroom first, then came out to wait on his newly acquired prize to exit the ladies' room. When she came out, she pulled him into a private alcove and pressed against him with a deep kiss, grabbing his crotch. If the deal to go to her flat wasn't a sure thing up to that point, she sealed the deal then and there.

Waiting around the corner was a non-descript Toyota Prius so common to many Uber drivers. But this wasn't an official Uber car or driver. It was another operative on Turner's team. Ottosson's full attention was on the female operative and none of the precautions that a professional operative would take were even considered. He was totally and completely at the mercy of his goal to conquer this woman.

On the drive to Alexandria, she continually had to fight him off in the back seat from roaming hands and advances. For the female operative, she couldn't get there quick enough.

The Uber driver told them he was within a few blocks of the address she had given him. She reached for a garage remote for a one-door garage that opened when she pressed it. Inside the garage was a minivan.

"We'll go in this way," she told Ottosson. He followed her like a puppy dog as she hit the button on the wall for the garage door to close. She pulled him to her once again to deliver another deep kiss.

As the garage door closed to the ground, four men jumped out from behind the minivan, dressed all in black, with ski masks. They tackled Ottosson. Immediately they restrained him as one put a washcloth full of chloroform over his mouth and nose and the other three held him down for the thirty seconds it took for the chemical to knock him out.

They quickly bound Ottosson's hands, feet and mouth and loaded him into the back of the minivan where the third row of seats had been removed. One of the men gave her the signal and she hit the garage door button again, and the four men backed out of the garage, waiting on her to exit the garage before it closed. Once all were in the van, it backed up and sped away.

The female operative took out a small flask of mouthwash and took several swigs of the liquid and spit it out as she rolled the window down halfway.

"The things I do for my country," she lamented.

Within thirty minutes, Ottosson regained his senses but the chemical mixed with the chloroform made him nauseous. The van drove for two hours to a remote, small warehouse in the Monongahela National Forest in West Virginia.

The crew pulled Ottosson from the vehicle and immediately strapped him to a chair in a room that had the eerie look and feel of a torture chamber. There were instruments of torture hanging on the walls and stains that looked like blood on the walls and concrete floor. Ottosson remained gagged and tied. Every time he made a sound, someone would slap his face smartly and tell him to be quiet. They also referred repeatedly to waiting until the "boss" arrived.

What Ottosson did not know was that everything in his field of vision was staged. The blood was from pigs. The torture tools had never really been used, but he didn't know it. For an hour, he sat in silence as each one of the operatives would pick a tool from the wall and adjust it, sharpen it or make some other kind of reference to it. Ottosson, who had no experience whatsoever as an undercover operative, was becoming terrified at what might be in store for him. Just a few short hours before, he thought he was about to have his way with a very beautiful woman he picked up at a bar.

All were sitting quietly as the sound of a car pulling into another section of warehouse could be heard, along with some loud voices.

The door of the room Ottosson was sitting in suddenly swung open. A man, dressed all in black and a mask, walked in carrying a small sledgehammer.

"Mr. Ottosson, these next twenty-four hours will either be the worst of your life or you can cooperate with us and you will be returned to your home," the man said. "Now, remove his shoes."

The others quickly took off his shoes and socks. They then removed his gag.

"What the hell is going on here? Do you know who I am? I have diplomatic immunity. Do you know who I know in Congress? Hell, I know the president! Who the hell are you people?"

"Mr. Ottosson, I am going to ask you some very direct questions, many of which we already know the answers to. If you lie to us, it will be painful. The problem for you is you don't know what we know. Do you understand me?" said the man with the sledgehammer, now referred to as the boss.

"Go screw yourself," Ottosson answered.

Before he could finish the sentence, the boss swung the short sledgehammer, slamming it on the little toes of the Swede's right foot. Ottosson let out a blood-curdling scream, trying mightily in his restraints to get free.

"Like I said, Mr. Ottosson, we can do this hard or we can do this easy. Take off his pants and underwear."

"Am I going to die today?" asked Ottosson.

"That is totally up to you. I have a mind to just put a bullet in your head right now and be done with you, but you could be of some use to us."

The crew cut his pants and underwear off him.

"Roll in the battery charger."

The crew went to the next room and brought in a large battery charger used to boost the batteries of large diesel truck engines.

"Mr. Ottosson, the next wrong answer you give me, I'm going to instruct my friends here to connect those boosters to your balls. Do you understand me?"

Ottosson, eyes wild with fear, nodded.

"Do you know a Russian operative named Volkov?"

Ottosson hesitated. He knew that disclosing *any* information about Volkov was akin to him signing his own death warrant.

"Never heard of him," Ottosson claimed.

"Lying on the very first question, Mr. Ottosson, sets a very bad precedent. Hook up the boosters!"

"No, no, no. I don't know this man you speak of!"

The next thing Ottosson felt was the sharp pain of one of the booster clamps, like a battery charger cable, clamping onto his scrotum.

"Nooooo! Ouch! No, no. Okay, I know him. Take it off, take it off right now!"

"Take it off. I think Mr. Ottosson is willing to participate now," said the boss. "Now, when was the last time you spoke with him and when was the last time you saw him?"

"I saw him in Alexandria several months ago at a pub. Honestly, that was the last time I saw him."

"Why were you meeting with Volkov in Alexandria? What was discussed?"

"He was working on a project for us," Ottosson said, nervously looking around to make sure nobody was picking up anything to use on him.

"What project was that? What was its name and what was its purpose?"

Ottosson tried to divert away from the subject. "I don't know. I'm just a messenger. I was just told to meet with him and arrange payment obligations."

"Bullshit, Ottosson. Pull that booster over here! Gag him! I don't want to hear his screams!"

The team pulled the booster to him and this time put both cable clamps on his scrotum. Ottosson was screaming in pain.

"You think that's painful? What until we dial up the voltage."

"No, no, no. Okay, okay, okay! We were discussing *Madison*! Please, please take these off!"

The boss turned to the female operative and looked at her to make sure the video recorder was capturing everything. She nodded affirmatively.

"What was *Madison*?"

"It was a project to change public sentiment to eventually overturn the 2nd Amendment. Please, please take these off! I'll answer your damned questions!"

"I want you to think very clearly before you answer this question. Were you on the Ida Kay when Chief Justice Noyner drowned?"

"Yes, yes, I was there."

"How did he drown?"

"He fell out of the boat and we couldn't save him!"

"Hit him!"

Another blood-curdling scream came out of Ottosson's mouth as the booster was flipped on to its lightest setting for three seconds.

"I bet no woman has ever given you that kind of thrill up your leg," laughed the boss. "That was only three seconds, Ottosson. You are apparently not a fast learner. We will increase the voltage the length of the boost each time you continue to lie to us or give us non-answers."

"Okay, okay, okay! Please take them off. I swear I'll tell you!"

"Then tell us what really happened on the Ida Kay?"

"He was injected with a neurotoxin that made it look like a heart attack. He did actually fall out of the boat, but he was already convulsing."

"Who injected him?"

"Please, I'll tell you! Just take these off now! Please!"

One of the operatives stepped back over to the booster as if he was going to turn it back on.

"No, no, don't! Volkov was on the boat. He injected him!"

"Let's go back to *Madison* for a minute as you are taking this trip down Memory Lane. Who orchestrated the mass shooting in Dallas?"

"I'm begging you. Please take off these cables! Please!"

"Mr. Ottosson, I'm not going to ask the same question twice. If I have to ask any question more than once, it will really piss me off and we might forget to turn the booster off once we turn it up. I really don't give a shit if you die today. Do you understand me?"

"Okay, sir, okay! *Madison* was Volkov's project! I wasn't involved in the planning. He used three or four of his own people to pull that off!"

"I'm going to take a break. In the meantime, keep these booster cables connected and, if he makes so much as a whimper, hit him with 120 volts."

The boss and two others left the room and closed the door behind them.

When they got out of the room, two of the men pulled off their ski masks.

"Damn, it's hot in there," remarked Beard.

"Not as hot as it is for Ottosson. What a wussy. He was singing before we even hooked up the cables," said the third operative as he chuckled.

"That's what happens when you've got no principles or belief system. This guy is a total whore, a sellout who's only in it for monetary gain. He's no ideologue; he's simply a lobbyist playing spy games," said Will, also known as the boss for this interrogation. He pulled off his mask.

"We've got a lot more questions for him. We will edit the video and get it ready. This should exonerate Zach and get him out of custody, right?" asked Beard anxiously.

"We've got to be smart about it. This is banana republic kind of shit. It will throw our entire system into a tailspin. So, no media. Everybody understand? We are going to use this information strategically," commanded Will.

"Got it," they both said in unison.

"Let's go have some more fun," said the third operative.

Ottosson was doing his best to remain still as the three men returned with their masks on, but the clamps from the battery booster were causing immense pain to his scrotum.

"Mr. Ottosson, tell me about the crash of the Texas governor's plane," said Will.

"I wasn't there," Ottosson answered painfully.

"That's not what I asked you. Were you involved?"

"No, I wasn't. Please take these cables off me. Please!"

"You're lying again! Hit it!" yelled Will.

Five seconds is a very long time when you are getting shocked on your scrotum. Ottosson's screams were guttural. He writhed grotesquely in response to the pain.

"Stop! Now damn it, Ottosson, I thought you were learning your lesson. My bullshit detector is like nothing you've ever experienced. Hell, the U.S. government was thinking about using me to replace their polygraphs!" Will joked to Ottosson. "Now, I'll ask you again what happened to the plane?"

"Volkov was there. He's an expert at that kind of thing. I don't know exactly what he did but he promised he would take that plane down."

"And what about the mechanic and his family?"

"Volkov," Ottosson said flatly.

"Jesus, Volkov killed the wife and the small boy?"

"Volkov doesn't leave loose ends – of *any* kind."

Beard stepped up in front of Ottosson to ask the next set of questions.

"There was a Texas state senator named Milsap that was murdered execution style in downtown Austin. Is this the work of Volkov too?"

"Yes, it was Volkov."

Beard turned and looked at Will.

"Why in the hell would you have this guy killed? He was about to leave office," said Beard.

"We had secrets on him that compromised him with his wife, but he told her before we could. We had to make sure we had the numbers," Ottosson said as he grimaced and tried to get comfortable.

"I'm going to have these cables taken off you. If for a split second we think you're lying to us again, they are back on and this time it ain't shutting off after five seconds. Do you understand, Mr. Ottosson?" Will asked.

"Yes, sir. Please, please. Take them off. The pain is unbearable."

Two operatives reached over and removed the clamps. Ottosson was sitting in a small pool of blood where the clamps had penetrated the skin of the scrotum.

"A little blood, but he ain't going to bleed to death," said one of the operatives.

"Mr. Ottosson, you were using leverage on State Senator Milsap. What were you using this leverage for?"

"To kill the Texas independence referendum vote."

Beard and Will turned and looked at each other. Surely, this move wouldn't have been Ottosson's alone.

"Kill it? By whose orders?" demanded Will.

"My superiors."

"Boys, get those cables ready!"

"Okay, okay, okay. The administration wanted it defeated, by any means necessary," Ottosson revealed.

Will stood up and looked back at the operative who was manning the video camera to make sure she captured this moment. The operative nodded affirmatively.

"Mr. Ottosson, I'm going to ask you very plainly about this in particular and you had better give me very straightforward answers. Do you understand?"

"Yes, sir."

"Where did the orders come from to assassinate Milsap?"

"We didn't get *exact* orders like this to take anyone out. How those orders were executed was up to others."

"Who ordered the Texas independence referendum vote to be stopped by any means necessary? Who was it?"

"The White House."

There was complete silence in the room for a few seconds and Will again looked back at the video recorder to make sure the red light was on, indicating it was still recording.

"Who at the White House, Mr. Ottosson, ordered the vote to be stopped by any means necessary?" demanded Will.

"Chief of Staff Weingold."

"We had you tracked and our records showed you were at the White House nineteen times total with President Johnson's administration and now Bartlett's administration. Who were you meeting with at each one of those meetings and what was discussed?"

"During the Johnson administration, it was mainly Attorney General Jamail Tibbs."

"Did you ever meet with President Johnson?"

"Yes, one time."

"Why? What was discussed?"

"It was a formal introduction and a celebration of sorts when Congress approved funding for our voting software."

"That was it?"

"Yes, sir," Ottosson said.

"What was the context of the meetings with the attorney general?"

"Mostly to report on simulated elections when we were testing our software."

"Mr. Ottosson, this is another booster cable moment for you. Do you understand?"

"Yes."

"What was done in those simulations?"

"We produced varied outcomes in simulated elections."

"Am I understanding you to say that you manipulated votes in those simulated elections?"

"Yes."

"These were all simulated elections?"

"At first, yes. Then we actually did live test runs in *actual* state and local elections."

"So, in effect, you changed some election outcomes?"

"Yes."

"How many elections during this testing phase did CIS impact?"

"I honestly don't remember, probably twenty or so."

"Who told you who should win those elections?"

"The attorney general."

"Was the software successful?"

"We failed to produce the desired outcome in two of the first five, but once we fixed our algorithms in the tabulation coding we got it right every single time after."

"Was your CIS corporate headquarters in Sweden aware of this manipulation?"

"Not at first; we had some rogue programmers who got paid on the side to hijack the systems in place in the states. The Johnson administration was very successful in promoting the software and orders were streaming in from most of the states."

"Are you saying CIS corporate later became aware of the reason these orders were coming in? At what levels in CIS were they aware that you were being asked to manipulate voting results?"

"I assume at the very top, although I've never spoken with the CEO directly about it. Sales of the software and support were sensational. If he had a clue, he didn't ask, but there were others in management that turned a blind eye as the bonuses started to roll in," admitted Ottosson.

"Here's another booster-type question for you, Mr. Ottosson," began Will. "Was the last presidential election modified or altered in any way by the CIS voting systems?"

"Yes."

"How so?"

"Bartlett was losing in most of the battleground states. We changed the coding algorithms late in the evening to adjust the vote tabulations," replied Ottosson, almost as if proud that they were able to do so without being caught.

"How can that go undetected?"

"The coding tabulation is done at the precinct level. This was a very tight election and a few counties in a few swing states were all Bartlett needed. We knew it would be a tight race and we were prepared for weeks ahead of time to adjust what was necessary."

"I don't understand. The Bartlett comeback was really unbelievable. Why not make it look simpler and therefore more believable?" reasoned Beard who was fascinated by what he was hearing from Ottosson.

"I was told to stand down on this until very late on election night. I don't know this for a fact, but it is my understanding from Weingold that Bartlett really wanted to win this outright, without our manipulation. When it became clear that she could, in fact, lose, Weingold had us initiate our plan. It was later than we would have liked, but it did make for a great story."

"A great story that wasn't real, and a story people like us who have seen this government work, didn't really believe," retorted Beard angrily.

"So you have firsthand knowledge President Bartlett knew this election outcome was manipulated?"

"Well, no. I have never spoke to the president about any of this. My dealings were with Weingold only."

"But you have every reason to believe the president knew this plan to change the outcome was in fact operationalized?"

"I have every reason to believe she did," answered Ottosson flatly.

"What was CIS' reward for this outcome?"

"More government contracts, but not just the election systems. Operating systems for many government functions. We also got approval for a $2.6 billion overhaul to the IRS systems."

"Let's go back to the Texas vote for a minute. How many people did you get to?"

"We had dossiers on every state legislator and state senator. We got to about twenty-five in total. Some had girlfriends, some had boyfriends, some had other secrets and a few, Volkov simply threatened family members."

"And the White House was involved in this also?"

"Both administrations, yes."

"Tell me about Senator Simpson? Have you had direct contact with him or with Governor Strasburg?" asked Will.

"We've met with both on numerous occasions about getting the voting systems into Texas. They have both been in meetings I have been in with Weingold."

"Do you have firsthand knowledge of their participation or knowledge of *Madison*, the governor's plane, the assassination of the chief justice, or the stolen elections?"

"I've never had any direct contact with them on any of those items, nor have I been present when they were discussed with, or in front of them."

"But you said they were in meetings with Weingold?"

"Yes, but not at the White House."

"Which means they aren't on any official record or visitors log," stated Beard to Will.

"Are you aware of meetings they might have had with Weingold or the president when you weren't present?" asked Beard.

"Only to the extent that they stayed in meetings with Weingold after I had left."

"How many of those meetings were there?"

"I can't really remember the number, probably three or four."

"Did CIS contribute any monies to their individual election campaigns?"

"Not directly."

"What the hell does that mean?"

"It means we got creative about how we helped them. CIS had American subsidiaries and dummy individuals who could contribute themselves, but the money actually originated with CIS."

"Jesus, this just keeps getting better," said Beard sarcastically.

"Sir, please tell me I'm not going to die today," begged Ottosson.

"At the rate you are cooperating, probably not," answered Will. "Just keep doing what you are doing. We will want more details later."

"Let me ask you this, Mr. Ottosson," asked Beard. "In your best guess, how many officials in this administration knew the motives and players regarding *Madison*?"

"Probably five or six."

"Who would they be?" pressed Beard.

"Weingold, the attorney general, the president, and likely a couple of others."

"You're telling me right here and now that the president of the United States knew this mass shooting was going to occur?"

"What I'm telling you is she knew an event, or a series of events, was going to take place that would bolster her position on reversing or minimalizing your 2nd Amendment."

"That's unreal, but I think I get it!" said Beard. "So, something like this was in the works before y'all killed Chief Justice Noyner?"

"Even with the mass shootings that have happened in the past, the president's political party couldn't defeat the NRA and they couldn't overturn a conservative majority in the Supreme Court. It was a three-step plan. Make sure the majority of the Court was changed by electing Bartlett for future nominations, get rid of Noyner, who was the primary conservative, and sway public opinion in a massive way. You have to admit it was ingenious."

"Look, you frickin' scumbag. Don't get too cocky or I'll slap those booster cables back on your balls so fast your eyes will bulge out!" yelled Will, irritated at Ottosson's cockiness and willful disregard for American laws.

"Mr. Ottosson, can you tell us how many members of Congress and the Senate are familiar with any of these operations you have spoken about today?" pressed Beard.

"About a dozen of them would be aware of one or more of these operations."

"Which ones? Would it be safe to assume that there are members of both parties that may have a hand in these?"

"You gentlemen must remember my main point of contact for all these operations was the chief of staff. Rarely was I at any meetings where any members of Congress could be trusted with the magnitude of these operations, but I can tell you that the leadership in Congress from *both* parties knew or was aware of some of these operations."

"Leadership from *both* parties?" Beard asked to confirm.

"Yes."

"How many members of Congress and senators did CIS funnel election campaign funds to?"

"Literally, most of them."

"What about state politics? Did CIS fund elections in individual state elections?"

"Most definitely. That was my primary job. I got forty-eight out of fifty states to buy our election software. CIS gave me a lot of money to spread around and there's nothing easier in life than getting politicians to follow the money."

"Do you have any direct evidence that President Bartlett was fully aware of all of these operations?"

"Only insinuations in conversations with Weingold."

"What about President Johnson?"

"Same answer, except in his case in conversations with Attorney General Jamail Tibbs."

"Was CIS' solution ever a legitimate attempt to sell *secure* voting systems?" asked Will.

"In the beginning. But Tibbs really pressed to find a back door. In fact, our big test was Johnson's re-election. That outcome was also manipulated."

Beard and Will turned and looked at each other again, shaking their heads.

"Roll that battery charger over here closer," said Will.

"I've been cooperating with you people. What the hell? Please!"

"These are your most important questions of the day," announced Will.

"Who paid Volkov and how much?"

"Volkov has been paid several million dollars. Most of it has come from CIS or your CIA."

"Damn it," said Will as he looked in another direction.

"How much were you directly involved with paying Volkov?"

"I've personally funneled over $3 million to him."

"Where did the money go?"

"Various offshore banks, with strict privacy laws, laundered under a host of different entities."

"Where is Volkov?"

"I swear I don't know."

"Last time I'm going to ask you. Where is Volkov?"

"Last thing I heard, he was flying from Houston to Paris after the Dallas shooting, but under some other passport."

"Where is he now?"

"I don't know. Honestly, I don't know. If he knew or finds out I'm telling you any of this, I'm as good as dead. None of you can protect me from him. What are you going to do now? If you pursue any of this information or it comes out I've talked to you, I'm a dead man anyway."

"Where is Volkov?"

"You can ask me that a hundred times and you'll get the same answer. Volkov is not going to tell me where he is. He never has and he never will."

"How did you meet Volkov?"

"It was arranged by Weingold and a contact at CIA."

"Our own government introduced you to Volkov?" pressed Beard.

"Yes, that's right."

"Where is Volkov right now?"

"Same answer again. I don't know."

Will stared at Ottosson.

"Clamp them on him."

"What? Why? No! Please, I don't know!" screamed Ottosson.

The team put the battery booster clamps back onto Ottosson's scrotum.

"Where is Volkov?"

"I don't know! I swear on my mother's life, I don't know! Please!"

"Three seconds! Hit it now!" ordered Will.

"Noooo! Ahhhh! No! Damn you!"

"I'll ask you again. Where is Volkov?"

"He doesn't tell me. I told you so! No! Please, no!"

"Five seconds! Hit him again!"

"God damn you! Ahhhhh! Stop! Please stop!" Ottosson contorted and writhed around in the chair.

"Where do you think Volkov is?"

Crying and in immense pain, Ottosson said, "Probably Russia or Chechnya. I don't know! Please stop!"

"Take the cables off. We've got what we need for today."

The team removed the booster cables. "You son of a bitch, I bet you've never had anything that hot between your legs!" said one of the operatives.

"Please, please just let me be. Please," begged Ottosson.

"Today's your lucky day, Ottosson. Really. You've given us enough information to keep you alive for one more day. Now this gentleman here is going to take you through a series of questions about your operations, your encryption methods, devices and security. I'm going to go eat my lunch. If I get interrupted because they tell me you aren't cooperating, we will replay these last five minutes with your friend over there." Will pointed to the roll-away battery booster.

Ottosson couldn't talk any more.

"Get him some water and some bandages for his balls."

Beard and Will walked into the next room and removed their ski masks.

"Wow! Who would believe any of this? I can't wait for this to get out. So much for those who think the *Deep State* is a conspiracy theory," Beard remarked to Will.

"I'm not sure if this is fixable, Beard. Our constitutional republic is dead as we know it. The Republic of Texas is sure looking like the only real option. At least we can use this to get Zach out of jail."

"What's our next step?"

"Keep interrogating him for the technical information you need," replied Will.

"What are you going to do now?" asked Beard.

"I'm going to try to reach Pops Younger."

CHAPTER 56

"The purpose of the Bill of Rights was to limit what the federal government could do. Any interpretation of a provision of the Bill of Rights as a grant of federal power is ipso facto wrong."

- L.A. Powe, Jr.
Centennial Professor of Law at The University of Texas

"They picked up Turner's wife and his kid, and he turned himself in so she could get bonded out," said a distressed Hank Lofton to his crew.

"They're blaming him for *our* bombings, and for the mass shooting," stated Jaxon Haines, one of his lieutenants.

"What the hell are we going to do about it?" demanded another of Lofton's crew.

"We are going to hit more targets," responded Lofton angrily.

"More? Is this to help exonerate Zach?" asked Haines.

"Partly, because it will confuse them. They will claim this is his team's response to him getting arrested. Unfortunately for Zach, it won't do anything publicly to help him. They haven't stopped their pursuit of us, so we won't stop our pursuit of them," said Lofton confidently. "We are going to impact their ability to conduct war against us. Every damned IRS employee should lose sleep over going to work the next day. They need to think about it. If we can impact operations by having at least twenty percent of the IRS workforce staying home, then we've reduced their ability to wage war on us."

"How violent are we going to get, Hank?" asked a concerned Haines.

Lofton stood up from his chair and, leaning over the table, he placed both hands flat on the surface as he got closer to Haines.

"They operate by invoking terror on U.S. citizens. We will turn the tables on them and invoke terror on them," said Lofton. His face reddened and veins in his temples bulged under his skin.

During the early morning hours of the next day, letters in envelopes were carefully taped on the front doors of dozens of television stations under the cover of darkness. The stations were carefully chosen by location where large IRS processing centers were located and for media who had provided extended coverage of the previous IRS bombings.

As early morning news crews began showing up to work on the east coast, the producers were faced with the dilemma of whether to make the letters public. All the stations contacted the FBI and other law enforcement agencies. The FBI asked all the stations that contacted them to not broadcast the letters; however, most of the stations felt it newsworthy and that they should make the public aware of the new threats.

At the ABC affiliate in Austin, the early morning show began its broadcast, with the letter they received, as the lead story.

"We begin today's broadcast with this breaking news. This station has received a letter that directly threatens all twenty-two-hundred IRS employees that work at the Austin processing center and various other IRS locations in the city of Austin. It is a chilling warning. We would like to warn our audience that the nature of this letter, this threat—is chilling and could be disturbing to some viewers," the host said with a concerned look on her face. "We have contacted law enforcement officials; however, neither law enforcement nor this station can confirm the authenticity of this letter. We will tell you that other outlets have received the same letter, but we do not have an exact count of how many television stations received the same letter."

She then looked down at a document in front of her and began reading.

"To All IRS Employees,

Beginning today and from this day forward, we have randomly selected various IRS locations across the country to target in response for your unapologetic terror of American citizens that, frankly, has gone on way too long.

IRS locations will be bombed from time to time. The previous bombings were purposely designed as a warning. By our grace alone, no IRS personnel were injured. Since the IRS and Congress have not acted since those bombings to stop government-sanctioned terror on our citizens by your continual violations of due process and the Fourth Amendment, we have no choice but to act.

Therefore, we consider every single IRS employee a terrorist. You cannot escape us. We will continue to bomb your facilities. We will place snipers outside your IRS offices and will shoot you as you go in or as you come out, on a random basis. We will target you as you leave your homes. If you choose to go to work to terrorize Americans, beginning tomorrow you are putting your life at risk.

For those of you in Congress who facilitate the terrorists at the IRS, you too will be targets. You will not be safe, nor will your families be safe. For those judges who operate in the kangaroo courts known as the Tax Courts, you need to immediately find another line of work before it's too late.

Our message to you is simple. You can no longer terrorize us without evoking terror on yourselves. By this time tomorrow morning, you will know we are serious.

Signed,

Americans for Freedom from IRS Terror

As the breaking news spread across the country, the attrition for IRS employees was noted, as more than thirty percent of workers did not go into their workplaces that morning. Some who showed up to work unaware of the broadcast of the letters left their posts immediately.

"We can't put folks' lives at risk," stated the worried manager at the main office in Austin, who had given his employees a choice to stay or go. "Look how close we came to a disastrous situation not too long ago from this same group. I don't think we can risk that. This time, it could turn deadly."

IRS Commissioner Ivan Stanislau issued a press release about how dedicated the people of the IRS were, and stated that no terror threats would stop them from doing their mandated mission.

"This terror group hides in the shadows," Stanislau announced to managers, "and they don't have the guts to pull off anything serious,"

The news of the IRS threats began to overtake the daily updates on the mass shootings on all media outlets throughout the country as the lead story.

Commissioner Stanislau, who was embattled by GOP-led Congressional investigative committees accusing of him of lying to Congress about the targeting of political enemies in the Johnson administration, particularly targeting Tea Party organizations, was especially combative and asked for a news crew to video him leaving his home in the University Heights area of D.C. to prove to his employees that it was safe to go to work.

At least three national television crews and two local stations positioned satellite trucks on the crowded street to broadcast with live crews. The commissioner's media manager had told the media outlets the commissioner would make a brief statement in his driveway before getting in his car and driving to the sprawling monolithic IRS headquarters on Constitution Avenue.

Ivan Stanislau was a weasely-looking fellow, with short gray hair, balding on top, and he wore round, silver-framed bi-focals. He didn't look like he had the intestinal fortitude to make such a public gesture in defiance of a terror group. A career bureaucrat, he rose in the IRS ranks primarily because of his record as a tough, non-compromising revenue agent who had gained fame in high-profile criminal tax collection efforts. Although his record of collection was impressive, he was often cited for his overly zealous tactics that raised eyebrows at Treasury. The truth was that, since the IRS operates literally without regard to the Bill of Rights, he commonly used practices that would have gotten both civil and criminal cases thrown out of normal courts instantly.

Walking out his front door, wearing a grey wool coat, suit and tie and carrying a briefcase, the commissioner waved to cameras with an awkward smile as he walked to a bank of microphones set up on his small patch of front lawn. The media had been forewarned that the commissioner was only going to make a brief statement and would not take questions.

"Good morning," Stanislau announced. "Like all dedicated IRS employees, I am going to work today to do the job the American people expect me to do. I, like my fellow IRS employees, will not be intimidated, threatened or terrorized by fringe, right-wing extremists, and we will continue to do our jobs. I want to thank my colleagues at the IRS, and I have full trust and confidence in the U.S. Treasury and Justice Departments that they will keep us safe and catch these lunatics in short order. Thank you."

The press tried to ask questions, but Stanislau waved them off. He walked about ten steps to his government-provided four-door sedan and opened the back door, reaching in to set his briefcase on the back seat. He then opened the front door and turned back to the cameras once again and waved.

Suddenly, a few of the reporters heard a muffled thud. The cameras caught Stanislau's head as it snapped back violently. His glasses flew off his face. Blood and brain matter splattered the door, windshield and inside the driver's front seat area.

With live camera feeds rolling, the commissioner's head snapped back upright, revealing a bullet hole right above the front left temple with blood streaming out. His face was expressionless. He remained standing for what seemed like seconds, then he slowly crumpled to the ground, his head hitting face first on the driveway. The back half of his head was mostly gone, and the grisly sight of blood, skull bone fragments and brain matter all over the car were exposed in plain sight of the cameras. Screams sounded in the background from the reporters and crews on the scene as the reality slammed into their collective consciousness.

The cameras continued to broadcast live to the world as chaos broke out and the live cameras were dropped or knocked over as the crews realized what had happened. Crews scrambled as they instantly became aware they were in some type of live-shooter scenario, not knowing where the next shot would come from or who would be the target. There was no police presence for the live taping of Stanislau's press event.

Lofton's operative ducked down behind a roof wall on top of an apartment building four doors down and cattycornered across the street. He unscrewed his noise suppressor and took apart his modified M24 sniper rifle, putting it into his backpack. He climbed down the fire escape to the ground, stepped into a walkway between two fence lines and walked two blocks to a waiting car. As soon as he got in the car, the sniper changed shirts, took off his wig, hat and mustache and a faux paunch belly. No one noticed him.

Many of the live television feeds were cut off by producers back in studio once they realized what they were transmitting to the world. Instantly, the video of the assassination of Ivan Stanislau went viral. Soon thereafter, a tweet on a Twitter feed from a brand-new Twitter account named "The Great Purge" stated:

"This is only the beginning. We warned IRS not to go to work terrorizing Americans. Let this be notice to all IRS employees from today forward. #thegreatpurge"

Within a few minutes, that tweet was followed by:

"The IRS commissioner has made a career of terrorizing innocent Americans and political enemies. That career ended today. #thegreatpurge

Followed a few minutes later by:

"There is no one we cannot reach. Do you hear that, Congress? President Bartlett? Close the IRS now, for good! #thegreatpurge

The tweets came from Hank Lofton as he sat on a concrete city park bench on the Galveston sea wall, looking out at the Gulf of Mexico. He stood up, about to walk down the steps to the vacant beach, when he decided to send one more tweet.

"Zach Turner, who the govt has in custody, is not associated with #thegreatpurge."

Lofton walked down the steps to the edge of the waves pounding the beach from the Gulf. After meticulously wiping it down, he took the prepaid temporary phone he'd used and threw it as far as he could into the water. One couldn't be too careful.

CHAPTER 57

"President Vladimir Putin could never have imagined anyone so ignorant or so willing to destroy their people like Obama much less seeing millions vote for someone like Obama. They read history in America, don't they? Alas, the schools in the U.S. were conquered by the Communists long ago and history was revised thus paving the way for their Communist presidents."

- Xavier Lerma
Russian columnist for Pravda
Source: Obamas Soviet Mistake, Pravda, 19.11.2012

Texas Rangers' Commandant Pops Younger had a decision to make. Federal arrest warrants had been issued for all of Zach Turner's known associates, including Will and Beard.

Both the government and the media had already tied the *Free Texas* movement to the IRS bombings and the mass shooting. Will knew that reaching out to Pops presented risks but, like Zach, he totally trusted Pops.

"Its Turner's wing man, Will," said Dyson as he handed the phone to Pops as they drove to the Dallas Fairgrounds for more investigative meetings with the FBI.

The news had just broken about Commissioner Ivan Stanislau being assassinated on national TV.

"Younger here," said Pops.

"Mr. Younger, this is Will Turnbow. Thank you for taking my call."

"Hello, son. I'm sorry I didn't get back to you last night. I'm going to ask you right off the bat…"

"No need, sir. We had nothing to do with this morning's events. Nothing whatsoever."

"Do you know who did?"

"I have an idea," hedged Will, "but I can't imagine it would have gone to this extreme."

"Hank Lofton?"

"I couldn't confirm this for sure," Will said. "His group doesn't communicate with us since he split with Zach. I was a little bit more convinced when I saw the tweets."

"What about the tweets?"

"Lofton always used the term 'purge' when referring to ultimately fighting back against the *Deep State*. It may just be coincidence, but I thought you should know."

"Son, I want you to know we are checking on Zach daily. His wife and son were reunited last evening and are headed to Austin as we speak. We know Zach has nothing to do with any of this. What news have you boys got for me?" Pops questioned.

"Mr. Younger, we have information that will exonerate Zach, but we also have some of the most incredible video testimony you will ever witness. Unfortunately, it will rock our constitutional republic to the core—and it goes all the way to the White House."

Pops pondered that for a few seconds. "Where did you boys *get* this information?"

"Ottosson."

"How is that possible?" asked Pops.

"Let's just say we had a nice sit-down chat with him," Will said.

"Really? Why am I suddenly worried how you boys *extracted* that information?"

"We *conveniently* arranged for Mr. Ottosson to meet with us."

"Son, be careful. Any testimony you get outta that scumbag that is acquired by questionable methods may be inadmissible later," scolded Pops.

"I think you need to see the video, sir."

"Who else has seen it?"

"Only my crew was present," Will told him.

"Where is Ottosson now?"

"He's our guest, for now."

"Your guest?" Pops chuckled. "I don't want to know any more about that."

"I understand," Will said.

"What can you tell me about the Russian?" Pops pressed.

"The Russian orchestrated the mass shooting."

"Of course, he did," Pops snorted. "Did Ottosson give you details?"

"Yes," Will said, "and these details go all the way to the Oval Office."

Pops paused to let that statement sink in for a moment, "What? Son, are you telling me the damned president can be implicated in the Dallas mass shootings? And... that you have proof?"

"I'm not only telling you that, sir, but this is only the beginning of the admissions made by Ottosson."

"How credible are they?"

"Seem credible to us," Will stated. "You'll have to see the videos and determine for yourself."

"I'm going to want to interview Ottosson, if he is still your guest," Pops said.

"We can bring him to you, or you can come to Ottosson."

"Where you boys at?"

"We are much closer to D.C. than we are to Dallas, sir."

"I'm coming to you. Don't tell me on this line where Ottosson is; just tell me where to meet you. I'll hand this over to Dyson. We will be there as quick as we can."

Dyson took the phone to arrange a different method to get the details on where to meet Will. After he got off the phone, he turned to Pops, "Did I hear correctly that the Russian is involved in the shooting and that the White House knows?"

"These boys are saying Ottosson is claiming the White House not only knows, but had something to do with it."

"Damn, Pops, how is it these boys have gotten to Ottosson? What did they do, kidnap his ass?"

"Probably. All I know is somehow we have been given the opportunity to interview him."

"Pops, if they've kidnapped him and we go wherever they're holding him, we could be accessories!"

"Damn it, Dyson, I know that. I also know we've got a couple of hundred murdered kids and a governor who's plane went down mysteriously, who just happened to be a personal friend! I'll be damned if I ain't following up on this lead. You know that boy Turner ain't done a damned thing. What the hell choice do we have?"

"Pops, the minute we step foot outta the State of Texas, the feds will reinstate that original warrant on *you* somehow. How the hell are we going to pull this off?"

"Nobody needs to know we are leaving. Tell command to make up an excuse for not meeting with the FBI today. Hell, tell 'em I got the damned runs or something!"

He continued. "We can't use any DPS aircraft. Get someone to charter us a commercial plane under some other name. Ain't no way I'm getting on a state plane, right now, anyway. We also don't want them to file the real flight plan. We can deviate and change course in the air."

Two hours later, a chartered Citation lifted off the ground from Addison Airport in north Dallas, headed to a private airport in the D.C. suburbs.

After fifty years in law enforcement, Pops was now faced with the decision of his life. Just going to where Will was holding Ottosson could put him at odds with the law he was sworn to uphold. What was even worse was that he had no idea how Will's crew had coaxed these admissions from Ottosson. Pops never believed in torture of any kind for prisoners of war, much less an American citizen on American soil. Few people realized that Pops entered the Korean War at eighteen years old and was captured by the North Koreans. He was held for ninety-seven days before he fashioned a daring escape that freed him and three other American soldiers. Pops was awarded the Silver Star for his valor.

While Pops was a POW, the North Koreans inflicted horrible beatings and torture sequences on him and his three fellow Marines. In Pops' mind and in his heart, torture of any kind was extremely difficult to justify.

CHAPTER 58

"The biggest threat to the American people today lies with the United States government. And while gun ownership stands as a barrier to potential, Nazi-like behavior, the long-term solution is to dismantle, not reform, the iron fist of the welfare state and the controlled economy. This includes the end (not the reform) of the IRS, the DEA, the ATF, the SEC, the FDA, HUD, the departments of HHS, Labor, Agriculture, and Energy, and every other agency that takes money from some and gives it to others or interferes with peaceful behavior. It entails the repeal of all laws that permit such conduct. And it means the privatization of most of the bureaucrats who work for the U.S. government."

- Jacob G. Hornberger
Future of Freedom Foundation 1997

Milton Weingold opened the door to the Oval Office as President Bartlett was on the telephone with the Prime Minister of Israel.

Bartlett liked to conduct many of her calls with heads of state from other countries without being monitored by her chief of staff or cabinet members. The calls would be recorded, then replayed later to determine whether to keep the recordings. Bartlett was very sensitive to criticism and did not appreciate any guidance that may come her way from inside the West Wing while a conversation was taking place.

Bartlett immediately noticed the look on Weingold's face, letting her know that his sudden entrance in the middle of her phone call wasn't appreciated and would likely mean he had disturbing or unsettling news. Bartlett ended the call abruptly. Few outside of Bartlett's close associates knew of her vicious temper that could flare with the slightest provocation.

"I'm sorry, Madam President. I've received several calls from CIS, members of Congress and the CIA regarding Ottosson. He's nowhere to be found."

"What the hell does that mean, Milt? I've told you people before that he was a liability because he can't keep his damned prick in his pants. He's probably shacked up with some whore somewhere on a drinking binge. Why in the hell are you interrupting my call for something like this?"

"Whenever this has happened before…"

"Before? How many times has this happened?" Bartlett asked.

"It has happened before, but the difference this time is the CIA always knew how to get in touch with him. Even the CIA has not heard from him in three days, and he *always* answers them."

Bartlett looked at Weingold, who still had a very pained look on his face.

"What are you not telling me, Milt?"

"The CIA detected incursions into the messaging system and files they have on Ottosson. Somebody has breached Langley's systems to acquire highly confidential files on Ottosson."

"How is that possible? What the hell are you *really* telling me, Milt?"

"It means someone has possibly gotten access to highly sensitive information. In the wrong hands, it would be extremely damaging."

"Milt, why in the hell would we keep that kind of information stored anywhere?"

"We don't, exactly, but we are being told that CIS systems have been breached also. It's the combination of those two breaches, coupled with Ottosson's absence, that has our attention."

"Can we tell what they acquired in the breaches?"

"No, but Langley is saying the methodology of the breaches is consistent with the unlocking of different security protocols in succession. It's like following a trail, and the trail leads ultimately to places we don't want anyone to go. Also, we were confident in CIS' ability to lock down data in the past, but whoever is doing this is getting inside information of some kind."

"Are you telling me Ottosson has turned somehow?"

"I doubt it. He's gotten rich. Why would he do anything other than protect his own interests at this point?" Weingold questioned.

Weingold and Bartlett had an unspoken agreement never to discuss Volkov. Bartlett didn't even know his name, but she knew the CIA connected a Russian intelligence operative with CIS and the results, for their purposes, had been spectacular.

"What about the Russian? Could he have been turned?" asked Bartlett reluctantly.

"I guess anything is possible, but he had indicated his desire to completely disappear after Dallas. He was paid handsomely and will continue to get paid with each month that goes by. He has no reason to turn or divulge information at this point," Weingold stated quietly.

"Do we know what they know?"

"No, we don't know anything other than what I am telling you. We've checked on Ottosson's passport and he hasn't left the country, as far as we can tell."

"Damn it, Milt, look how far we've come. We are right on the cusp of major reforms. We've got the Court turned. We've quashed the Texas thing. We are turning the majority in Congress with each election with the help of CIS. Hell, we are about to turn the 2nd Amendment on its ear. We cannot afford a setback; do you understand me?"

"Yes, Madam President, I agree. There's only so much we can ask Langley to do. We have to remember there are still a few Boy Scouts there, Madam President. We can't afford a complete investigative resource effort of the CIA or FBI or send signals to alert the inspector general of each department. We have all the directors and their subordinates on board, but all it takes is one of those Boy Scouts divulging something to the press, and we are in big trouble."

"Who knows how to reach the Russian?"

"I do not, but I have a CIA resource who likely can. If anyone can, he can. But remember, Madam President, he vowed to retire and completely disappear after Dallas. He stated on numerous occasions that, if the money kept coming, we'd never hear from or see him again."

"Part of his deal was we would keep paying him as long as the investigation went as planned and none of his compatriots were arrested or charged, right—for years to come?"

"Yes, Madam President."

"If we are paying him monthly, then somebody knows how to reach him."

"I'm not sure about that, Madam President."

"If you can't find him in the next twenty-four hours, then quit paying him," Bartlett snapped. "This will flush him out and force him to reach out to someone. Since we have been told he is the best in the world at what he does and, if we haven't found Ottosson in the next twenty-four hours, his continued payments are contingent upon him finding—or *dealing* with Ottosson."

"Madam President, are you sure this is what you want me to do?"

"Milt, you can't find Ottosson, right?"

"Not at the moment."

"You're telling me CIA and CIS systems have been breached to the point someone may have intelligence or evidence against us?"

"Possibly, Madam President."

"Do you have another plan, Milt? Right now you aren't presenting me with many options."

"Madam President, the Russian is highly volatile."

"Damn it, so is Ottosson, for different reasons. But is he reliable? Isn't that what you have been told?"

"Yes, reliable is an understatement."

"If you can't locate the Russian to help us find Ottosson, then turn off his access to money."

"Yes, Madam President."

"Have you provided me an alternative?"

"No, ma'am. I've only giving you the facts as they stand at this moment. But, Madam President, let me express my utmost reservations at stopping the flow of money to the Russian."

"If you've got a better plan, Milt, now is the time to tell me."

"I do not, Madam President."

"Then why are you still standing there?" Bartlett barked. Weingold dropped his head and replied before answering sheepishly, "I will implement this immediately."

"I want hourly updates, Milt. I want the CIA director in my office within the hour, along with the NSA director or anyone who can tell me how we are going to find these two people," she ordered Weingold as he was leaving the Oval Office.

"Yes, Madam President. I will make this happen."

Weingold slunk out of the office, his tail figuratively between his legs.

CHAPTER 59

"A society of sheep must in time beget a government of wolves."

- Bertrand de Jouvenel (1903-1987)
French Philosopher & Economist

"Right now, I don't want you to take me to Ottosson. I want you to show me the videos you took," Pops told Will as they met at a pre-determined location about twenty miles from where Ottosson was being held.

"Pops, before you watch this, you must understand we did what we had to do to get Ottosson to give us this information."

"Son, if you did what I think you might have done with this scumbag, I'm not sure how reliable the information will be. I've seen men who have had the snot beaten out of them and would give their captors any information, true or not, just to stop the pain. Doesn't mean it's real."

For the next two hours Will and Beard showed Pops and Dyson the videos of Ottosson's interrogation. Pops winced, then got up from his chair from the very first moment Ottosson was struck on the foot with the sledgehammer.

"None of what you will see from here forward is life-threatening to him," said Will. He couldn't help but notice how uncomfortable Pops was with the blow to Ottosson's foot.

"Boys, I've seen this method before, and I'll tell y'all right now that most men will say anything you want to hear to stop the pain."

"Sir, we asked him open-ended questions that we either knew the answers to or ones in which we had some evidence he was connected," offered Beard.

"Go on; show us the rest of the tape," directed Pops.

Pops and Dyson watched the rest of the tape without much emotion except from Dyson, who got very uncomfortable with Ottosson's guttural screams when the voltage was ramped up on his scrotum.

"What do we do with this information now that we have it?" asked Will. "We've got to get Zach outta jail. This should do it."

"Except that it will put you two boys in jail. I'm glad I'm seeing this outside my jurisdiction 'cuz I'd be obligated to haul you boys in."

"Hell, Pops, this is learned behavior by these CIA spooks. They do this crap all over the world, I'm sure," commented Dyson.

"Sir, no disrespect, but I'm not sure if we have time to argue the morality of enhanced interrogation techniques. I will tell you it has helped us avoid serious terrorist attacks you don't even know about. We've got a mass shooting of eight hundred people, many of whom were kids, and there's evidence that ties this directly back to the White House," said Will.

"Son, we understand that. It's not been proven that the stories you get as a result of torture are consistently reliable. Not to mention that some poor innocent son of a bitch could be tortured. It completely skips due process and, as much as you boys are protectors of the Constitution, I would imagine that would be important to you."

"It is, sir, believe me."

"Ya know, son, I think of the Constitution kinda like the Bible. You can't pick out that piece there and this piece here to suit your fancy," Pops told them. "I'm sure the CIA taught you this was acceptable. King George, Stalin, Hitler, Mussolini and other tyrants tortured their people. Terrorists torture people." Pops turned from Will and Beard toward Dyson, "Damn it, Dyson, exactly when the hell did this country fall to the dark side? We used to be better than this? We won the *Big War* without torturing anyone," said Pops, shaking his head.

Will didn't want to argue with Pops, but was intent on having Pops see things his way. "Sir, now that you have this information, what do you want to do with it? The damned *Deep State* is so vast, I'm not sure who we can trust. Do you have people in law enforcement at the federal level you can trust?"

Pops pulled his paper cup up to his mouth to spit some tobacco juice, generated by the pinch between his bottom lip and gums, into it as he pondered Will's question. "I know this. If you turn Ottosson loose, none of us will ever hear from him or see him again. They'll get rid of him. Now, if Ottosson was somehow in Texas where we could arrest him and keep him in protective custody, that would be the first step. There are very few Yankees in D.C. I can trust. You gotta remember that most of them boys at the FBI would love to do to me what you just did to this Ottosson fellow. The damned governor is no help; he's part of the problem. He has too many ties to D.C. and I don't trust him as far as an armadillo can piss."

"We understand. We can get him to Texas, Mr. Younger."

"What about that Russian? If what Ottosson claims is true, and I believe it is, I want that son of a bitch." Pops stopped, glaring at them. "Surely your spooks across the pond can find this nut job terrorist?"

"Sir, he's the best we ever faced in the CIA. If he's been handsomely paid and has decided to really disappear, then we will have a very hard time finding him. Outside of Osama Bin Laden, he's the most wanted man by the CIA for twenty years, but the public will never hear his name. He's killed at least six of our operatives over the years and dozens more from other countries. He's smart, very smart, and he's brutally effective."

"He may be smart but, like all criminals, he'll make a mistake. When he does, I plan to be there to make him bleed for taking down the governor and those poor kids," Pops vowed.

Pops and Dyson got back on the Citation to take them back to Dallas. They sat quietly in their seats without speaking for nearly thirty minutes.

Finally, Dyson spoke up, "The Pops Younger I've known for forty years would have slapped handcuffs on those boys for kidnapping and assault."

"Yep, you're right, Dick. In normal times. *These ain't normal times.* You can consider us undercover, waitin' for the right opportunity to *take it all down.*"

"That was a lot to take in, Pops. You can't carry this burden alone. We've got to find some help."

"There isn't *any* at the federal level. I used to laugh at this *Deep State* thing as some invention of conspiracy wackos. Hell, the proof of how deep and how wide this thing runs is we've got nowhere to go with the information we just learned. Who the hell do we trust? We have Senator Perez and that's about it," complained Pops. "I think we need some trusted sources in the press. If those boys end up with Ottosson back in Texas, then we can make some progress. That video's credibility will be challenged by the torture. Damn, I really wish they hadn't done that."

"The IRS commissioner's assassination will ramp up the search for Will and the rest of Zach's crew like never before. I give them even odds to make it back to Texas with Ottosson," said Dyson.

"They've got a network of fellows just like them. They'll make it."

"Sounds like you have a plan." Dyson glanced at Pops.

"Ottosson isn't safe, even when in custody. If the Russian knows we've got him, and if he doesn't know yet, he'll know soon enough, he's wily enough to reach him no matter where we hold him. It's very important that he be kept safe. And besides, Ottosson is how I can draw out the Russian."

"So you are going to use Ottosson for *bait* for the Russian?"

"Like a jackrabbit in a bear trap! Wherever he's holed up, as soon as he knows we have Ottosson, you can bet the Russian will not be far away."

Pops and Dyson continued to discuss strategy, all contingent upon them successfully transporting Ottosson to Texas. Pops informed Dyson that the only safe place he knew to put Ottosson was in the Death Row Unit of the Huntsville State Prison in Texas.

"The Death Row Unit is a maximum-security facility," said Pops. "What could be better?"

Surely, Volkov couldn't reach Ottosson there…

Dyson received a call late in the evening from Will. The van carrying Ottosson, along with Turnbow, Beard, and four others, were in Texarkana and would be in Dallas in the wee hours of the morning. They decided on a rendezvous point in Dallas, and the Texas Rangers were going to escort the van another two-and-a-half hours south to Huntsville. Then, and only then, would Pops rest. He would have Ottosson secured away to plan the next steps of how this damaging information to the entire Republic could be divulged.

By 3:00 a.m., Pops and Dyson both were getting concerned that they had not heard from Will. He was an hour and a half late at the rendezvous point in south Dallas. The Texas Rangers had staged six vehicles along the route to fall in line in front and in back of Turnbow's van to lead him to Huntsville.

At 3:21 a.m., the Rangers could hear Garland police radio transmissions regarding a vehicle crash on a bridge over Lake Roy Hubbard on Interstate

30 inbound. It was the same interstate that Will's van was traveling from Texarkana.

"Get on the radio and find out what vehicles were involved," Pops ordered one of his Rangers.

"They are reporting multiple fatalities," answered another Ranger.

Dyson and Pops looked at each other. Certainly, this couldn't be them, but Pops had a gut feeling something was wrong. Will was exactly like Zach Turner, punctual as hell and very good at communication. He would have gotten a message to them if he was going to be late, even with a communications lock-down. This was way too important.

Then came the news. The Garland police were reporting over their radios that the accident was a single-vehicle accident in which a gray van rolled several times before careening into Lake Hubbard. Divers were on the scene preparing to dive in twenty-six feet of water. One body had already been recovered.

"Get me there now!" yelled Pops to Dyson and his Rangers. They sped the fifteen miles from the rendezvous point to the scene of the accident.

Garland police were surprised to see Texas Rangers appear on the scene, and even more surprised to find it was the legendary Pops Younger.

"What the hell is Pops Younger doing *here*?" asked one of the police officers.

"I heard something about *national security* from one of the Rangers, but hell, it's Pops Younger here on our accident scene. Wow," uttered a young police sergeant.

"Why the hell aren't those divers in the water?" demanded Pops to the local police.

"We need daylight, sir. The lake is so murky, the lights they brought to dive with aren't strong enough to see six inches in front of their faces."

"Damn, can't they at least get to the vehicle?"

"We haven't found it yet. All we have are eyewitness accounts about the van. We have a body over there on the grass."

Pops and Dyson hurriedly walked over to the body covered by a sheet.

"Go ahead." Pops motioned for Dyson to pull back the sheet.

"Son of a bitch, that's Beard. Damn it! Son of a bitch!" barked Pops.

Pops turned quickly to the Garland police officer in charge of the accident scene, "Where are the witnesses? I want to speak to them right now."

Pops was led over to a small group of people who were standing around, talking to police and anxiously waiting to see if the divers could come up with anything. Pops talked to several of the witnesses, who only saw the van flip and careen off the bridge into the lake but didn't see how it happened or what caused it to lose control. They reported lots of sparks flying, but Pops mentally noted that it was before the van flipped. They all claimed they didn't see a second vehicle enter the lake, so the police were treating it as a single-vehicle accident.

Eventually, all the Texas Rangers who had been staged at various points on I-45 to escort the van containing Ottosson to Huntsville made it to the accident scene. Dyson had his Rangers start their own investigation.

The entire interstate was closed going westbound to Dallas while the accident investigation and recovery of bodies was underway. The police were looking for skid marks and any clue they could find. The Department of Public Safety officers, under the command of the Texas Rangers, showed up to help with the accident. It suddenly occurred to Pops that they had only closed down the westbound side.

"Close the damned eastbound lanes," he ordered a DPS officer, who wasn't entirely sure why Pops wanted the lanes on the other side of the freeway shut down. With the morning commute coming, at least the outbound lanes would be open.

A few minutes later, the closure of those lanes wasn't happening fast enough for Pops.

"I said shut down those damned lanes!"

"Sir, we are waiting for other patrol cars to come up and divert the traffic one exit ramp back."

"I'm telling you right now to immediately close those lanes. If you have to climb over the damned guard rail and stop the traffic yourself, do it!" barked Pops. "I want it closed a mile and a half back east and west! Does everyone understand me, or am I stuttering?" yelled Pops, who was physically shaken by the death of Beard, whom Pops had grown fond of, and the possible loss of Will and a key witness.

The sun came up at 6:36 a.m. that morning and the divers entered the water. Thirty-five minutes later, they located the van. The divers came to the shore to report five bodies were in the van. The van was lying on its side at the bottom of the lake. One by one, divers pulled up bodies and brought them to the shore. Pops and Dyson were beside themselves to see if Will and Ottosson were among the dead.

Four bodies were recovered; however, none of them were Ottosson or Will. Dyson had also grown to admire and respect Will, despite his misgivings about his CIA past and differences early on. Somehow, some way, they both hoped the next body recovered was Ottosson and not Will.

Finally, the divers brought another body to the shore. It was Will.

Pops knelt down next to Will to view the body of his newfound friend, trying to do his job and not get emotional as he looked for any signs of what happened. Will had an obvious massive head wound from the crash but no other signs of foul play.

"There's got to be another body in the lake," Dyson told the divers. "We know for a fact there was another person in the van, six in total. Keep looking."

A Texas Ranger came running up to Pops and Dyson. As he tried to catch his breath, he blurted, "Sir, I have six .223 shell casings back there on the ground about five hundred yards."

"On the other side of the freeway? Outbound or inbound side?" asked Pops.

"Outbound," said the Ranger.

"Now you folks know why I wanted the outbound lanes closed, too! There's evidence over there. Have everyone form a line and walk the entire scene. I'm talking a half mile either way. Do you understand me, men?"

"Yes, sir," answered the Rangers and DPS officers.

As Pops and Dyson waited anxiously for the cranes to pull the van from the depths of Lake Hubbard, the combined law enforcement teams formed a line and walked, step by step, on both sides of the freeway, identifying eighty-six empty shell casings scattered around, on both sides of the freeway. Every shell casing was marked on the spot where it lay. Pops' attention immediately snapped back to the lake. The crane was starting to pull up the van, and it slowly emerged from the water. Meanwhile, divers were scattered at different points in the lake, looking for the final body that would match Pops' information about the number of passengers in the van.

As the gray-colored van slowly began to emerge from the lake, Pops walked to the edge of the water, followed by Dyson, his Rangers and various law enforcement officers from the area.

"Geez, Pops, look at that," Dyson noted.

"Sons of bitches. Damn," said Pops.

The crane swung the van, which had water pouring out of it from all the windows, to a predetermined area along the shore.

The gray van had no windows or glass whatsoever. What caught their attention as soon as the van was fully visible were the bullet holes down the driver's side of the van; lake water poured out of the perforations. As they walked around the van, they saw that the entire van was riddled with bullet holes down both sides, in front and in back.

Pops instructed his team to immediately look for any cell phones, laptops or other equipment and to take any they found to his SUV. To Pops' disappointment but not his surprise, no cell phones or laptops were found.

"Sir, this is consistent with some wounds we have found on some of the bodies," a Texas Ranger said.

"Don't you think it's strange that the bullet holes are on both sides? Does that mean their assailant changed lanes or that there was a high-speed chase?" asked Dyson to nobody in particular.

"Look at the direction of the holes on the driver's side. These shots were fired from an oncoming vehicle or someone in the median on the opposite side," Pops stated. "The holes on the passenger side are pretty much straight on, meaning someone pulled up on that side and let loose."

"Who the hell is that?" asked Dyson, as two black helicopters, with the thud-thud-thud of chopper blades, moved toward them. One chopper hovered while the other set down on the empty interstate. As it got closer, the emblem on the side of the chopper became evident.

"FBI?" Dyson stared at the ominous birds. "What the hell are they doing here?"

Six men in suits emptied out of the first chopper as the second one landed about fifty yards away. The men walked straight toward Pops and the contingent of law enforcement surrounding the van.

"What the hell do you want?" Pops asked Regional FBI Director Michael Jarvis.

"It's my understanding this accident involves several individuals wanted in connection with the IRS bombings and the murder of the IRS commissioner. We consider this a crime scene and will take over this investigation. You can have your people stand down. In the meantime, I'd like you to brief me on what has been done so far and what evidence you have," Jarvis ordered.

"When pigs fly," Pops stated flatly, taking a cigar out of his front left pocket, chewing the end off it and spitting it at the feet of Jarvis.

"Excuse me?" Jarvis looked astonished.

"I said, when pigs fly."

"Younger, I don't need any more of your homespun Texas wisdom. This crime scene is now under federal jurisdiction."

"Whose bodies do you think are over there being loaded by the coroner?"

"Those are likely suspects in multiple federal warrants."

"We haven't called you boys in. How the hell do you already know who these victims are?"

"We're the FBI, Younger," snarled Jarvis disrespectfully. "We get *paid* to know these things. How many bodies do you have?"

"We've recovered all the bodies," said Pops.

"Then why are there still divers in the water?" asked Jarvis.

"Just being thorough," snapped Dyson, who was also bent out of shape because of Jarvis' attitude.

Jarvis turned to the FBI agents behind him and nodded his head. Like automatons, the men turned to the van and went to take a look at it.

"Looking for anything in particular?" asked Pops.

"Of course." Jarvis stared at Pops, insolence oozing from him. "Evidence of a crime. Who's in charge of these divers"?"

"I am," Pops told him in a calm voice.

"They will now take direction and orders from me," Jarvis retorted.

"When pigs fly," Pops answered again.

"These men were under federal warrant. This is now part of a federal investigation. This is a national security investigation." Jarvis started to join his men. "I need my team to look at the bodies and see if we can identify them."

"You take one step toward those bodies over there and I'll put a pop knot on your head so fast, you'll think you were in a New Orleans whorehouse." Pops fixed his steel blue eyes on the director's dark eyes.

"Younger, I've got orders."

"I don't give a shit. This is *my* crime scene." Pops took a step toward Jarvis. "Now take your boys and git your candy asses back on that bird, or you and I are gonna dance."

"Younger, you're playing with fire. This is now a national security case. My orders come from very high up."

"Unless you got written orders from God himself, you ain't touching my crime scene. This is my jurisdiction. Now scoot your ass outta here."

Jarvis turned and motioned for his men to come back from the van. They all walked back across the inbound lanes of the interstate and stood near the choppers. Two local police officers couldn't help themselves and started clapping for Pops, to the dismay of the FBI agents.

The divers continued to scour the lake for another body.

Pops motioned to Dyson and walked away from everyone so nobody could hear their conversations.

"Where the hell is Ottosson?" asked Pops.

"He's got to be in that lake somewhere, unless he got out before the van got riddled," answered Dyson.

"There's no way Will let anyone nab Ottosson—under *any* conditions," Pops said confidently. "Instruct the divers to also look for laptops or cell phones. If they find anything, I don't want them to bring it up. Just mark the location. I don't want any further evidence brought up while they are here." Pops nodded to the FBI crew.

"Got it, Pops," Dyson said, walking over to the lake with a slight smile on his face.

For the rest of the day, up until dark, the divers continued to search for another body and any further evidence, like a laptop or cell phone. Pops knew Beard always seemed to have multiple devices and, so far, only one had been recovered. He had no idea if that laptop could be saved or its contents recovered. He needed the video confession of Ottosson.

The divers came back to shore at sunset.

Ottosson had not been found.

CHAPTER 60

"There are no necessary evils in government. Its evils exist only in its abuses."

- Andrew Jackson (1767-1847)
7th US President

ABC News reported that the prime suspects—in the IRS bombings, in the mass shooting at the festival, and IRS Commissioner Ivan Stanislaus assassination—had been killed in a high-speed chase in a Dallas suburb. The anchor reported that white supremacists in the *Free Texas* organization, which had ties to the Texas independence movement, various Tea Party groups and other radical right-wing zealots, were involved.

Hank Lofton and his crew moved their base of operation out of Texas after they knocked off the IRS commissioner. Lofton and his crew heard the news while in their new hideout deep in the Atchafalaya Swamp in southern Louisiana.

Lofton's crew remained somber because, if the news report was true, it would mean their lifelong Special Forces friends who didn't agree with their approach to fight the *Deep State* had suffered the consequences that were meant for them.

"Damn, Hank, I feel terrible," said one crew member.

"It ain't right. No doubt about that. We need to confirm this is true. We have to send another signal, one that will confuse the feds and show them they got the wrong guys," announced Lofton, rubbing his eyes and his forehead, as the stress of being hunted by the government was only surpassed by his grief over the loss of his good friend Will Turnbow.

They had fought back to back in Afghanistan and other hotspots around the world.

"I agree. They need to know those guys weren't the only ones fighting the *Deep State*. There are more of us, and our numbers grow every day," chimed in Jaxon Haines.

"We've sent the message to Washington. Now it's time the message was sent to Austin," said Lofton. "It's time to rid Austin of the carpetbaggers, RINOs and liberals."

"Ha, you'll have to kill most of the residents to rid Austin of liberals!" laughed one of the crew.

"Gentlemen, we have essentially rendered the IRS incapable of operating, simply out of fear. If we cut the head off the snake of the *Deep State* in Texas, we effectively do the same thing. We all know Governor Strasburg is a D.C. lackey. We will never get an independence referendum with him in office. This also needs to be very public. Hell, it might even make Austin weirder by nudging the liberal nutcases to move back to California!" joked Lofton.

"Hank, they had zero evidence connecting Turnbow, Beard and those guys to the IRS commissioner. I'm just sick about this," said a despondent crew member.

"This is why you cannot forget our cause here, gentlemen. The feds will murder innocents. We've all seen this in our Langley operations, overseas and here on our own soil. I don't believe for a second they believe they got the right people, but the story looks good and it boosts the prospects of Bartlett and those in power. Let's send them another message they won't soon forget and dedicate our next move to Will and his crew!" announced Lofton vehemently.

Pops remained close to the accident scene for two days, hoping they would find some clue to the whereabouts of Ottosson's body or recover more of Beard's or Ottosson's devices. One more laptop was retrieved from the depths of the lake but it wasn't clear yet whose it was.

A black Jeep pulled up on the right median of the interstate, but was stopped by DPS officers. The inside lane of the inbound side of the interstate had been reopened, but the right two lanes were still closed. A man dressed in army fatigues got out and handed a note to a DPS officer, addressed to Pops Younger, and insisted that it be delivered to Pops at once. It stated:

Please give me five minutes. I am with Lofton's crew.

It took about ten minutes to get the note to Pops. He opened it, read it and then asked, "Where is this guy? Bring him to me at once."

A few minutes later, Lofton's crew member was face to face with Pops. "Sir, Lofton has no idea I'm here talking to you."

Pops looked at Dyson and said, "Get his vehicle outta here. Son, come take a walk with me." The two started to walk along the edge of the lake, away from all the activity around the dive. The FBI agents, who had staked out a position not far from the accident scene, were straining to see who Pops was meeting with.

"Don't worry, sir," said the crew member as he glanced to the FBI tent. "They can't trace that Jeep to me."

"Son, are you telling me you stole a vehicle and drove it right up here among all this law enforcement presence? You're either a dumb shit or you've got an incredible set of huevos," chuckled Pops.

"Well, sir, something like that." The guy grinned.

"First, let me ask you if you were part of that execution of the IRS dude?" asked Pops, who followed with the question, "and I'm sure you ain't had nothing to do with the Dallas shootings?"

"Let me just state this, Mr. Younger. There is more bloodshed coming and it's going to land right on your doorstep in Austin. Now, I'll be honest; I became enraged when they arrested Zach and took his wife and kid. My family's neck also came under the bootheel of the IRS. They took everything I had. My family has no money. All I ever did up to that point was support Texas independence."

"I understand, son. We can always debate the right way or wrong way to handle that situation, but you are obviously here to tell me something," pressed Pops, who always had the ability to get right to the point.

"Sir, there is an operation going down in Austin tomorrow and, to be honest with you, I can't participate anymore in this. I deeply believe in our independence but I gotta think that all of these actions, if the truth ever comes out, will eventually have the opposite effect, turning Texans against the cause," the crew member admitted.

"I suppose you are right, son. What is it I need to know?" asked Pops.

For the next thirty minutes, Lofton's crew member laid out the details of Lofton's next operation.

"Dick, tell them to get the damn truck. We gotta hightail it to Austin," Pops yelled to Dyson.

Dyson was shocked that Pops was willing to leave the accident scene. "What the hell is going on? Why are we leaving?"

"Son, this is Commander Dyson. I want you to tell him exactly what you just told me. We are headed back to Austin." Pops barked more orders to his Rangers on site, leaving explicit instructions on what to do if Ottosson's body was found or any additional device evidence showed up in the lake.

"Son, what about your Jeep? You can't just leave it there," said Dyson.

"Y'all might want to get it back to its rightful owner," said the crew member, making it clear that he had just "borrowed" it.

The next day, Texas Senator Simpson was due in Austin to meet with the U.S. Chamber of Commerce at the historic Driskill Hotel in downtown Austin. Texas Governor Strasburg and many notable Texas politicians aligned with the Republican establishment were scheduled to be there as well.

Simpson and Strasburg were keen on trying to rebuild the relationship with the Chamber after it cut ties with the Texas chapter during the *Texas Crisis*. This was a high-profile meeting designed to show the world that the *Texas Crisis* was over and business was back to normal.

Lofton arrived in Austin with his crew the night before to make preparations. Strasburg and Simpson were his targets. The plan was to take out the governor as he left the governor's mansion for the short trip to the Driskill, while Lofton had another team prepared to intercept Simpson's drive to downtown Austin from his arrival at the Austin airport. Four other Texas politicians, who were considered GOP RINOs who had vehemently opposed the independence referendum, were also targeted. Lofton had prepared statements to be sent to Austin TV stations, similar to the letters that went to TV stations across the country that threatened the IRS. Lofton's headquarters for the operation was an old rented house on Austin's east side, only four miles from the downtown area.

Pops and Dyson spent the entire night preparing the Rangers to intercede, and the crew member was told to go back and join Lofton so as not to create suspicion that could cause Lofton to cancel the operation.

With all the Rangers, Austin police and DPS officers in place, Pops' response went into action as soon as Simpson's private plane touched down. Simpson was traveling on a Texas grocery store magnate's private jet, accompanied by other Chamber business leaders.

Pops sat in an SUV positioned just two miles from the rented house where Lofton was to stage his operation. Pops' plan was to intercede as soon as Simpson arrived, before he could be in jeopardy. Dyson was dispatched to the area of the governor's mansion to monitor progress there. Pops and Dyson debated for an hour whether to give the governor advance warning, but both decided Strasburg was so unreliable that he would blow the cover somehow.

At exactly 9:05 a.m., the Texas Rangers and Austin SWAT moved into position to swarm the safe house. The Lofton crew member who had disclosed the operation was inside the house and in charge of monitoring communications, including police scanners. Pops had directed the entire team to radio silence other than cell phones. It would be relatively easy for Lofton's crew member to alert Pops' Rangers when the time was right to storm the home; however, Pops was fully aware of Lofton's experience and ability to fight back—under any scenario. He knew full well that the likelihood of a raid like this on Lofton was almost certain to result in bloodshed.

There were only four crew members in the house with Lofton. At 9:15, SWAT officers were to launch tear gas canisters through the home's windows, along with percussion grenades to disorient Lofton and his team. At the exact same moment, other SWAT and Rangers would descend on the snipers positioned near the governor's mansion and on Lofton's mobile team, whose plan to take out Simpson was to pull up beside Simpson and his entourage. It was critical for the raids to happen simultaneously.

One minute before the raid was to take place, the crew member who had approached Pops drew his weapon on the others in the safe house. He knew how Lofton would react with a SWAT raid. He knew people would die. He immediately called Dyson and told him to stand down on the concussion grenades and tear gas. He asked them to enter the house quickly, as he had a gun drawn on Lofton and the others.

Lofton was incensed and he figured at some point he would make a play for his weapon, but he never did. He continued to shout at the crew member as SWAT and the Rangers stormed the home and quickly restrained him.

Lofton was placed in handcuffs as he shouted "Traitor" to his crew member.

At the exact time the team entered the east Austin safe house, the Rangers executed their plan on the other two operations meant to kill Strasburg and Simpson. Their raids were also successful, and they arrested Lofton's crews without a single shot being fired. Simpson and Strasburg were stunned at the turn of events. Simpson was brought to the governor's mansion, where both met with Pops and Dyson to be debriefed on the situation.

"I demand to know why I wasn't informed of this plot!" yelled an enraged Strasburg. "Did you use me and the senator as bait, Younger?"

"You're welcome, Governor," said Pops simply.

"How long did you know about this?" asked Senator Simpson.

"Less than twenty-four hours," answered Dyson.

"That was certainly long enough for you to tell us. I should relieve of you of your command right this minute, Younger," snarled the governor.

"That's certainly your prerogative, sir." Pops calmly pulled out a small chunk of Copenhagen and put it in his mouth as if he didn't give a crap what the governor was threatening.

"Governor," Dyson interjected, "we simply didn't have time. If you would have changed your schedule in the slightest manner or added security to your detail or done anything differently, Lofton would have sensed it and we would not have been afforded this opportunity to arrest him and his crew."

"Still, we should have known," Strasburg retorted. "It doesn't mean we would have changed a thing. You Rangers still think you are cowboys who can chart their own course, do what you like. I can assure you that's going to change."

"Are you finished yapping like a damned Chihuahua now, Governor?" Pops asked. "We've got a good man in federal custody and I'd like to clear his name as soon as possible, and get him out of jail and back home with his wife and son. I believe you will find Lofton quite the witness. He's damned proud of his actions and will admit to all the IRS shenanigans," said Pops.

"They aren't letting Zach Turner out if that's what you think, Younger. He's still a suspect in the Dallas mass shooting," stated Simpson.

"You both know I've been doing our own investigation of that shooting, separate from the feds. I think we both know who's behind that shooting."

"You're out of your mind, Younger. You should have retired long ago," snapped Strasburg.

"Let me tell you, Governor, how the cow ate the cabbage. By the time we are done, both of you are going to wish Lofton had been successful in his little plot. At least then both of you would be considered some sort of heroes and at least be given a state funeral. From what I know, you both are going to be wearing those little orange jump suits for a very long stretch," laughed Pops as he started to walk toward the front door of the governor's mansion.

"You've lost it, Younger. I want your resignation on my desk by 0800 tomorrow morning," demanded Strasburg.

Pops turned back to the governor and walked right up to his face and fixated his steel blue eyes on him, "Strasburg, let me tell you somethin'. I ain't never quit nothin' in my entire life. But I will tell you this. If my last official act as a Texas Ranger is to fit a pair of shackles to you, then I'll leave the Rangers happier than a pig in a poke!"

Pops then turned and walked out the door with Dyson and his Rangers.

CHAPTER 61

"It is seldom that liberty of any kind is lost all at once."

- David Hume (1711-1776)
Scottish Philosopher & Historian

The media pounced on the story coming out of Austin of a major assassination attempt on the Texas governor and U.S. Senator Simpson. The left-wing journalists seized on the opportunity to denounce the Texas independence movement as far-right wingnuts who were racist terrorists.

There was no hiding the fact that the media and politicians were using this latest news story to call for more gun control. They continued to ignore any evidence whatsoever that the *Free Texas* movement didn't have a single link to the Dallas mass shooting.

The anti-gun fervor had crested to a popularity level never seen before in the United States and even the GOP sensed the public shift of sentiment start to cave—similar to the huge swing in acceptance of gay marriage, only much, much faster.

The White House indicated that the president was going to speak to the country live at 7:00 p.m. the day after the Austin arrests in front of a joint session of Congress. The administration knew it could seize on the opportunity to present what appeared to be a consensus between Congress and the administration in front of all Americans.

In amazing fashion, staunch 2nd Amendment defenders—especially those on the right—started contradicting previously held positions, even going so far as to refuse future donations from the NRA. The once-powerful NRA lobby was beginning to lose its grip on congressmen and senators who had vigorously defended them before and in return received donations. A sea change in a fundamental piece of the Bill of Rights was beginning to be shaken to the core.

Similar to a State of the Union address, Bartlett made her way down the aisle of the Joint Session of Congress, glad-handing all those who acknowledged her. It took almost ten minutes for her to make her way down to the main podium.

"Mr. Speaker, Mr. Vice President, members of Congress, distinguished guests and fellow Americans:

"The Declaration of Independence eloquently stated, *We hold these truths to be self-evident, that all men are created equal, that they are endowed with certain unalienable Rights, that among these are Life, Liberty and the pursuit of Happiness.*

"For too long, similar to our country's dark period of slavery, those inalienable Rights were not allotted to *all* Americans. Children go to school scared of the next mass shooting. Just a few short weeks ago, a far-right Texas nationalist militia group killed over eight hundred, including hundreds of children, at a literacy fair. Our nation has the most gun violence in the civilized world.

"The violence has reached a tipping point. We have witnessed the death of federal agents in a state that has proudly embedded the gun culture into its society, which was a factor in those deaths. This same culture evolved into a serious Constitutional crisis, which I'm proud to say this administration has solved.

"We have witnessed the assassination of IRS Commissioner Ivan Stanislau. Just yesterday, a diabolical plot to murder a sitting governor, as well as a U.S. senator who supported our efforts to quell the crisis, was averted by the quick actions of law enforcement. This same group terrorized federal employees with bombs at local IRS offices.

"Enough is enough. Americans have had enough of this gun culture. Congress has had enough of this gun culture. And, frankly, I've had enough of this gun culture."

The entire body of Congress stood up and gave Bartlett a five-minute standing ovation.

"Of all of the Bill of Rights that were so brilliantly crafted, the 2nd Amendment has always been one that was left open to broad interpretations. For those that want to see it literally, instead of as a living and breathing part of the Constitution, I'll just say to you that the Supreme Court has allowed limitations and regulations, and we are confident that new regulations will stand the scrutiny of the Supreme Court."

Another round of applause occurred, but this time only about half of Congress stood during the ovation.

"Tomorrow I will sign an executive order dealing with new gun regulations, which will be the most stringent and strictest in our country's history. These measures will include:

- "The immediate ban on assault weapons as defined in the order. This includes the sale and possession of assault weapons and semi-automatic weapons.

- No longer will any local law enforcement agency be allowed to issue permits for machine guns or suppressors.

- New federal firearms applications will now have a means-testing component for any weapon that contains a magazine or can fire more than six shots. A citizen requesting a permit or license to own a firearm that is not identified as a firearm used for hunting purposes and has more than six shots, such as a revolver, will have to prove they have a legitimate need for the weapon.

- All concealed handgun and open carry laws from any of the fifty states are hereby rescinded. You must reapply for any firearms you intend to keep. If you receive a permit for a firearm, it must be stored in your home or place of business, have a trigger lock attached at all times, and be kept under lock and key.

- Gun manufacturing companies will now be potentially liable for damages for all accidental and intentional shootings. I will ask Congress to enact legislation to this effect immediately."

Congress again erupted in applause. Bartlett waited for the applause to die down before continuing.

- "Parents or guardians whose children access any weapons at home and commit a crime or an accidental shooting will be subject to criminal penalties.

- Any unregistered firearms are now required to be registered.

- The transfer of any firearm privately will require a federal background check or both parties will be subject to criminal prosecution.

- Gun shows will no longer have this private transaction loophole, as every sale will have to have the FFL check. Gun shows will provide a registry of attendees that is maintained by the ATF.

- The purchase of ammunition will be limited to no more than twenty-five rounds every six months, except shotgun shells for hunting that shall be limited to one hundred for the same period.

- Ammunition purchases will also require an FFL permit.

- Ammunition manufacturers will be required to inscribe each ammunition round produced with a unique serial number for tracking purposes within twelve months."

Bartlett paused again to allow for applause, then continued, "If some of these measures had already been in effect, these militia groups that took the life of heroic federal agents would likely not have been possible," she stated. "Our Founding Fathers, who saw the need for the 2nd Amendment during the birth of our nation from a tyrannical king, could never have envisioned the advancement of these weapons that literally took several minutes to load and arm to these high-powered automatic and semi-automatic weapons used to kill American children. I'm sure if they were with us today, they would be standing right behind me, urging me to sign these orders and imploring Congress to act."

Again, Congress stood and applauded, with the exception of a smattering of congressmen, congresswomen, and senators who knew their constituencies would have major issues with these orders.

"And finally, I will ask Congress to move to call a Convention of States in order to permanently fix the 2nd Amendment so that future generations never have to face what American children have faced in their schools and on those fairgrounds in Dallas!"

Now Congress roared, although catcalls came from the gallery, and congressmen and congresswomen from some Southern and Western states.

Pops Younger sat in Dyson's office, chewing on a cigar while watching the president's address with Dyson and several other Texas Rangers at DPS headquarters in northwest Austin. Later that same day, as fate would have it, were the funerals of Will and Beard in Houston.

"Have we really come so far that we have Congress standing up and applauding the demise of the frickin 2nd Amendment?" Dyson wondered out loud.

"I guess those kids were right about that *Deep State* thing," Pops responded.

"Never would have figured, but they sure have the numbers at the Supreme Court to shoot down challenges to Bartlett's executive orders. That little event out there in the Gulf had far-reaching consequences," said Dyson.

"It'll never stand here. Never. Probably not in a few other places, either," stated Pops as he pulled on his handlebar mustaches.

"It's diabolical, the whole damn thing," reasoned Dyson.

"I'll tell you this—just about the time she thinks she's solved this *Texas Crisis*, she does the one dad-burned thing that will stir it back up again like a rattler in a basket full of yellow jackets. She thinks she's gonna take Texans' guns? I'll never git to retire," lamented Pops.

"Couple that with Ottosson's admissions and we'll have a full-blown crisis on our hands, Pops, that makes the last one look as tame as a yard goat. I sure as hell wish we'd get a call telling us they found Ottosson's body in that damned lake."

Later that day, at the funerals of Beard and Will, their families were not only distraught by their deaths but also by the way the media and law enforcement were painting them as criminals and linking them to the Dallas mass shooting. Kymbra and Colt Turner also attended, still worried about Zach, as the feds only let her and Colt visit him once while he was in custody in Houston. He had since been moved to an undisclosed location.

While good friends and family members were focused on consoling the surviving family members, the buzz in quiet conversations at the funeral was Bartlett's direct assault on the 2nd Amendment and the confiscation order of guns. The sad nature of the funerals was mixed with a very resolute anger from those who believed Bartlett's move on the 2nd Amendment was a direct challenge to every Texan.

Also attending the funerals was Evilia Flores, the mother of the heroic teenager, Amanda Flores, who died at the hands of federal troops after trying to cast her ballot on the Texas independence referendum that sparked the *Texas Crisis*. Her homemade Texas flag, where she had sewed "1789" on its white bar (referring to the ratification of the U.S. Constitution and Texans' call to return to the document) was picked up from a dying Flores by Texas hero Chuck Dixon, who was also killed by federal agents while clutching Amanda's flag, which became an endearing symbol to the Texas independence movement.

"Mr. Younger, I've never had a chance to meet you, but I wanted to thank you for honoring my daughter and for your fight for what Amanda believed in," Ms. Flores said as she grasped Pops' hand with both of hers.

"Ma'am, I'm sorry I never got to meet her. I will tell you that all Texas is proud of that little lady."

"Please tell me, Mr. Younger, please, that her death was not in vain. Please tell me that we aren't done and that Amanda's cause is every Texan's cause? Surely it has to be?" she begged, looking deeply into Pops' eyes.

"Ms. Flores, I'll tell you what I can. Your daughter was fighting against something that is as purely evil as the devil and something that has gripped this country to its very core. It cannot stand—and it won't if I have anything to say about it," promised Pops. "God bless you."

"And God bless you, Mr. Younger. God bless Texas."

CHAPTER 62

"I would remind you that extremism in the defense of liberty is no vice. And let me remind you also that moderation in the pursuit of justice is no virtue."

- Barry Goldwater
(1909-1998) US Senator

The call came into Dyson on his way back from the Houston funerals with Pops. They were calling off the search for any more bodies at the accident site at Lake Hubbard. It appeared as though Ottosson's body had simply vanished somewhere in the depths of the lake.

As distressing as this was for Pops and the Rangers, what was even worse was that Pops' computer forensics team back at DPS headquarters could not retrieve the video feed from either of the two laptops that were recovered from the lake.

The Texas Rangers kept Hank Lofton and his crew in their custody, refusing to turn them over to the feds. Pops' team had finally secured a videotaped confession from Lofton regarding the IRS bombings and Commissioner Stanislaus' assassination, but still the feds would not release Zach Turner.

Dyson was trying to arrange a prisoner swap—Lofton for Turner—but the feds were still trying to convince themselves that Zach was involved in the mass shootings. Without Ottosson's videotaped confession, Pops had no clue how to exonerate Zach, except by capturing Volkov, who was long gone and not even in the country anymore.

The next day, U.S. senators and members of Congress lobbied to be at

Bartlett's signing ceremony of the executive orders at the Oval Office. Of course, Texas Senator Simpson was front and center and brought along his fellow establishment buddy, Texas Governor Strasburg. He was the only governor at the signing. It was a strategic move by Bartlett, who knew her orders would be controversial and a tough sell to the average Texan.

Throughout Texas, locally organized militia groups began planning next steps to counter Bartlett's orders. Local TV stations throughout Texas aired interviews of everyday Texans on the street who vowed, "They'll *never* take my guns!"

At least two dozen Texas sheriffs vowed publicly not to enforce any of the orders, citing their oath to the Constitution. Similar stances were taken in several Rocky Mountain states and most of the old South. CNN and MSNBC were constantly showing polling data that depicted eighty-three percent of the country wanted these changes to occur, trying to reinforce Bartlett's actions.

Legal analysts were divided on the subject, as were most on the interpretation of the 2nd Amendment. Many resigned themselves that, no matter the interpretation, the country was moving to support a Constitutional amendment to further restrict, or to altogether eliminate, the 2nd Amendment. Even some GOP leaders embraced the winds of change dictated by mob rule and public sentiment that they could not withstand politically.

An Illinois county had a literacy fair of its own, duplicating the Dallas mass shooting event where admission was free with the voluntary turn-in of a firearm on the Bartlett ban list. The media loved the story and many other counties, cities and townships considered copying their gesture as a way to honor the Dallas victims, incredibly including Houston, Austin and San Antonio city councils.

Even the mighty NRA couldn't stop the momentum.

The Dallas mass shooting was the last straw for many, and most politicians simply couldn't be on the wrong side of the seismic shift in gun control that had enveloped the entire body politic.

A rural Texas county sheriff interviewed on CNN claimed that any forced confiscation of firearms would re-launch the *Texas Crisis* and pit Texans against the rest of America, and even Texan against Texan.

Senator Perez reasoned in vain for Bartlett to suspend the orders, stating drastic changes were not advisable when emotion had overtaken reason. Those in the opposite camp of Perez screamed for immediate action due to the inability of Congress to deal with any gun control changes from any prior mass shooting. Perez was fighting a losing battle in the court of public opinion in every place but Texas.

Pops and the Texas Rangers called for an emergency meeting of Texas county sheriffs, police department chiefs and other law enforcement officials in Texas for a meeting in Austin. Most of the large urban center police departments in Houston, Austin and San Antonio planned to publicly boycott the meetings. They criticized Pops for his past participation in the independence referendum, and his actions in Austin and at Ellington Air Force Base against federal agents. And then there was the highly publicized stand on the International Bridge in Laredo, that was broadcast worldwide, where he single-handedly took on advancing Mexican federales.

Some, even those who favored Bartlett's swift and dramatic executive orders, were pleading for a moratorium or an opportunity to ramp up the new restrictions over time. The left was having none of it.

Bartlett, Weingold, and others in the administration, with first-hand knowledge of the carefully crafted *Deep State* chess game that had led them to this point, were not going to let this opportunity evaporate or delay it for a second.

The *Deep State* now owned Congress, the White House, and the Supreme Court. Although acquired by unthinkable means, it was a clean sweep of all three equal but separate branches of government. To the *Deep State*, the end always justified the means, no matter how it was obtained.

Finally, without warning, the feds agreed to do a prisoner swap with the State of Texas. This is something people would normally see between two separate countries, not between a state and the U.S. Justice Department. Pops had not been willing to hand over Lofton to the feds unless he was able to obtain the release of Zach. With Lofton readily admitting to the IRS bombings and the assassination, and the feds having no evidence to link Turner to Dallas, they reluctantly agreed to the swap. The feds got Lofton and his ten-member crew, minus the crew member who assisted Pops in the raid on the safe house. Not trusting the feds would give him consideration for his assistance that prevented the additional loss of life, Pops refused to hand him over to the feds for now. The feds were more than happy to get a nine-for-one swap.

Turner was unceremoniously dumped at Reagan airport in D.C. with a plane ticket to Houston. When he arrived at Bush International Airport,

Kymbra and Colt were there to meet him, along with some surviving members of his crew. With Zach's exoneration from the IRS crimes, Operation Ghost had been lifted, and a few of his crew who were able to make it back to Houston greeted him warmly.

Zach was ecstatic to be home, but his thoughts were with his best friends, Will and Beard, who had been killed at Lake Hubbard. After spending some time with his wife, he informed them he couldn't even think about going home until he paid his respects to Will and Beard's families. The entire entourage went with him to each family home. It was a tearful reunion. Zach promised them all that he would get to the bottom of their deaths and dispense justice to anyone involved. They believed him.

The next morning, Zach got up early to drive to Austin to meet Pops. He had a lot to catch up on and a lot to tell Pops. More than anything, he wanted to know how his buddies died.

"Damn, son, it's about time you got finished with your vacation," quipped Pops when he laid eyes on Zach.

"Yeah, some vacation. You should try it sometime," Zach joked.

For the next several hours, Pops shared what they knew about Lake Hubbard and the Dallas mass shooting. Pops and Dyson described to Zach what they saw on the video from the interrogation of Ottosson. Zach winced.

"Pops, I know how you feel about this, but this is how our government trained them. I'm not a fan, but I understand the intent," offered Zach.

"I just don't see how the information can always be reliable when obtained this way. I saw men in Korea say anything to stop the pain," Pops said.

"Do you believe anything you heard?" asked Zach.

"Unfortunately, I think it's all true," admitted Pops.

"Now, damn it, Pops, we don't know that for a fact. The problem is, even if we had the recordings—which we don't—you're gonna have people say the same thing, that these outlandish tales were made up by someone being tortured to stop the torture. The evidence will be discounted heavily," reasoned Dyson.

Pops' desk phone rang, interrupting their conversation.

"Younger here."

"Is this Pops Younger?" asked the caller.

"Yeah, this is Younger. Who the hell is this?" asked Pops, who always seemed to be irritated when he had to talk on the phone, especially when it interrupted a very important discussion with Zach and Dyson.

For a brief second, Pops thought he recognized the voice and the accent, but he couldn't place it.

"Mr. Younger, I need your help," said the accented voice over the phone.

"Hang on," said Pops as he hit the speaker button on the phone so Dyson could also hear.

"Okay, who is this?" Younger asked.

"Mr. Younger, I have no one else to turn to. I need your help, sir."

"Holy shit," Dyson said, but Pops was still trying to put the voice to his memory. Dyson immediately knew who it was. It was a Swedish accent.

"Mr. Younger, this is Nils Ottosson."

Pops immediately stood.

"How do I know you are who you say you are," asked Pops.

"Sir, I know you knew I was held somewhere in West Virginia. I was tortured. I was with the *Free Texas* guys when our van got shot up and flipped into the lake."

"Where the hell are you? You are in incredible danger, son."

"That's why I'm calling you. I have nowhere else to turn," Ottosson pleaded. "Will and Beard told me if anything ever happened in our ride to Texas that you were the only one I should trust."

"Where the hell are you? We will come get you right now and make sure you are safe. Where do we go?"

"I got out of that van somehow when it went under. They were still spraying bullets when the van went in. I literally dogpaddled away into the night and got a kind old lady who owns a lake house to tend to my injuries. She found me on her dock the next morning."

"Jesus, son, give us your address and we will get you to a safe location and get you some medical treatment. Who was shooting at the van? Did you get a look at them?"

"Hell, it all happened so fast, I didn't see anyone."

"Who do you *think* it was?"

Zach stood up and interrupted their conversation, "Guys, I guarantee the feds are monitoring this phone. Don't give us your address, Mr. Ottosson. I see your number on his caller ID. We will call you back on a secure phone."

Both parties hung up immediately.

"Good thinking, son, I just can't believe this. The son of a bitch is alive!" yelled Pops.

"We have to assume the feds know this now, too. It's a race to see who gets to him first," Pops said in about as an excited a tone as anyone ever heard from him.

"My phone is secure. Calling him back right now," said Zach as he furiously dialed the number.

"Younger here again. Who do you think was shooting at the van?" pressed Pops.

"It's either the Russians or the CIA dispatched by the administration."

"The Russian is back on U.S. soil?" asked Dyson.

"I have no idea if he is, but he's more dangerous than the CIA. Can y'all come get me?

"On our way, son. Hang tight. We will keep you posted every step of the way."

Dyson immediately got on the phone to the Texas Rangers' field office in Dallas. The Rangers could be to this lake house within thirty minutes.

"Fire up an aircraft; let's go," said Pops, already walking out the door.

"Geez, Pops, not too excited to take a state-owned aircraft, if you know what I mean."

"Screw it already. Charter the fastest jet you can find."

"I'm on it!" Dyson exclaimed.

"Sir, I've got operatives in Dallas. Does your team need support in any way?"

Pops hesitated for a minute, then remembered that Zach's team was very adept at covert operations.

"Give them cover, son. Set up a perimeter; keep your folks at a distance but in communication."

"Roger that. Tell your boys so we don't end up shooting each other," ordered Zach.

Regional FBI director Lawson got a call on his cell phone.

"Sir, Langley just called and they are seeing a flurry of communications between the Texas Rangers HQ in Austin and their regional office in Dallas," said a voice from FBI headquarters in D.C.

"Do we have any transcripts yet?"

"No, sir, not yet, but working on it."

Another voice interrupted. "Sir, one more thing. We've got eyes on two Ranger SUVs that left downtown Dallas, heading northeast on I-30. They are in an awfully big hurry."

"Hmmm, I-30?" Lawson said to himself. "I-30, I-30, crap—Lake Hubbard! Are there still any dive crews on the lake?"

"No, sir, not for days."

"Somebody has found some evidence. That's got to be it. Dispatch everyone we've got. Somebody has found a cell phone or pulled up a laptop or something on a damned trot line. That could be the only thing causing this level of activity. Get a bird in the air but at a distance on those Ranger SUVs."

Pops began thinking about Zach's claim of eyes and ears everywhere.

"Dick, send our team to the crash site." he ordered.

"The crash site? The house he's at is damned near entirely across the lake. That will delay them. Why, Pops?"

"I think our boy here is right," Pops replied. "We have to figure these turds in D.C. know our every step. Zach, can you get your boys out to pick him up? No one will detect them. Hell, they just came out of hiding, right?"

"That's a great idea, Pops. I think we better be safe," Zach said. "You better figure they have a chopper following them right now if they were monitoring your phone. Sending your team to the crash site is ingenious. What if I had one of my guys meet them there and give them a laptop?"

"Do it! It will buy us time to get him out of there."

Pops paced incessantly at the private hangar as the Citation jet and crew were being readied for the short flight to an airport in Addison, a suburb just north of downtown Dallas. The crew told him it would be a twenty-eight-minute flight once they got airborne. Pops, Zach and Dyson would not be able to communicate with their teams on the ground while in flight. It would drive them crazy to be in the dark that long with the fate of the most valuable witness in American history within their grasp.

The two black Ranger SUVs pulled up to the original crash site, then pulled into a gas station parking lot on the next exit. As they waited, unmarked FBI, ATF and Homeland Security units were nearby waiting on orders to intervene at a moment's notice.

Shortly thereafter, an old yellow Nissan pickup truck pulled up, and a guy with a camo ball cap and scruffy beard got out, holding what looked like a laptop. Two Rangers from each SUV got out and approached the man, who was standing next to his pickup truck with the laptop.

Suddenly, vehicles screamed into the gas station parking lot. Officers jumped out, and the federal agents drew weapons on the four Texas Rangers and the man with the laptop.

FBI Regional Director Lawson got out of one of the SUVs and approached the group.

"We are Texas Rangers, sir. Tell your people to holster their weapons NOW!" yelled the Ranger in charge.

"I believe you are in possession of federal evidence pertaining to national security." Lawson walked over and took the laptop from the Ranger

"Keep your hands up, gentlemen. I'm instructing my men to shoot you on the spot if you so much as twitch an eyelid. Sir, you there, come over here with me," Lawson said as he motioned to the man who furnished the laptop.

"Sir, what is that that you handed to those gentlemen?"

"A laptop computer," said the man, who was one of Turner's operatives.

"I can see that, sir. Why do these gentlemen want it? Where is it from?"

"I found it right over there."

"Where? Point it out to me, please."

The man pointed to an area near the crash site.

"How did you find it?" Lawson demanded.

"I hooked it on a spinner bait when I was fishing." The man looked confused.

"So it was under water?"

"Yes, sir, it was," the operative replied.

"How deep was the water where you found it?" Lawson wanted all the details.

"Well, I'm not exactly sure, sir. My spinner bait hooked it. I would say maybe just a foot or two deep."

Lawson looked at his crew. They knew why. How was it that both Pops and his teams missed this evidence.

"Who told you to call these men, sir?"

"Well, I knew it wasn't good anymore, but someone pumping gas at the marina told me there was a reward for any electronic devices found in the lake and I was to call a certain number if a phone or anything like that was found. Do you know how much the reward is?"

"No, damned if I don't," said Lawson, irritated that Pops' men had the foresight to offer a reward if anything was discovered later.

"Sir, this may be evidence in a crime. I don't know about any reward, but how much were you looking for?"

"Heck, I don't know. I'd be happy with a case of Budweiser," said Turner's operative, who was turning in the acting performance of his life.

"Get him some damned beer, all his contact information and get this back to the lab immediately," said Lawson, instructing one of the agents to take the laptop.

"Gentlemen, I'll ask you to keep your hands in the air until we are out of the parking lot."

"Sir, there will be hell to pay for this. Pops Younger ain't going to take kindly to you federal boys drawing down on us like that," said the lead Ranger. "In fact, I ain't real fond of it myself."

"You can tell Mr. Younger thanks for doing business. Tell him he owes me a case a beer. I paid his reward for him! See you gentlemen later." The agents retreated to their vehicles and screamed out of the parking lot.

While this scene was playing out at the Shell gas station, less than a mile away, Turner's operative swooped in and picked up Ottosson, literally. Ottosson still could not walk on his feet, which had been broken by the sledge hammer.

He had convinced the kind old lady who had taken care of him to stay quiet, and that Zach's operatives were actually his cousins. Ottosson's charm with the ladies proved to be very valuable to his survival the first night on the lake. Even bloodied and hurt, he convinced the woman to take him in.

Zach's team was streaking to the Addison Airport to meet Pops' jet. He instructed the pilots to keep the engines running, telling them they could file a new flight plan upon arrival once he had loaded a few more "guests."

On the way back to the FBI lab in Dallas, the agent holding the recovered laptop in the back seat began to carefully inspect it. It looked pretty clean to him for a laptop that had been at the bottom of a lake for days, even if it was only in a couple of feet of water.

Lawson was feeling pretty good about himself. He had outsmarted

Pops Younger. Heck, he might even get a promotion and get back to FBI headquarters in D.C. over this. He had never seen the Bureau so focused on recovering evidence, so much so that he was fully aware the attorney general, and even the president, were briefed on progress daily. He couldn't wait to tell his superiors.

Lawson's cell phone rang.

"This is Lawson."

"Sir, we have a call from the manager of a private FBO at Addison Airport. He says there is a chartered Citation sitting on the tarmac, engines burning, waiting to pick up some additional passengers, but hasn't filed a flight plan yet."

"Probably just some corporate suits who can't decide where they want to go next or waiting for some strippers to join them on a flight to Vegas. What's your point?" Lawson asked.

"Sir, another pilot remarked that Pops Younger is on that jet."

"Say that again? You are saying Younger is on that jet? How do they know this?"

"The captain of the charter was chattering away to other pilots in the air that he was carrying the famous lawman. Couldn't wait to get his autograph."

"Where are those Ranger SUVs headed right now?"

"Let me check, sir," the man said. Moments passed and Lawson's head began spinning. Surely Younger was there to personally pick up the laptop, but why the charter? Why not a state-owned aircraft? And surely he would know by now that his Rangers were minus the evidence. He'd likely just return empty-handed and sore as hell, he figured.

"Sir, the pilot just confirmed with the FBO on tower availability, runway length and runway lights at Huntsville Municipal Airport."

"Huntsville, Texas? Where the prison is?"

"That's affirmative, sir."

"What the hell is he up to?"

"Sir," said the agent from the backseat. "I popped open the battery compartment and it says Property of Mesquite Independent School District. I'm not a certified computer guy, but from what I can tell, there isn't a hard drive in this computer. Looks like it was robbed of parts at some point. Where in hell would any information be stored on it?"

"Son of a bitch, we've been duped. Younger is still there waiting on some other kind of evidence to be delivered. That whole scene at the crash site was a ruse. Call Addison tower and tell them to turn it all off—all of it! Turn all units to Addison Airport now! Right now!"

"Sir, I don't understand. Tell them to turn what off?"

"The runway lights, the tower—everything! Do not let that plane take off!"

At the same time Lawson was screaming into his cell phone, two Ford crew trucks pulled up to the gate of the FBO, telling the girl inside the tail number of the aircraft that was waiting on them. At an FBO, its customary for a vehicle to go through a gate and drive right up to the plane to deliver occupants for the flight.

The FBO manager now had his interest piqued. Something was going on here and he was determined to see what it was. When the two pickup trucks pulled up, it took three people to lift another man, who couldn't walk, into the aircraft. He called the FBI back and told him what he saw.

"What in the hell are they doing? Who are they loading into the aircraft in such secrecy?" Lawson's mind searched for answers.

"Oh, my God, they've got Ottosson! That's got to be Ottosson!"

"Sir, should I call it in? Want me to call D.C. right now?"

"No, we don't know for sure." Lawson wasn't confident enough to alert D.C. What if he was wrong? He'd rather just be the hero and snatch him away from Younger.

The Citation was already taxiing to take off into a south wind. The taxi would take a few minutes as they were at the far south end of the runway, and they needed to taxi for two miles to point back south. When they got to the end of the runway, the pilot asked for clearance from the tower to take off. Suddenly, the runway lights went dark.

"Sir, the tower is telling me they have a power failure and it will be several minutes for the back-up generators to supply power and light them back up."

Pops peered back at Ottosson, who looked to be in pretty bad shape.

"Tell them we have a medical emergency on board and to get those lights powered back up!" Pops instructed the pilots.

Dyson, Zach, Pops and two of Turner's operatives were getting more nervous by the minute.

"I don't like it, sir. I don't trust it one bit. What are the odds the lights go dark on us like this? They know something!" yelled Zach.

"Uh-oh, we've got company, sir!" yelled Dyson as a flood of flashing lights could be seen entering the tarmac from the south side, heading directly toward the plane.

"I'll be damned. No way that carpetbagger is that smart," said Pops.

"Someone informed them. No way he figured this out." Dyson glanced at Zach.

"Surely, after all of this, you think one of my guys would cooperate with them?" demanded Zach.

"We'll have time for that later, but we've got to figure out how to get out of here with him," said Dyson.

"Call the Texas National Guard commander right now. I want our Apaches at Huntsville now," said Pops, referring to a squadron of Texas Air National Guard Apaches stationed in Conroe, Texas, just thirty minutes south of Huntsville. This group was under the ultimate command of the governor. "This is a direct order from me. No need to call Austin."

Pops stood up and walked bent over with his large frame to the cockpit and got right between the two pilots.

"I need you to take off immediately. Do you understand me?"

"I'm sorry, sir, without runway lights there's no way."

"Maybe you didn't hear me. You've already got this bird pointed in the right direction. Now take off!"

The captain was extremely flustered with all the goings-on, but the young co-pilot didn't seem to be fazed.

"Son, how many seconds does it take for this thing to scream down the runway and take off?"

"It depends sir, on wind, weight of the aircraft…"

Pops pulled out his pearl-handled revolver and put it to the captain's head.

"I rightly apologize for my behavior, but I'm telling you right now, the weight of the western world is on your shoulders. If you don't take off this very instant, the world as you know it is over anyway, so I might as well go ahead and put a round into your onion so you don't have to see what you caused!"

The aircraft lurched forward as the young co-pilot powered up the engines.

"I just have to keep her straight. I've got these floodlights but we'll get going fast enough to outrun them."

The Citation jet began roaring down the dark runway. The tower was screaming at the pilots to stop. It reminded Pops of times as a kid when they would drive down two-lane highways in west Texas as teenagers and turn off the headlights until somebody would lose their nerve and flip them back on. Only this time, the Citation was screaming down the runway at peak speed of one hundred eighty miles an hour with a light head wind providing lift to the wings.

"Am I seeing this? Am I seeing this? Is that aircraft taking off in the dark?" yelled Lawson at nobody in particular as they were speeding directly toward the Citation on the taxi runway. "Can't the tower do something?"

The event was happening too quick to get a reply. Lawson had an initial thought of jumping over to the Citation's path, but it was clear at the rate it was approaching them that the jet would have no way to stop, even if they were in the path of it.

As the co-pilot powered up, the captain was still not functioning, overwhelmed in the moment, plus Pops had a gun to his head. Pops ripped him out of his seat the second they started rolling down the dark runway and was now sitting in the captain's chair.

"Fix him a damned drink or something, but keep him the hell outta here," he instructed Zach.

Inside the cabin of the jet, everyone was white-knuckled as the jet roared into the darkness directly toward the flashing police lights.

Lawson knew it was too late to stop the aircraft, although he was amazed Pops would try to take off without runway lights.

"Stop, stop!" he yelled at his driver as he jumped out of the SUV to see if the Citation was going to make it.

Less than a hundred feet from him, the jet being flown by the co-pilot reached the airspeed it needed to lift off slowly.

As Lawson looked at the aircraft, there was Pops Younger with his straw Stetson cowboy hat in the captain's chair.

Pops looked out the pilot's window, with the cockpit lights still on, looked at Lawson directly and tipped his cowboy hat as the jet slowly rose.

"*You've got to be kidding me?* Did we just see that, sir?" asked another FBI agent.

"Hell, even the tower saw that. Did any of you know Younger was also a pilot? Damn, you've got to admit, that was something," said the agent holding the laptop they thought was the prize.

"Shut the hell up!" Lawson screamed. "Get on the radio and get units to Huntsville Airport. I want them there before that plane lands. Get busy; I want that plane tracked in case they go somewhere else. We've got what, about twenty minutes?" figured Lawson.

"The FBI office in Houston is an hour away at least. They'll never get there on time," said Lawson's second in command.

"Call the local sheriff. This is a national security matter. I'm calling Washington. Maybe they can scramble an F-16 or something to escort them in."

"Good job, son! Way to go!" Pops said to the young co-pilot. "Huntsville is still the destination, but I need you put on your afterburners or whatever you call it to get us there as quick as you can."

"Sir, I'm getting radio traffic from the FAA demanding that we return to Addison, Love or DFW. I'm being told they are scrambling F-16s and they will shoot us down if we don't land. Holy crap!"

"Dick, where are the nearest F-16s? Can they beat us to the spot?"

"Damn, Pops, there's some at Ellington, some at Fort Hood, and maybe a few Texas Air National Guard squadrons here or there. Would they really shoot us outta the sky?"

"Mr. Dyson, please recall that the *Deep State* killed hundreds of kids as a means to an end. I guarantee you that our *cargo*," he nodded toward Ottosson, "is so potentially damaging to them that they wouldn't hesitate. Remember, they are telling everyone this is a national security issue. They will have a built-in excuse. We better get there in a hurry," said Zach.

The co-pilot's eyes became as big as saucers.

"Are y'all really serious, or are you bullshitting me?" he asked.

"Maximum power, son. Maximum power," Pops urged the co-pilot to stay focused.

"We've got two F-16s scrambled on orders of the president!" announced Lawson to his crew. "They are lifting off from Ellington Force Base south of Houston. It's going to be close."

"What's their orders, do you think?" asked the agent still holding the laptop".

"My guess is, if it's that serious, which it appears it is, they'll shoot it down."

"Pardon me, sir, for being just a little bit skeptical, but shooting down a civilian aircraft with Texas Rangers on it? What the hell would Pops Younger be involved with that would threaten national security?"

"Agent, you're not here to question orders. You're out of line. This is not my decision. You just heard; it comes from the president herself. Dismissed."

CHAPTER 63

"Are we at last brought to such a humiliating and debasing degradation, that we cannot be trusted with arms for our own defence? Where is the difference between having our arms in our own possession and under our own direction, and having them under the management of Congress? If our defence be the real object of having those arms, in whose hands can they be trusted with more propriety, or equal safety to us, as in our own hands?"

- Patrick Henry (1736-1809)
Founding Father, American Revolutionary Hero & Orator

"Seven minutes out, sir," said the co-pilot.

"What do you show on radar?"

"I've got four low-flying aircraft directly in our path about eight miles south. Not moving too fast."

"Can you tell what kind of aircraft?" asked Dyson.

"My guess is choppers. Going too slow to be anything else," said the co-pilot.

"Is there a tower there? I don't remember," asked Pops.

"There is, sir, but it's not manned this time of night," the co-pilot answered.

"Is the runway lit?" asked Dyson.

"As soon as it detects my transponder, it will light up. Should see it very soon. Sir, the choppers are splitting up, two going east and two going west."

"Friendlies?" asked Dyson.

"It would appear so to me, knowing what I know. Those are likely our Apaches, sir," stated Zach confidently.

"What do you think the FBI's plan is?" asked Dyson.

"If I was that carpetbagger and I couldn't get my people to the Huntsville airport in time for our landing, next thing I would do is call the local Walker County sheriff," chuckled Pops.

"Why is that humorous?" asked Zach wryly.

"Me and that sheriff go back a long way. Hell, I served in Korea with his daddy. He's probably the most Yankee-hatin' SOB wearing a badge in Texas! If he was alerted by the FBI that it was me on this damned bird, he'd lock down that airport tighter than a prom queen," announced Pops.

"I hope you're right," said the young co-pilot.

"He's shootin' straight," reassured Dyson.

"There's the runway!" shouted the co-pilot, sharply banking the Citation to the east to make his final approach.

"What ya got on radar now?" asked Pops.

"Still got those choppers. Appears they are hovering at a couple hundred feet and have spread out around the airport, but they have left us a lane to land."

"There's a lot of flashing lights down there," noted Dyson.

"Sir, they've got the towers manned now. I'm getting a signal from the tower," said the co-pilot. "Uh-oh... I hope that's not what I think it is," said the co-pilot, pointing at the radar screen after he zoomed out to show a larger viewing area, indicating two blips approaching and moving significantly faster than any other aircraft viewable in the Houston air traffic corridor.

"I'm sure those are F-16s. We need to put this thing down now!" stressed Zach.

Everyone got quiet as the Citation descended to the runway a couple of hundred feet below them. All of them, including Ottosson—who was now awakened and slightly coherent—were doing the math in their heads to see how much time, if any, they had to reach the ground before the F-16s were close enough to use their air-to-air missiles.

"What are they packing and what's their range?" asked Pops.

"If they are AIM AMRAAM missiles, they are effective up to thirty miles. If it's Sidewinders, a little less," said Zach. "What's their range now?"

"Looks like thirty-two miles but closing fast. Hang tight; I'm coming in hot, with a little more speed than normal. Buckle in, folks," ordered the co-pilot.

"Patch me in with the tower," said Pops, still sitting in the captain's seat.

Embarrassed at being ripped out of his seat, the captain remained quiet but attentive.

As the wheels touched the runway, Pops picked up the radio mic. "This is Pops Younger, commandant of the Texas Rangers. Who has arranged this fine party for us?" he asked.

The Citation's occupants stared out their small windows to see dozens of emergency vehicles and police cars."

"Younger, is that you, you old coot?" A deep, scratchy voice sounded over the radio.

"Damned if it ain't Sheriff Scotty Robbins. You mean the fine folks of this county ain't gotten any smarter and re-elected your damned ass again?" Pops chuckled.

"It's the devil they know, Pops," laughed the sheriff. "I got a call from some high-falootin' FBI dude up in that cesspool they call Washington, asking me if I'd arrange a little welcoming party for ya, so here we are. Says were supposed to arrest you and your traveling party as well. Somethin' about national security?"

"That's damned nice of you, Scotty, to arrange this little shindig. I'll tell you what; you can tell them you took us straight to jail. I need a lift for a few of us in here straight to the Death Row Unit, if you don't mind."

"Damn, Pops, I ain't even gonna ask. Must be serious. By the time you taxi over here, I'll be there to escort you personally. If you ain't noticed, we've got some friendly Apaches in the air who will make sure your ride to the prison has air cover."

"It's damned serious, Scotty. But I gotta tell ya, you've never seen a cowboy so happy to see four Apaches take the high ground," laughed Pops.

The Citation pulled up right next to the small-town airport terminal.

"Guys, those Falcons are going to be right on us any minute. Personally, I'd like to get off this thing as soon as possible. Let's get our Swede and get out of sight ASAP!" ordered Zach as everyone picked up the pace and got off the aircraft quickly.

The two F-16s were flying barely above tree-top level, but pulled up as they approached the airport to make sure they were clear of the Apaches.

While all these events were occurring, President Bartlett, Chief of Staff Weingold and several cabinet members were assembled in the Situation Room below the White House. Two members of the Joint Chiefs were also in attendance.

"Madam President, the private jet landed before the F-16s could reach them," said the first Joint Chief. "They did not get a visual on the occupants, but apparently they have vacated the aircraft. There are four Texas Air National Guard Apache helicopters on location but airborne, apparently hovering at a very low altitude. We did not call them and we don't know why they are there. The F-16 pilots are attempting to make contact with them.

"Why are they there, Milt?" asked the president.

"Madam President, Pops Younger has many friends in Texas. That unit reports to the Texas governor, and you know for sure he didn't send them there, so my guess is Younger called them in," said Weingold, referring to Governor Strasburg, who was as much a part of the *Deep State* as any of those in the Situation Room.

The F-16s banked steeply and came back low over the terminal, sending a message to Pops and the Walker County sheriff.

"We need to play the shell game, sir, and do it in intervals, but even that might not be enough. Even if the Falcons see two dozen police units departing the airport in different directions, they could still get lucky. I don't like it at all. It's not a safe play, but I'm not sure what the alternative is," lamented Zach.

"Are you suggesting those fighters will fire on us and our escorts on the way to the prison?" asked Dyson.

Zach leaned toward Pops and said quietly, "This Swede knows *everything*. He knows the elections have been a fraud. He knows the government is complicit in the Dallas shootings, the assassination of a Supreme Court chief justice, the fatal crash of the governor and who the hell knows what else. I'm telling you right now, it's enough to shake this Republic to its very core. Hell, yes, they would kill every single one of us by any means necessary to protect the damned *Deep State*! Gentlemen, I know firsthand what this government is capable of."

"The Apaches are telling us the F-16 pilots are demanding they land and that no vehicles should leave the airport or they will be fired on," said Sheriff Robbins. "Pops, what the hell is going on here?"

"Scotty, I've got you and your men into one hell of a rodeo," said Pops.

"If that's the case and you need to get outta here, I can arrange some *alternative* transportation if you don't mind a little discomfort," said Robbins.

"A little discomfort sure beats a missile raining down on our heads," replied Pops. "What ya got in mind?"

"I'm going to call my brother-in-law right after I take this call from the FBI," said the sheriff. "Yeah, I got them here. I'll hold them here until your boys from Houston arrive. They ain't going nowhere," winked the sheriff.

The sheriff hung up and made another call as he walked out of the small waiting area to the vending machine room, then came back in. "Your rides will be here in just a few minutes." he announced.

Pops and the rest were now very curious about how the sheriff was going to get them out of the small terminal so they wouldn't be sitting ducks for the F-16s that continued to buzz the airport. While all this was going on, the Apache pilots were very unappreciative of the high-stakes buzzing they were experiencing from the F-16 pilots, much less being told to ground their choppers. The pilots of the Apaches and F-16s were not exactly friendly to each other.

CHAPTER 64

"Freedom is never more than one generation away from extinction. We didn't pass it to our children in the bloodstream. It must be fought for, protected, and handed on for them to do the same, or one day we will spend our sunset years telling our children and our children's children what it was once like in the United States where men were free."

- Ronald Reagan (1911-2004)
40th President of the United States

"How long until the Houston FBI agents arrive?" Weingold asked the group in the Situation Room.

"Fifteen minutes, maximum," said the FBI director.

"What are our orders if they take off before the FBI arrives?" the Air Force general asked the chairman of the Joint Chiefs, who immediately looked to the president.

"Madam President, I must have our pilots prepared. What are your orders if they attempt to leave?"

Bartlett was extremely uncomfortable with the question, and her body language changed immediately.

"Let me remind everyone in here of the national security implications, much less your own personal careers if this damned cowboy is able to secure Ottosson. We still do not have visual confirmation that Younger has him, but the FBI is convinced they do. It's the only thing that makes sense. Do your jobs!"

"Madam President, your orders please?" the general asked again.

"You neutralize them immediately. The local sheriff has them, correct?"

"Yes, Madam President, it appears so, but I need to cover all contingencies."

"And you would minimize any collateral damage, correct, General?"

"To the extent possible, yes, Madam President."

"We'll worry about that later, General. Remember, this is a national security issue, so explaining any collateral damage won't be an issue if we are presented with such a situation," reminded Weingold.

Sheriff Robbins walked back into the waiting room.

"Pops, your chariots await," he said, taking a half-bow. "Follow me, gentlemen."

Pops, Dyson, and Zach helped Ottosson stand.

"We're going to get you to a very secure place," assured Dyson.

The sheriff led them through a side door that took them to a metal hangar attached to the terminal in which maintenance was done on aircraft parked at the airport permanently. Through a side door came four Polaris four-wheelers. The sheriff welcomed his brother-in-law, who owned the four-wheelers.

"We took out the bulbs on the tail lights so the machines can't be seen. I suggest you let me lead you boys outta here as that trail is narrow and you've got about four miles to go down the high-wire trail until we get to the two-lane highway leading to town. I don't know what y'all got going on here tonight, but these are my three boys." He introduced them. His oldest boy was nineteen and his youngest was fifteen. The boys recognized Pops Younger from the famous scene on the Laredo bridge.

"Pops, the tall pines will keep you out of sight of the fighters, but my crew down south of town just radioed and told me the FBI convoy from Houston is blazing up I-45 and just reached the south edge of town. If you're going to go, you need to git right now!" advised Sheriff Robbins.

"Much obliged to you, Scotty. Much obliged to you, too, sir—and to your sons," said Pops.

Pops and Dyson climbed onboard two of the four-wheelers while Zach suggested two of the boys double on one. He let Ottosson get on the last four-wheeler first and climbed on behind him.

"Keep your hands right there on those bars and let me drive. Put your feet up there on your fender and don't try to steer or drive. I'll do that. Just hang on," Zach told Ottosson. Ottosson had a tough time lifting his legs and getting his mangled feet set.

"Hit the lights!" instructed the sheriff to turn off the lights in the hangar. He didn't want the fighters to see the four-wheelers traverse the twenty yards into the trees and onto the trail. There was no chain link fence surrounding this small town airport except on the runway that ran parallel to Interstate 45.

The fighter jets roared over again.

"Now!" said the sheriff as the four-wheelers took off into the darkness of the East Texas piney woods. As soon as they hit the trail, they couldn't be seen.

"Turn them back on!" yelled the sheriff, referring to the hangar lights as he fixed his cowboy hat and hurriedly went into the terminal.

"What the hell are you doing, Sheriff"?" asked a deputy as Robbins ran out the door.

"Time for me to play rabbit!" the sheriff said.

"Scotty, you heard what they said. Those fighters are likely to come down hard on any vehicle leaving here. Please don't!" said another deputy.

"That's my brother-in-law and his three boys risking their necks because I asked them to. They don't have a clue why, only that I asked them. The least I can do is divert attention from them being seen," shouted the sheriff. He jumped into his SUV, flipped the lights on and looked into the sky.

"Come on, you sons of bitches, where the hell are you?"

Twenty seconds later, the two fighters roared over the terminal again.

"Here we go!" the sheriff yelled into his radio. He flipped on his sirens and headed in the opposite direction that the four-wheelers were taking into the woods.

Robbins announced on his police unit radio that he had the Citation's occupants with him and he was leaving for an undisclosed location.

"Madam President, there's a police unit leaving the terminal at a high rate of speed!" announced the general, a grave look on his face.

Weingold stood up in the Situation Room and took a deep breath, "Madam President, they are making a run for it. We cannot allow them to get Ottosson out of there before the FBI arrives."

"How far away is the FBI? Why are they not there yet? Why is the sheriff not following our orders to stay put?" demanded the president.

"They could have subdued the sheriff or taken a hostage. Who the hell knows? We needed about five more minutes," said the FBI director.

"Can't you divert your men to follow the police unit?" she asked.

"Yes, we can, Madam President, but you take the chance that Ottosson is somehow tossed out of the unit or they transfer him to another vehicle. Those fighters are too fast to stay on him and follow him like a helicopter could. They won't have nonstop eyes on him," responded the general.

"Madam President, you have to give the order. I know it's hard, but you must think of how bad the alternative is!" pleaded Weingold.

"Milt, we don't know who's in there," she replied.

"Madam President, the sheriff just radioed in that he had them! Do we have your order for the fighters to take out that vehicle, Madam President?" repeated Weingold. The tension in the Situation Room was palpable.

President Bartlett dropped her head and took another deep breath.

"Do what you have to do, General," she said reluctantly.

"I will give the order, Madam President," the general confirmed.

Pops and the group on the four-wheelers finally made the four-mile trek through multiple trails in total darkness, simply on knowledge of the trail by the sheriff's brother-in-law and his sons. Most of them had abrasions from small tree limbs and thorn bushes they couldn't see that overhung the trail as they sped along in the darkness. When they got to the highway, they waited at the edge of the woods for a pickup truck that was going to pick them up.

As they rode through the darkness, Zach's mind wandered to the man he was sitting behind on the four-wheeler. This scumbag was the focal point of the *Deep State's* diabolical schemes. He was indirectly responsible for hundreds of deaths.

"I should put a bullet in his head right now," Zach thought to himself.

As they waited for the pickup truck, they all noticed a flash of light and a sound like thunder in the distance, then saw one of the F-16's afterburners in the western sky.

"What the hell was that?" asked the brother-in-law.

"I don't know for sure, but it can't be good," said Zach. "Where's our ride?"

"There he is."

The driver of the pickup flashed his lights twice as he approached.

"Thank you, sir, and thank you, boys," said Pops. He shook their hands and piled into the cab of the four-door truck. He introduced those with him by first name to the driver, who was wearing his gray prison guard uniform from the Huntsville State Prison.

The pickup truck drove up to the main gate of the massive, sprawling fifty-four-acre Huntsville State Prison complex. The Death Row unit had been moved to Livingston, Texas, but the old prison with its famous huge red brick walls, also known as the Walls Unit, still contained highly secure death row cell blocks. This secure location was the only place Pops felt he could hold Ottosson long enough to get him some medical attention and get his taped testimony without any associated torture. It would make it very tough for Volkov or the CIA to permanently silence him.

News spread quickly that Texas legend Pops Younger was in the prison, and many guards temporarily left their duty positions to get a glance.

As soon as the group entered the prison, Ottosson was taken into custody and shackled at feet, waist and hands. Pops was taking no chances. Ottosson had to be taken in a wheelchair to the medical unit to be evaluated and treated.

"We finally got him here. Hell of a journey, Pops," commented Dyson.

"Dick, stay with Ottosson. Do not let him out of your sight. I've got to go find out what that explosion was and see how Scotty's troops are doing at the airport. Surely the FBI has arrived by now," said Pops, deeply concerned about his friend.

The scene at the airport had turned into an angry mob of law enforcement, paramedics and airport employees who believed they had witnessed a United States Air Force F-16 deliberately launch a missile on a Texas sheriff's truck.

When the FBI finally pulled up, they were met with anger and disgust. Under orders from the deputy sheriff, nobody was allowed to leave to see if the sheriff was dead or alive. They had to rely on reports from the Apaches. "Tell those two Apaches to immediately vacate the area and return to the airport or they will be fired upon," said the general into the conference phone on the table in the Situation Room.

"Sir, the Apaches are not cooperating. One is touching down right now in the vicinity of the target," came the direct voice of the lead F-16 pilot over the speakerphone.

"Do you see any movement out of the destroyed vehicle? Any signs of life at all?" asked the general.

"No, sir, none. The vehicle is totally destroyed."

"We don't want them moving anything. The FBI has diverted units from the airport and is trying to locate the vehicle now. Warn them to lift off in the next two minutes or they will be fired upon!"

"Uh, sir, can your confirm your order"?" asked the pilot.

"Give the Apache on the ground two minutes to lift off and vacate the area; otherwise, you will fire on them."

"Affirmative, sir."

Pops' cell phone rang.

"This is Deputy Crawford, Mr. Younger. We think the F-16s fired on Sheriff Robbins."

"What? Where is he?" Pops asked. His heart sank, thinking the explosion he saw and felt might be related.

"He took off toward Interstate 45 west to divert attention from you folks leaving the airport. We've got a really bad situation here."

"I'm on my way!" Pops hung up.

"Pops, it is extremely dangerous for you to go back to the airport. They would like nothing more than to have an opportunity to kill or arrest you," pleaded Zach.

"Look, Dick is in there with Ottosson. I need you two to protect him at all costs. Do not let anyone get to him 'cuz as sure as the sun comes up tomorrow, they will try," said Pops. He looked at the prison guard who delivered them and said, "I need your truck."

"Yes, sir, here's the keys. It actually belongs to the prison. Here you go, sir. Be safe."

Pops climbed into the pickup truck, then checked both his pistols to make sure they were fully loaded—a common habit he had when he figured a confrontation was coming.

The prison truck had a police radio in it and Pops immediately got on the radio, "This is Texas Ranger Commandant Pops Younger. I need the FBI agent in charge at the Huntsville Airport immediately."

Pops waited a few seconds, then heard the crackled reply on the outdated radio speaker.

"This is Agent Herforth." He sounded stunned to hear Pops on the radio. He'd thought Pops was in the burning sheriff's vehicle out on the two-lane highway heading west.

"I need you to stand down. I'm coming back to the airport now. Again, I repeat. Stand down," commanded Pops.

"Sir, are the other occupants that arrived with you on this private jet with you right now?"

"No, they are not. I am headed your direction and you need to stand down immediately!" Pops repeated.

"Mr. Younger, I need to know where your other occupants are," demanded Herforth.

"They left the airport with Sheriff Robbins," said Pops, purposely trying to throw them off.

The FBI agent turned to the deputies standing near them, "Did you see anyone else get in that vehicle that left with your sheriff?"

"Sheriff Robbins left from the other side of the hangar. We did not get to see who went with him. He left in a hurry," said the deputy.

"Yeah, right. So who is not in that terminal that came off that plane?"

"Couldn't tell you, sir. None of us were in the hanger. That's where it taxied to originally and where the occupants exited."

"We're coming in to interview the pilots."

Pops could hear the entire conversation on his truck-mounted radio.

"Herforth, you will stand down until I get there. You are not to enter the terminal," commanded Pops.

"My orders come from Washington, Younger. They don't come from some hayseed has-been," said the frustrated lead FBI agent, who was also getting pressure directly from the national FBI director from the Situation Room to get into the terminal and find out who was still there and to arrest the pilots.

"Deputy, do not allow anyone access to the terminal," ordered Pops over the radio.

"Roger that," confirmed the deputy, glaring at the FBI agent, who was outnumbered by sheriff's deputies and Huntsville city police on the scene. All those officers were visibly shaken and angry by what seemed to be the fate of their popular sheriff.

A few minutes later, while a stand-off appeared to be happening at the terminal, Pops drove in and locked his brakes right in front of the terminal entrance. He got out and walked directly to the FBI agent in charge.

"Who's running this shit show? I want to speak to him right now!"

"Sir, Texas Ranger Pops Younger is standing right here and would like to speak with you." The agent handed his cell phone to Younger.

"Younger here."

"Mr. Younger, this is General Thomas Southerland. I have you on speaker with FBI Director Nelson in the room. We need you to defuse the situation there, allow our people into the terminal, and to surrender your weapon to Agent Herforth."

"Did you instruct the Falcons to fire upon Sheriff Robbins?"

"Our instructions were that no one was to leave the terminal. We had no idea who was in that vehicle, which left at a high rate of speed. We had no choice. Do you know who else was in that vehicle?"

Suddenly, another explosion rocked the sky, and a small fireball lit up the night sky.

"What the hell was that? What the hell are y'all shooting at now?" demanded Pops.

"Sir, the Apaches are calling in saying the F-16s hit the Apache that landed to check on the sheriff! No word on the pilots! Jesus Christ!" said the deputy sheriff.

"What the hell is wrong with you people, General! Did you give this order?" demanded Pops.

"Mr. Younger, our instructions are not fuzzy. They aren't in a foreign language. We've told your people down there to stay the hell in place. If they don't do as instructed, people are going to die. The chopper was warned and he didn't obey. The same thing will happen to any of you who do not follow our direct orders," snapped the general.

Weingold and President Bartlett received word that events were unfolding in Huntsville and were rushing back down to the Situation Room.

The chatter over the frequencies used by both the F-16 pilots and the Apaches was intense. What the Apaches didn't know was that both the pilot and weapons officer aboard the Apache that landed had gotten out of it and were near the sheriff's vehicle to see if there was any chance the sheriff had survived.

As the F-16s banked back toward the Huntsville airport, the fighter pilots were heard warning the three remaining Apaches to land immediately. "It's your final warning," they said ominously.

"Stand your boys down, General. There's no need for this to escalate. Do you hear me?" yelled Pops into the phone as the F-16s approached low and tight over the tall pine trees.

The Texas Air National guard commander in Austin had given the Apaches permission to defend and to fire if fired upon. The F-16s were way too close to launch any missiles on the Apaches and seemed to be making another low fly-over for intimidation purposes as they had already done a few dozen times.

The Apaches were not readily visible in the night sky. They could be heard but not seen. There were no running lights. The jets screamed over the terminal, quaking everything in sight, with the FBI agents and sheriff's deputies covering their ears. The planes started to bank west at the end of the main runway.

Since nobody could see them anymore, those standing outside the terminal didn't realize the Apaches had all dropped down below a tall stand of pine trees less than fifty feet off the ground at the end of the main runway. As the F-16s banked, the Apaches rose up above the trees. The F-16s were now exposing their bellies to the powerful choppers.

All three Apaches let loose with their 30 mm. chain guns, which are effectively automatic cannons. The entire crowd of people winced, shrieked and turned to see the tracers leaving the Apaches and striking both F-16s.

The first F-16 immediately exploded into hundreds of pieces as the cannons hit the fuel tanks in the wings, the ordnance it was carrying, or both.

The second F-16 was on fire and rapidly heading to the ground as the pilot tried to eject. The plane hit the runway and tumbled in a fiery heap for hundreds of yards. The body of the pilot could be seen easily from the glow of the burning wreckage as he glided a short distance to the earth.

"What the hell is happening there?" the general shouted. "Younger, what the hell is going on?"

"Son of a bitch, damn it, General! This is what happens when you let a situation spiral out of control. Your birds are down!"

"What do you mean, down?"

"I mean the Apaches just blew them out of the sky is what I mean," said Pops, a trace of sadness in his voice.

President Bartlett had just walked in and sat down, only to hear the last two sentences by both men.

Lead FBI Agent Herforth was screaming at Pops, at his agents and the deputies, as total chaos unfolded quickly.

"You think this is over, Younger? I can have twenty more fighter jets there in ten minutes or less, and you and your people will be grease spots on the prairie when I'm done with you," yelled Weingold at the speaker phone.

"Everyone here is under immediate arrest. Take their weapons and place them into custody now!" shouted Herforth.

In one fell swoop, Pops dropped the phone, reached over to Herforth, grabbed him by the scruff of the neck, pulled him toward him and yanked one of his pearl-handled Colt .45s from its holster. He pressed it hard into Herforth's temple.

"Back off! Back off now! All of you put your damned weapons in the dirt!" he yelled to the dozen or so FBI agents. "Tell them, damn it!" he screamed to Herforth.

At the same time, the sheriff's deputies pulled their service weapons and trained them on the agents. The agents put their arms and hands out.

"Git 'em out, boys. Drop 'em!" screamed the deputies.

"Deputy, get your EMS crew dispatched over to tend to that pilot and see if he made it," Pops directed, referring to the ejected pilot.

There was no doubt about the outcome for the second pilot.

"Now give me that damned phone again," Pops said. A deputy picked it up and handed it to him. The FBI agents dropped their weapons as the sheriff's deputies began placing handcuffs on them.

"General, I want to speak to President Bartlett, right now, or I'll blow the noggin off this sorry piece of shit I'd hate to waste good lead on!"

The general, FBI director and Weingold paused and looked at the president.

Bartlett hesitated, then announced herself.

"This is President Bartlett. I suggest you surrender yourself and end this crisis you have going on there, Mr. Younger."

"You and your administration have caused unnecessary bloodshed and death here, Bartlett. You killed my friend Sheriff Robbins, a great man with a great family, for no damned reason."

"Mr. Younger, I can assure you…"

"Shut the hell up, Bartlett. I've got Ottosson. Do you hear me? He's confessed to the plot to murder Chief Justice Noyner. He's confessed to his involvement in the death of another friend of mine, Texas Governor Brahman. We know about how elections were rigged through CIS. And, worst of all, he's informed us of ALL the co-conspirators in the murder of the kids at the Dallas Fairgrounds!"

"Younger, you're a lunatic!" interrupted Weingold.

"Listen, you little metrosexual piece of jackrabbit shit, all of you are going down. Do you hear me?"

"Shit, Younger, that hurts!" stated Herforth. Pops pressed his .45 pistol deeper into the skin of Herforth's temple the madder he got.

"Mr. Younger, please relax. Mr. Ottosson is obviously not of sound mind," begged the president.

Everyone in the Situation Room was now standing. The cat was out of the bag. Surely dozens heard what Pops just claimed.

"Take this piece of shit and bag him!" Pops shouted as he pushed Herforth to the nearest deputy. "Cuff his ass!"

"Before you think about doing anything further, General, just know this," Pops said back into the phone. "Ottosson is not here and he's safe. No matter what you might do here, all of you are getting exposed. Do you hear me?"

"Mr. Younger, let's be reasonable here," said President Bartlett.

"I was in Dallas shortly after the shootings conducted by the Russian with your full knowledge and blessing. You know it and I know it. There were dead kids still lying on the grass, horribly mangled by the bullets. You have no heart. You have no soul."

"You're out of your mind, Younger!" screamed Weingold.

"Listen closely, you bastards. Texas is done with all of you. You hear me. The *Great Purge* is coming. The *Deep State* is over."

"You are certifiably a nut job, Younger!" yelled Weingold again.

"Listen, you slime ball, I used to tell folks like you that Texans can forgive, but they never forget, but I can't say that anymore."

Pops lifted his straw Stetson, took a handkerchief from his pocket, wiped his forehead and then his handlebar mustache.

"But, in this particular case, Texans ain't about to forgive."

CHAPTER 65

"The pursuit of Liberty is never convenient and often demands blood as the price to achieve it—and to keep it. Liberty is never permanent, for to believe in its permanence is most assuredly its ultimate destruction."

- *David Thomas Roberts*
Author

The sound of blaring sirens started to envelope the entire city as every imaginable police car and firetruck within miles responded to what seemed to be a disaster of some type at the National Mall.

The Lincoln Memorial was bathed in a deep orange glow as the reflection of the burning wreckage of Marine One was strewn across the steps from the Mall and into the Memorial. The low cloud cover producing the light snow reflected the fires and lit the entire area.

Texans Chris and Connie Flores, who just moments before were tracing the name of their grandfather's granite-etched name on the Vietnam Memorial, and who witnessed the downing of Marine One and two accompanying choppers, were running for their lives. For all they knew, a nuclear bomb could be the next thing that hit Washington, D.C.

Chris had an ominous sense of the happenings around them, even more ominous with what they had just witnessed with their own eyes. After seeing two men in wool ski masks that just ran by them, he realized they were carrying some sort of tube.

"Connie, let's duck down back here. I'm not sure who those guys were, but I don't know what we've just seen. I'm not even sure if we should be seen. Quick, get back here!" Chris pointed to a big green trash dumpster behind a small office building.

The trash dumpster at the end of a parking lot was positioned almost all the way to a concrete barrier from another parking lot, to another building that was about four feet higher than the parking lot the dumpster was in. This allowed them to crouch between the dumpster and the barrier, below the adjacent parking lot.

"What do you think is happening? Are we at war or something?" asked Connie, who was visibly shaking.

"Are you cold? Do you need my coat and scarf?" asked Chris.

"I don't think so; I'm just scared to death. What the hell is going on?"

"Whatever it is, it's bad. Really bad, but I know this. We don't need to be here but, until we know what's going on or see the police, let's stay put," he advised her.

"Uh-oh," she whispered to Chris.

Three men wearing similar ski masks were running into their parking lot and directly toward them.

"Don't move. Don't move a muscle or make a sound," Chris whispered.

The men went straight to the concrete barrier and handed some type of tube that looked like it had a trigger mechanism to someone with outstretched arms above the guard rail on the concrete barrier. Those arms took the tubes while the three men latched onto the guardrail and pulled themselves over the barrier. They got into the back of a van that backed into a spot right above them.

The brother and sister were hidden by the dumpster lid, which had been left open and was laying across the barrier. Chris motioned her to stay quiet, putting his forefinger over his lips.

Less than thirty seconds later, two more men dressed the same did the same thing when they reached the barrier.

The siblings could hear the men talking in quiet, excited tones, even going so far as slapping hands, like a high-five gesture.

Chris got a better look at the tube devices. He wasn't a military expert, but he first thought the deep, green tubes looked like some kind of bazooka and had the stenciled letters "Слова."

The men in the van closed the rear doors and drove away. Chris took a close look at the van but could only see that it was an electrical contractor's van.

As soon as the van pulled out of the parking lot, Connie turned to Chris and asked, "Who the hell were they? What were they saying, and were those some kind of guns they were carrying?"

"I couldn't really tell. Looked like bazookas, but had strange writing on them," he answered.

"Also, what language was that?"

"I'm not sure about that, either. Let's get out of here and see if we can find the police." They got up and lifted the dumpster trash lid so they could get out of their hiding place.

At almost the same exact moment in time, Marine One went down with President Annabelle Bartlett aboard, and other calamities in D.C. and across the country started to be called into various law enforcement agencies, adding to the sudden chaos.

In D.C., Sally Ferguson-Haverton, who was just named chief justice of the United States Supreme Court, was killed outside her Georgetown flat by a single bullet to the back of the head as she was taking her springer spaniel for an early morning walk.

Chief of Staff Weingold was decapitated and his head was stuffed into his master bedroom toilet. His headless body, clad in a velvet robe, was found on his kitchen floor in a large pool of deep red blood.

The two generals from the Joint Chiefs who were in the Situation Room with President Bartlett the night before met similar fates, along with their wives, while sleeping in their beds.

GOP Majority Leader McCray and his wife of forty-six years were taken out as they got in their car to go to Sunday morning Mass.

The heads of the NSA, Homeland Security, FBI, ATF and the U.S. attorney general were assassinated with incredible precision.

Texas Governor Strasburg's SUV was riddled by bullets at a stop sign in Austin as he was on his way to a Methodist church service, killing him, his wife and two staff aides.

Texas Senator Simpson was found slumped over on his toilet with his hands still clutching the *Washington Post* at his apartment in Alexandria, two bullet holes in his chest and one in his forehead.

By the time it reached noon on the East Coast, one hundred forty-two members of Congress and twenty-nine U.S. senators, along with eighteen state governors and various other political and public figures, were found dead. The assassinations included both Democrats and Republicans.

Throughout the date, the breaking news' momentum built steadily.

A Special Report news bulletin came out on CNN as the host exclaimed, "I am sad to inform our viewers that President Bartlett has died in a crash of Marine One. Officials believe from eyewitness reports that it was *not* an accident. I repeat, it was *not* an accident. It appears as though *The Great Purge* is upon us. We are getting reports from all over Washington, D.C. and other locations throughout the country that a dastardly and systematic plan has been implemented to murder elected officials. No group has accepted responsibility; however, this would seem to be the work of a domestic anti-government terrorist group such as the *Free Texas* militia. We will stay right here as we bring you up-to-the minute news."

As the electrical contractor's van crossed over the state lines in West Virginia, it pulled into a rest area where the occupants abandoned the van and split up into two other vehicles whose drivers were waiting on them. The large tubes were now in duffel bags and loaded into the trunks of the cars.

As the first car sped up and entered the interstate, one of the men reached over to the passenger in the front seat to shake his hand.

"Congratulations, Comrade Volkov! The Americans must learn to pay their debts!"

CPSIA information can be obtained
at www.ICGtesting.com
Printed in the USA
LVHW04*0912120818
586656LV00001B/1/P